BLOOD

Maggie Gee has written fifteen books to great acclaim, and her work has been translated into fourteen languages. One of Granta's original 'Best of Young British Novelists', she is a Fellow of the Royal Society of Literature and has been short-listed for global prizes including the Orange (now Women's) Prize and the Dublin International IMPAC Prize. She writes novels, short stories, memoir, poetry and journalism. In 2012 there was an international conference about her work at St Andrew's University. She is a Professor of Creative Writing at Bath Spa University and a Director of the Authors' Licensing and Collecting Society. Maggie Gee was awarded an OBE for services to literature in 2012.

Blood

Maggie Gee

Fentum
Press

Sold and distributed by Global Book Sales/Macmillan
Distribution and in North America by Consortium Book Sales
and Distribution, Inc., part of the Ingram Content Group

Copyright © 2019 Maggie Gee

Maggie Gee asserts the moral right to be identified
as the author of this work

A CIP catalogue record for this book is available
from the British Library

ISBN (paperback) 978-1-909572-12-6

Typeset in Albertina by Lindsay Nash

Printed and bound in Great Britain
by CPI Group (UK) Ltd, Croydon CR0 4YY

For Katherine

Revenge is a kind of wild justice; which the more man's nature runs to, the more ought law to weed it out.

FRANCIS BACON, 'ON REVENGE', 1605

When the President does it, that means it is not illegal.

RICHARD NIXON, INTERVIEW WITH DAVID FROST, 1989

Silent enim leges inter arma
(Law falls silent in times of war)

CICERO, *PRO MILONE*, 52 BC

Part 1

Family Problems

1

The Ludds. Artistes of awfulness. I'm one of them. I share the bad blood. And yet I have my softer side – as you'll see if you stay with me. I am more sinned against than sinning.

Some facts. Five years ago, our brother died. Fred was twenty-four, and a soldier. I wanted a party to celebrate him. All were invited, the whole family. It was a chance to make amends.

Only our father never showed. He didn't bother to turn up.

Very soon after, Dad was dead.

Dad is dead, and I've never liked him. Yes, it's true, I was heard 'making threats' –

I am a teacher, a Deputy Head, a respectable citizen of East Kent. I'm a good teacher, I love my job, I keep violence to a minimum in the classroom.

(The kids are splattered with violence every day, internet videos of vile beheadings, Defend British Values picketing mosques, blood in London, Paris, Brussels – Kabul, Nice, Nairobi, Glasgow – bodies exploded like burst packages, balaclavaed heads popping up like hydras. Their parents blank them, hugging their phones. Naturally, the kids do violence to each other, compass-points in arms, knives in back pockets, shoves and trips and dark moments in the lavs.)

I deploy violence myself, preventatively, you understand, propelling my enemies out of the room with just a hint of pressure on their elbows, but because I'm a big woman, their feet are off the ground, and obviously, afterwards, it never happened.

No, don't judge me until you've been there. In the end, there is only survival, under the ice, once you fall through. Then haul yourself back up to the surface. No education without order. The kids need me, Kriss, Deniece, chubby Abdul whose voice broke late. I am their teacher, I keep control. Some of what I teach them makes a difference.

I called in sick not long ago, before I went on the run, that is. That morning I was down to teach Shakespeare, and then a session on Sex and Relationships, SRE, to the girls of Year 10. I love those kids, I was letting them down, but this was a matter of life and death.

'Family problems,' I told Neil, the Head, who sounded surprised: I never take time off. The news about Dad had not got out.

'Your mother, I suppose,' he said helpfully when I declined to elaborate. 'Of course we want to be supportive. We all have families, Monica.'

'Uhhmmnn,' I offered in return.

'Problems at the Home?' Ma's in a Home.

'Problems at home, yes, got to go.'

But no, other families are not like mine.

When I try to explain to a new acquaintance, they sometimes say, trying to comfort me, 'All families are awful. Mine is!' Their evidence is trivial, like 'Someone was mean to someone else at Christmas'. I nod my big head and bare my teeth. Sometimes I laugh inappropriately, hahaha, hahaha.

The main thing is, Neil accepted it – you'd almost have thought he was relieved.

And so I was free to make my escape. Or try to escape. If anyone can.

I zoomed along at sixty down the wintry cliffs of Thanet, only half-listening to the five o'clock news. They were talking about another 'incident'. Central London was closed to traffic after a suspected bomb at Oxford Circus. A man with a beard had fled the scene. Was he a hoaxer, or incompetent? Was it a response to the attack on the mosque? Which was the seventh 'terrorist outrage' this year – the seventh *in Britain*! It's come to this! Law and order were at a crossroads.

How lucky we were to live in the country. Though no-one could call East Kent uneventful, not after the suicide bomb in Sandwich. And now the murderous attack in Margate. On my own father, in his own home. (Maybe Dad had annoyed a *jihadi*? Monica, unthink that thought.)

The radio was droning on about Brexit. Will we, won't we; he said, she said; endless stallings on dull committees. The referendum seemed decades ago.

Yet Thanet had felt a new vigour, having 'sent a message' to London. What was the message? Fuck off suits! Fuck off foreigners, and politicians!

Yes, got it. And so, what next?

Off to hell in a second-hand car. I was driving faster than I normally do. But everyone was driving faster, fewer people were paying taxes. I, Monica, know words like 'fewer', I, Monica, am on a pay roll, and I, Monica, have lived in Paris. I feel it, though. There's a Brexit spirit. Mon, drive carefully, beware of anarchy, life is cartwheeling out of control.

I was making for somewhere special that day, somewhere the

police didn't know about, getting to know the way the big old car, which was 'borrowed' (*stolen*), handled the road. Full speed ahead to Dad's holiday house, and for a moment my heart lifted, as if the nightmare hadn't happened, as if we could all begin again, as if we could be a family, but then the red curtain of horror fell. No, we could never begin again. But maybe I'd get a few days of grace?

Sun on the road was dazzling: it curved, empty, ahead of me, and to my right, the blue line of sea that always seems to promise absolution from guilt, worry, my heavy body – sometimes I swim for hours in the sea.

Grace: I do believe in it. I have known it as I sit in sunlight and sense blind life pulsing through me. I feel it sometimes when I write my diary, making words link hands and dance. I might do a book, when everyone's dead. I didn't read Seneca and Webster for nothing.

I can make life, or take it away.

2

Let's start again. I have a story to tell. There was a day on which bad things happened.

That day, it's true, I was not at my best. I had a hangover. I hadn't slept. No-one's at their best when they haven't slept.

Fact: my father was found covered in blood, one eye horribly punched back in its socket, his knuckles raw as chicken-bones. His pyjama jacket was pulled up over his shoulders so his head was like a cracked egg in a bag.

I looked at him and almost vommed.

Of course, I had to get away. That day I went charging through the undergrowth, swearing, wreathed in blood and snot and brambles, axe in my hand, towards the fields.

Who did that to him? Who?

Not me, at any rate.

Nor Ma, of course. Poor little Ma.

Ma is still afraid of him.

You don't need to be, Ma, not any more.

3

'Did you ever contemplate violence against your father?' the policeman asked me, later that day when, upon request, I accompanied him and his doddery colleague into the station. I sat in the back. Someone whistled in the car, which suggested one of them was feeling cheerful. Nobody had noticed the axe in the hall. I was not arrested, I was a witness. This was carefully explained to me, so I would like you to note the distinction.

The policeman was one of those smug graduates, making an effort to sound worldly-wise, and failing. He was a detective, or a superintendent, at any rate, he was in charge of things, or thought he was in charge of things. I asked him if I needed a lawyer, and he snorted, an unpleasant habit. I was going to say 'unattractive habit', but, bizarrely, the man was not unattractive. Testosterone alert, Monica! Yes, I do use exclamation marks – punctuation's my *métier*. In the right place they are most effective; and semi-colons are safe with me.

'You're here voluntarily, aren't you?' He smiled at me. He had a bouncy quality. It started to feel like a fencing match, but I was too tired to fence with him; that day I had seen my father, dead, though I didn't intend to mention it. 'Really it depends, Mrs Ludd.

How formal do you want this to be?'

What was he saying? Would it be kecks off?

He had red hair, which is a defect. And not enough of it, which is another. And pale blue eyes which looked small and polite. Almost grey. Almost friendly. Then when you didn't expect it, they sharpened. He wore a tie, which was perpendicular, as if he had sewn it to his pants.

'Did you ever contemplate violence against your father?' he asked. 'By the way, I'm not recording this.' He waved a dismissive hand at the machine. 'No need to write everything down in my day book either.'

The room was small, and smelled faintly of socks. Not his, I assumed. He was suave and dapper, though I generally prefer fully follicled men. How tall was he? He was certainly – sturdy. His thighs strained at his moleskin trousers ..

My concentration must have flickered, because he asked the question again. 'Did you consider violence against your father?'

'Of course I did – doesn't everyone?' was certainly too truthful an answer. The police dislike it when you question them, particularly about their own boiling minds. But then, I am habitually truthful. Or in your face, as some might say.

For a moment I thought I caught a flash in his eye, a flash of amusement, or even friendship, but no, I must have imagined it.

'A difficult man, your father,' he said. 'So I gather. Would you agree?'

I said nothing. What a fucking nerve! Was he a social worker, as well? But my head was nodding on its own. My head had found Dad difficult.

'By the way, remind me of your home address. I think I'll drop by again tomorrow. Don't bother to tidy up,' he added.

'Why, do you want to search me – officer?' Something about that sounded arch. Did it suggest 'search crevices'? He didn't answer. 'Your address,' he repeated, though he'd just been there, he should have known it.

I told him, and he wrote it down. (Small intense writing, pudgy hands, bowed pink scalp with that ant-path circling it, a failing stubble of auburn hairs.) The teacher in me wanted to shout at him: 'No one will be able to read THAT.'

He stopped writing and stared straight at me. 'I heard that. I'm not deaf,' he said. 'I would caution you to change your attitude.'

'I must have been thinking aloud. Sorry.'

Thought is free. No, it isn't.

'You could be in trouble,' he said, with a grin. Something peeked out on the left of his smile, some incongruous dental detail.

Did you consider violence?

I'd seen Dad battered so many times, in the secret dirty rooms of my dreams, and now I had seen it in broad daylight. My error was writing everything down, and now, oopsy, I've done it again, though I mean to hide this so far out of sight that only God and I will read it.

I'm not crazy, but I have imagination.

No, not crazy, but I do have blind spots.

Taking the axe on the bus was crazy.

I should have buried it far away. I didn't expect the police so quickly.

So many errors. I had no practice. One chance at it, one: the electric instant when all the detail falls away and you're there, surfing a wall of desire, black and dazzling, he's there in front of you, blood is pounding in your head –

Sometimes you just have to go over.

I left in shock, with my bloodied axe.

So much to explain, so little time. Then again, least said, soonest mended.

I shouldn't have said, as we left for the police station, 'I wasn't there, I know nothing about it.'

If you never lie, if you're a bad liar, don't do it when you're in a tight corner. In the end, 'The truth is best' – Dad's banal mantra did make sense, though he normally backed it up with a false-hood: 'I have never told a lie.'

(He lived in a land of perpetual repetition, because Ma never challenged him. His words must have sounded empty to him, bouncing futilely off the mirror.)

I have told lies, Dad, since you died. Lie after lie, and then some more. Just to get from breakfast to supper. Just to stop them arresting me the first time they came round to mine, when they turned up looking all cross and excited, until I said I was a Deputy Head.

'The truth and nothing but the truth.' *So help me, Dad.*

Help me, Dad. You know the truth, in the land of the dead.

4

Why have the police left me at large? Do they hope I'll implicate someone else?

It gives me time to set my story straight. So many stories, all jostling for space: Fred's story – *Story of a Quiet Hero*. Dad's story – *The Villain's Tale*. My story – *Unjustly Suspected*.

So let's begin with a picture of me. Then I'll attempt my sisters and brothers.

I'm thirty-eight years old, in my prime. I'm blessed with height, at six foot one. Monica is an amazon, strong, deep-chested, solid haunches, long muscular legs. The staff biscuit-tin belongs to me. Call me FAT, but that's better than skinny.

Don't call me fat. If you do, I'll have you. Larger women are more attractive. Male eyes feast upon my breasts. Then they dip towards my hips and try to slip around to my buttocks. Can I bounce those juicy jouncers!

When I want. When I choose to seduce. Otherwise, boys, better look away.

My brows! Yes, caterpillar brows are having a moment. One more thing other women envy! Though they seem scared to meet my eyes, after that second of shock at how tall I am. My brows do merit a second look.

Black, thick and marked, a dark wood on the brow-ridge. Maybe I have Neanderthal genes – they were sensitive giants who buried their dead. If I frown, half my face is in shadow.

It's a long face, a strong face, with a long strong well-cut FABULOUS nose. (I won't apologise. *Lusus naturae*! Nature has played a game with me.)

I'm currently single, though I do like men. Lovers, bless them, not sure how many – more than twenty, fewer than two hundred…

Monica – Monica. More heart, less speed. I have had loves. And I have longed.

I can't help being sexually desirable, can I? I have my needs. And sudden impulses. Sometimes they've got me into trouble. Maybe I do take after my father.

In my twenties I tried to be a man. I think I wanted to be so strong that Dad could never hurt me again. I had a loud voice, my limbs were like tree-trunks, I powered down the middle of pavements. At social occasions I took no prisoners, stroked no egos except my own. I learned to do wiring, roofing, swearing. Being a six-footer helps, of course. I learned maleness from my two big brothers, the Terrible Twosome, Angus and Boris, who were a dozen years older than me. Terrible Twos, we called them for short –

Time to introduce my siblings, the eldest first: Angus and Boris.

Twins, absurdly identical, till Angus dyed his hair blond five years ago, which made them scarier to everyone, except us Ludds, who felt affronted. They were impressive, my two big brothers. Beer-barrel limbs, size 14 shoes, shoulders wide as snooker tables. Built like Dad, only one size bigger. They were slow to speech, but quick to rage, till Boris found ways of repressing it. They did maths and physics as easily as breathing. Angus was fractionally cleverer than Boris, but Boris was better at managing the world, half an inch taller and three kilos heavier. Angus was bonkers. Stark, staring. He understood numbers, but not language, and needed Boris for protection.

Boris must have invented the name for the software firm they started in their twenties, with shining new identical PhDs from MIT: *Buoyant*. They were forced to go it alone so young because Angus hit the managing director of the Californian IT outfit that took them on. They'd only been at work for five hours. The man told Angus to use deodorant a second before his nose got broken.

Boris had girlfriends: Angus did not. Maybe the great dorks only loved each other. Their firm ended up employing a thousand people, selling for millions in 2008 just before the market imploded.

Then they came 'home' – laughingly described as. They meant to stay in a London hotel and day-trip to Margate to visit us, but Dad was so scathing on the phone – 'Too good for us now, I suppose?' – that partly to prove the old bastard wrong they agreed to stay with Dad and Fred. One furious row later, they had moved out, paying cash for a vast green cliff-top palace near the park Moses Montefiore left to Ramsgate. Sir Moses Montefiore, Ramsgate's greatest man, who gave money to children, and schools, even churches, despite being a famous Jew, and hand-outs to poor Muslims in Jerusalem. Why couldn't I have had a dad like him?

But no, I had to be the dentist's daughter, and got no pocket money at all.

There are three of us girls, three sisters, three daughters, Anthea, Monica and 'Fairy' Sarah. I'm the middle daughter of Mum and Dad, the only middling thing about me.

Anthea's seven years older than me. Glamazon Anth, in advertising, with her brands and concepts, her leopard-print heels, her stashes of cashmere ('I can't stand *cheap* cashmere') and leather jackets and gym-bunny joggers and must-have Thai spa holidays, her giggling walkers and work crises and 'Oh my God, do I need a massage!' and blonde extensions and what is the new thing, *balayage*, fucking *balayage*? I think it means primping your bush with a paint-brush. If you ask me, Anthea's gay – always going off on 'girls' trips' with 'a friend' to Vienna or the Virgin Islands. Apparently she needs to 'de-stress' – from advertising? Let her try teaching!

Yet the bitch had the nerve to tell me I 'looked like a lezzer' when I made the mistake of cutting my hair off. I only did it once; my features looked HUGE. 'It's just a joke; don't go off on one,' she said, as I chased her round the room. 'Say sorry,' I said, pushing my face into hers, which involved a bit of stooping on my part. 'Sorry,' she said, 'though it is a bit butch. But everyone knows you're a slag, not a lezzer.'

One day

She'll pay.

Anthea and I never took to each other (though I definitely disliked Fairy more). But Anthea is not all bad. Once when our father had knocked me down, my big sister protected me. Aged eleven, I announced it was unfair that he had two bathrooms all to himself while the rest of us shared one freezing lav. I didn't get to the end of my sentence before a great howling wind hit my ear, and then his other paw whacked my nose. Pain in a wave and prickling tears. Anthea came and took my hand and yanked me to my feet again. Dad shouted, 'Leave her alone, it's none of your fucking business, Anthea,' but I was spouting blood from my nose, all over my sister, all over the floor, and perhaps our father was taken aback. He yelled, 'The pair of you make me sick,' and thundered upstairs. For a second we were friends.

Later, I would take boxing lessons.

Although I don't like her, I remember it. When all's said and done, Anth's my sister. An older sister is easier, they're part of the world before you arrive.

But Fairy is fifteen years younger than Anthea, eight years younger than me, Monica. She was christened Sarah – but her nickname suited her. As a kid she was hardly human, tiny and trembly with transparent skin and limbs like the wands of Japanese mushrooms. Her eyes were sky-blue and aslant, like elves' eyes, and constantly brimming, two teary pools, even when I didn't torture her. As a toddler, she hid by the sofa, not toddling.

'Come on, Fairy, give it a go!!' Clinging to life by a single thread that might snap if anyone shouted. I always shouted, perhaps I am deaf, people have suggested it, yet I hear insults, even in whispers.

Wand-thin Fairy actually loved baking, the only one of us to copy Ma. She even cleaned up after her. Whereas I, her hungry older sister, scooped up spoons of her raw cake-mix, *Burr-rr-p, sorry!*, kicked the oven door and stomped from the kitchen with a multipack of KitKats.

Anthea and I both bullied her. I more than Anthea, because it was enraging to be followed, as a giant, by a pretty little fairy. Which meant our big brothers picked on me, because it was easier to haul me off Fairy than ask what she had done to annoy me.

Looking like she did. That was Fairy's worst fault. She stole the hearts of our father and mother, and the Terrible Twos, my brothers, adored her.

She was a trouble-free baby, but a deadly dull child, which Ma misinterpreted as 'being good'. Fairy wasn't bright, academically – I, of course, was always first at English, Anthea was all-round competent, our big brothers were geniuses – nor did she have friends, at primary school. She was too fragile to play rough games, too selfish to listen, too weird to smile.

But at secondary school she came into her kingdom. No longer weird, she was suddenly a beauty. She shot up to be one inch shorter than me, though she never seemed to get much broader, and her lips and eyes became bigger, if possible. She grew her curly hair down her back in a tangle of sickly-sweet natural blonde, yet Ma never tried that maddening trick she'd played on me when I was adolescent, pursing her mouth into little pleats and mutely stretching out a hairbrush.

YOU'RE RIGHT, I HATED MY LITTLE SISTER.

But I was proud of her, as well. Fairy was a phenomenon. People stopped talking when she walked into a room. And so, the modern fairy-tale – she went to London for the day, from Margate, with her friend, Anita, a plump, pretty black girl with a lisp, and they strolled into Top Shop to look at boots, and a talent scout from Storm spotted her. She was fourteen years old. It was the beginning. And the end of her friendship with Anita.

We expected Dad to veto the modelling, but no! He hoarded photographs of Fairy, piling up copies of glossy magazines on the sitting-room sofa where he watched TV. When Ma complained there was no room for her, he moved them out into his den. Ma said, 'She's young, men can't control themselves,' and he said, his voice getting harder and rougher in the way we all knew too well, 'You're not going to spoil this for her, April. She's not the sharpest knife in the box, she might as well sell her pretty face.'

I told the little show-off what Dad had said, because I thought it would be good for her. (Well yes, OK, because I was jealous.) Her delicate, faultless skin turned pink, her ear-lobes and her elvish cheek-bones. It made me feel powerful, watching that happen. Then, like a lamia, her sharp tongue flickered. 'I'd rather be thick than bright and ugly,' she hiss-whispered. 'Do you know what they'll be paying me?' She left school with two GCSEs and was crafted into a news story. While the other Ludds bored on in Thanet, she was termed 'THE NEW KATE' and 'THE NEW DARYUSHA'.

All of us felt the reflected glory, though when she visited we tried not to show it. (Why had she left home ahead of me? I was doing A-levels, then uni, and Dad still treated me like a great gooby.)

She changed her name from Sarah 'Fairy' Ludd to plain 'Fairy', at Storm's suggestion, her 'Ludd' lopped off. We felt rejected, but the name was short and international. She started phoning from distant hotel rooms. Once she sobbed for an hour from Tokyo. Ma said, 'You should never have let her go', and Dad poured black coffee over her hand.

(Why didn't she stand up for herself? No, unfair, don't blame the victim, although, let's face it, victims are vexing.)

Fairy's trips home were brief, and Dad behaved oddly well around her, as if she had become a different person along with her new name, so we had to follow the rules for strangers – no actual violence; no throwing food.

The starry rise of my little sister seems more astonishing now it's peaked and is sliding away into soft focus. She's thirty now, which is fine for a model if you're Naomi Campbell or Anna Pyre. But Fairy was always half water and air: she's started to shrink, minutely, and shrivel.

The *Vogue* covers have dried up, like her. She's lovely from a distance, fine from a distance. The catalogues would be thrilled to use her, but that would be a humiliation. (I buy from catalogues: I have to. Only catalogues have things in Extra Plus Extra.) Fairy's hanging on to the side of the hill, and her nails dig in but she's still sliding down, little by little, hour by hour.

I don't want to see it. In a way, I love her. Though obviously I can't stand her. Anthea, ditto. And of course, the boys.

Now you have met nearly all of us. Angus and Boris, Fairy and Anthea. That leaves only Ma and Fred. It's an effort for me to remember that name because our father dubbed him 'Ferd' when it turned out he was hopeless at spelling. We all copied; Fred became 'Ferd'.

Maybe it mattered. Of course it mattered. Was I a good sister?

He sat on my lap. When he was small enough, not as an adult. I cuddled him, shared chips with him, on the wonderful days when Ma ordered in chips. My chips: I didn't always steal his. I held him in my arms, my brother.

5

Time to record some facts about Dad.

His dental practice is, or was, in Old Town, Margate, northeast Kent. There is a receptionist, Esmeralda, who's been with him for nearly half a century. Way back at the beginning of his career, Dad was 'a pillar of the NHS. I did my time,' he would proclaim. 'I had the biggest practice in Thanet.' Yes, too right, though there was more to it, but I won't tell the bad stuff all at once. Lately he only took private patients.

Dad was one of the first British dentists to offer one particular service: all out, all temporaries in, in one day. He had a website: he advertised. A photo of a model he had never treated, grinning out with great fright-white fangs:

The Perfect Smile
between lunch and dinner.
Be the one you always wanted to be –
that younger, better, brighter you.

Dad had a few difficult patients. 'Never let anyone in,' he told us. The ferrets guarded his bolt-hole at home, which no-one but Ma was allowed to enter, back in the day when we all lived together. (Who's feeding them now? Don't think about that. What will they do if they get desperate?)

Dentistry has served Dad well. He bought two properties in Boom Town, and a series of great fat dentists' cars, big fuckoff Range Rovers or Jaguars.

Margate is a dump, some opine, but this view is out of date. The *Daily Telegraph* saw merit in Kent. Property prices went zooming up like tower-blocks over stinking water. Margate has Tracey Emin, who filmed herself riding a big horse over the sunset sands, some of the longest sands in Britain. We have the Old Town, now the bit with new money, tall Georgian houses and the Turner Centre, a brutalist white box with all the beauty inside, and cheap antique shops and sparkling clean cafés that sell tiny cakes at tiny tables.

I hate those midget cafés which make normal, healthy people like me feel, well, outsize! Whereas Fairy, my sister, Queen of Anorexia, hovers above the little gold chairs like a dragonfly in a pool of sunlight. Fairy is a model. So could I have been! But I preferred to use my brains – Fairy didn't have that option.

Dad also owns one of those Georgian houses in one of the new 'best squares in Margate' (*Telegraph*, September 2017). Dad and Ma – how quaint that phrase sounds now, when they've been apart for fifteen years – bought it when they were in their twenties. It probably cost them a few thousand pounds; a bed-and-breakfast full of fire-doors and basins, which Dad wrenched out to make a 'family home'. That was where most of the bad stuff happened. Ma had taste, so they preserved the features. Now it's said to be worth £2 million, which divided by five, as we have to, fair's fair, even though my brothers don't need the money, and nor does Fairy, and nor does Anthea – makes £400,000 each.

You think me mercenary? Not at all. All of us make those calculations.

Though I fear the value of the house may plunge. People don't like the smell of a crime.

And I'm in trouble, dreadful trouble, with far to go before I sleep…

Deep doggy-doo.
Cock-a-doodle-oo!

6

I've never known what to say about Ma. But when she left home, she abandoned Fred. Left him to his fate with Dad.

Oh, I'm one of five, but we should be six. Three brothers, three sisters, five live, one dead, and the dead one, the source of all the grief, is Fred. Frederick, to give him his proper name. He was the youngest and should have lived longest. My youngest brother, our youngest boy.

What happened to Fred cannot be undone.

I started explaining this to the policeman. 'My father killed my brother,' I said. The ginger's pale-blue eyes popped open. 'In Afghanistan, I mean.' I saw he now thought me completely insane. 'That is, Dad bullied him into the army,' I added, and his pupils relaxed.

They called Fred 'Pizza Face' at secondary school. Like Fairy, he failed the eleven-plus, the fence which all Ludds were supposed to soar over. Teenage Fred was pale and spotty and never bothered to stand up for himself. The few times he did, though, the results were surprising. He was fit, Fred, and a marathon runner. Once set on an action, he didn't give up. Which is why he won races, and why he died: he just kept going, he never gave up. I'll tell you that story when there's more time, and when I can – when I can –

When I can bear it.

What was Fred like? People said he was 'kind'. People at his funeral, they said that. Yes, good-natured, when we left him alone, and weirdly tolerant when we didn't. A good-natured Ludd! It puzzled us all. He agreed to most things without complaint, and then he just got on and did it. He didn't want to go into the army but, once he was there, he was a good soldier, so his commanding officer affirmed in a letter sent us after his death that told us where and why he died.

But we knew Fred, we had always known him. Anything he started, he followed through.

I was fifteen and he was five when I made a Kleenex sandwich for him, and he trialled it without a murmur. Look, I was having a 'scientist' phase, and this was an experiment! And no, I never did it again. Not *that* experiment, at any rate. He was small and brave and he smiled through the fibres, and wouldn't stop eating when I told him to, he kept on chewing and smiling and choking, with curds of tissue all over his teeth and something blind and mad in his eyes…Maybe he was a Ludd, after all. But later that day when Dad hung me out of an upstairs window to punish me, little Fred cried and begged for my life, which was fortunate, because I refused to.

He lacked the Ludd aggressive streak: hadn't the guile to defend himself. Should we have defended him? Hard enough to survive ourselves. Why am I crying? My poor raw nose's roots are stinging at the back of my throat.

Fred said he wanted to be a farmer. None of us took him seriously. There had never been farming in the Ludd family, not that we knew what our forebears had been, there were no records, no memory. 'A farmer? Here? Are you mad? They're rich bastards,' our father roared. 'They inherit land. There isn't any land left, in Thanet.'

He was wrong, of course. There are wide white beaches. The best beaches this side of the Bahamas, the sea that links us to the world, or cuts us off from it. And there are still stretches of rolling green: Pegwell; Cliff's End; the North Foreland. Dad never shifts his great hams out of the car, what would he know about *terra firma*?

'I want to go somewhere different,' Fred said, not meeting Dad's great red scornful eyes. 'There would be fields. I could run, as well.'

'Where?' said Dad. 'You know nothing, twat.'

'Cornwall,' he said. 'Might be a shepherd.' He'd been reading some book about a shepherd's life.

'I'd rather see you dead,' said Dad.

Fred went back to the Pfizer factory. Shortly after, he was sacked (again) because they couldn't put up with his marathon training. This happened in the handful of days when Boris and Angus were living at home after coming back rich from the USA. It was teatime but, without Ma, no tea.

Fred was doing press-ups by the kitchen table. Dad said the Army would make a man of him. Fred went on to a hundred reps and didn't seem to hear Dad's goading, but afterwards, Dad wouldn't let up. 'The army, that's what you need, you pussy, that's what would make a man of you!' Angus picked up a big wooden chair and made for Dad with murder on his mind but Fred and Boris pulled him away, and that was when the Twins left home for ever – well, they moved as far as Ramsgate.

Soon afterwards, Fred went and joined up. Probably he couldn't bear Dad's jibes, or maybe he looked forward to army marathons. He did come second in an inter-services run, and never told us – that was in his officer's letter, too.

Our brother Fred died in Afghanistan, fighting a war only idiots believed in. Five years ago; five years dead. Fred who had been our pale lean baby, draped like spaghetti from lap to lap, amiable, harmless, no trouble to anyone – Fred was stopped by a bullet in the back. What was it like? What's it like to be killed? A sledgehammer blow, the ground slamming up?

Did he have a flash of us at home?

That one split second was the crux of it all, the moment when we were tipped towards – what? An act of justice, or a murder?

No, don't think about the Kleenex sandwich, the way Fred's pale face wouldn't stop eating, Monica, don't blame yourself – we blame our father, we blame Dad! Yes, and he thought it would be forgotten, as all his other crimes had been.

The rest of this story follows from that. One death, then another death. Soon there will be bodies all over the landscape.

7   Adoncia

My name Adoncia, in fact. At first he say, 'Such pretty name. I love it! A-don-cia, A-don-cia!' He singing as he put the drill in my mouth, and he watch me jump, just a little bit, and I see he laughing, and I know he trouble, but I like his smell.

Oh OK, that first time, yes, I willing, actually. My young man Luis been out too much, come back too late and sleep like baby. I love my Luis, but maybe I lonely. Maybe I want to feel sexy again. I like Albert's thingy – big and red. Stick up so hard it bang at his belly. He breathe loud and funny like a big pork pig. And he smile big smile with his big white teeth. His big white teeth and his red *salchichón*. My appointment always at end of day; he send the dental nurse away. And then receptionist, Esmeralda, like tiny monkey, *demasiado* lipstick, small nose sniffing like she not approve of me, Albert say, 'You go home early.'

Later of course Albert grew bore. He start to call me 'Dunce' and 'Donkey'. I let him. Yes, I hook by then. I wish I never let him do it. Because a name, you know, very special. Adoncia. I love my name. My father choose it, before he in prison. So, Albert disrespect my *padres*, actually. 'Come on Donkey, let's get going.' 'YEE-ha, the Donkey in the chair!'

He the one not human. He the one stupid, because he not see what coming to him, Señor Albert *hijo de puta* Ludd.

I the one coming, Mr Albert.

Part 2

Fred's Party

8

11 p.m., hour of the witch. No sleep for Monica, not tonight. Come to my aid, hags and vixens, witches, viragos, devil-women, bitches.

Tell my side of things before they arrest me.

I took the lead in arranging Fred's party because I never quite gave up on my family. We were different, you see. Not like other people. My enormous twin brothers with their brilliant millions; Fairy, our elegant giraffe; business-class, high-gloss Anthea with her high-intensity exercise and her coke habit whizzing like a trapped hornet.

Angus and Boz were going to be fifty, Anthea was pushing forty-five, Fairy was trembling on the edge of thirty. All of my siblings were born in winter, on the dark side of the year, November, December, so I told each one that the party was for them, 'And for Fred, of course. To remember Fred.'

We all need to be special, don't we?

When Anthea was fifteen and I was eight, my sister told me I was 'special needs'. That made me proud, till I told my teacher.

Everyone's special, but I don't always feel it. Mostly when someone has sex with me. Just before it happens: that moment of wonder: they want something and think it is me.

November 1 was Fred's twenty-fifth birthday. Would have been…could have been. Instead he had been dead for five years.

The perfect day for a memorial.

Ma. I can't put it off any more. Ma, so hard to think about.

We had to invite her to the Party. She was Fred's mother. Plus, she might find out – the Cliffetoppe's receptionist-owner was a gossip. We thought we could invite Ma, because she wouldn't come.

Did I mention that Ma always drank? Did Dad sense, when he married her, that she had a weakness? He liked cracked vessels. The young, the foreign, the desperate to be beautiful, which included most of the implant patients, bashed on the jaw by the ugly stick.

Not long ago Ma gave up drinking. I went round to the Home to see her. We had our routine. 'Shall I pour you a sherry?'

'There's none in the cupboard.'

'I'll go out and get some.'

'Don't.'

When I asked her how she had managed it, she simply answered, 'The switch turned off.' Why couldn't she have done that decades ago, which might have made her less shit as a mother?

'I'm going on a health kick,' said the sweet little voice out of the sweet little face with the porcelain skin that Fairy had inherited. 'Nikki is helping.'

'Who?'

'Nikki.'

'Oh.'

Yes, the windbag in reception, who wrote us letters about 'our residents'. The fucking stupid spelling of her name made me unable to remember it.

'And I'm taking up weight training,' she added. She pronounced it 'Wee-ate Treening', with one of her teeny trills of elocuted vowels.

'Have you been got at by Anthea, Ma?' My sister favoured Tai-Chi with dumb-bells.

'I've a mind of my own, though no-one has noticed,' Ma answered, drawing herself up in her chair. Her neck, for once, was supporting her head.

'We're throwing a party in November,' I said. 'I know you won't come, Ma, but, course, you'd be welcome.'

Her curranty eyes had blinked wide with shock. 'Party? What for?'

'Ferd,' I said. Then I corrected myself. 'Fred. You'd hate it, Ma, you'd get upset.'

'Fred was my baby,' she said. 'Where is it?'

'School hall. Nothing remotely exciting.'

'Is your father going?' she'd almost whispered. 'I'm coming if he is, you can't stop me.'

'Stop you?' I said. 'I was inviting you.' Damn, damn, now there would be trouble, but no, no, she would forget.

'I'll buy a frock,' she claimed, wildly.

'Of course you will. You'll be gorgeous,' I leered. I happened to know Ma had no shoes, so the dress would have to go with furry slippers and one of two pairs of reindeer bedsocks.

'By the way, how IS your father?' Now her little eyes looked sharp and suspicious.

'Cheerful.' (Because of his girlfriend, obscenely young, a hideous fact we had hidden from Ma.)

'I know he's fucking fucking a trollop,' she spat, her white neck rearing up like a cobra. I had a kid did a project on one, as part

27

of detention for spitting himself – the Nubian Spitting Cobra on his YouTube clip was less alarming than Ma that day. My mouth dropped open. I stared at her. It was one of the rare times I had heard her swear. 'Mo-*ther*,' I said.

'You swear,' she countered. 'Why am I the only one in the family not supposed to? He's got some whore. Nikki told me.'

It was obvious Dad had to attend Fred's party, to compensate us for his crimes, to show respect, for Fred, for us, but there was no way he could bring the Girl.

Only Anthea and Fred had met her. We all referred to her as the Girl, though her name was Veronica Karlin. Anthea went home unexpectedly one day and found Dad in a state she couldn't bear to describe with a girl she just said looked like a schoolgirl. 'Glasses? Frown? Big tits? White bra? Went bright red, and Dad yelled at me?' Half the girl's family was Orthodox Jewish – after the father went to prison, her brothers started reading the Torah and both acquired those spaniel locks.

(Neil, our mealy-mouthed Head Teacher, bridled when I used that phrase to him, describing the hilarious band of Jews who make an annual pilgrimage to Ramsgate because the great Sir Moses lived here, and visit the synagogue in Montefiore woods, then actually go bathing in their dreary dark coats – one of them drowned at Broadstairs. Yes, tragic, but get your kit off! 'That phrase might be culturally sensitive?' he quivered. 'Which one?' I said, out of devilment. 'Spaniel locks,' he whispered, anxious. I just wanted to make him say it! 'Most people think I'm insensitive,' I laughed, but no, Neil was still 'unhappy'. 'It's a metaphor, Neil,' I insisted. 'But we have to ask, is it the right one, Monica?')

Back to the Girl. I must not be distracted. We assumed she was blind and soft in the head because she was going out with our father, but then there was the question of our parents' house, and we weren't going to let the fat tart inherit.

'The family's religious, I'll have to marry her,' Dad said. 'She's got some problems. Well, a health problem.' The over-explaining suggested he knew we'd view the project with disfavour. Health problem? She was probably pregnant. Fred must have been traumatised by knowing his father was fucking a girl not much older than him. (We think Fred was a virgin when he died. It made his death sadder. *I hate my father.* He had to have everything, the house, the power, the sex his son was debarred from having.)

Obviously the Girl couldn't come to the party. But none of the others could say this to Dad. I got lumbered, as I usually did.

Anthea and I had gone for a walk to thrash out some details about the Party. The tide was low, autumn sunlight, the sea was crawling towards our feet. 'The whole Party thing was your idea – and any way, Mono, you're not scared of him?' Anthea insisted, incorrectly, using the rising twang she loved, borrowed from Australia, and idiots. 'You're his favourite?' she added. 'No, you ARE!'

But then, Anthea was in PR.

Oh treacherous heart! Part of me swelled with joy to think I might be my father's favourite. On the horizon, a tiny boat, its sails neat white triangles, was scarcely moving towards Dover.

'Why do you say that, Anthea?' Of course, I longed for some evidence.

Long pause. My heart began to shrink again, back to black pickled-walnut size, and a caul of grey cloud shrouded the sun. I could see the tangled roots of Anthea's extensions.

'I don't know, but you look like him. You are like him.'

'Fuck off, what an insult!'

'Just ring Dad and tell him not to bring her. Don't tell me that you're scared too?'

Fear: pride. Great tides crashing. 'I'm not afraid of the old bastard,' I lied.

I fooled them all. Perhaps I was brave, because that's what it means, to be afraid but to rush the gate where the machine-gun's blazing. His bloodshot eyes, his bullish jaw. *But were we slaves? Could we live like slaves?*

When he picked up Fairy by her bush of blonde hair, when he chased the boys upstairs, roaring, viciously belabouring their great raw calves, when he snatched Anthea's new palette of make-up (she was seventeen, it had come by post, she was too in love with it to hear Dad's order to 'get her fat arse off the sofa', and he snatched the palette and snapped it in two down its pink, weak, glitter-plastic hinges, she was weeping and pleading as he chucked it in the bin), when he made Fred kneel to apologise for dropping Dad's favourite mug on the concrete – 'I'll mend it, Dad, please don't hit me' – in a blaze of red, I stood up to him: and they all believed I was not afraid.

It was the shame that made me oppose him, the shame of living under a tyrant, with Ma unwilling to do anything.

The morning after that chat with Anthea I sat for an age palping the phone. Then my hand punched in his number on its own.

Silence, and the sullen, heavy breathing of a man with people he didn't want to talk to.

'All right, Dad?'

He grunted.

'Ripping plenty of teeth from their jaws?'

'I am an excellent dentist, Mono.'

Long ago, when I was a teenager, Dad had given me work experience after all my other interviews ended in failure – some people asked me to talk more quietly, some said I should sit a little farther away. Dad drove me to his surgery next day, the usual manic ride in the Jag, with him speeding up whenever people tried to overtake us. There I got to know Esmeralda, his receptionist, now our honorary aunt. The paperwork was all off-limits: I spent my time checking in the appointments. Afterwards Dad was more than usually aggressive. 'So have you learned anything, Mono?' he roared. 'Have you learned anything about hard work?' 'Why didn't you pay me? Other girls got paid.' 'Well other girls managed to get real jobs. I only took you on out of pity.' One afternoon about five years later I ran into Esmeralda on the beach in Broadstairs, and found she had a problem with drink. She went and bought a bottle of wine, then sank another without blinking. And talked. She knew too much about Dad. I may have asked a casual question. Dad's NHS practice was all smoke and mirrors. The dead, the unborn, they were all registered. Finally, the police grew interested. Dad had gone private just in time.

'Plenty of implants?' I prompted him, now.

'A few,' Dad said slowly, with an overtone of threat. 'Are you sniffing round for a loan, Mono?'

I could hear the angry smile in his voice, I could see him baring his jaws at me, the tombstone teeth in their shiny red gums, their enamel as white as his dental coats, bleached by Esmeralda, one for every day. A meat sweat of rage and horror rushed through me. 'Did I ever ask you for money?' I said. 'I am a Deputy Head teacher. I don't need money, I have my own money. It's about the party we're planning, Dad. Make sure you're there –'

But my father interrupted. 'Esma-*fucking*-ralda put it in the diary. Is your mother going? I need hardly ask.'

'We invited her. She won't go though, will she?'

'No,' he said. Was there a hint of regret?

If there was, I would leap on it. 'Not least because *you're* going,' I lied.

A sharp intake of breath. I heard the smile increase, a great shark smiling before it gashed me. 'Your mother won't go because she's senile. You don't want a drooling mong at your party.'

'You learned that word from that girl,' I snapped, outraged, as he intended.

'That girl?' he said. 'Careful. Veronica is my fianc*ée*.'

He put ridiculous emphasis on the last syllable, either to suggest irony or, more likely, because he knew no better. Anapests are wasted on my father. Yes, the anapest, *da-da-DUM*.

'Don't bring the whore to the party. Don't,' I shouted. It was out, too fast. I'd wanted to sound firm, mature, objective. 'Angus will kick off, you know he will. Could you for once consider your children?'

'You're a stupid – ugly – spinster, aren't you?' Dad asked quietly. 'Consider my children? *Consider* them? Family's everything to me. I've sacrificed my life for you. Did you think I wanted to be a dentist? No, I wanted to be in the army, but kids suffer when their fathers are away and the mother is incompetent. You lot lived off the fat of the land because your father put food on the table. Do you think it was easy living with your mother? A *man* needs a proper *woman*. Your mother was never a normal woman –'

'Stop insulting our mother,' I shouted.

'– whereas Veronica, now, she's a normal woman. A normal woman, with normal *needs*.'

'Don't tell me about your disgusting sex life!' I yelled. 'Don't bring the cow to the fucking party!'

'You swore at me,' he said, sounding happy, his voice overlaid with silken calm. 'I'll wait for you to apologise.'

With that, our father put the phone down.

The terminal hum of the severed line.

Four months went by without me speaking to him.

9

This seemed to count against me with the ginger detective. I was in my home, being interviewed, the day after their first knock on my door.

'How long is it since you saw your father?' he asked me.

'Not for a month. Two months. Four.'

'And yet you say you loved your father? He didn't live very far away.'

'He's very busy. He's a dentist. I often call to find him out.'

A very old joke made me want to laugh. *The vicar called and found you out.*

'Is something funny?'

'Just indigestion.'

'You didn't like your father,' Ginger said.

There was a pause while I assessed his eyes: small, blue-grey, intelligent. Something there I did not dislike. Something he wanted to say to me. Instead of bluffing, I sat and waited.

'Other people might agree with you,' he added, after what felt like minutes. 'Why might people dislike your father?'

I sidestepped it with a quote from Dad. 'Family was everything to my father.'

He frowned with annoyance and tapped one finger. 'I asked you why your father was hated. Why you didn't see him much. Yesterday you claimed you saw him a lot. Have you forgotten what you told me? Luckily, I have a note. You said that's why your car was parked there. You told me you like to power-walk home. Six miles or so. That's what you told me.' He said the words 'power-walk' with a wealth of irony. Yes, he was enjoying himself.

'I was upset, I must have mis-spoke. Sorry, that's ungrammatical.' He nodded; his eyes were faintly impressed. He passed over my lie, as if it were a detail.

'Your father had a reputation,' he said.

Surely, he was leading the witness? (Was I a witness or a suspect?)

'People don't tend to like dentists,' I stated. 'We were all upset. By my brother's death. Perhaps it had caused a coolness.'

'Ah, a *froideur*.' That note of irony. Or was he just correcting me? Mon is an English teacher, Sunshine, plus I spent six months in Paris.

'I rang to ask Dad to our party. He didn't come. That was his choice.'

'He didn't come to your brother's wake. Some might think you'd be furious.'

That amused smile, those small blue eyes, small shiny pebbles with a fringe of pale lash.

What does he want? It's as if he knows us. Is he just waiting for me to say, 'It's a fair cop, OK, arrest us'?

10 Adoncia

'Family's everything to me,' he saying. That *fucking* bastard with his five children (me, I have one. She dwarf, and lazy, she never leave Malaga, live in a Home. Luis say I mean but it cost a lot of money. I always pay, but who love a dwarf? Who going to marry my poor Juanita? *De hecho*, I have no family. Family mean future. Family mean baby. Yes, Albert guess I have no family.) 'Don't never mess with my children,' he say, when I ring him, one time only, at the house. 'You don't know who you're messing with.'

He don't say so much about his *fucking* kiddies when he tipping the dental chair back almost to the floor, then climb on top of me, like is his right. He rip a button off his white coat because he can't wait to get his *porra* out. Foreplay, to him, was ride on the chair. 'I give you a little discount,' he say.

'Discount?' I smile at him standing there. When they in that state, they do anything for you. I pull up blouse and show him my boobies. They nice booby, I always know. 'Better be *fucking* free, my friend.'

'Maybe this once,' he say.

And he mean it.

After that, he just make small discount. 20% for oral, 30% for fucky-fuck, but free, he say, after the first time, only for my *culo*, and that, I tell him, I NEVER give him.

In the end, though, I make him an offer.

11 Monica

Suddenly it was the day before the Party, and everything was going to plan.

I, Monica, supplied the venue. Our school hall was a brutal-ist hangar, with strip-lighting and steps to the playground. There was a stage where we could make speeches. Anthea was doing the 'decorations', which sounded ominous to me, but she explained it was Halloween. 'Give or take a day, Mono? You'll love it, believe me?' she carolled in that maddening Sydney sing-song she'd learned in the years when she escaped Margate and lived beach-side in Australia and worked in bars; years when her hair turned curly and blonde and she gained tanned biceps and, probably, girlfriends. And there were twangs of LA in there, unconvincing borrowings from Hollywood films. I should have been used to that voice by now but part of me wanted to bawl, 'Come off it.' Her teenage voice had been cold and nasal and her hair a bear-pelt of greasy brown. As a child I must have needed someone to look up to, but Anthea was a poor role model.

Looking at it from her point of view (a namby-pamby habit I try to avoid – empathy, that lispy, whimpery word), she was probably longing to baby me when I burst into the world, weigh-ing fifteen pounds, sporting a rug of coarse black hair which made me look like a chimpanzee, as the single remaining pho-tograph proves.

No-one told me I was beautiful. A beautiful baby. Imagine it.

One day I'll have a baby too, once I have trapped a source of sperm.

No, forget it, back to the Party.

'Pull together,' Dad always said. Did the Ludds pull together for the Party?

No. The others just did their own thing (except Angus and Boris, who did everything together). It was my school, for heaven's sake, so I offered to help Anthea decorate. 'No, Kelly will help me. Let us get on with it?'

Kelly. Her current friend, or girlfriend, who rode pillion on the motorbike that Anthea kept at Dumpton Gap in the same garage as her Japanese jeep. I met her for the first time that day, in Anthea's kitchen, a white-and-chrome copy of the monstrous kitchen on TV's *Masterchef*, though Anthea can't warm a tin of baked beans. Kelly hung round us with a nose like a button, tiny and shiny and annoying. I wished the silly bitch would eff off, so my sis and I could squabble uninterrupted.

'I was just offering to help,' I said.

'No, you weren't, Mon. You're a control freak?'

'It's MY school hall,' I said, reasonably, or maybe I was yelling a bit, because Kelly looked up and smiled her meaningless smile.

'You've got enough to do with the food,' said Anth. 'You're always late?'

'I'm never late,' I shouted. This was a lie.

'You're always late.'

She knew it annoyed me when people said I was late, but she poked the snake. I said, 'Your face is orange.'

'It's a healthy tan?'

'Well, where the fuck did you get *that*, in Thanet?'

'Don't swear?' said Anthea. 'It's none of your business,' but her smile had faded, my shaft had hit home. I knew she bought bottles of fake tan by the case. 'Do you want to squabble over Ferd's grave?'

Good move, Anth. I felt a pang. 'Fred's grave,' I corrected her.

'We have to remember our brother?' she continued, in a churchy voice that came through her nose, the chiselled, improved Australian nose that I, with my handsome proboscis, envied. Tempting to land a punch on it.

Kelly, who was making tea ten miles away at the end of the

work-top, sauntered over and smiled insanely. 'Little birds in their nest agree,' she said. 'Mon, the party's such a great idea.'

'She knows that.' Anthea cut Kelly off.

I gave the little squirt a look. 'I never said you could call me Mon.'

'She definitely didn't,' Anthea agreed, her glottal-stop in temporary abeyance.

'Sorry for existing,' Kelly said, amiably, put two mugs of builder's tea on the table, and swung her narrow hips out of the room. 'You Ludds always stick together, don't you?'

'Bollocks,' I shouted after her.

Kick-off was supposed to be eight o'clock, with speeches planned for half-past nine. I had promised to bring the food at 5.30. At six, I roared into the car-park, plates and dishes groaning and clashing in the back with a final mad slither as I braked too fast. I shoved the food back on to the dishes in the dark, licked my fingers, and carted it to the door.

My God, the hall was looking terrific. At every window, there was orange crepe, and spreadeagled against it, a black skeletal figure. Anthea had turned the hall into hell.

Every table held a small white skull. Orange marigolds burst out of the top like a fright wig. Candle-flames flickered as the wind sneaked in behind me and tweaked the cardboard skeletons in the windows. The corners of the room swarmed with shadow.

My sister was halfway up a ladder passing a plastic bat to Kelly at the top. Anth's bushy hair was sprayed virulent green, sticking out like a halo of spiralised sprouts above her strong, snaking body, encased in a sheath of silver scales. We are a prodigiously well-muscled family: she could have killed a chicken by coiling around it.

'Is thith the latht bat?' she was asking Kelly. There was something wrong. Had she been to the dentist?

'Bloody hell, Anthea,' I said. 'It's me.'

She turned and her face looked perfectly normal, i.e., botoxed, shiny, faintly blurred by fat injections and minor surgery, the face of a well-off 45-year-old impersonating 38. Then she opened her mouth and two tusks pronged forward, long white incisors with scarlet points. 'You think it'th OK?' she lisped through the teeth.

'Dad's going to love those gnashers,' I said.

'I've got a thet for all of uth? They're hell to wear, but it'll make him furiouth.' She climbed down and sashayed towards me. 'They're not very nithe to wear. Let'th put them in at the latht minute.'

There was the usual split second when we wondered whether or not to kiss, but the incisors settled it. 'Respect, Anth.' I waved around the room.

With difficulty, she spat out the teeth. 'It's taken weeks of planning,' she announced.

'She's not slept for a week,' Kelly added, crowding behind her, nodding inanely.

'She's never not slept in her life,' I said flatly. 'We Ludds are brilliant sleepers, Kelly.' (It used to be true. But nevermore.)

'Got to get on,' said Anth, blandly. 'You think the Boys will like it, then?'

'Yeah, the family will love it.'

'Good job Ma's not coming, though. Good job she's not capable.'

Anthea hadn't seen our mother for a while. Hard to

remember, once you've seen someone old, everything pale and shrivelled and tiny, that once they were normal-sized, with normal-coloured hair, and did whatever they wanted to. Hard to believe some return from the dead.

How much of what happened should we blame Ma for?

Sometimes I wonder about our mother. Sometimes I think they were in it together...

Erase those words! Poor little Ma.

12   *Adoncia*

I not know he crazy till we get to business. 'My wife is beautiful,' he hissing as he push his *porra* into me. 'A family is a beautiful thing. Adoncia, do you have a son? I father sons. I have three sons.'

Somehow the *cabrón* know I don't get a son. But he talk about wife as he start to fuck me. What kind of sick fucking bastard do that?

At first he just do the usual thing – yes, in the chair and on the chair. He fill me with the anaesthetic, he fill me with mercury, he fill me with sperm. Later though he get too ambitious, actually... He get ambition with my *culo,* he get ambition with my teeth. He see the pound sign in my mouth.

'Implant,' he tell me. 'We do the lot. You'll be beautiful. I can see your smile. The Perfect Smile. Discount, £20,000.'

He see a smile. I see red.

13   *Monica*

6.30: The food was on the trestle table – I frightened a stray sixth-former into helping. Anthea accused me of 'slopping it', but in arty semi-darkness, how could she know?

'Because Kelly nearly slipped on it. Why do you think I'm on my knees mopping up?'

Yes, I had opened a few bottles of wine, but the most I had drunk was what, an inch? – The most I had drunk was two or three glasses.

6.40: I was suicidal. 'No-one ith going to come!' I said. 'All thith food, and no-one ith coming. Nobody R-Eth-VP-ed to me.' I felt so sad I took my teeth out.

'No-one RSVPs any more,' Anthea said. 'Of course they'll come. My mates from London. The Boys have asked half of Marija's family, who've invited all the Latvians in Thanet. Fairy is bringing her new boyfriend, my homeopath has asked her line-dancing friends –'

'Oh Christ,' I said. 'No line-dancing –'

'– the line-dancers are totally cool? – I tried to keep up with their class, and couldn't? – '

'Not the Latvians!'

'– Latvians have very good manners. And that ex-Army woman, what'shername, who run's Ma's Home. Put out more forks.'

'Not the gobby dyke from the Home,' I said, 'What if she brings Ma?'

Dad was more of a worry. We hadn't spoken since the row on the phone.

6.55: The Boys arrived. I felt my usual mad surge of pride. The Twins were bigger than anyone else. They came through the door side by side, like a tank, in their immaculate, sober pin-stripe suits, Latvian Marija between them like a gun turret, on six-inch stiletto-heeled duck-egg blue boots, her hair tweaked up into a peculiar white-blonde unicorn horn on top of her head.

Boris looked around the room. 'My God,' he said. Marija's horn quivered in the light, a long elegant organ sensing the air. 'MY GOD,' said Angus, a millisecond later, and both of them stalled, a yard inside the door, their faces ticking over as they tried to understand it.

Then 'Love eet,' shrieked Marija, and tugged them on into the room behind her.

This was an occasion for a hug. Solemnly, we all hugged each other. Puzzlingly, Kelly stood in line, but no-one took any notice of her.

7.10: Anthea put on the music and she and Kelly had a practice jive, which made my brothers stare in wonder. 'Why is that woman dancing with Anthea?' asked Angus. 'Why she fucking shouldn't?' Marija asked, and then got up and joined them on the floor, dancing like a high-speed hungry spider, pistoning her limbs, her white horn tossing. Left alone, the two boys looked large and lost. Of course they made for the bar, and started drinking.

7.30: The first civilians arrived – the first ones if you didn't count Kelly, and I didn't count Kelly, that waste of space. Two shy neighbours of my father's. Yes, the Germans, Hans and his wife. They began a lumpen conversation about the longer-term consequences of Brexit. 'At least we'd get rid of some Germans!' I quipped, but they looked hurt and melted away.

Normally I keep *schtum* on the topic, but Hans was boring, and I was tempted. (Neil had approached me in the staffroom one morning to 'clarify my stance on Brexit' – parents 'had complained', as usual. I said, to make him go away, 'Neil, you can hardly think I'm pro Brexit.' His little rosebud lips fussed and fluttered. In fact, I loathe foreigners, like everyone normal, specially the ones with weird habits, but I loathe British people more, and with Brexit fewer Brits will leave for Europe. 'I take a balanced view,' I said. 'Balance,' said Neil, 'that's what the children need. Maybe you have been misquoted.'

Actually, what those kids need is order. So does my family; so do I.)

7.45: The room was over half-full. Most people were speaking Latvian. There were jokey screams and laughter at the decor. People were thronging round Anthea, who was camping it up by a skeleton.

Every so often, though, we looked at each other, we four children, across the dim room, past the splashes of light that lit teeth and wrinkles, thinking about the ones who were missing. Fred, of course. Missing for always. Ma, we hoped, was safely packed away. Dad had to come or the event was pointless. And where was Fairy? She had better not bottle it. Fairy had promised orange cupcakes.

7.50: The swing doors crashed again, and there she was, the Ice Princess. My skinny, wide-eyed, supermodel sister. Fairy, in white, yes genius – all in white, despite Halloween, dangling a red ruched bag like a wound, swinging across her on a scarlet thread. The artificial light bounced off her skin, which still looked perfect porcelain. Her icy glitter stilled the room. Fairy, even fractionally damaged by time, Fairy at thirty, Fairy on the slide, sent a whisper and a shiver through the populace, 'It's the model, isn't it? Fairy, look. Used to be Sarah when we knew her. Wow. But wasn't there a story – was she the one photographed snorting cocaine?'

I crossed the room without noticing I'd moved.

'Hi,' she breathed, blinking blindly at me, 'Oh hi.' From her half-open lips there crept a little breathy voice. She didn't have that voice before she was a model – she used to sound estuarine, tinny and whiney.

I could do the voice. I COULD DO IT ALL! – if I were half my weight, with different features. My brows are perfect – better than hers. I have the brows! I HAVE THE BROWS!

I found myself hugging her. She smelled of patchouli and vomit. OK, so she was still throwing up – but she was Fairy, she was my sister, my frail, filthy rich, bulimic sister, the Ludd family's celebrity, the only one of us touched with stardust.

Was there the tiniest answering squeeze from the silk-wrapped bundle of bones I was clutching? Maybe this time we would really talk. Maybe that tense knot of tenderness I felt when we were little and she fell, and hurt herself, over my foot into a box full of Lego and got a few Lego-shaped dents in her face, would finally yield its load of love. I'm not a monster, though my feet are large.

'Cakes,' she said, extracting cake-tins from another great bag with a Hermes logo. 'I made three dozen. Butterfly cakes. Ferd adored them. Coloured with Dr Oetker's Orange. Probably

44

organic,' she said, vaguely, looking to me for approbation, but I had prised off the lid of one tin and was helpfully stuffing a cake into my mouth, so she didn't hear me say, 'Who gives a shit?'

Then the door crashed open and shut again. 'This is Rupert,' Fairy whispered. 'He wanted to come. Monica, you've got icing on your chest.'

My God! There he was, Fairy's boyfriend. He stood there like a young James Bond. Dark lashes dipping over too-bright eyes, clean-cut jaw, lipstick-red lips – *maybe he was wearing make-up?* – but he was all man, I had to have him.

Trying not to stare at him too much, I uttered, full of *savoir faire*, 'Hallo, fuck, are you a model?'

'This is Rupert,' Fairy whispered, and to him, aside, 'I warned you, I mean told you, about Monica. And no, he's not,' she concluded repressively, and, 'Stockbroker,' he brayed at the same time.

'Lovely to meet you, Rupe,' I said. I shook his hand and didn't let go, just pulled him gracefully towards my aura – nice for him to get to know his girlfriend's sister!

Anthea came and spoiled the moment, or as she said later, 'saved the situation'. 'I've got some vampire teeth you can borrow,' she told him, holding out some plastic fangs. Turned out Rupe had been to Durham Uni where they like nothing more than dressing up. Soon we had him in full skeleton kit, which involved my helping him out of his trousers, and Anthea constantly trying to take over.

('Monica, please leave him alone!'

'Go away, I'm helping him.'

'Monica, you're actually panting.'

'Only because I'm bending over.')

Rupert zoomed off like a bat into hell.

9 p.m. It was already nine! Esmeralda arrived, escaped from the Perfect Smile Centre. Hard to recognise her out of uniform. Dressed up for the occasion, she looked even older. Tight black skirt, bandy little legs in knee-length, skin-tight black leather boots, blue-red lips and bleached white teeth, our father's handiwork. Blimey! Fuck! Trussed up like – what? That low-cut top hugging wrinkled-apple breasts. I tried to think who she reminded me of. Oh dear, it was a prostitute. Yet underneath it, she was Aunty Esmeralda.

'Aunty Esmeralda, hell-o-o-o!!'

We Ludd children were short of aunts, Dad's one sister died aged ten – in a calor-gas fire, how did that happen? – and Ma was the last survivor of nine. 'Dad's not here yet,' I blurted, worried. 'What do you think he's up to, Esmeralda?' (I didn't say, 'What *do* you look like?')

Esmeralda knew Dad better than anyone. Rather too well; our father is vile. She'd played some role in Ma leaving home. On the fortieth anniversary of her becoming Dad's receptionist, he had insisted she come round to dinner. Afterwards, there was a row between our parents, I heard Ma screaming and ran downstairs just as Dad threw the toaster at her. There was a line of blood on her cheek. Ma was jealous, of course she was. But Esmeralda's link with Dad went back a lifetime.

To the darkest places in rural Kent. *There is darkness here, but we struggle towards light.* There are a lot of unsolved crimes. The nights can be long. People don't go out.

I remembered Esmeralda, drunk on the beach, the evening when she told me, a furious schoolgirl, about the fraud at Dad's surgery. I cried and said, 'I hate him, he's a bully and a cheat,' but she rounded on me as if I'd hit her and slurred severely, 'DON'T SAY THAT! He's still your father…You understand nothing.' Then it all spilled out. Esmeralda's mother knew Dad's when the two of them were kids. 'He grew up like an animal, farmed out from one caravan site to another…he never knew his dad and his mother was *rough* – even my mother looked down on her. Mum said your grannie was a junkie and a thief and a few other things I won't repeat. She was always being picked up by the police and leaving your dad with anyone who'd have him. He must have had two dozen so-called uncles. Bad things happened. I never really asked…There was one bloke, though. Tosher. We all knew him. He ran bare-knuckle fights between boys. Loved your dad because he always won. One day there was a terrible fight between the two of them and Albert refused to go back any more. But somehow or other, he passed his exams. He always said he would make it out of Medway. Sheer grit, he's got. He never gives up. He's done his best. He's kept his family together. Your precious ma's never worried about money…' (she would never have said 'your precious ma' if she were sober). 'He gave me a job and he always pays me.' Yes, peanuts, I happened to know.

But she stood by Dad and she'd stand by us. Thank God for Aunty Esmeralda.

Plus, we had nothing to explain to her, and nothing we needed to lie about. I smiled upon her like a visitor from heaven, though all of us were off to the other place.

'Do you think I look peculiar?' She squeaked, anxious. So OK, I'd spoken that thought aloud. 'They were the only black things in the cupboard. This outfit was my mum's, in fact. So probably it's her I look like.' Behind her bony head, skeletons scampered, leering and clacking their jaws at the past.

'No-one else is wearing black.' She peered around her. 'They ought to be, to show respect.' Her little forehead creased, crestfallen.

'You look…amazing?' Anthea tried.

'Fucking astonishing,' I agreed. I had more important things to think about. 'Dad's got to get here in time for the speeches. Maybe there's been an incident?'

'An incident? Don't swear, Monica.' She peered at me, short-sighted, anxious.

'Terrorist incident, I mean. There was a false alarm in Waitrose yesterday, they tried to close the store when I was searching for dips. They told us to leave without our purchases, but no, I told them, no surrender. In the end they let me through the tills.'

She hugged me, arms raised, face pressed to my bust because she was so very small. She looked up, her sharp nose red with cold, or from bumping into my push-up bra. There was something white and slippery on one nostril. I realised it was Fairy's icing. Great, it was no longer on my cleavage!

'Good girl, Monica, you've done him proud.'

'Fred?' I asked her. The party was loud.

'No, your father.'

'Oh. Thanks. Why isn't the old bastard here?'

'Language. Your father's always late.'

On school Speech Days when we kids won prizes he'd barge in at the end to assume the credit; he burst in to funerals midway through, with all of us running white-faced behind him, as if he were leading in a cadre of terrorists – yes, I got lateness from my father.

But this felt late even for him.

The party had got into a feeble swing. My colleagues at school were not lively people, but I had invited them to make up the numbers, and they'd all turned up, looking smart and nervous. Maybe they were scared to turn me down? They stood around shyly eating their peanuts in little frozen clusters of acquaintances.

'Have a drink,' I shouted. 'There's enough to float a battleship.'

'Oh, I'm not much of a drinker,' said one, and others joined in with, 'I'm OK, thanks, Monica,' and, 'Only popped in for a few minutes.'

'No, GO AND GET A DRINK,' I instructed them, and pushed one gently in the small of the back. Suddenly they were all off to the bar, falling over themselves in their eagerness to please me, or maybe in their eagerness to escape me, as I must have pushed her a bit harder than I meant to.

9.15: The Latvians were dancing in earnest. Marija was surrounded by a cohort of blondes, all of them thin, intense and hyper, an army of crazed Latvian robots.

They call me mad! I don't dance in public. No-one in the Ludd family will deign to dance, I told myself, we're above gyrating, though sometimes, if truth be told, in my bedroom, I give it up, give it up, to the glass as I boogie on down to 50 Cent –

(And was there another memory, once? My father saying, 'Stupid, giants can't dance!')

Either it was me, or the whole room was revolving. It was full by then, and the noise level was stunning, and every now and then I looked for my brothers, I looked for my sisters, and they looked for me, and our faces said – *Dad isn't here.*

Then Anthea and Kelly came up hand in hand, and Anthea said, her Australian up-twang sagging unhappily into statement, 'Dad's still not here? He's not going to come?'

The glut, the glut of glottal stop. 'Anthea, are you speaking English?'

There was a crackle from the microphone, followed by a tone-y, resonant thump. A woman was on stage, at the microphone. There was a deafening wave of howlround.

Fairy! I recognised the legs, the only part of her lit up, longer and skinnier than anyone else's, in a towering pair of silver shoe-boots. Then someone made an adjustment to the spotlight. A wave of 'shushes' washed the room. White heart-shaped face, wide cloud of hair.

'What's she think she's doing?' I asked, too loudly, and Rupert turned and stared at me. There was definite electricity between us, and yet his eyes did not look friendly.

'Hallo,' she breathed into the silence. 'Some of you know me as Sarah Ludd, but now, well, I'm Fairy. Thank you, everyone, for coming.' (She was saying the words I had planned to say, but done as a torch-song, damp and breathy, a Margate Marilyn Monroe.)

There was a pause. The microphone sighed. Then she said, 'We're here for our brother, who…died. Frederick was five years younger than me. My kid brother, who I grew up with.'

And of course she started blubbing. Fucking hell.

'He dy-eed for his countr-ih!' somebody shouted. Oh God, it was Rupert. 'He dy-eed for ENGLAND!' Rupert, baying from the foot of the stage, waving the fluorescent bones of his arms. A low, growling cheer went up from the room – Thanet is very patriotic.

But Fairy had stopped sniffing and was back on the mike.

'That's sweet,' she whispered. 'Thank you, Rupert. I hope my brother believed that too. But actually…'

Agonising pause. That milksop mouth quivered. It was her looks held the room in thrall, pale face and silver chrysanthemum of hair. Then her voice strengthened and she stopped shaking. 'It was thanks to our father,' she hissed, furious. 'All – thanks – to – our – FATHER!'

I thrilled to the sound of distilled hatred, but the rest of the room didn't understand. Three feet away from me, one of the Latvians explained to another and her English boyfriend, 'Now she's thanking their father.' 'Oh? It's nice.'

'Our father made him go into the army,' Fairy spat.

But someone started clapping. Yes, it was Rupert. 'Well done!' he roared, and the room followed, a wave of demented patriotic clapping swept like pigeons over our heads, and Fairy's face lost its grief and anger and became lifeless, a mask on a stick. She whispered something like 'Whatever' and faded from the stage like mist.

So it was up to me. I had always known it. Sixty minutes till the hall had to close. I found myself ploughing across the room, crashing on delicate bones and toes, snagging trouser hems, mangling ankles, but apologies are for weak people, and besides, the Latvians wouldn't stop dancing and so deserved to get trodden on…

I had a speech written out in my handbag. To be heard by Dad, heard in public, because however much families try to lock the doors, in the end the secrets storm out of the cupboards.

Where was the old bugger? Where was Dad?

I was halfway up the steps to the stage when somewhere out of nowhere, another voice was shouting. There was a scuffle by the door. Anthea and Kelly were fighting with someone! Had the Margate alcoholics arrived?

'Albert?' a screechy young voice was shouting. 'Albert, they're attacking me!'

The Girl. Must be her – first time I'd seen her. Veronica was shiny and red-cheeked and ordinary, and young, horribly, sickeningly young, with glossy black hair pulled back in a bun, younger than Anthea, than me, than Fred. She had dared to show up, and call Dad 'Albert'!

'What are you staring at?' she shrieked into the silence. 'I'm Albert's – fiancée! He's expecting me!' The hubbub resumed. This was normal for Margate.

Then an elaborate chase began, the Girl escaping through the revellers, pushing with the strength of a twenty-year-old, the crowd closing behind her like water, with Anthea and Kelly in outraged pursuit, though stopping periodically for a chat. I had made it to the stage, so I had a good view.

I was on the stage. I had the mike. The speech was a ball of hot paper in my hands. But Dad wasn't there – we had no Dad. Mum wasn't there. We had mislaid our parents just when we needed to call them to account. I stared at the meaningless moil of people. I had a sudden vision of my younger brother as he would have been half a dozen years ago, hanging out with the gaggle of boys he'd grown up with, computer-game kids, thin and bowed, Fred a bit stronger and more wiry than the others because of years of distance running. The army had broadened him and straightened him up – but he never had time to grow out of the acne, never had time to grow up completely, or stand up to the bloody old tyrant who killed him, who sent him to Iraq, then Afghanistan.

Dad, not Saddam. Daddam, damn him. Damn them to hell, the wicked old men.

'Where is he?' the Girl was still shrieking. 'Albert!'

I reached out for the microphone.

14

I spoke. Which is to say, I must have bellowed, from the way people stopped and stared at me. 'We're here to honour our brother Ferd –' I caught myself. 'To honour *Fred*. He was only twenty-five. What was the point of him dying?'

A few ragged offers from the audience. 'He did it for us' – probably Rupert.

'He didn't die for us. He died for his ' I couldn't say 'comrade' No, I was choking. My voice jack-knifed. I clung to the microphone, hard, for support. Something under my finger clicked. Perhaps I should have done a sound check.

'He died for a soldier blown up by a landmine. A boy of nineteen he had known for two weeks. The lad was probably already dead, but Fred wouldn't leave him, he had him in his arms, he wouldn't put him down and the man was heavy, apparently Fred just kept going, everybody else had run away but he just kept walking. Like a fucking – moron.' (Did I say that?) 'With the bloke in his –' *arms*. But I couldn't say it, I was choking again. 'He was – carrying him. He wouldn't give up. That was Fred all over. Once he got an idea…He was kind, Fred. He was the best of us.' (Dimly, I saw Anth waving at me, waving support, good, go on.) 'It wasn't his idea to go in the army. Fred never should have gone in the army. Our father bullied him into it. I want to tell you something not many people know. Our brother wanted to be a farmer. Thanet used to be farming country. But Fred could never stand up to Dad. He'd be alive if it weren't for Dad. He did have friends, though. He always made friends. He tried to carry his friend back home. And the sneaking lying Taliban shot him in the back. So Fred was a hero, in the end.'

Now more people were waving and shouting. I tried to ignore them but then I saw Boris and Angus in sync at the back, yelling and pointing like a couple of prophets. I stopped speaking and peered at them. 'Mike,' they were shouting.

'Who the hell's Mike?'

'THE MIKE'S GONE OFF!'

Oh no. Oh fuck.

I'd said it all, and no-one had heard.

That fatal click must have switched it off. Adrenalin deserted me. My body felt enormous, and weary. 'Raise your glasses,' I heard myself saying, though I'd never used that phrase before, it was something other people's uncles said at weddings – 'raise your glasses to my brother Ferd. *Fred!* Frederick! RAISE YOUR GLASSES!' – and then I remembered, *go for Dad*, tell the world whose fault it was, but it was too late, glasses surged upwards, they chorused 'FRED!' The moment had passed.

Idiots! Cretins! Morons! Fools!

But no, it was me who had failed Fred.

Lump. Oaf. Failure. Fraud.

I looked round the room. It was shutting down. Fairy was leaving early, with Rupert, the Boys were tossing down shorts at the bar.

My great head of steam had leaked away.

*

I needed Dad's face to do it right. If he had been there, I'd have pulled it off, I'd have checked the mike, it would all have worked.

I was fourteen. I burned with rage.

Now the evening breaks down into staccato seconds. I must have started drinking. Gone on drinking.

The feel of glass after glass in my hand.

I was helpfully finishing other people's glasses left half-empty on the trestles. And then Veronica was kicking off. A last glimpse of her flying from the room with Anthea and Kelly propelling her, she was curiously clumsy, her legs were too big; was that the little defect that had drawn Dad to her? – a scream of fear as she fell down the steps and the double doors crashed to behind her – funny, the old lady watching her go flying and laughing with a friend in the corner bore a resemblance to our mother –

Christ, it *was* her – Cheers, Ma! She was in a wheelchair pushed by the frizzy-haired gossip who ran the Home, but then she was out of it, leaning on the bar, her white head jerking in time to the music – fuck's sake, Ma, bit of a raver –

Marija was having a go at Boris, shrieking at him in a loud thin wail and then clopping past me on weaponised stilettos –

Angus shouted something after her, then Boris and Angus were dancing together, a fast, muscular, practised jive. (Can this be true? Did I imagine it? Why ever did I think that Ludds don't dance?)

Now Anthea had switched the main lights back on and the few survivors looked small and ugly, except the Twins, who looked huge and drunk. Jessie J was on at shattering volume.

That was definitely Ma. She was not in her wheelchair. I must remember the name of that woman.

I was right beside her. 'Glad to see you, Lizzie! – it is Lizzie?' 'No, it isn't.' She got quite huffy and left the room. Then I was trying to help pack the glasses, oopsy, whoopsy, I'm dropping them. Anthea was holding my head over the toilet, and I pushed her off me so violently that she fell and cut her lip on the basin.

'Clumsy!' I told her as she struggled up, and Anthea may have been feeling tetchy, someone came in and alleged we were fighting, but after we punched her, she went away.

Soon we were all leaving with our arms around each other. There was a spray of blood on the steps from the Hall. Actually, it was more of a pool. Ma was laughing and pointing – 'That was the Girl!'

Could it REALLY be Ma? Yes, between Anthea and Kelly, laughing so much she almost shook them off, then Anthea was by her jeep and shouting, 'She's wet herself, I'm not taking her back.' 'Ai've got may own transport,' Ma said with dignity. Now she was in the wheelchair again. In, out, it was confusing. 'My friend from Cliffetoppe's is here somewhere.'

And yes it was true, now I remember, it was probably Lizzie (?) who we punched in the bathroom.

Under the cruel arc-light in the car-park, we paused, waiting for Ma to be collected, big clumsy children without a father. When Lizzie turned up, she said she was 'Nikki' and drew attention to her black eye, trying to blame it on me and Anthea, but no-one took any notice of her.

I was the one who voiced the general feeling – 'If Dad hasn't got a good excuse, he's a dead man.'

I didn't threaten him, I stated a fact, whatever the police have made of it. An anonymous witness says I was 'ranting', but actually I felt calm and settled, as calm as immense drunkenness permitted.

I'm a big girl. I can hold my drink. As I walked up my path to my little house I may have been shouting some highlights from the speech I didn't give. Some of my neighbours are nosey-parkers, lights went on, curtains twitched. All I recall (it comes back in flashes, uncomfortable flashes of minute detail) – is shouting, 'I'll kill you, you fucking old bastard!'

Later that turned out to be important.

Part 3

Day of the Dead

15

So, on the morning after the party, I woke with a sledgehammer blow to the head. Great rocks of pain bowled through my skull. Switched on the radio as normal, but nothing was normal. Guitar music strummed. Then I heard the words, 'the Day of the Dead'.

And just like that, my head cleared, I cheered up. Yes, this would be the Day of the Dead, the Day of the Dad, the Day of Reckoning. I crunched down three paracetamol with three fried eggs and five rashers of streaky. A slug of black coffee left me supercharged. Broadstairs to Margate takes fifteen minutes, but I swear that day I did it in five. I drove like a maniac – in fact, like Dad.

The house I grew up in looked much as usual, that deceptive Georgian wedding-cake sweetness. If he were inside tied up by burglars, I would forgive Dad, but not unless.

Brrrr, Brrrr, BRRRRR, BRRRRRRRRRRRRRR, I slammed my hand flat on the bell. Then held it there for good measure. On the top of Dad's steps, I was ten feet tall, I was Kali, Hindu goddess of war (I knew about her from multi-culti assemblies), I had ten arms and a necklace of heads, but there was still space for a big one, Dad's. Come out, you bastard. Come out and fight.

No answer.

I started to hammer with my hands on the door, interspersing it with more jabs at the doorbell. I hardly realised I was bruising my hand.

Up above me, the thud of a sash window shooting up. I craned my neck. I saw blinding yellow hair.

There was a woman at Dad's bedroom window.

I couldn't see her face, which was black against the sunlight, fringed with the halo of acid yellow, but her voice was gravelly, smoked out, foreign. 'Go away,' she said. 'He in bed. Don't disturb.'

'Who are you?' I could hardly get the words out, not just because the angle of my neck cut off my voice-box.

There was a pause, and then – 'I the cleaner.'

'Well I'm the DAUGHTER! Fucking let me IN.'

'I busy,' she said, or perhaps, 'We busy?' With that, the window slammed shut again.

I thought, I'll tear down the house with my hands. I tugged the letter box, impotent. I rang again. And then again. Sound of feet lumping down the stairs.

The door opened. It was the woman. She was old, despite the yellow hair. She barred the doorway. I almost hit her, though I didn't know her.

I remembered I was a Deputy Head. Non, Mon, you can't hit a cleaner. Very surprising that he had one. Several had quit, afraid of the ferrets.

She had had botox, now sunk into whorls, faintly recalling tribal markings. Those bright white teeth looked wrong in her face, which was tan-coloured, almost expressionless. She was cleaning in a filmy transparent dress.

'I've come for my father!' I said or shouted. Her hair was so yellow it was almost green. Oh look, she had cut her finger. A trickle of blood ran down from the nail.

'He doesn't come.' Her voice was foreign.

'Why not? Do you know you've hurt your finger?'

Why was I bothering with her? *Who was she?*

'He in bed.'

'It's eleven o'clock. I am his daughter. Is he ill? I need to see him.'

She had strange light eyes, pale blue and stunned. Maybe she was wearing a nightie. There was a hot sharp smell, like geraniums. A hideous suspicion stopped me breathing. The sun was very bright and everything went slowly, my hangover was back in force, this had been going on all my life and *no, I'll stop it once and for all.*

'What do you want?' she asked, robotic. 'I take a message.' She was closing the door!

'Take a message? Who the fuck are you? You're not the cleaner. You're wearing a nightie!'

'Is dress,' she said.

'IT IS FUCKING NIGHTIE!' I tried to grab hold of it, she backed away.

'I am...patient,' she said. 'I am private patient. I get the treatment, now I recover.'

I made to push past her but she was faster, the door was closing, the door had closed!

It was outrageous. 'A private patient'! Since when did Dad's patients come here to recover? He couldn't escape them fast enough.

Another harlot. Another whore. Yes, I would take revenge on him. He had disrespected Fred for a floozy.

And so I went and bought an axe.

Yes, I just meant to make a point, I'm almost sure, I'm pretty certain.

I wanted Dad to sit up and take notice.

Then I meant to chop him down.

No, you're a Deputy Headteacher.

The first two ironmongers were crowded so I ended up driving round to Ramsgate, leaving the car some way from the shop.

'Depends what you want it for,' the man remarked. His nose was red and exploding with buboes. He stared at my breasts, but everyone does. 'Logs or kindling?' he prompted, idly.

Necks was obviously on my mind. 'A nice big one,' I said. 'Yeah, big logs. Or maybe what I want is a machete.'

He gave me a look that said, 'There's always one,' and solemnly put on his glasses. '"Matchet"'s how *English* people pronounce it.'

'I'm an English teacher, by the way.' I pushed my jaw out and stared at him, but he was too stupid to understand. 'Pronunciation's my special subject.'

'Bushcutter, Miss?' He indicated a long, slender blade, but it looked too delicate for me, Lizzie Borden.

'What kind of axe would be good at slicing through, well, you know, really tough things?'

'Such as?'

Silence. I didn't know what to say. 'Trees,' I improvised. 'Big, old, tough ones. Hardwood,' I added. 'Lots of them.'

I was hungover, and wild with temper. Why was he annoying me?

'Have you ever done it before?' he asked.

You can only kill your dad once, I wanted to say, but didn't. 'Course,' I assured him. 'Lots of times. Let me see that one,' I said, repressively, pointing to the biggest, sharpest axe I could see.

He handed it over. 'Try it first.'

It felt heavy as death, serious: it felt expensive. The actual axe stopped me dead in my tracks, so heavy compared to what I expected. Panic gripped me; a flood of cold sweat. I imagined swinging it, how it would hit, the second flesh and bone would slow it.

He must have noticed me wavering. 'Yes, that's a heavy-duty tool, and pricey, more suitable for males, if I may say so, if I'm allowed to talk plain English. There are firms who can do this for you, you know.'

Professional killers? I felt like asking him.

Oh dear, my lips had moved. 'Professional tree surgeons,' he said.

'I don't trust them.'

'Why not?' He was stubborn. We eyeballed each other. The world flashed red.

Because he opposed me, I pushed it through. 'I don't have time to debate with you.' I nearly wavered; I nearly stalled. I might have walked right out of the shop, and driven home, and it would all have been over.

But no, I counted out my cash. He re-counted it twice, which felt like an insult. 'You will take care of that, young lady,' he muttered as he shafted the monstrous axe in cardboard, laid it reverently in my hands.

'Am not a young lady, fuck off,' I said as I charged through the door, which felt liberating, but was an error – it might have made him remember me.

Into the passenger seat it went, lying on top, that is, not embedded. My car scorched back from Ramsgate to Margate, leaving a trail of indignant cyclists, shunted motorists, scared pedestrians – laying a trail of evidence. I didn't care, I was incandescent.

The axe was meant for both of them, the yellow-haired woman, my disgusting dad, wave it around, make them frightened – yes, I just meant to frighten them.

But nothing went to plan that day. Day of the Dead, Day of blood.

As I bounded up the steps for the second time, axe in hand, ready to rumble, I noticed a tiny red petal in the sunlight. Dad must have bought red flowers for the whore and never for our mother, that was unforgivable, but when I looked again, after ringing the doorbell, I saw it was changing colour, growing duller, a small geranium of blood.

Just as I was poised to stab the doorbell again I noticed the door was open, just a crack – a crack of black, a slit into hell, and my axe nicked Fred's paintwork as I crept inside, for everything, now, went into slow motion, it was happening, the sequence from all my bad dreams. It was sharp cold daylight as I stepped on to the path –

the narrow path from which none returns

I smelled the woman in the dark on the stairs. I thought, perhaps she only just left. In too much of a hurry to close the door?

My feet slowed further as I reached the landing. There was a banging sound inside.

My God, the floozy was still in there with him, they were at it, at it, in broad daylight! Yes, kill them both, avenge my brother, avenge my mother, avenge us all –

With a yell of 'DAD! BASTARD!' I burst through the door, tripped over the bedclothes, a long entanglement, my feet tied together then OOOOOHHHHH I was falling, my face hit the floor and my teeth clashed together in a jarring rictus. A moment of blackness. I had dropped the axe, which thwacked into the floorboards and stuck there, quivering. I lay beside it, looking up at it. No breath in my body, stunned and winded. The room was quiet. Perhaps I'd passed out.

Pulled myself upright and saw the horror.

16

Dad, dead, obviously dead, slumped on his back on a pile of pillows, both hands up like some forties' minstrel, his head smashed, his head broken, his mouth twisted, his eye enormous, a slimy, quivering, orb of blood. The window-blind banged and banged in the wind.

'Dad,' I said again, differently, my voice shredding, sick in my throat.

I scanned the room. No sign of the woman. Blood was everywhere, in spots and sprays. And little clots of squashed red fruit. Red, red. That bare male room. It smelled sour, of shit, of wrongness.

There was a loud clatter, my heart thumped then stopped, but it was just the axe, falling on its side, splintering the floorboard as the blade pulled out, the handle falling in a pool of bright blood. I wrenched it out clumsily; blood on my hand, and wiped it furiously on my shirt (yes indeed, I did make errors).

I had to get out of there to be sick. I'd wanted to kill him but come too late, the job was done for me but, *uuurrgggh*, the horror, surely I couldn't have wanted this?

One last look. So horribly changed. He was driving the bed

like an enormous car, propped crooked in the driver's seat, his face a monstrous blind tomato.

He was my father. He was dead.

Shock, dumb pity gave way to hatred. Dad had stolen a march on us. Now we could never, ever get even.

Could it have been the Girl who did it? He'd stood her up, he'd let her down, it wasn't just us he had betrayed. If she had found him with that woman, the ancient floozy with her yellow hair –

I wanted to vomit, I had to get out, I could not look at Dad again. I stumbled halfway down the stairs, was forced to lean against the wall –

And then, with horror, I remembered my axe, I could not leave it there in the room, there was some dim thought to consequences, I turned and lumbered back up again.

Into the room, retrieve the axe. I paused, dizzy, on the landing, eyes clenched against the sun-blazed bedroom, *do not look on the nakedness, the battered nakedness of your father.* God hovered somewhere, furious. Something monstrous had occurred. Here it came, the flood of terror, tidal wave that blacked out sunlight. Yes, the death of kings, tyrants. Yes, some ultimate taboo. Darkness lay upon the land. I bowed my head, my shoulders crumpled, yes, my father, yes, the horror, I stood there, shaking, my eyes pressed shut.

Monica, don't drop the axe. Monica, you must get out.

My eyes felt odd and my cheeks were wet.

It was Dad's fault I had come to kill him – anyone normal would have done the same. But now I was stuck with a corpse and a weapon. I had to escape, I had to get home –

No, I had to look at him one more time. I forced my gaze towards the bed. So red, so dark, the bloodied gargoyle. Some trick of the light made it look as though the intact eye was slightly open, a venomous live slit staring at me.

I remembered: *you're supposed to close their eyes.* Something about a final duty.

I have never, never been a good daughter.

Just as I thought that, something horrible happened, there was a low, long-drawn-out visceral trump which made me scream and clutch the axe as Dad, alive, lurched to one side and for a millisecond the eyes seemed to move, a kick of terror, those childhood nightmares where you kill the bogeyman and then he comes back –

his mouth gaped sideways as if to accuse me, but no, it was gases, it was gravity, the body lay there motionless.

Out, out, Monica, get away, and my body jerked, my body turned, after the scarlet chamber the stairs were black, all of a sudden I missed a step and help, I was tipping headlong forward, hitting a wall, the banister, saving myself then lurching onwards, no, I had gone, there was no more hope, it was time to die in our father's house, my constant fear as a little child –

Then I was on my shattered knees, sprawled, winded, in the dark of the hallway.

Everything hurt. A ringing silence. Had I broken my neck? My ankle was twisted. One of my wrists was trapped beneath me. The hall tiles were deadly cold.

Just seconds later I heard the sirens and knew a police-car was outside.

(I didn't know then it was driven by Ginger. I didn't know Ginger. There was just fear.)

Raw and total. They would see my car.

They would find me, bruised by falling downstairs, and think

I'd been in a fight with Dad. I tried to get up, I was on my feet, I had no time to count my wounds, the sirens screamed in my brain like panic, then the nee-naw stopped, must be parked outside, I charged down the hall, making for the garden, out through the back door, I'll abandon the car, limp down the lawn, damn the axe, why did I choose such a heavy one, but if I leave it here they'll think I did it, it was smittled with finger-prints, smeared with blood, I scrambled on to Dad's barbecue table which was a hazard, a gleet of wet leaves, but in a second I was over the wall and into the German neighbours' brambles, fear had made me immune to pain but I did have a flash of Hans's pink amazed face and then his wife's long, sad one as I staggered at speed across their lawn, yelling, 'Hi, how are you, Hans, and Mrs Hans, sorry if I caused offence in our little chat about Brexit last night, got to dash, I'll explain later,' hauled myself on to his ride-on lawnmower clad in its vile green winter cover, 'So-rree!' and flung myself over the next bare hedge, Pepita Upward's fucking flowering currant, ouch, it scratched me, I landed short, bounced myself on into her wheelbarrow, *clang*, the blade of the axe hit the painted metal, I tried to steady myself but no, it tipped me on to her compost heap – did I see Pepita's pale fat features floating balloon-like in her music-room window? – 'Hello, Pepita, hello!' – my coat now sported an exploded tomato and smears of something like decomposing leek, possibly rotted celery – but over the next hedge, I could see fields, open ground, sheep, greenness, if only Fred were here to enjoy it –

I tore my jeans on hidden barbed wire as I landed on the other side. Sheep in Thanet I was not expecting, they looked like a solid wall of mutton, yellow-greyish, muscular, barring my way to the opposite hedge beyond which was my road to Ramsgate, and I screamed at the herd as I ran towards them, 'Get out of my way, you fucking fuckers,' and the first one wavered at the sight of me and a millisecond later the whole lot turned and became a deluge of dirty white wool, soft as clarts on their silly little legs which always remind me of burnt matchsticks, and I cleaved effortlessly through them, the axe whistling past their matted curls. Hedges were nothing to me by now – up, rip, pain, down – *baaa, baaa*, they were noisy buggers – but speared on a twig I saw a plastic bag and, on an inspiration, grabbed it, and wrapped it clumsily around the axe –

Thanet District Council almost certainly had some snivelling policy against weapons on buses.

Ah yes, the bus. Squat, low, normal, the Margate–Broadstairs–Ramsgate Loop bus in its dayglo-orange ugliness, but to me that day, beautiful, gorgeous. Soon I would be safe home with my axe. I got on that bus full of hope and warm feelings, but something about me made the driver stare.

'Are you all right?' he said, a second or two after I climbed aboard.

'Yes, are you?' I may have sounded short.

'Well are you just here for a chat?' he asked.

'What the fuck is the matter with you?'

He went even redder in the face and spoke very slowly. 'Are you a foreigner?'

'Are you fucking UKIP?' I shouted, not loudly, but the queue had started to mutter behind me.

'YOU HAVEN'T SHOWN A PASS OR PAID FOR YOUR TICKET!'

Oh, that was why he was staring at me, oh, oh, the humiliation, I dug into my handbag and brought out lipstick, brilliant magenta, insanely red, the top had come off during my pell-mell flight and all my possessions were smeared with crimson – *Dad, his hurt body propped on the bed* – combs, hair, tissues, pens, the coins were at the very bottom but I scrabbled, desperate, they resisted me. I finally thrust them through the driver's porthole. 'Sorry.'

He nodded and I stumbled forward two paces before he called me back again. 'Don't you want your ticket? Or your plastic bag?'

Now the whole bus was staring at me. Some people were sniffing, too. Yes, my encounter with the compost heap. I'd hastily brushed off most of the tomato but the celery, or leeks, were impossible to shift. I was boiling hot as I sank on to a seat. The woman next to me was staring at the floor and casting sideways looks at me behind her thick glasses. Ugly people like her should stay at home. Then she was staring at the floor again. No, she was fixated on my carrier-bag. Oh God, the axe had hacked itself a hole, a silver shark-fin glinting in the sun.

''Scuse me,' she said, half-standing up though the next bus-stop was minutes away. I thought of pushing her down again, but in the end I let her pass and I saw her talk eagerly to the driver as the bus slowed for my own stop.

As I barged past, both of them pretended not to be talking about me, and behind me, other passengers made little faffing flurries of motion, I had bothered the bus-going burgers of Thanet; the vehicle was still stopped dead as I panted on down the road to my house. Error, error, one after another.

I hurried up the path to my home. The axe swung heavy as a wreckers' ball and every part of me had started to ache, every part of me was bruised or scraped. (*Poor Mon. No-one to comfort me.* That whiney voice. I throttled it.)

It had really happened. Dad was dead.

In through the door. Dump axe in porch. Hang up coat, which more or less covered it.

Then I was standing in the blue bathroom staring at my wild, lead-pale face, scratched straight across the forehead and my left cheek, suture-like marks of ragged crimson – God bless words, my mad brain clutched them, 'sutures', yes, so much better than 'stitches'.

Save yourself, Mon. One part of my brain was cattle-prodding the bits that were frozen. *Wash off blood. Run a bath.* Hot tap on full. I stared at it as it pelted down and the steam filled the bathroom. Take off clothes. Call cab to Manston Airport.

No no no, the airport had closed, no more planes swooping up like great moths and carrying me off to safety in Holland, no more ferries hoving over to Belgium. Globalisation has abandoned Thanet, and then they wonder why we voted Brexit!

I was on my own in the middle of a nightmare.

Dad, dead. *Dead, Dad. Dad, dead,* but I didn't do it. My heart kept thudding the words in my ear, the weight of the words, his great heavy body, the flickering crack of his accusing eye.

What was I to do? If I had actually killed him, my half-formed plan had been to go to the police station and dob myself in, to save everyone time. But this was different. Could I actually dob someone else in for doing what I had always longed to…? (and yet, a part of me wanted them punished. Dad was OUR father, let US sort it out)

Was blood thicker than water, then?

I peered at my image in the mirror but steam from the bath

had misted it over, just a vague pink being I had never seen before. No longer Mon, I was disappearing.

Maybe, just maybe, nothing had happened, this morning's events were a long bad dream, and I clutched the basin and listened to the water and closed my sore eyes, just for a second.

I must have been asleep on my feet, the last twelve hours had been abnormally tiring – I jerked awake to the house phone shrilling and it all came back, I felt drugged and hurt, *the bath*, my God, it would have overflowed, but I turned, it was empty, the water ran cold, I had forgotten to put in the bath-plug, my life was running down the hole.

Oh, thank God, the telephone stopped.

I had no right to feel – what was it, grief? Something was shrieking with pain in my head.

Had Dad mattered, in some mad way?

I washed the bloodstains off my hands in cold water and plastered make-up on the marks on my face. Luckily, I've always been a quick healer – it looked like a peppering of midlife acne.

The police would come, because my car was there.

Why shouldn't it be there? I was a dutiful daughter. Naturally I'd pop in to see my father.

My mind was whirring in decreasing circles.

I went downstairs. I was horribly hungry. I opened the fridge and started eating bacon, looping a rasher over my hand, before I remembered you had to cook it. Most of it projectile-vommed on to the floor, but some of the fat had gone down too far. But raw pork-flukes were the least of my worries, I swallowed, burped, it would make me stronger.

And strong is something I have to be.

It was late afternoon, not time for bed, but a primal drive to sleep took over. I went upstairs and put on a tracksuit and lay on the bed for a moment's shut-eye. Instead I slept like the dead for four hours.

Then I sat bolt upright, my heart pounding.

There was a split second before I remembered.

Dad, dead. His lopsided red body. His poor squashed eye and stoved-in mouth. After a lifetime's torment, I had lost my father. Yet I felt as if something appalling had happened.

There were so many suspects, but who had done it?

That blonde foreign floozy on Dad's doorstep. She was squat and sturdy and her eyes were weird. When she'd said, 'We're busy,' she didn't mean 'fucking'. She meant 'I am midway through murdering your father. Go away, please, I've got to crack on.'

Hahahaha, why am I laughing?

But no, *the Girl was the one with the grievance*. He'd asked her to the Party, then hadn't turned up. Yes, young and fresh with those short fat legs that made her look innocent and clumsy, but according to Jane who teaches swimming there, Veronica was a ferocious forward at hockey who had been suspended three times for fighting, and finally banned – Jane didn't know the details, but 'there was an incident with lots of blood'. While I was away buying my axe, she could have ousted the blonde and bludgeoned Dad.

Then my mind went blank. I was right out of time, for my doorbell rang like electrocution, the letterbox clashed and gnashed like cymbals.

I stumped downstairs to stop them breaking the door down.

Mon, I thought, you're for it now.

17

I was nearly there when I remembered the axe, which I'd dropped in the porch under the row of coats, oh no, too late, would the door conceal it? – but I was already flicking up the Yale.

There they stood, a uniformed old loon and the younger man I now know as Ginger, red-haired, squarish, tallish, nearly as tall as Monica. He had sharp eyes that ran over my body (I had no bra on under my tracksuit; breasts like mine are an ice-breaker.) Yes, he looked authoritative.

The axe was hidden by the open door, but when I closed it, wouldn't he see it?

'Good evening, officers,' I said.

They gave their names. I heard nothing but 'DI Something and Sergeant Blur.' I think I managed not to say, 'Speak up!'

'Is there a hearing issue?' The old one said.

'Oh dear, no. Do come in. Is this something to do with school?'

'School?' said the white-haired fool blankly.

'You probably know I'm the Deputy Head.' I should have said, 'Acting Deputy Head' – Neil wouldn't give me the permanent job. 'Of our local school. Cup of tea, officers? What is the problem?' They followed me stolidly into the kitchen. My tracksuit, I knew, would count against me, so my demeanour was extra regal.

'Check the address,' said the younger one and the white-haired one started tapping his mobile phone.

'It's the right address, but I dunno,' he grunted.

'Are you Monica Ludd?' the sharp-eyed one asked. Ginger. Now I know him as Ginger.

'Guilty!' I quipped, but neither of them smiled.

'I'm afraid we have some bad news,' said Ginger, eagerly, pink-cheeked, grim-eyed. No uniform, so I knew he was a detective. 'Your father has been attacked.'

'Attacked?'

I summoned up my Sarah Siddons side, sinking into a chair and gazing wild-eyed, one hand spreadeagled on my mighty chest.

'Where?' I asked, then suppressed a snigger at the possible meaning, *flank or buttock*? I turned it into an attempted sob, which sounded more like a belch than anything. Then I smiled, with dignity: tragic, brave. 'May I go to him?'

No, I just sounded fucking stupid, an escapee from a 1930s film.

'That won't be possible,' said the older man. 'He's…'

'The attack was very severe,' said Ginger.

'I'll put on the kettle,' I said, sniffing.

'No tea, thank you. We'll be interviewing you.' Their eyes were flicking round the room.

'This is such a terrible shock,' I said, tugging the zip of my tracksuit down, I was hot with guilt, I longed for aircon, maybe I should move to America? The zip was stuck, I tugged harder, it suddenly plunged towards my navel, whoops, blimey, a strawberry nipple, I dragged the zip up again in a temper. 'Have you ever been to America?'

They looked at me blankly. 'Would you like to come with us to the station?' said Ginger.

'I don't really see how I can help you.'

'I have to go outside, Grills,' said the older one, urgently. 'Call coming in.' (What kind of name was 'Grills'? Or 'Grillz'?) He went out through the front and I waited for him to spot the axe in the hall, the bloodstained handle under the coats, but I heard nothing, and flushed with relief.

'Smoker,' said Ginger, 'filthy habit.' He was still reeling from my zip, perhaps. Then he seemed to regret confiding in me. 'Do you have any questions?' His voice was hard. There was something odd about one side of his mouth.

'I'm a bit overwhelmed.' I made my voice quaver. (I *was* overwhelmed! What a day I'd had!) 'You're going to tell me he's dead, aren't you?' There was a silence, and I tried again. 'Officer, please, don't toy with me.' That frightful voice again from 1930s' films – true, I watched them a lot on DVD. Joan Crawford, Bette Davis.

'We found your car outside his house,' he said bluntly.

Now it was my turn to be silent. His bright piggy eyes. I stared him out. 'I often leave it there,' I said. 'I like to drop by, I'm a good daughter.'

'I've had a word with some neighbours,' he said, but the clear implication was *you are a liar*. 'You leave your car outside your father's house? That is a twenty-minute drive away. It must be inconvenient.'

My mind was whirring frantically, trying to make sense of my ridiculous claim. 'I like to walk, so I come back on foot. I use the road when the tide is in. Otherwise I power-walk along the beach.'

'Eight miles?' His eyes flicked over my thighs again, as if assessing if I could power-walk. The letterbox rattled: the other one must have finished his fag in the front garden. I went to let him in, but before I left the room, the detective said, in a level voice, 'I'm treating you as a witness, Miss Ludd.'

'Ms Ludd,' I said, rudely, which was unwise.

'*Muzz* Ludd,' he said, with emphasis. The title annoyed him, for some reason, when the corpse had left him perfectly calm. 'Be grateful I'm not arresting you! I am treating you as a witness, not a suspect. I'd like you to come in to the station now. We'll be contacting your sisters and brothers.'

'They'll be devastated. As I am. Thanet is becoming very violent.'

'Interesting choice of film,' he said, indicating the DVD on the table. Damn, it was *The Revenant*. 'By the way, I can't place you, but you look familiar.'

I'd had the same nagging feeling about him, but maybe all gingers look alike. 'Why am I a witness?' I improvised. 'I wasn't there, I know nothing about it.'

'General witness. Generally of interest.' He thought he was smart, but he walked through the porch to join his colleague on the doorstep and never noticed my guilty weapon, my shark of steel, my haft of oak. I clawed up a coat and followed them.

The room at the station was bald like Ginger. I did my best to parry his thrusts. Halfway through, he had an urgent call. He was telling them to 'apprehend' someone. Apprehend? What kind of word is that? Perhaps my presence made him self-conscious.

That evening, I hardly registered his questions. He said he would come to see me in the morning.

And so a night of hell began. I lay in bed and shook with terror. What had I seen? What had we done? The battered head, the bloodied pillow.

I woke at one, two, four a.m., went to the window, stared at blackness. Dad was dead. There was no more order. While the sea stayed warm, the boats slid in, into the quiet Kent night, packed with desperate men, veiled faceless women and their touchy religion. *Come to Margate, your home from home.* Across the Channel, Europe was sinking. Yes, we would leave, and it was going under, there were no more rules, no more borders (or so I thought, in the middle of the night). And I, Mon, must abandon my post, fail to turn up to teach my class. Outside the gate, the barbarians massed. *Après Monica le déluge. Mea culpa* for dumping you in it, oh sad centurions, supply teachers.

Ginger would be back to see me in the morning. Maybe bringing other, harder cops. I thought I saw a police car just out there, under the street light – watching, waiting. The fucked-up, flickering street light of Thanet. Around it, the leaves were wet and bright, red as a bloody fingerprint.

There weren't enough cars, there weren't enough policemen, Border Force had small rubber boats which bob-bob-bobbed against the power of the ocean, bob-bob-bob, I was falling asleep, Dad's head was slowly slipping sideways, red, red, and one eye staring, was he trying to speak? – icy cold, I jerked awake.

18

To catch me out, Ginger came at eight. I was still in my apricot-silk nightie, which was not in itself a bad thing, but I had had no time to hide the axe. Damn, damn, but he walked straight past it. Nothing felt real. I was sick, and dizzy, and somehow light-hearted, adrenalin-fuelled. I had not had breakfast, yet wanted to vom. I swallowed it, and smiled at him. He looked surprised – maybe my smile had curdled – and did not return it. I tried to look sad. At least I had a dressing-gown on. Maybe I was still in shock, for part of me felt – almost randy.

'Where were you on Sunday morning, Mrs Ludd? Remind me.'

I am rarely attracted to ginger men. Square bald gingers, treble fault. And he was trying to annoy me.

'I am not Mrs Ludd. That is my mother. I can give you her address. She is in a Home.'

'Yes, yes. We needn't waste time. Where were you, Mzz Ludd, around midday?' He buzzed the 'Mzz' with excessive energy.

'I don't know why you're asking me. Probably I was on my walk.' I let the dressing-gown fall open. The flicker of apricot silk caught his eye. He saw me noticing him noticing.

'May I go and put some clothes on?'

'Be my guest.'

'Don't you want to accompany me?' Someone had taken over my voice. It was deep and throaty. What was I doing?

He stared at me nonplussed, but not entirely displeased. Suddenly I felt like laughing. Looking back on it, I was still in shock.

'In case I destroy some evidence? That's what always happens in films. You know, policemen have to watch people get dressed.' I was twinkling at him, which I hadn't practised. 'Or would that be violating my human rights? I teach half a module on that to our sixth form.'

'I suggest you get on with it.'

I waited and listened at the top of the stairs. Sure enough, I heard him walk back down the hall. There was a clatter as the axe fell down. He had found the axe, so I was done for.

And so it began, as I walked across the landing, the new world that I live in now. I didn't mean to descend into hell. I did nothing wrong (not recently!), but I'm trapped by the facts and the falling axe, a cascade of facts piling on to my lie, the stupid lie that I knew nothing about it.

Yes, truth is best, truth will out. Start with a lie and there's no way back. I had no alternative. I had to plough on.

When I came downstairs, Ginger said nothing. He didn't mention a murder weapon, he kept that up his sleeve for later. He let me make coffee, leaned back in his chair and contemplated me as I served him. My white wool sweater was slightly see-through. Too bad I had chosen a black push-up bra!! My Atlas Mountains strained at him. His small blue eyes had a slightly fixed glaze. Perhaps he'd been up all night as well.

'What shall I call you?' I simpered, gamely.

'Try my name. DI Parkes-Woods.'

I instantly forgot it. 'It seems so formal.'

'Yes, Mzz Ludd. Taking a witness statement is quite formal.'

'Your colleague of the other day called you "Grills"?'

'That was a nickname. I do not like it. Can we get on with things, Ms Ludd?'

That was a real spurt of anger. I made a note not to forget it.

Some of his questions gave me pause.

'Did your father have enemies?'

'He was a dentist. I am a teacher. Dentists and teachers have enemies.'

'Facts, please, not philosophy.'

'I also teach philosophy.'

He stared, with a mixture of annoyance and interest. 'I didn't know that featured in today's comprehensives.'

'It isn't Hegel, or Husserl. I have abandoned the actual course. We talk about things they don't understand – ethics, mostly. Morality.'

Why did I bother to be frank with him? Frankness usually gets me into trouble. But he nodded, faintly, and almost smiled. I processed something I had noticed before, that flash of metal in his mouth, something that didn't fit in his face, which was pink and shiny and neat-featured. There were two gold teeth on the left-hand side. 'What kind of thing do you talk about?'

'ISIS. Climate change. They're scared. We talk about the end of Europe. Some of them don't know where it is.'

He looked sceptical. 'Scared? Your lot? Really? You have had problems with knives at Windmills.'

'Some have knives. They also have nightmares.' He said nothing, just looked at me. I had a sharp pang of missing my job; normally I would be preparing the classroom, rubbing badly drawn genitals off the whiteboard.

'At first they take the mickey, but soon they start talking. What do you do about total violence? Why it starts. How you can stop it. Like this latest thing in Canterbury Cathedral. They would have killed the priest, if the police hadn't showed. Thank heavens your men were there, officer.' It sounded creepy, but I meant it.

'And you are qualified to talk about violence?'

I wanted to say, 'Try living with my father,' but held my tongue just in time. It was tempting, though. This almost felt like a date. Or like the dates I would have liked to have had, where you talked for a bit, before you did it.

OK, I said it. 'Try living with my father.'

I had a sudden urge to confess. Not to the killing, to our family shame. The whole story of the Ludd family.

'So your father did have enemies? And it was to do with his line of work?'

'Policemen probably have enemies too.'

'It's not the time for speculation, Ms Ludd.'

A bird was singing, singing in the garden. The usual one. I was annoyed with nature, interrupting my concentration. Probably a stupid robin, people get sentimental about them, I prefer cut flowers: the rose, the geranium. *That tiny spot of blood on the step.* Why all these questions about Dad's practice?

'He did have enemies. Nothing but. The only people who weren't, didn't know him.' Once again, I spotted a repressed smile.

'Ms Ludd, I caution you against being flippant.'

'I wasn't being flippant, officer.'

He wrote avidly in his notebook.

'You seem to be saying you disliked your father.'

'Dislike's not the word.'

'What is the word?' I said nothing. There were two words: LOVE, HATE, the knuckle words. I wanted Dad to love me. He didn't, so I hated him.

'Your father was violently attacked, at home in bed.'

When I hesitated – there was so much to say! – his irritation surged up again, he was not as even-tempered as he pretended. 'We know you were there. Do you want to confirm that?'

Did they know I was there? I had denied it. But I looked him in the eye and saw something important. Curiosity, but no blame. No actual sense of repulsion, no terror…the man must know I didn't do it. Despite the axe, despite the car…

He had another suspect, that must be it, that's why he hadn't arrested me. He was just trying to make me nervous. 'There's nothing to confess. I am innocent. I wasn't there. I had been for a walk. I went early. Afterwards…' My mind stop-started. 'Afterwards, I was gardening.'

'Do you like gardening?'

'Yes I do!'

'I note you have no plants at the front.'

'It is November.'

'The earth is bare.'

'I just prefer to keep things tidy.'

The questions continued, and I sidestepped them. Sometimes I didn't see the point. Why was he obsessed with Dad being a dentist? It was more important that dad was dead. Once or twice I told the truth, to confuse him.

'Were you a happy family?'

'No.'

'Did any of you have a grudge against your father?'

'All of us had a grudge against our father.'

'How would you describe your childhood?'

Just for the hell of it I said, 'Very happy.' (And yet, in fact, there were happy moments. Life's bizarre, there are no right answers.)

'Was that an attempt at a joke, Ms Ludd?'

'Why would you think so?'

'Your face looked peculiar,' he answered, spitefully. I wanted to laugh. Ginger and I had things in common, but this was a strange way to start a friendship.

'Was your parents' marriage happy?'

'You'd better ask our mother, not that she'll remember.' (Yet she had seemed sharper since she stopped drinking.)

Hours of it, while he noted it all. Time passed by. Was it nearly afternoon?

Every now and then he would take calls from the station and I listened, trying to piece a picture together. The DNA results would take a few days. There was someone they wouldn't be able to interview 'for several days, perhaps weeks'. That must be the other suspect. My siblings were being hard to track down. (I'd told him, truthfully, I didn't know their numbers. 'And yet you seem intelligent? By the way, what is your mobile number?' 'Oh, I have never owned one, officer.' His ginger eyebrows shot up his forehead. 'Everyone has a mobile phone.' 'I'm mindful of the research on cancer. And social media is not for me.')

So far, of course, he hadn't swabbed the axe, and nor had he looked in my washing machine, where the clothes I had been wearing still sat in the dark, sopping wet and perhaps still blood-stained. Damn, any fool would think of that, but I have a blind spot when it comes to housework.

'It's time for us to talk about the weapon.'

'Weapon?' My voice sounded horribly fake.

'There was a large axe concealed in your hall. I'll be taking it away, as evidence.'

'Oh, that axe. Yes, I just popped it down there. Of course, it is meant for chopping trees, as the man in the shop where I bought it will confirm.'

'When did you buy it?'

'I can't remember.'

'You say it was meant for chopping trees?' At that point Ginger left the room and came back swiftly with a discontented air. 'There are no trees in your garden, Ms Ludd. It doesn't help if you make wild claims.'

'I was going to chop for a friend,' I claimed.

'Would your "friend" be able to confirm that?' He said 'friend' with light irony.

'I haven't had time to let her know that I am planning to help in her garden.'

His pink face reddened slightly with temper. 'So you bought a very expensive axe to help a friend who knew nothing about it.'

'You sound sceptical, but yes.'

'Why?'

'I am one of life's altruists.' I swear I wasn't trying to annoy him, but a mad part of me enjoyed the fencing.

Tell me the name of the friend.'

I thought fast – friends, gardens, I didn't really give a fuck about either – and remembered moon-faced Dr Pepita Upward, who lived three doors away from my father, the violin teacher who disliked my father because he had tried to stop her practising. 'Can't you stop that bloody caterwauling, woman?' he had yelled when she burst through his tolerance threshold, one Sunday morning when I was a child. 'Mr Ludd, it's my profession,' she answered. 'I don't ask you to stop being a dentist.' After that run-in, she had smiled sympathetically whenever she passed us kids in the street and we usually responded by pulling vile faces. All the same, I hoped she didn't bear a grudge. Yes, she may have seen me climb over her hedge, axe in hand, but I did say, 'Hello!'. With luck she wouldn't peach on me.

'Pepita Upward. She's a doctor.'

'What kind of trees does Mrs Upward have?'

'I don't know the name of them, but they're enormous. Dark,' I added vaguely, gesturing dimensions.

'The type of tree would help,' he encouraged me.

I hate it when other people are sarcastic although, it's true, it's a vice of mine. All I could remember of her garden was the hedge. Yes, the bare twigs had stuck into me. 'It's a…hedge-type tree. But enormous. Pepita can't care for it alone.'

'If I think you aren't trying to assist my enquiries, I will have to take you down to the station,' he said, and the look he gave me was cynical. Powerful! 'I am the SIO on this case. Senior Investigating Officer.'

I felt a frisson of sexual excitement, I have a thing for dominant men which one day's going to get me into trouble, I tell my sixth-form girls to avoid them. 'I'm tired, officer, that's the trouble. I need some rest. Could we resume tomorrow? It's been a simply dreadful few days, what with our father dying, which is naturally distressing.' That frightful, hammy voice again.

'I have not told you your father's died.'

'Is this a trick? Why else are you here?' I could feel the colour, heavy as blood, rush to my cheeks and spread to my temples (and I saw Dad, for a split second, on the bed, broken, awash with red). 'You know he's dead. Let's not pretend.' Why did I suddenly want to howl? Big tears pressed in my eye sockets.

'Why don't you tell me what you think happened?'

'What's the point of guessing, officer?'

We eyeballed each other. He was no fool. His features were symmetrical, despite being pink. He was growing on me, yet I had to thwart him.

'Let's leave it till tomorrow,' he said suddenly. 'I need to talk to your family.'

'Happy to oblige.' It sounded odd on my lips, though men had sometimes found me obliging, and yes, Ginger, I was ready to oblige you.

Yes, you only had to ask.

After he left, the manic energy sagged. I crawled up to bed and lay on the covers.

Why was my family not here to support me? Boris and Angus were never alone, Anthea had Kelly to cry on, Fairy had Rupert, I had no-one.

Once I had hundreds of Facebook friends, once I de-stressed with Instagram and Twitter. I like to think I was popular, I used to get dozens of Laughing Out Louds. Then Neil produced a 'social media' policy. 'What's this fresh nuisance, Neil?' 'Oh, you know, Monica, our Windmills values, responsibility, accountability.' Although he swore it wasn't aimed at me, it managed to ban everything I did. 'Feel free to go on "tweeting", Monica,' he said, with nervous quote marks around the verb. 'But parents are sensitive to abuse.' 'Neil, I would never abuse our parents.' 'Governors queried "moron" and "twat"…governors feel quite strongly on this one.'

That night I took down all my accounts. If I lost my job, I would have nothing.

I've still got no-one, is the bottom line. Mono the monster. Poor sad Mon. Lying all alonesome upon my bed in the bedroom with the pink upholstered bedhead. It used to be Ma's, when she stopped sleeping with Dad, but before she left him altogether. I nicked it from the house when she went into the Home.

Yes, I, Monica, loved my mother, it's a weakness of childhood, you have no choice. I kept the bedhead to be close to Ma. She must have cared for me, she must have fed me. She's all I've got, I must love my mother.

We Ludd children have never been normal. We hang around Thanet, not far from our parents. Where are the grandchildren? There must be a curse. It's almost as if we haven't grown up. Boris and Angus: autistic, unmarried; Anthea: gay, with a stupid accent; Fairy, bulimic, anorexic. Only Fred has escaped completely.

And where were my siblings? Why not at my side?

Were they all ganging up on me?

I've a sudden longing for the Terrible Twos. I lunge across the room to pick up the phone, barking my shin on the Victorian foot-stool which always entangles my feet, like a dog, and the pain reminds me how bruised and battered I already am from my fall down Dad's stairs, my flight through fields, fences, hedges. There are cuts and sorenesses everywhere. Lucky that Ginger declined to look at my great hurt body as I got dressed. One day, though, I might offer a viewing. If he returns to ask more questions.

Yes, I have hopes and plans for Ginger.

19   *Adoncia*

The old *puerco*, he like to talk. He never listen, but he like to talk, he like to make his patient listen.

'Implant,' he always telling me. 'Make your teeth beautiful. Make you young! You show young Luis a thing or two. All the men will be crazy for you. We do the lot. Easy, in one. The Perfect Smile. Special Discount.'

He go on talking as he fuck me.

I'm a dunce, though, like he say, a big fool, because in the end I let him do it. All out, all in, the same day, everything, and then I suffer like never before. When the drug wear off, I crazy with pain.

I don't look beautiful. I don't look young.

20   *Monica*

Angus answered the phone, which almost never happens. He sounded jittered but relieved it's me. Almost instantly he started to whisper. 'Monica, the police are questioning Boris. Did you do it, Monica? We think you did.'

Angus was always suicidally direct.

'Who's "we" when we're at home?' I barked at him.

'You said you would kill him, we all heard you,' he hissed in my ear.

'Stop whispering!'

'Shhh, Monica, we think our phone might be bugged.'

How did they ever make so much money? Some basic understanding was lacking. 'Angus, whispering will make no difference. How's Boris? Can I talk to him?'

'He's a bit upset, Marija's gone home. All the way back to Riga this time. But did you do it? He'd want me to ask.'

'No, Angus, I didn't kill him.'

He sighed happily. 'That's a relief.' Typical Angus: he lived on the surface, he didn't understand shades, or lies. 'I'll tell Boris, don't worry,' he said. 'And we'll be your witnesses to the police.'

'Angus, it doesn't work like that. You can't say you saw me not doing it. You can't be sure if I did it or not.'

There was a pause while he tried to digest it, then his voice roared up to its normal volume. 'But did you, Monica, did you? Monica, you can tell me the truth.'

'Angus, I've told you. I'm innocent.'

'Have you seen him?' he said, which was a weird question that left me tongue-tied. I had seen Dad, I would never forget it.

Then a loud, strange noise began in my ear, something

animal but mechanical. For a second I thought it was something on the line, and then I realised that my brother was crying. That Angus should cry was terrible, and I found that I was doing it too, some giant, unstoppable machine took over and forced the grief and anger up through me, shaking my ribcage, crushing my chest.

'Love to Boris,' I roared, like a normal sister, and crashed the phone back into its cradle.

21

I knew what to expect when I rang Anthea and, shortly after, Fairy. I was eating great handfuls of crisps at the time, I had missed my lunch, I had missed my tea, and as usual they pretended it was hard to hear me. I heard them though, I have good hearing; they all seemed to have decided it was me.

Yes, superficially, I see their point, unwise of me to make death threats in public, but I am Big Mon, their own sister! They'd never known me to commit a murder! As I said to Fairy, whose voice was thin and wretched, the sad, nasal voice I remembered from her youth, and Rupert was barking away in the background, giving her instructions not to talk to me, I guessed.

'I never killed anyone, Fairy, did I?'

Pause. Then she said, 'What happened to my rabbit?'

This was a grievance from a hundred years ago, when she was adolescent and I was still at home, and a boy had bought her a fluffy white rabbit with blind pink eyes and an 'adorable' nose. It *was* adorable: Fairy adored it.

The rabbit had been parked in a cardboard box while the

adults decided what to do with it. For once, our mother stood up for one of us. 'The child won't eat. The school will report us. Miss Smith is already sniffing about. Let her have the rabbit, it might help her.'

'She'll eat if I tell her to!' Dad shouted. In fact, I know he was frightened too, I had seen him staring at Fairy's legs which were thin as arms, and only grew thinner as she stretched up white and wan and leaning over – she had no periods until she was sixteen! I laughed like a drain when she told me that. 'You're an alien,' I told her. 'You can never have babies,' which was harsh, I agree, but someone had to tell her. There was no blood in her, no flesh, no 'go'. And then she got the rabbit, and, with it, beauty.

She stood out in the garden with the baby in her arms, its white fur haloed with sun, like her hair, cooing and singing in a strange high voice. She was suddenly happy. She called it 'Flopsy'. She rushed home from school early to play with it. She started eating tea with Flopsy in the garden, one mouthful for her and one for the rabbit, and she looked less fragile, and her colour improved.

It was unjust that she should have such a jewel. Dad never allowed us older ones to have pets, however much we scrimped and saved up to buy them and begged and promised to care for them ourselves. Now, just because Fairy was given it, Ma was insisting she be allowed to keep it.

'Let her keep the rabbit. It'll save trouble. You don't know what Fairy might have been saying. Have some sense, Albert! If the rabbit goes, I go,' Ma screamed bravely in her sad kitchen for which he would buy no dryer or dishwasher (we got them both after her departure).

'*You're* a bloody rabbit. You'll never go!'

'One day you'll find out –'

I was listening in the hall. Then I heard it happen, the familiar sound of pushing and falling and Ma's small gasps of hurt and terror.

I ought to remember she stood up for Fairy, even if only from fear of Fairy's teacher, who had started talking about social workers. *But why didn't she stand up for me?*

The rabbit stayed, and the Terrible Twos, by then climbing fast through the stock markets, sent an expensive hutch as a present.

Flopsy lived safely in her hutch in the garden until one morning we were eating breakfast and Fairy burst in, a tall fountain of tears. 'Flopsy's gone. There's fur on the lawn.'

No-one ever discovered what happened to her, but somehow Fairy believed it was me, though I pointed out it was much more likely that Fred, then ten, had left the hutch door open, because he was always visiting it, 'whereas I always hated your disgusting rabbit'. Of course that made her suspect me more –

(OK, yes, I let Flopsy go walkies, but I wasn't to know the fox would eat her.)

Dad never allowed her to get a replacement. Probably my sister became less trusting. That must have helped her in the modelling world! The twat should thank me for the learning experience.

Instead, she thinks I'm a murderer.

'The rabbit's history. Dad's not a rabbit.'

'Rupert says I shouldn't talk to you.'

'Oh Rupert, Rupert! He isn't a Ludd. He doesn't understand, like you.'

There was a long pause. The call of the Ludds, the Ludd blood. *We had suffered together.*

When she spoke again, her voice was different, it had warmth in it, it had blood in it. 'I understand, Mon. I don't judge you. In fact –'

But Rupert took over the phone. 'Your sister would prefer you not to call,' he said. Did I hear a feeble sound of protest? 'We're all exhausted. Let's get some rest.'

With that, the line went cold and dead.

I needed dinner but the cupboard was empty so I ate what I had, half a loaf of bread (vitamin B is good for stress; I recommend bread to the A-level girls who believe dieting aids concentration) and opened my emergency bottle of gin. Every bone in my body hurt and cried as if I had been in a giant battle, and yet the enemy was lost in fog; I had not fought, but Dad had died.

He had died, hadn't he? Of course he had. No-one who looked like that could have survived.

I drank down the tumbler of gin in one – I'm a big girl, it takes a lot to slake me, with my large frame I can't get drunk, it's just a waste of time to add mixers. Then I rang Anthea, who didn't answer, which doesn't surprise me – she's a Xanax Gal. Dead to the world beside Kelly.

22

Trying to sleep in the middle of the night, tangled in my hot duvet.

Shouldn't there be someone to pray to? When we are little, we all believe in something huge that will protect us. I prayed to Jesus but he looked the other way, Dad raged on, I grew ever larger, my pubes sprouted, Mum ignored us, and soon I stopped believing in Christmas. In our house, Christmas was a day of rage; Dad, disappointed with his presents, furious with Ma for a half-cooked turkey. The cranberry sauce dripping down the wall. Ma sent Fred to get a cloth. On Fred's thin fingers it looked like blood.

Yes, our mother. I prayed to her. Once I actually got down on my knees, 'Please, Ma, can't we leave him?' I was five or six, I hoped for better. But in the end, she left without us. Did she love us? Did she hear me? All of us needed to believe in her.

Weak, hateful, but all we had.

Fuck off, Ma.

Ma, we love you.

Ma, defend me against bad dreams.

It's like praying to a soft-boiled egg!

I had left the light on on my landing, but in my dream there was no light, and when I woke, I could not find it, that strip of light under my bedroom door that meant there was something, sanity, hope, that I wasn't totally alone in the dark and thirteen years old and Dad was there, outside my room, panting, angry –

I couldn't escape, I was not awake, the narrow thread of light was back but he was on it, there were two black dashes that meant two feet, two heavy shadows, two hooves of evil, he was pawing the floor outside my door and of course no door could keep him out, he would break it down and come for me

He had never died, he was not dead, he was huge, huge, I could never escape him

And then I realised it was Fairy he wanted, with simultaneous fear and relief, I would offer her, then, my baby sister, and at least this time I would escape. I opened the door, he was old and fat and had no teeth but his hands were enormous, red and huge and dripping blood, but why was I bleeding? The blood was everywhere, all over the sheets, I had to hide them from my father.

Fairy had started her periods, she was wearing a dress of pale rabbit fur and she looked exquisite, like a Christmas Tree fairy, and Ma was there, but that was only more frightening, she was tiny and white and hung from the ceiling like some horrible glistening legless grub, moaning slightly, 'I can't do anything' – and Fairy vanished, and I was alone, and he raised his hands and came for me and his weight was a dead cairn of stones on my chest –

I woke. I woke. Yes, I survived him. Was I having a heart attack? Slowly my heart stopped hammering.

Dad was dead. It was 4 a.m.

23 *Adoncia*

I meet the old goat ten years ago, when Luis and me, we start the café in Margate. Happy Days! My hair still nice, my leg very nice, my boobies nice. I still feel pretty. I am rich, actually, café mostly something keep me occupy and my young man busy, my nice young thug who need something to do so he don't bugger off back to Spain. Keep Luis happy and out of people's houses, for he have a little habit, he get into trouble in Malaga, so I invite him over here to live with me, and he fly here so fast, I see he love me.

(But maybe here just better than prison.)

At first we do nothing, just spend my money I get from this and that in Malaga, and also from last will of stupid husband, who not agree with me, and die, unfortunately, yes, *desafortunadamente*. In Kent I have connection, people know me, I always like this little bit England. Yes, we do business, Malaga–Thanet. Many lorries bring fruit, vegetables, blah-de-blah everything 'nice and legal', *asi se dice*, 'nice and legal'! But under the *pimientos*, we put people. Some very nice, teacher, doctor, one nice *marroquí* doctor, some not so nice, but no-one poor. No, this a service for high class-people.

Seguro, some suffer, it chilly in there! But most not die, so it worth the money. We only try to help people, give them new life away from warzone or whatever fucking problem they escaping. But police get more nosey, so we hide them deeper. Maybe it colder, but not our fault.

Then three four die and stupid young woman who never tell me she was pregnant, my husband unhappy, he go to priest, *entonces*, I and he disagree – I tell him, I not the one who drive the lorry! I not the one who choose to do it, hide in refrigerator, break the law! *De hecho*, we just help, like social worker! – I tell him, never trust a fucking priest, they the worst of the lot, they friend with policemen.

But no, my husband fucking have regret, he never going to shut up. In middle of the night he snore and cry, big bag of wind, *para que sirve esto*? What good old man's bad conscience do anyone? I warn him once, I warn him again, but in the end I have to sort problem.

So quite soon I am widow with plenty of money. Interpol a little interest in me. Time for a holiday, I tell myself, and I think

of Margate, when we young and happy and just starting business we spend a week for holiday. Adoncia need new man for
company.

This time I choose Luis, someone different, not old man talk too
much with stupid pot belly and *rimordimiento de conciencia*. Luis
have the empty head, he just like me, happy, and never worry.

Margate nice enough, house very cheap then, price soon shot
up, fucking cold and smelly, but food enough to make you sick,
so I think, why I not open restaurant? Very nice job, no-one
get hurt. I call myself 'Ada Smith', *entiendes*, and *restaurante* have
British name, 'Smith's Snack-Café', see, very clever, no-one guess
I Spanish! '*Smith's Snack-Café*' do *tapas* and ice-cold beer, I call
young Luis *gerente*, manager, he lazy but it give him something to
do. Not too hard, he get up midday and *normalmente*, we close at
four, besides Margate people too stupid to eat there.

Luis go to the gym every evening. After a bit he start saying,
'I look after myself, Adoncia. It very important, Adoncia.' I start
to hear what he really thinking, 'Look after yourself, Adoncia.
Don't get old. I younger than you.'

So I think about that, because I love Luis, and I look for a dentist, because teeth not OK, and I go to the *cerdo* because he near
me. *Cabrón, cerdo*. Thank you, Mr Dentist.

At first, his place look terrible. He mean, too mean to see the
front look cheap, cheap as shit, or chips, you say, with horrible
door, dirty blue paint, and sign like sign on building site, and
inside seats for patient, crack red plastic with yellow wool from
sheep falling out. I tell him he have to join the 21st century or
no-one come except the tramps with their stinking mouth, and
I don't want his tool in them then me. He say, and he laughing, he

97

not care if they come. 'This country pay you when patients not coming, they pay you for patients not even alive, this socialist country, this socialism,' and then he laugh some more, but later I remember, I add two and two.

Soon I tell him he have to do private. I tell him big money in cosmetic. 'Nice for you, Albert, all the patients women.' My own fault, maybe I start him thinking.

I talk to Esmeralda sometime, poor skinny bitch, she out in the cold. Esmeralda and I talk about business. I always a good businesswoman. Too bad he not notice I a clever woman. He suck up ideas and think is his own.

But Albert refurb himself, yes. 2005, he get new name, *The Perfect Smile*. Thanks to Adoncia, is why, though Esmeralda pretend is her. He should have given me 50 per cent. Now the dirt pig had Perfect Smile.

Then I go wipe it off his face.

Part 4

A Leak from the Past

24

My last police interview pressed me the hardest. I was getting ready to make my escape when Ginger arrived with the white-haired sidekick.

'Been busy?' Ginger said, when he arrived and heard the dryer whizzing at the back of the kitchen. 'We'll take charge of your washing, thank you, Mzz Ludd.'

So then I knew they would find Dad's blood. But, matching DNA takes time, doesn't it? Time was what I needed, to work on my story.

I had told Neil I wasn't coming in, though I didn't like letting down my Shakespeare class. I knew he'd adore to get rid of me. But I wasn't leaving. I love those kids, the little beasts, the brats, the buggers. No, I would never abandon them. Yes, in odd moments I was missing them, when not busy avoiding arrest.

'I think we'll take a walk into the garden,' Ginger added. My cheeks were flushed, I had just come back in, I'd been hiding my laptop in a sealed plastic bag at the bottom of the beehive at the bottom of the garden that the family who lived here before me left. They were lovely people, with bees and veggies (they were boring, boring, stiff with vitamin C, but I smiled upon them and told them I'd look after their 'lovely home', their 'super veg patch'; there were several of us competing for the house). I like to eat meat, I despise lettuce, but I kept the beehive, I don't know why, I thought it was an amenity.

The day was sunny, unseasonably hot. I wandered after the policemen across the lawn. The petals of one sickly rose still shone pink near the guilty beehive, and by lucky chance, a few half-frozen bees were listing and weaving overhead. I said, as the police veered in that direction, 'My bees, officers. I hope they won't sting you!'

They rapidly returned to me. Ginger was whistling, trying to look untroubled.

Men are cowards, except our father. Maybe no-one has lived up to him? But isn't it cowardly to hit the weak? Wrong to hit someone smaller than you?

So everyone says, but I have learned different. Attacking someone bigger is risky. I myself left Boris and Angus alone after Boris gave me three Chinese burns for stealing Angus's virtual pet, and 'overfeeding' it until it died. He managed to revive it! Tamagotchi Immortal!

I don't like the thought of the dead coming back.

That day Ginger asked about my 'early years', after the white-haired policeman was gone. The Early Years of Monica Ludd! I could write a whole book about that, but I didn't want to waste it on my detective.

'So was your father an attentive parent?'

'He noticed things, if that's what you mean.'

'What things did he notice?'

'Mistakes, weaknesses.'

Oops! That hardly proved I loved my father. 'In order to help us correct them', I added, 'because he was a caring parent.'

'Your brother Boris says he was unkind. Specifically, unkind to you.'

That stupid stupid grief again, grief for myself as I heard the truth, boo-hoo-hoo. Monica, pull yourself together.

'My brothers felt protective, it's normal, officer.'

'Your brother Boris has divulged a nickname.'

Divulged! Blimey, good for you! Ginger went up in my estimation.

'My father gave us all nicknames. It was a kind of affectionate joshing. My nickname was kinder than some.' But I told myself I would never reveal that our father had dubbed Angus, 'Anus'. Never reveal your family shame! Except when trying to save yourself. 'For example, he called my brother Angus, "Anus". It was all good fun.' I grinned again.

He looked at me, incredulous. 'He did? Most people would consider that shocking.'

'Our family is not like other families. We are unusual. But very loving.' I forced the rigid muscles of my mouth into what I hoped was a depiction of tenderness.

'You looked strange for a moment, are you upset?' Ginger asked.

'No, I just had a stab of toothache.'

I saw he was sweating lightly, a film of moisture on his bald pink forehead and glistening on his boyish upper lip. He leaned in slightly, as if for the kill. We sat facing each other in the dining-room with a folded gate-leg table between us, and I kept imagining erecting the leaf so it crashed against his sturdy knee-caps.

Would I have to have sex with him? He was quite formal, but he had a sense of humour. I'd seen him staring at my breasts. I would offer if I had to, at least a gob job. Policemen probably don't get many offers. DI Dickhead, the ginger plod. Was he thirty? Twenty-eight? Thirty-eight?

With a superhuman effort, I managed to smile. 'Our father had an unusual sense of humour. For example, he called our brother Fred "Ferd", because poor Fred was severely dyslexic.'

'Wouldn't you call that cruel, Ms Ludd?'

'Our brother Fred looked up to our father.' The glib lie – with a truth in it, because Fred had often been knocked to the floor. I had seen him cowering, staring upwards, protecting his face with one thin arm – sounded false as paint, even to me. Ginger said, 'That's not what I asked.'

I thought, he is a graduate, one of the new breed of clever policemen, but not as clever as me, Mono. And yet, I was upset, and short of sleep, and Dad was dead, I was not myself, and the dining-room felt claustrophobic. Soon I would distract him with an offer of coffee, and up it, if need be, to *cafetière*. I have lived in the fifth *arrondissement*, I can always deploy my *savoir faire*.

'Let's talk about your father's nickname for you?'

'I don't remember, it was decades ago.' For some reason I felt uneasy, though you will remember I quite liked my nickname.

'Sometimes people repress things for a reason.'

I stared at him, and once again I had that nagging sense he was faintly familiar.

'I'm quite unrepressed, so people tell me. It was "Mono". From Monica. It means something like "single-minded". That's how I became a Deputy Head.' I thought it was time to remind him of my status, respectability, innocence.

'Is that what you believe?'

It rattled me. He was looking complacent, and there was a definite glint in his eye.

'My father's dead, and you ask about nicknames? You should be catching the murderer.'

'So you keep insisting,' he said, with a smile. I didn't like it when he smiled, I liked him to look pink and frustrated.

'Mono means "ape",' he said casually. 'It's the word for "ape" or "monkey" in Spanish.'

It hit me in the solar plexus, it hurt my belly and my back, and something old and almost lost was stirring, stirring at the back of my throat. I looked at him anew. I hated him. I wanted to slap him, but no, that wouldn't help my case.

'Do you even speak Spanish?' I managed to ask him, but I could hear the odd timbre of my voice, deep and creaking and off-balance, a monster bellowing underneath, roaring with pain, badly wounded. The trouble was, I didn't speak Spanish. My degree was French and English. The trouble was, our father did. He had learned it as a labourer in Valencia, after he ran away from home, before he came back and trained as a dentist.

'I'll bring a dictionary along to help you,' the bastard said, with a small, tight smile that half-revealed small even teeth, sharks are known for their even teeth, and then that glint of gold to one side.

Ape, monkey. So that's how Dad saw me. I had always liked Dad using my nickname. At primary school the kids called me 'Ape-arms' until I punched Barry Jones on the nose and made it bleed all down his grey jumper. His mum was mad and I got detention, but the name-calling stopped and the boys feared me.

So I was called 'Ape' by my own father. Worse, I was actually grateful, and liked it.

'How old were you when your mother left your father?'

'Are you psychoanalysing me?'

'Answer the question.'

'Grown up. It didn't affect me.'

'You were twenty, you were at Kent University, but you still lived at home. I know because your name was mentioned in a report of an incident at that time.'

He leaned in too close, I could smell his breath. Fish last night, or else for breakfast. Smoked haddock. So he had a wife?

'Yes, there was an incident.'

The detective was tapping his pen on the table. It was new and shiny. I stared at it. It made the leaf of the gate-leg quiver and emit a low faint rattling sound like an earthquake happening miles away in Margate or a rattlesnake slipping in from the garden, in through the door, rearing behind him –

'There was an incident,' he prompted. 'No prosecution was pursued.'

'Marriages break up all the time.' That telltale creak in my voice again, a crack, a creek, a leak from the past, a gulf of horror I try not to enter.

25

Mum had talked about leaving for months, until I started to think it wouldn't happen. It couldn't happen. That's what I thought. How could our mother leave our father? They were the pillars of the universe. Home life was vile, but it went on for ever. I had long ago outgrown my childish dreams where Ma would spirit us kids away to a peaceful land beyond the rainbow.

I couldn't imagine Dad without Ma. Who would contain his terrible rages, his desperate need to be fed and comforted? If Ma left, I left, or I would be finished. I hadn't forgotten what he yelled at the boys as he chased them upstairs or out into the garden, 'I'll break you boys, I'll finish you!'

I'll finish you. Those terrible words. A father finish his own children.

It was a normal Friday. I had been to a seminar on 'The Literature of Courtly Love', where I had contributed a lot, as usual, because I'd done the work, unlike the others, posh students are fucking lazy! I had strong opinions – 'It's a load of bollocks' – but I think my tutor liked me because I spoke, even though the others did it in French. The tutor only told me to stop talking because she didn't want the others to get jealous.

'When men don't get sex they are maddened,' I explained. 'In this courtly-love business, they just accept it, they pledge their troth, and they don't hate the women, the men don't rape them or knock them about. I love the language, the language is great –'

'*Il faut l'employer donc, Monique,*' she said. 'Monica, why don't you use it?'

'– but I don't believe a word of it,' I said, and making an effort, '*C'est incroyable.*'

'It doesn't rhyme with "employable".'

'Same difference, *c'est incroyable,* in a nutshell. Men will only stop raping if we biff them, hard. Or bang them up. Or hack their balls off. Courtly love's never going to do it.'

A few male students whinnied and sniffled, and, 'Rape is never acceptable,' dull Beth informed us, but who would rape her? I had heard my mother struggle with my father.

In any case, I was feeling cheerful as I rode the little train back from Canterbury to Margate. I'd bought some scones to take home to Ma so she would let me talk about my day – never having gone to university, she often failed to grasp my stories.

In through the front door, that peeling Georgian door that teenage Fred had to paint sky-blue, and then re-paint two or three times, 'Not good enough, you lazy tyke!' I heard a sound like a dozen mice scurrying, but thought nothing of it, I knew what it was, Ma would be preparing the evening meal, chaotically, in the untidy kitchen. How often had Dad thrown it back at her, his whole loaded plate, obscurely insulted. 'Bubble and squeak? That's pauper's food.'

'Ma! I'm home!'

'Monica, quick, come and help me.' Her small pale face in its nest of white hair peered down on me from the landing above. 'I'm leaving him. He's doing a root-canal. He'll be home in an hour and a half. Hurry.'

With that our mother disappeared, and I knew that normal life was over, the dreadful normal I was terrified of losing.

'What if he comes back and catches us?' I hate to admit how scared I was as we packed and folded, folded and packed. 'What if he comes after you.' But her face was set, her movements determined. Every so often she looked at her watch and threw things faster into the trunk, I didn't know she had that energy in her.

'Ma, I never thought you meant it.'

'I said I would leave, and now I'm doing it.'

There was a crash downstairs and we halted and stared, my eyes reflected in hers, blank terror, but no footsteps followed and then I remembered, 'It's my bag, I propped it on the banisters,' and we giggled – yes, we actually giggled, despite the gravity, we wept with laughter, and then she said, 'Only half an hour left, he'll have removed the nerve, he'll be cleaning up. Run and get my overcoat, it's hanging in the kitchen.'

I flung myself downstairs and snatched up her coat. On my

breathless trajectory upstairs I reflected. 'Why are you cooking? There's a stew on.'

'I thought I would leave Dad one last meal.'

She didn't see how strange this was. But she'd cooked every day, ever since she met him, cooked and washed up and cleaned up the mess.

'Ma, are you sure? He'll, you know, go mental. What'll I say?'

'Say I've taken the car and gone to Tesco.'

'Why?'

'To get the food for the barbie tomorrow.'

'Ma, you won't be at the barbie! And I can't do the barbie without you!'

'Monica, there won't be any barbie. Besides the barbies are hell, remember.'

Yes, but it was the hell we knew. Barbies were the one space my father cooked in, and he regimented them like dental operations, making us stand in a queue for hours so we didn't keep his sausages waiting.

There was another crash from the hallway. We froze, watching each other's faces. We could thrust the suitcases under the bed, she could dish up supper, we could cover our tracks, the Ludd family would remain intact…

'Quick, go and see,' she hissed at me.

I tiptoed out on to the landing and peered down through the dizzy spiral, fearing to see his hot eyes stare up, we'd be discovered, crushed, murdered.

But no, it was just a polythene-clad parcel an idiot had pushed through the door, Christmas Cards by Toe-Painters.

Ma finally managed to shut her cases fifteen minutes before his ETA. I, Monica, heaved them downstairs. On the doorstep

Ma turned and kissed me on the cheek with her own soft, dry, lips. She so rarely kissed me.

'Don't say anything. Don't give me away.'

'Ma. Won't you tell me where you're going?'

'Tesco's. Better you don't know, Monica. I'll get in touch once I'm there, I promise.'

'I'd never tell him. I won't betray you.'

She left her note solemnly on the hall table. 'GONE TO TESCO. MA. BACK SOON.'

'What should I do?'

She looked puzzled, as if it had never occurred to her that leaving would have implications for others. 'What? Oh, why not go abroad to your brothers?'

How did she think I would pay the airfare?

'If you get your things, I'll give you a lift,' she offered. 'But no, I suppose it'd take you ages – I can't hang about. It isn't safe.' She was on her way, she had already decided, she would save herself and sod the rest of us.

I lived there. She abandoned me. Her daughter, still at university.

'I'd be quick, Ma. But there's my college stuff.'

'Don't ask me, Monica.'

'It's all right, Ma.'

After her engine roared away from the house a strange lead weight made everything slow, so by the time Dad returned exhausted from his labours I had still only packed my dictionaries and textbooks. When I heard his key, I rushed downstairs. He found me panting in the hall, staring blindly at my mother's note.

He gave it a cursory glance, then, 'She's gone to Tesco's? Stupid cow. I've told her to get the meat from the butcher's…Why are you smirking? What's up with you?'

'Nothing.' In fact, I was grinning with fear.

'Why are you still living here?' This was normal for Dad, mere badinage. I stood there waiting for the world to end. But instead he started ranting about his root canal, who had needed three lots of anaesthetic – 'I had to hold her down. She kept coming round!'

He loved to regale us with brutal feats of medicine, but that day I didn't pretend to listen, just walked away upstairs and got on with packing.

It was six o'clock. At seven the shit would hit the fan, when he started to realise that all he had left was lamb stew in a slow cooker – and he had never liked the taste of lamb.

And so I moved into frantic motion, throwing everything into my enormous rucksack, advertised as 'Used by the SAS'. I meant to walk straight out of the house, without a goodbye, and never come back.

(And you see, it does no good to come back. Look what I found. Horror. Blood. All over the bedroom, my father's blood which was also mine, all over the sheets, all over his face, staining the carpet.)

The rucksack became hugely heavy. At ten to seven I tried to lift it. It was like shifting my own body weight. I couldn't heave it off the ground, but there was no time to unpack anything. I was sweating with effort, panic, grief (MA HAD GONE!). Ma had gone, and Dad would go mad, and I was stuck in the middle of it, and my heart beat fast as I set off walking, dragging my whole world along the floor, through the bedroom door, out on to the landing, then bump down one stair, bump down another, the sound of a heavy life saving itself, and then that sound, so horribly loud, was drowned by another one, louder, angrier, Dad in the dining-room yelling blue murder, 'Where is everyone? The table's not set! MONICA! WHAT'S HAPPENED TO YOUR MOTHER?'

Bump down bump down on through the yelling which protected me, because it deafened him, bump down bump down three steps to go –

And then he burst up from the stairs to the kitchen and stood in the hall and blocked my path. 'Where the hell do you think you're going?'

'Out.'

'What've you got in that bloody rucksack?'

'Stuff.'

I can still see his eyes, red with fury as he started to scent the end of things, but he would never let it happen, and I looked away so he couldn't read my face which must have been crazed with fear and triumph.

'Stop right there. Put that fucking thing down.'

It *was* down actually, I couldn't lift it, but I went on dragging it towards freedom, just two metres of hall to go before I was out, and I mustn't look round; in one last lunge I managed to grab the snib of the Yale, but as I yanked it back, my father clubbed me, a great fist-blow on the side of my head. 'Where the fuck do you think you're going, Miss?'

I was dizzy with pain. He had caught my ear. 'To stay with a friend.'

'A fucking boyfriend! You whore! You tart! I'll have no prostitutes in my house.'

I was twenty years old, I went to the gym, I was an inch taller than my father, but grief and terror turned me into a clown. He didn't realise I was a virgin; it wounds you in your secret centre when your own father thinks you're a whore – is it any wonder that I became one? We were falling out of the door together –

we were on the front steps, I tried to fight him off and defend myself but the bag made me stumble, and all I could see was his furious face, his jutting jaw, the veins erupting from inches away as he grabbed my shoulders and tried to shake me and then we were crashing down the steps together and I thought, clearly, 'Now he will kill me,' but he must have hurt himself in the fall because, though winded, I was crawling away, dragging myself along the pavement with my huge bag bumping behind like a corpse and his insults blaring out for everyone to hear, 'Come back, you little whore, I'll kill you!'

And then he was kicking my legs and ankles, all his life he wore ankle-high boots, great shiny black things, winter and summer, with stiff leather soles, metal heels and toe-caps, my father was booting my ribs, my back –

No, too dangerous to remember this, some horror pushing behind my eyes and in a split second I would be sobbing –

26

Ginger was bent forward, elbows on the table, pale eyes predatory, pin-sharp, the table minutely a-quiver with life. I recalled myself to my present danger and thought, for the first time, 'He's very attractive,' and now I consider, it was partly the fear, the fact that my genitals were tight with terror, yes, my genitals, they do cause trouble, surging into action at unexpected moments, so do not judge me when you hear what happened.

'Somehow I got involved in it, yes.' I was surprised to hear my voice, cool and collected and in control. But Ginger was looking at my hand, which was shaking, and I moved it slightly on the table. My hand and his were only inches apart.

'Tell me more, Mzz Ludd.' He was still buzzing.

Yes, I was fine. 'There was some kind of struggle. I fought him off. One of the neighbours called the police. They wrongly thought I was a "vulnerable adult".' I tried to smile. 'Ridiculous!'

'What I remember from the record,' said Ginger, 'is that some-one reported you "had never looked normal".' Ginger actually laughed at that.

After a moment, I joined in, louder, so loud it unnerved him, and he stopped; but all the same, I felt a pang of interest. Yes, we did have a lot in common. A sick sense of humour can be a bond.

'So as a twenty-year-old you were fighting with your father. It is also true he blacked your eye and pulled your hair out, with "numerous contusions" elsewhere on your body? Did you give a statement to the police saying your mother was "in fear of her life" and asking them to refuse your father's request to trace her?'

Yes, he had read the whole write-up.

Dad had set the trap fifteen years ago.

I pulled back my shoulders, relaxed my hands, and realised I must be thrusting my chest out, because, for a breath, Ginger's eyes darted down.

I do have big breasts. Yes, it's a fact. They're in proportion, or maybe a little out of proportion, but men love that, and so do I. OK, I thought, I have to change tack. I pushed them out a little more. 'Can we take a break? These questions are exhausting.'

His snake eyes flickered briefly, surprised, in a calculation he hadn't made before. I injected a little more meaning to my voice. 'You're looking hot. Should I turn down the heating?'

Surely I had overdone it. Was it an offence to seduce a policeman?

You may not believe a large woman is seductive, you may have been conned by the fashion pack, but real life is not a cat-walk, and I was giving Ginger an eyeful. Remember, a woman of the world has wiles. Believe me, Monica knew what she was doing.

'Would you like to take a break…officer?'

'I would like you to answer some more of my questions.'

But he'd seen me noticing him noticing me, we were entangled in a net of sly glances, a net of secret intelligence, and once again there was something between us that might save me if I played it right – though the net wasn't strong, and I couldn't quite trust it, I was high in the air, swinging closer each time but not yet sure that his arms would catch me.

On cue, he put them behind his head, either relaxing or feigning it. His chest was barrel-like, muscular, his biceps pressed against his shirt. I stopped minding that he was bald and looked at the vigour of the hair in his brows and curling red over the backs of his hands. Signet ring, third finger. Unmarried?

In any case, the married ones are easier to take, ripe fruit longing to be plucked from their branches.

'Would you say you had good relationships with your siblings?'

'Very.'

'Do you see each other regularly? Keep in touch?'

'You'll remember we had the big family party.'

'That was not what I asked you, Monica.'

(He'd started saying 'Monica' after coffee. Strong and black, with the offer of chocolate, which he refused, but with enough reluctance for me to know that he was tempted. He had looked again, for a fraction too long.)

He used my name frequently, like a suitor. Yes, of course, I liked the attention. The kids at school only call me 'Miss', my family all call me 'Mono', and awful knowledge has poisoned that.

Ape, Monkey. Yes, he had to die.

Would there be a funeral, would we all go, would I have to stand at the back in handcuffs?

Ginger and I were getting closer. Just before teatime I appealed to him directly, interrupting his questions by avowing my innocence. Me on the sofa, with a hint of sprawl, him in an armchair, erect, attentive.

'I didn't murder my father, officer.'

'I don't believe I have accused you of murder.'

'I can take a lie detector test,' I continued. 'I am innocent as driven snow.' I saw the blood spurt out over the snow, great skeins and hanks of it, spreading, staining, flooding my great strong thighs and thick ankles. 'You should be questioning my father's – partners. Girlfriends, whatever.' I didn't say who, I still felt obscurely complicit with whoever had whacked Dad's head like an eggshell.

He nodded; for a second I thought, 'He believes me, this is a formality.'

No, alas, that would have been too easy. 'But you *were* at what we call the scene of the crime. Contrary to what you have told us, Monica. There is closed-circuit-camera footage of your car arriving at the house mid-morning,'

I took a few beats to absorb this information. 'Oh, yes, the car,

I had forgotten, I may have got my timings wrong, I'm so used to leaving it over at Dad's and going off on one walk or another. Maybe I was gardening the day before. I'm a very physical person, officer.' Again, I allowed myself to hold his eyes.

'Go on. Sunday morning. We are almost there.'

'I was telling you about my usual walks, I go round the coast, Joss Bay, Bone Bay, it's glorious, along the beach, past the Thirty-Nine Steps, have you read John Buchan's novel?' And forestalling his protest, 'Eight miles or so. That's what I call a proper walk. Do you like walking, officer?'

'No. I admit I do like John Buchan. There's a proper writer, Monica.' For the first time, his smile relaxed, briefly he was just another human being, not that I like those, but I needed a friend.

He leaned back, his arms behind his head again, the glint of his ring against the crimson of the chairback, people like bright colours, nothing wrong with that, but the red was too bright, too much of it, and I'd always meant to get them re-covered. Ginger continued, 'Yes, I like John Buchan. Flight, pursuit, that kind of thing, murders, crimes. Justice, Monica.'

I yawned elaborately and shifted on the sofa from one mighty thigh across to the other. Fighting was tiring. We needed a rest. What had I to lose? Absolutely nothing. I had lost it all when Dad called me a whore.

'Sunday morning, please. You were there.'

'I feel silly calling you "officer". Do you have another name I could use?' I leaned across the sofa, smiling, and planted my hand on the crimson velvet.

'DI Parkes-Woods. I did introduce myself.'

'Parkes-Woods is a bit of a mouthful.' I ran my tongue over my lips. My genitals twanged like bedsprings, ready for the decisive moment.

He seemed to teeter on the brink of something, and then he said defensively, 'Well, it's my name. My mother was a Parkes, my Dad was a Woods. Which is a peculiar bit of grammar.'

He bobbed up again in my estimation.

'But some people call me Ginger.' And he looked guilty, or suddenly boyish, as if he was afraid of loss of status, and his mouth straightened, and he folded his arms.

'Is it all right if I call you Ginger?'

He looked maddened, and circled his head erratically between nodding and shaking, as if trying to dislodge an annoying bee.

Ginger! I'd been calling him that all along within my imaginary fencing-ring. 'Ginger, there's a lot that I want to tell you.'

His head steadied into greedy nodding. Yes, spill the beans, I could sense him thinking (but, of course, I wanted him to spill his beans, all over my face, if necessary!).

'My father imagined I was sexually active long before that was actually the case. Why would you say he imagined that?' I opened and closed my thighs, slowly. 'I was a virgin, officer, Ginger. Of course, that was a long time ago.'

'Mnnmnn,' he said. 'Get to the point.' He was looking flushed, and slightly shiny.

'I became unusually promiscuous. Ginger, I hope you will not judge me.'

'Hmmmm.'

'After the traumatic day I left home –'

'We dealt with that,' he said, disappointed –

'I started sucking off everyone I met.'

His eyes opened wide, incredulous, and then he was mine,

of course he was mine. 'Language,' he said, as if his tongue was gluey, and then I saw he was starting to laugh, and that was why it sounded strangled.

'I'm afraid I still find it hard to resist.'

'Hard to resist? You do, do you?'

What do men want? They want eager women, women who do not need persuasion, women who do not rebuff them.

His nostrils quivered. My Ginger was suddenly sharp and sly and intensely focused, and our eyes met, and that was it. In seconds he was on the sofa beside me and I stretched out my hand and undid his zip.

Oh Monica! You fell, you fell! Well, in fact I just knelt down in front of him, I'm laughing with glee as I remember it, his joyful face, his anticipation, the pleasant pink tower that arose before me as my tongue lapped, lapped around its shore –

to the point where I abruptly pulled away, leaving thumb and fingers gently circling the base. His cock was a thing of bounding energy, twitching inches from my face, a transparent seed-pearl of hope at its tip.

'For God's sake, Monica, you can't stop now.'

'I hope you've got a condom, Ginger.'

Yes, it was a risky calculation, but he groaned and said, 'I don't carry them around; you're the first nice woman I have met in ages.'

Note, please, that he said 'nice woman'. No mention of 'slag', 'whore', 'cock-tease'.

'I don't mind going, you know, bareback,' he said, but the way he said it made me certain Ginger had never said 'bareback' before. 'Not much risk with, you know, oral. As it happens, I haven't had sex for a year.'

I shook my head sadly. 'You have to remember I teach Sexual Health to the children at school – part of the Sex and Relationships course – but I can direct you to the nearest chemist.' And I gave him two more licks, for luck.

Sighing, he forced it back in his pants. 'No trying to abscond,' he said, tensely. 'And this is just between us, obviously.'

'Yes. I won't share it with any other policemen.'

'Monica, you're too good to share.' For a moment his face was soppy with gratitude. Then an edge of suspicion crept back in. 'You can't go anywhere, you haven't got a car.'

'Exactly. You policemen have impounded it. I suggest the Boots near the seafront, you'll be back in twenty minutes and I'll be waiting.'

'I think I'd better take you with me.'

'Think of my reputation,' I pleaded, rising briskly from my knees. 'I'm a Deputy Head. I can't keep being seen with policemen.' I brushed off the fluff with deliberation and blinked demurely at my sheepskin rug.

Ginger got dressed in record time and then did something I wasn't expecting: he ducked his head and loomed towards me and for a moment I flinched from a head-butt – Dad had once head-butted Angus to the ground, leaving a great blue-blackening bruise on his cheekbone – but no, the man gave me a peck on the check. Then we both looked at each other, surprised. 'Do you want to take my house-keys?' I asked him. 'You could even lock me in.' I had three sets, it was just to reassure him.

He shook his head and cleared his throat. 'Monica, there's something I should tell you about your father –'

'Let's not talk about Dad just now. Come back soon. Tell me later.' And he went haring out of the door.

I warmed to Ginger. Of course I did: he trusted me. He didn't lock me in.

Yet as soon as I heard his engine revving, I leaped upstairs to grab my bags.

Yes, here they were, Gunilla's keys, where I had concealed them at 5 a.m. My neighbour Gunilla, an industrial chemist who went to Sweden for three months every winter, always left her car locked up in the garage, and she would be happy to do me a favour.

Quick, quick, out to the beehive to rummage for my diary, dew on the garden from the melting frost, and my house, as I pounded back through the grass, suddenly looked a little reproachful, *Monica, why are you spurning a cup of tea with a friendly man?* But Dad was dead and everything was different. Forget about Ginger's disappointment, why should you pity a fucking policeman?

(And yet, with men I had always played fair. If I don't want them, I make it clear. If I beckon them, I come across.)

My last act as I left the house: I scrawled 'Sorry' on a scrap of paper, and then, even stranger, I added a kiss. This in my moil of haste and fear.

What if her garage door doesn't open? But after a pause, it swung up silently, rat-trap mouth too slow and stately, but behind it, the smiling eyes of her Volvo. Yes, yes, my friend, my ally. (Surely Gunilla was a kind of friend? She'd dropped off the keys soon after she moved in, saying, 'I hear you are a teacher.' True, she asked for them back again. Sensibly, I refused to return them: she could get another set of keys for her daughter! But all the same, I think we were friends.)

Her big car drove me away from Ginger, away from our road, away from Broadstairs.

Would he assume I was in the bathroom and, slowly souring, wait for me? Would he be vengeful? Forget Ginger.

And yet, he had been kind to me, kinder than any man I recently remembered. That moment when he bobbed his head and, as I flinched from the blow, kissed me –

Sex. Love. Their energy. The Ludds had too much energy, most of it going in the wrong directions. What if sex and love went together? Sometimes they did, in other lives.

Mon, forget him. Concentrate. Sex, love, these things are over. Dad is dead, the chips are down. Save yourself and save your family.

Escaping, I did feel almost happy as I drove fast down the sunlit road, past the neat rows of inhabited houses, peaceful cubes with autumnal creeper, a white-haired gardener clearing for winter It almost felt like a holiday, driving off like this on a weekday, the 'borrowed' car more roomy than mine. Then I switched the radio on.

No-one had been charged for the attack on the mosque. (Probably Defend British Values, buzz-cut knob-heads with union jacks.) Terror alert at Oxford Circus. Three more Islamic schools being built (poor young girls with their heads in hoods! But the BBC was excessively respectful). Brexit, Brexit, going on and on.

In someone's garden, a man was shouting.

Silver-gold birches were shedding their leaves. I hoped I had remembered a book to read.

Odd that none of us Ludds has left Thanet. Some of us tried, but it drew us back.

Part 5

One Day She'd Pay

27

Yes, I enjoyed that little drive, even with Ginger somewhere behind me. I like the country I grew up in. I pass that on to the kids at school, both the new arrivals and the natives, though they just giggle and gawp at me. Most of them don't learn pride from their parents. The people of Thanet pretend to be cynics, putting themselves down before anyone else does.

Yet Thanet has the best beaches in England, serenely curving, sandy, empty. Other, less fortunate, places have pebbles. I walk these beaches, I have graced them all. I have swum at dawn and in summer twilight, and watched the occasional sunbathing family roasted maroon in their search for beauty, the toddlers too, tiny islands of pain. I have remonstrated, and not been thanked.

Yet the people of Thanet are kind, and will help you: if you fall down they will pick you up. Maybe not if you're splashed with blood, and probably not the bus drivers, not if you're carrying a lethal weapon...

True, Thanet's very hard to escape from, and difficult to navigate. The sea surrounds you on every side, because it's a peninsula. Whatever you do, don't make for the sea: glimpses of blue are counterproductive, an *ignis fatuus* that tells you nothing. There are few road signs, and all of them say either 'QEQM Hospital' or 'Westwood Cross' – Westwood Cross is our shopping centre. Most roads lead to death or shopping, but unpredictably, in no order.

Safest to know where you are going, with a head start on your pursuer.

Westwood Cross is a dead loss for clothes – if you are Junoesque, that is. Elsewhere you can buy wondrous things in junk shops, charity shops, galleries. (Not just ladies' shoes, size 11, *and always leave those shoes for me.*) There's a glut, a great gamut, of artists and musicians, running round strumming and plucking and writing and shining like lilies of the fucking field and selling paintings on promenades; if I weren't busy I would love to join them, but no, I choose to be a useful citizen, teaching Shakespeare and Condom Use.

There are folk festivals, and jazz festivals, and firework festivals, and food festivals. Some celebrations get out of hand. Thanet has some very dark stories, occasional tales of Gothic murder that vary the local paper's staple of much-loved kittens cruelly stolen.

Thanet is the end and beginning of Britain; Thanet has always been the front line. Deniece's grandpa, aged eighty-six, has a scar on his forehead from a German shell that was shot across the Channel from France – the class listened awestruck when Deniece told us. Thanet saw the arrival of the Romans and chased them off a time or two, before they came in force and stayed. Ramsgate sent little ships out to Dunkirk; Ramsgate welcomed them home again. Fighters zoomed off from Manston Airport to fight the Nazis in the Battle of Britain. So Thanet is correct, it is 'Front Line Britain', though most people who say so are old and drunk and wouldn't know a Roman if one walked down the High Street. Neil's not interested in Thanet's history and won't have Latin on the Windmills curriculum. 'Monica, Latin is not for us.' Latin is for everyone! But Thanet glowers across the sea at Europe. Thanet wants stronger borders, and Brexit, and yes, it's tragic, it will end in tears, but, no-one can say they haven't earned it.

Brexit, Break it, Brek-ek-ek-exit! Gofer it, Thanet! Don't forward plan it!

Thanet does quirky, loyal, local. Thanet cocks a snook at London values, although it's crammed with ex-Londoners. Thanet does patriotism, piracy, and UKIP, which has let it down. Thanet is near a university, but many people think degrees are a con. I didn't fall for that, I got my degree and I urge the brighter kids to raise their expectations...although their parents are afraid for them.

And so am I, and so am I, but I am a teacher and must hide it.

Shipwrecks fill whole bookshelves in Thanet, *The Heroes of the Goodwin Sands* and other volumes. Thanet youth volunteer for the lifeboats. Just offshore gleam the Sands themselves, low and white and always moving, a glimmer of beauty that sucks ships down, though they look welcoming and tender.

The sea washes round us; the sea forgets. It wears down the cliffs, and creeps towards us. It lands dark shapes in the middle of the night. It throws up dogfish, and heavier bodies. When you least expect it, the sea remembers.

Don't come to Thanet unless you're tough. For some people it's the end of the road, the end of their tether, *Thanatos*, Death.

But I, Monica, just keep going.

Stupid of me to be distracted by Ginger.

28

10 p.m. The house phone hasn't rung. The police have not come looking for me. Which must mean no-one knows I'm here. If my sibs guess, they haven't peached on me. My heartbeat has steadied, my breathing has slowed. It's like the golden clearing in *The Great Escape*, that moment in the film where the recaptured Brits stand briefly sunlit before their execution. What have I got? Hours, days?

Dad bought Bay House around 1980, when I was ten, and the twins were twenty-five. He was a few years into private practice and had discovered how to rake in the money (or Esmeralda had, more likely. Dad always said that Esmeralda was a business genius, 'except regarding her own wages', which he muttered with a pleased little chuckle. Yes, he was fond of Esmeralda! *No*, the bastard exploited her). The property market was depressed at the time so Dad had picked up the house 'for a song', a big 1920s building on the cliff above Bone Bay, with a margin of impenetrable scrub before the cliff-edge, in summer a tangle of yellow flowers and unripe pink and red blackberries – 'and I've just put in some whatdoyoucallits, Leyland something, to keep us private'. 'Leylandii, dolt,' said Ma, very quiet, but fortunately, we children heard her. Some of my traits must come from her.

That afternoon I came up the path again, decades later, a great strong woman, the car tucked away in the woods at the back so no-one will notice anything different. For some reason I approached the door carefully, crab-wise, darting from one tree to another.

It's hard to explain why I like to visit. It's still, I knew from deflated balloons I'd found in bins or by washing-machines, the place where Dad brings the Girl for a treat, and maybe others, like the yellow-haired floozy or murderess I'd disturbed him with – *past tense, past tense, never any more, whatever Dad did, it's finally over.* So when I've come here – maybe three times a year? – I always arrive with my heart in my mouth.

So why come? The thrill, the fear, Monica sleeping in the lion's mouth. So close to him that he would never see me, yet if he did, I knew he would kill me.

Maybe that would have been a relief, the act ending the fear of the act. Though this is just the psycho-babble I've had to learn to be a teacher.

Bay House needs refurbishing, because Dad is mean – Dad *was* mean. When I was a teenager I started to despise it, but now I detect the 1920s vibe. Art Deco chairs, sub-Omega screens hiding square, working fireplaces, and everywhere the original curtains, some almost in tatters, with runnels and star-shaped ravages of moth through which light pours in the early morning, and patterns of ersatz Clarice Cliff flowers. I'm a cultured woman who can name-drop Clarice Cliff, even if I only own a sugar bowl, and OK, even that lacks a lid. Was there an echo of Manderley? I can name-drop *Rebecca*, too. The rooms were bigger than our house in Margate. Too many photos of my sister – Fairy, of course, not Anthea. Fairy aged eight, ten, twelve. Around fourteen the pictures stop.

Not a single photo of me. Except at the back of one group photo where Dad had ordered me to go. 'Back row, Mono. You're too fucking tall.' I know he actually meant ugly.

We didn't know Dad had bought Bay House until he had owned it for a while, long enough to furnish it and landscape the garden, which had been a wilderness. He had no taste: leylandii, scarlet roses, big and unscented, and bright orange marigolds everywhere. 'I don't like marigolds,' Ma remarked. For once, Dad didn't lose his temper. 'They're good against pests, so they told me, April. Maybe they'll sort out these little buggers' – indicating us kids, and the two of them laughed.

The summer-house had been there for decades and the people before had painted it pale green. I loved it. 'Dad, Dad, can that be mine?' 'That shed? Are you mad? I'm going to knock it down,' but I begged and begged, and for once he listened, probably because it was less work to leave it. Yes, it was the thing I fell in love with, the first summer he took us there. (Anthea, seventeen and sulky; me, aged eleven, getting rapidly bigger; Fairy, seven, insignificant; and Fred, a tiny, quiet baby with a straggle of black hair and watchful eyes.)

The shed was where I could be safe, and alone. Anthea was afraid of spiders, Fairy was too young to turn the handle, and besides, they didn't trust me on my own with her after the incident in the cupboard, which I simply don't have time to go into.

There had been bad arguments all that spring which ended once Dad announced this trip, and we all sensed that Ma had won. Now I put it all together, Dad must have bought this house so he could fuck other women here. That would be it. And Ma protested.

Yes, whatever, I refuse to whine about trauma caused by our parents' sex life. I am thirty-eight. I am full-grown! To put it mildly. Six foot one.

Yet why have I always lived alone?

I remember that first family holiday. 'Do you know how lucky you lot are?' Dad demanded. He was actually smiling at breakfast that day. 'I never had a holiday, as a boy. But I slave all day so my kids can have fun. So we can have fun as a family!' And he sang in the car as we drove to the house, and didn't get grumpy when Ma complained. 'You're going to love it,' he instructed us. 'It's a holiday home. Well-off families have holiday homes. Thanks to me, we're a well-off family.'

The holiday was too late for the Twos, who were in Manhattan making a glittering mountain of money. We girls were thrilled and awkward together, punching each other in the back of the car, above the head of Fairy in the middle, though she pretended I was hitting her. I could only share my excitement with Anthea, and she could only share hers with me, yet she despised me as her junior, and I resented the contempt she showed for the books I read (Tolkien! Dickens!). The only book we both liked was *Rebecca*. She preferred health and beauty magazines. Although Anthea was my older sister, I already knew she was different from me, obsessed with nail colours and temporary hair dyes, de-pelting her legs and curling her lashes with stainless-steel toolkits that came through the post.

Fred was irrelevant because he was an infant. You may not know 'infant' means 'not speaking'. And so he couldn't speak up for himself.

Infans, infantis: Latin: mute. A child who can't talk can't protect itself. I mean to give birth to a talkative baby. At thirty-eight, I am not too old.

(Oh Fred, dead. I still don't accept it. Whereas 'Dad, dead' – I'm getting used to it. Hurts my head to think about him. He's split into two, or in the process of splitting. The normal heavy, meaty figure who shadowed my life since I was a girl, and the man on the bed, unnaturally brilliant, drenched in sun and scarlet blood, don't think about him, don't let him get in, his battered head, his eyelid flicking, just for that second, staring at me. No, no, go back to the past.)

It was summer when we first came to the house and my summer-house had a small window at the back that looked out over this delicious wildness. I had an exercise book in which I wrote poems. Red and black butterflies and small pale-blue ones spun and hovered. Perhaps they were mating. Left alone there, I was totally happy.

A twinge of pain when I remember that summer, I was eleven, I was still hopeful, I assumed I would have a mate of my own and probably a brace of children. There were five of us. The Ludds, the Ludds. We were a big family, but now we've shrunk. "No, none of us kids has reproduced," I had said to Ginger, and his eyes narrowed. I knew he had come to some conclusion. A dying family. We were dying out.

Stick together, said Dad, and *club together* – there should have been more of us by now.

That holiday was the first of several but, in my mind, the happiest. We used to roll up in a packed, noisy car, Dad shouting at us to 'Unpack first! Get the car sorted before you go exploring!' – and we shot from the car like corks from Prosecco and, loaded like pack mules, went rocking and giggling in cocky procession up to the door.

Obviously no holiday went quite smoothly; my father banned us from the rooms he favoured and forbade us to take ice-cream from the freezer and shouted at Anth when she wore a bikini, and had occasional rows with Ma in the early morning, a rumble from the bedroom which left her white-faced until lunchtime; but he also played French cricket with us, whacking the ball at the walls and trees and shouting with laughter when we dropped catches, our hands stinging from the force of his batting, and one day when I bowled him out he came over and ruffled my hair and said, 'Well played, my little Fatso.'

His hand on my head, not hurting me.

And much of the time we escaped our parents and played on the steps that led down to the beach and climbed the big trees and were mindlessly happy and dozed in deckchairs with a book (that was me), and later, Fairy and Fred tagged along and Anthea left and I was the leader and yes, as we lorded it over the queue of tourists at the beach café buying crisps and cornets and Strawberry Mivvis, and batted the wasps in the tourists' direction then ran, ran, ran for the sea, and danced holding hands like an enormous jellyfish, yes, I believe that we were happy, we Ludds were happy, I do believe it,

If we were happy, here was the place. So maybe I know why I've always come back.

This time, though, there's nowhere else.

29

I'm sitting on what Ma called 'the verendaah', a word which had poetry for her, some kind of echo of India, although of course she had never been there. 'Tea on the verendaah!' she would sometimes cry, a thin lost cry for a life of beauty, or did it just show her sad pretentions? – weak little Ma, one thing was certain, tea was the only meal she managed efficiently.

Ma had grown up in a family where the last meal of the day

was bread-and-butter with fishpaste or cheap strawberry jam, and the occasional flourish of jelly for afters. It's what Grandma gave us when we visited.

So Ma didn't cope well when her husband first demanded 'High Tea', which added ham and salad, then 'No sliced bread', which added to the work-load, with 'proper home-made' blancmange or trifle, not the Angel Delight to which she added water, and then finally roared, as the nineties arrived, 'You will have to cook dinner! I am a dentist! I work hard for you lot, and I deserve it! You're living in the past, you stupid cow!' (Never forget that he adored her. Yes, I know, it's complicated; life's complicated, get over it.)

Dad took a belligerent interest in the menu. 'Cod?' His face was a picture of distaste after the first mouthful. 'You know I like plaice.' 'It's just that the girls refuse to eat it.' 'So they decide the menu now, do they? Who pays for the food, I'd like to know?' (I am grinding my teeth in ancient fury as I hear my father's voice in my head.)

A moment later the horror had happened. Our mother's face streamed with grey liquid, the lukewarm sauce she had put on the fish, she had fish and potatoes all over her hair and a necklace of carrots and peas down her jumper, and Dad's plate crashed off her lap to the floor and broke on the tiles of the verandah.

'Albert, how could you?' her smeared mouth managed and her poor white hands dabbed liquid from her eyes and, impotent, dabbed at the mess on her chest.

'Clean yourself up!' he roared at her, then, 'What are you staring at, Monica? Sit down and eat your food, you great lummox,' for I had got up, without thinking, to protest or protect or follow our mother as she limped, half-blind, away into the house. 'Monica Ludd, get back in here!'

Alas, I obeyed. Do not judge me. I was thirteen. It won't happen again.

He will never frighten us all again.

And yet as I push my chair back from the table where long ago he assaulted our mother and hear the noise it makes on the tiles, like the bark of a seal, a great heavy seal, and seals are dangerous, they can gore or crush you – my skin is crawling, my arms, my neck, my intimate places, are wind-chilled, frozen. It's cold, the verandah where our family brawled, cold and empty and everyone gone.

By day it's a glassed-in corridor of sunlight that overlooks the lawn and the roses, usually shared with basking flies. At night it's a wide window on the trees, their blue-black shadows in constant motion, and one trapped insect high up against the glass, buzzing, buzzing to get away.

11 p.m. Time for bed. Only the weak are afraid of dreams. But no-one is – immune to them. OK, I'm scared that when I put the lights out, Dad's ghost will come for me. Or else the police, blue lights and sirens, dragging me out of my vulnerable sheets, sneering at the hot-water bottle I always take to bed with me.

A blush of shame as I remember my last – sexual contact, the one before Ginger. Under the duvet I threw back to accommodate the lout I'd picked up, there it was, horribly revealed, last night's hot-water bottle, not quite cold.

'Why use that thing? You're a big girl now,' the lout leered, cheery but faintly dismayed.

'Meaning?' I said to him, my arms akimbo over the bosoms he had been happy to lick and tweak.

'Bit old for a teddy-bear hot-water bottle, aren't you?'

'Who are you calling old, Fatty?' I only meant it as badinage, but now it was his turn to hide his belly.

'Mary, it fucking creeps me out.'

'My name is Monica.'

'Yes, whatever.'

'You'd better fuck off,' I heard myself saying.

'Bitch, I'm already getting dressed.'

I thought about Ma as I went into the kitchen and put the kettle on for my bottle. Would anyone have told her what had happened to Dad? Telling people things was usually my job. A brief pang of guilt I wormed aside. In recent years when I came through the door she'd tended to switch the TV on, loud. So why should *I* be the messenger?

11.15. Excellent. The comforting glug-gloo of liquid in my bottle – that's a hot-water bottle, not gin. Bedtime, maybe my last night of freedom.

Is the window steamy, or is that mist?

A noise outside. I jump, for no reason. The curtains are left open, so the sun can wake me. But that lets me see where the trees are stirring, dark shapes moving against the sky.

I know there's no-one hiding in the garden, sneaking up the path, watching through the glass...

30

Right on cue, the foghorn began.

I had locked all the doors and done my best to remember how

to set the burglar alarm, but numbers have never been my forte. I wouldn't need the code, no-one would come, but the foghorn boomed like a cow in pain, louder and louder, on and on.

Fogs sweep away the lines that divide past and future, land and sea, lines between people, parents and children, lines that parents should never cross, lines that protect fathers and daughters, lines between bravery and terror. Lines, as an adult, are the things which have saved me. Lines, in my childhood, too often went missing. Then the thick blinding fogs of Thanet reduced all things to a swirling nothing, there were no boundaries, they could all rush in –

come on Dad, time to break the door down

Suddenly, I am thirteen again.

I was sitting in the summer-house writing a poem and hadn't heard Dad calling me in, I didn't know I was late for dinner, all I registered was a roar like a train and then he crashed through the door of the summer-house scattering glass stalactites everywhere, random daggers of rage and pain, he had gashed his hand and there were drips on the carpet, drops of bright blood, he was leaking scarlet and yelling, 'I'LL BREAK YOU, MONICA!' – 'What's the matter, Dad? Help, no please –' but he was roaring too loudly to hear me, he hauled me up by my neck and hair (yes, I was heavy, but rage is powerful), then chased me up the path into the kitchen where the rest of the family sat mute and scared. Ma's little face was mouthing something but, 'I don't want to hear it, shut up!' he snarled and, 'She'll have to learn!' *I would have to learn* though I had no idea what lesson I was learning. 'Get upstairs, just get upstairs!' and he pounded after me hot on my heels yelling, 'You will obey me!' punching my back, my legs, my bottom, *was he going to kill me*? and pushed in after me, into my bedroom, my private place, my private places, my breasts, my back, my poor plump thighs, beat me black and blue as I lay there, curled like a helpless grub on the bed, my big weak arms trying to protect my head, which was smeared and spattered with our blood.

It happened, yes. I was innocent. Dad had called me to dinner. I didn't hear him.

Shortly after, the worm turned. Monica Ludd took up weight-lifting. I was also the first girl at my local grammar to sign up for after-school boxing lessons. The teacher thought I was joking, at first, and totally ignored me for the first two classes, but when he saw I kept turning up, he started to take me seriously. 'You need to be lighter on your feet,' he said, 'but you've got a good eye, and good rotation.' Much good it's done me. I was good at it, but how many people want a fair fight? I've imagined it, often. Jab, uppercut. Neil is lying limp and bleeding. Any violence and you lose your job.

Now I switch off the light and stand for a moment, getting used to the dark, trying to find my night vision. Outside the glass, just the thresh of the leaves on the long branches nearest the house, then the dark of the leylandii slowly creeping higher, then everything dissolved in fog.

No, I am safe. Yes, nothing.

31

I usually slept in my childhood bedroom which had the bed where the beating happened, but when I opened the covers to insert my bottle, I saw two smudges of beigey-brown. Then I put on the harsh overhead light and the smudges sharpened into two dead moths, silky, furry, tiny, repellent. I am a giant, moths are nothing to me, and yet they were horribly intimate, they had crept inside and silently mated and laid their smear of eggs and died.

With a thrill of repulsion, I yanked up the bedclothes to cover the corpses and stormed on to the landing. Right, I would sleep in the master bedroom, which was on the other side of the house. It would have had sea-views before the trees grew up; it had a wooden balcony Dad had repainted over the rot, on which a cream table and chairs slowly rusted, overshadowed by a shiny-leaved tree with big, lemony-scented white flowers, yes, Ma called it a magnolia, and Dad always threatened to chop it down. The windows were big, so it would be cold, but I'd pile on bedding and turn up the heating. The door was closed, and hard to open, I had to push it past the sticking point, it yielded and I fell inside. Large. Dark. Curtains closed.

The furniture showed how tight Dad was – a wardrobe-and-dressing-table matching set that might have looked luxurious in 1950 but he must have picked up in a charity shop, orange-gold walnut with extraordinary psychedelic whorls of mirroring knots and grains where the tree-trunk had been cleaved in two and skilfully crafted into symmetry. Had you folded both pieces down a central line, the two sides would have matched exactly. Something frightening about reflections. I was in him and he was in me – someone once said we looked alike,

I've forgotten who, some myopic fuckwit.

The wardrobe had an enormous keyhole and a dark, solemnly elaborate key from which there hung a luggage label. The dressing-table had three mirrors, the flanking ones slanted so if you stood close you would disappear into a hall of mirrors, a repetition that went on for ever as your life receded, getting smaller and smaller; yes, I was lost, I would never escape them, they got bigger and bigger till I disappeared.

No, rubbish, it was just an old mirror.

I had never slept in this room before; it was the forbidden, our parents' bedroom, but hey ho, no Oedipal cringing, I stood there in the glass, dead centre.

Monica Ludd. A person. A woman. No longer just a middle daughter. Monica Ludd, no more a punchbag.

The bed was made up, the sheets looked clean. I sniffed them suspiciously for a moment but all I could smell was flowery detergent, and I was tired, and the hour was late. I would just throw my things in the wardrobe.

The key turned with a jarring sound like the key of a medieval dungeon, loud and dangerous in the empty house. It made me jump; it made me pause. Would there be something bad inside? No, surely just my father's old trousers, now all his clothes were old and useless, and my heart felt heavy. I thought of his shoes, his empty shoes, and was wracked with sorrow. Would there be space to grieve for him? Two big tears ran down my cheeks. I was sorry for myself. I had lost my father. The only father I would ever have. And everyone so busy suspecting me of murder that I received no sympathy!

The wardrobe doors swung open with an ugly creak.

I couldn't make sense of what I saw.

Bright things, pretty things, cheap short dresses in girly colours, pinks and yellows and peppermint greens, and on the floor
of the cupboard, a stupid tangle of coltish shoes, straps and heels
and curlicues.

Was our father a cross-dresser?

No, it was the Girl! The fucking Girl! She had her things in our
parents' wardrobe!

'Bitch!' I shouted, and, 'Fucking fuckers!' And without thinking I was wrenching them out, pulling things furiously off their
hangers which crashed like doom against the hollow wood, yes,
yes, more noise, more anger, and ripping them where she had
wound the loops too carefully round a hanger's plastic hornlets,
the satisfying stretch and tear of cheap cloth; then I scooped out
the shoes into a landslide of rubbish,

I confess I kicked them. I am only human. I kicked her stupid
shoes around the room.

But it was nearly midnight, and I was alone, and my anger was
hopeless, and left me empty. Yes, she had made her nest with
Dad. Yes, she was young, and he was old, an old, incontinently
greedy man. Yes it was disgusting, a forty-year age gap, a woman
fifteen years younger than me, someone who could have been
his granddaughter –

But why was I bothered? Why should I care? Ma left him
fifteen years ago. I started tidying the mess I had made, I was
too old to sleep in chaos.

Then a sadder refrain began in my head.

It was wrong that the Girl should make this room her home,
the room which for me had always been forbidden. She'd been
allowed to replace our mother. Who was buying her clothes?
Dad was buying her clothes. The hateful dresses were bright

and attractive. No-one ever thought I would like nice clothes. *He should have bought clothes for his own daughter.*

I slept with the stupid thought gnawing my brain, lay there half-awake in the dark, listening to the birds' witter-whoo, hideous screams that might be foxes, the foghorn sounding again and again.

If I'd had nice clothes, would I have been different? Maybe I wouldn't have bored into my books and become a freak, a swot, a teacher?

Why, even now in my darkest hour, with my father lying with his head stoved in and the police on my tracks, was I taking the trouble to jot things down?

All work and no play, all work and no play, yes I had lived in the world of *The Shining*...

I tossed and turned and the foghorn snored and there was no escape from any of it and I knew the lighthouse would be throwing its beam out into the fog off the North Foreland, blink on, blink off, the great sweep of its shining...All work and no play makes me a dull boy...all work and no play made Fred a dull boy...all work and no play, all work and no play, all work and no play...

I woke unrefreshed, small birds were singing, a clutch of them crossing and recrossing the window, and there were still five of us, and should have been six, and I had a duty to talk to our mother.

32

It was a school day. My job was important. Probably time to check in again. Being on the run is a lonely business, though it had only just begun. And maybe I was missing the staffroom, though many teachers (I used to be one of them, before my rise to management) (hahahaha, hahahaha) opine, directly or indirectly, that it's no place for a Deputy Head. Could it be, actually, I even missed Neil, the happy arguments he always lost about whatever he was doing wrong?

My phone. Fearing Ginger would manage to trace it – my siblings were loyal, but Fairy was dim, and Angus might simply blurt out my number – I had switched it off and unplugged it, but yeah, thanks, now I couldn't ring it, and no, course, it had disappeared. Yes, thanks, impossible to find.

Searching for phones can make me impatient, though I am normally even-tempered. It was eight-thirty. Neil would be there.

Without so much as a cup of tea, I went straight out to the clifftop car-park to see if the phonebox still existed where we carved messages of love as teenagers. The fog had still not cleared from the sea. Yes, by the railings, the phonebox loomed, dim and red, a relic of the Britain we were trying to get back to by leaving Europe. It was full of rubbish. It smelled of wee. There was the cock and balls I had drawn, long ago when I was adolescent, scratching it into the paint with my nail file. Ahhhh! I felt quite sentimental. No time to waste, though, I must call Neil.

The dial was still working, creaking, slow. I gave my name to his secretary. Recently appointed, she was bland and dim; when I had time, I'd get rid of her.

'It's Monica.'

She gasped like a fish. 'I'll put you straight through.'

'Hello, hello!' Neil was there, sounding nervous and bright.

I thought: the police have been in touch with the school, and he has been told to play me along. 'My family problems are ongoing.' It was nice to have an audience, though. Good to talk. I began explaining, omitting any reference to blood or axes.

'Yes, I understand,' he started gabbling, before I had really got into my stride. 'Quite, quite, no problem this end, you don't have to apologise.'

'Good, I didn't.'

He pretended to laugh. 'Monica, you're so refreshing...where are you calling from?' Now he sounded cunning, though, honestly, he's not up to cunning.

'Oh, near the Home,' I said, vaguely. 'Why do you ask?' I wanted him to sweat a bit, why was he not offering support? 'A good school is a supportive school for staff and students,' the mission statement said, but now that I was on the run, fogbound, lonely, in a pissy phonebox, I didn't hear him offering to come and collect me.

'Oh, just to be sure that you're, you know, all right,' he said. 'Well, Monica, we will see you anon.'

'As soon as I can make it.'

'No, don't rush.'

The lonely tone after the line was cut off.

I stumped back to the house. My blood sugar was low, my spirits dipped at the fucking awful task ahead of finding my mobile. Throwing things around is always tiring. But actually it wasn't hard, I remembered my activities last night in the bedroom and the lightest kick to the Girl's clothes on the floor revealed my mobile under her shoe. I was glad to see it, yet I blamed her for it.

I switched on my phone. Ping, ping, ping! One after another, winging-in WhatsApps, but nothing from the police or Ginger.

'Monica, where are you? Worried' – Anthea.'

'Monica, come back and give yourself up, running away makes you look more guilty, we haven't given the police your number – Angus,' which I assume also meant Boris. 'Give yourself up': it was strangely old-fashioned, a plea from a childhood game of hide-and-seek where you did it to escape the beast panting behind you.

'Mon, Rupert says he can help with lawyers. Xxx Fairy.' You might think I'd be touched, but Fairy ended every message with kisses, usually two or more lines of cross-stitch though she was an air kisser, face to face.

My siblings had not forgotten me.

But nothing from Fred, never any more. *Fred, you are well out of it.*

I poured stale cornflakes into a bowl, trying to remember what happened in crime novels. Could my phone be traced now I'd switched it on once? Maybe I would throw my phone in the sea. I switched it off once, I switched it off twice. POWER OFF. At once I felt powerful.

I was Monica Ludd, I would stand my ground, I was here in charge of my father's house, sorry, that should be 'my parents' house'. Here I would stay and write my diary.

The tables in the kitchen and dining-room were bought by Dad as a job lot from Germany, three inches too high for the laptop user. That's why, only half an hour later, I was upstairs in the parental bedroom, laptop in the well of the dressing-table, when I thought I heard a door bang down below.

The door was locked, I hadn't been out, I told myself I must be mistaken, it must be the thud of junk mail arriving.

I went on jotting down my thoughts. 'My father was a man of intense, unbridled appetites.'

I thought of my father with a bridle in his mouth and little Ma on his back, like a jockey, so high above he could do nothing to her, so high above she was safe from him.

And then I heard a footfall on the stairs.

But no, of course it was those little brown birds, sparrows, or maybe it was squirrels running on the roof, and I shrugged my shoulder to deal with the stiffness and stretched out my legs, uncomfortably squashed into the gap beneath the dressing-table's shallow central drawer, which linked the two lateral towers of drawers together like an only child hanging on to its parents.

(Now I would never get a partner! It wasn't fair, but I knew suspicion would follow me like the whiff in our labs after experiments involving sulphur. Who would want genes from a family like ours?)

And then I caught a flicker in the mirror in front of me and everything tripped into total terror.

Someone was creeping down the landing outside.

The sun in the bedroom made it too dark to see –

Obviously I was imagining it. Yes, it must be curtains blowing, of course, I had left a window open –

Then another flash of colour or movement, a splash of red, *yes, something bad*, electrified the pool of the mirror and fear made me stumble to my feet so fast that I bruised my knees on the dressing-table as I ran to the door and there it was chocolate and scarlet, a splash of paint, rising, dipping, a dot of light, something alive, falling, staggering

It was a fucking butterfly! I had been frightened by a bug! Bloody Nabokov, what did he call it? – yes, Red Admiral, highly aesthetic, Latin name *Vanessa Atalanta* – just a bug left behind by summer.

I was trying to trap it in a large man's handkerchief I'd snatched up out of my father's drawer, leaning out dangerously across the banisters, probably I was trying to save it, yes, I would have caught it in order to release it, but no, I have promised to tell the truth, and the instant my handkerchief closed on it, two things happened in rapid succession, the banister dug me in the belly so hard that in reflex hatred I squashed the thing, the faintest grain of pain between my fingers, harder, harder, it had frightened me –

Then someone jumped me from behind.

33

As in all my nightmares, I couldn't breathe, two steel-strong hands were crushing my throat and I tried to shout but there was no air and I crumpled, moaning, to my big hurt knees with a monkey-strong, howling beast on my back.

Reaching behind me with a huge effort, I managed to grasp the hateful hands welded like metal claws to my throat and drag, pull, prise them away till I could choke in breath again, then I was kneed from behind in my private parts and that sneaky thrust into the core of me enraged me so much that I threw off the attacker as if they were thistledown, shouting, 'Get OFF me!'

And as I twisted, I finally saw her.

It was the Girl, the fucking *Girl*, how dare she touch me, my father's floozy, the landing was dark but she lay there winded on the landing carpet, red-faced and furious.

As if she were a hated sister I quickly sat on her and grabbed her wrists and held them hard down on the floor, both of us panting. I was so much bigger and I caught myself thinking, like Dad, 'I'll break her.'

'What the fuck are you doing?' I yelled at her.

'What the fuck were you doing in our bedroom?' she shouted, but was made hoarse and feeble by my weight on her ribcage and her hopeless position, flat on her back.

'It's not your bedroom! And you attacked my father!' I hissed at her, spitting a little; I didn't mean to but froth leaked out –

But at the same moment the Girl was panting, 'Get off me, Monica, you're a maniac! I know it was you who attacked Albert!'

'I AM NOT A MANIAC!' I roared. I realised I was sounding like a maniac.

Simultaneously, I thought, 'Perhaps she didn't do it.' Very mildly embarrassed, I shifted my weight so I wasn't mashing her wrists into the carpet, though I held them loosely in case there was trouble.

I did know her name, though I had never used it. 'Veronica,' I said, 'why did you attack me?'

'I couldn't see,' she said. 'And you're enormous. It was dark in the bedroom, you were just this figure. I thought it must be whoever attacked your father,'

I am enormous, but no-one should say so. At least she had admitted he was my father, not her usual mewling, miminy-piminy '*Albert* this, *Albert* that'.

'I will let you sit up,' I said, reluctantly. 'I think you attacked him because you were jealous. He stood you up at Fred's party.'

'Everyone thinks it was you,' she said. 'Especially now you've run away.'

'I didn't fucking *run away*, I escaped. Well I think it was you, Veronica.'

But the truth was, I had already changed my mind, there was something so authentic in the way she had accused me. She wasn't clever enough to play a double game. (What else had my colleague said about her? She had a gang, she got in trouble for fighting, she lurked at the bottom of the academic stream, her father was in prison, she may have been abused, she had 'turned herself around' in the sixth form and got a place to read sociology at Essex, though only thickos read sociology.)

Neil has forbidden me to use the word 'thicko', though I only apply it to members of staff.

A tiny part of me was glad to have company, even if it was Veronica's.

Now I was sitting on her, I had someone to talk to. And she might update me on police enquiries. I let go her wrists and sat up straight, though I was still straddling her hips. Fuck, I had failed to kill the butterfly. High above my head a small doodle of disquiet, a red dot circling its prison of sunlight. Actually, I was pleased to see it. Yes, more life to everyone.

Except my father, obviously.

'We could have a cup of tea,' I said tentatively. 'We could agree not to attack one another. The only thing is, I haven't any milk.'

'I hate tea,' she said, with venom, which clearly just meant she hated me. It was hardly fair, we had never really chatted, if we had, she might have got to like me. 'You can't just offer me a cup of tea, and go on about milk, after what's happened to Albert. You'd better not hurt me, either.'

That was so childish. 'Why not?'

'I've got a problem. A medical problem.'

That made me laugh. She was a strapping girl, half my age and a hockey player.

'Boo-hoo,' I said. 'All right, I won't hurt you unless you annoy me. But why can't we have tea?' I wanted some. I was used to getting the things I wanted. I let my thighs relax a bit so more of my weight rested on her body, and she gasped with discomfort. Her eyes registered defeat.

'I could keep you prisoner here,' I said. 'I think I will. Or I could let you go.'

'Fucking get off me. I will have tea.'

Slowly, I rocked back on to my heels, and she started to raise her shoulders from the carpet, but just for a joke, I gave her chest a little push that made her body collapse backwards while her head swung forward, which must have been uncomfortable, but well, she had to know who was boss, it's true of the kids at school as well.

'Only joking,' I said. 'Hahahahahahaha.'

Getting downstairs was an elaborate ballet, since neither one of us wanted to go first, which would have meant the other was a threat behind us. In the end I said 'After YOU' so loudly that she set off running down the stairs.

'Don't go too far,' I carolled, following, but when I got downstairs she was already out of sight, she should have listened, I gave clear instructions. I saw her through the hinges of the sitting-room door, flattened on the wall, outlined against the sofa, and I saw an expression of such terror on her face that I came in after her, my hands spread wide, trying to show her I was Mon the Innocent, Mon the Harmless, Mon the Kind, but I know my hands are unnaturally large and she screamed, 'Don't touch me, I'm calling the police,' and in a split second her phone was in her hand and of course I had no option but to throw myself at her and crush her fingers until she dropped it. I then disposed of it down the toilet, taking her with me, forcibly, arm in arm as if we were friends, and ignoring the fact she was making a fuss.

'That's all my contacts! I haven't backed it up!'

'Sorry,' I said, 'but you shouldn't have done it. We're both suspects, we're in the same boat. I know about the other woman. You probably did it because you were jealous.'

She looked at me, big-eyed and innocent, horribly young, uncomprehending. The whites of her eyes showed under the iris. Her skin was so fine I could see rosy filaments, as if the blood was too near the surface.

She leant against the wall, *flump, whump*, a puppet dumped by her puppeteer. 'You don't understand, I love him,' she said.

Part of me noted the present tense but filed that away to think about later.

I judged it might be safe to boil a kettle without keeping her in an arm-lock, but I thought a bit before I answered.

'No, you're right, you're practically a schoolgirl, I don't understand it, he was sixty-seven. He had grey hair and spinal arthritis.'

'None of you ever loved your father.'

This was, in fact, a slight untruth. 'Children are doomed to love their fathers. When I was little, of course I loved him.' I pushed a mug of black tea towards her. It tasted bitter, like an aftermath.

She sipped too deeply. 'I've burned my tongue.'

'Write it in the book of grudges.'

Now I sat down at the table opposite her for all the world as if we were pals, or normal neighbours airing minor grievances, but I had the killer blow in reserve, the yellow-haired tart in his Margate bedroom. The Girl looked so downhearted I almost pitied her. No, she was bereaved, I would definitely spare her, we'd have a nice chat, we really could be friends –

Or not. No, I thought not, on balance. 'So did you know about the other woman, or other women, Veronica?'

'You're making it up.' The second blow did it; she had managed not to take in the first.

'I saw another woman at his house that morning.' Mistake, it was another mistake, shut up, Mon, but I couldn't resist it, I must never tell Veronica what I saw, never tell anyone I was there.

'When? Where? You're making it up.' But the whine in her voice showed how deeply she was wounded, her mouth was wretched, downturned, thin, that pretty, small pale mouth he had kissed, oh horror, horror, the filthy fucker.

'She was blonde. Curvy. Experienced.' (Looking back, I was choosing my words to wound. I could have said, 'Dyed hair. Fattish. Getting on a bit.') 'Spanish, I think,' I added. 'Mature.'

Her face bounced back on hope's elastic. 'Oh, you mean Esmeralda, stupid. For Christ's sake, she's his receptionist. No-one could fancy Esmeralda.'

An ignorant young person might say that about me. 'Young woman, you have a lot to learn. *Everybody* could be fancied by someone. Esmeralda grew up in Medway, though her mother guessed her father was a Spanish waiter. But no, this woman was not Esmeralda. And yes, she was having sex with Dad.'

She was not drinking, just staring at the table. 'We were going to get married,' she burst out, suddenly. 'You probably despise me, but I wanted to get married! I'm not some tart! We were always serious! In my family, you have to be!' Two fat tears rolled down her cheeks.

I would not allow myself to feel pity. My neck was still bruised from her hateful fingers

One day
she'd pay –

and no point waiting, it was today.

'Dad would never have married you. Whatever he told you, he messed around. The only woman he loved was our mother –' (Her mouth had opened, desperate to speak, she rose to her feet, she was going to deny it, but patience is a virtue, she had to listen, I sat her back down on her plastic chair, she was mild as a lamb, the fight had gone out of her) ' – and well, I wasn't going to tell you, but he was with the woman on the night of the Party, that's why he stood you up,' I told her, kindly.

Miserably, she tried to recover, clasping her hands with their strong pink fingers, on one of which, I noticed, she wore a cheap ring, some gilded band with a pathetic glass stone, if Dad gave it her, he would have claimed it was a diamond. She saw what I was staring at.

'He's given me a diamond engagement ring.' Once again, that uneasy oddity of tenses. Two flies walked carefully over the oil-cloth on the table, which was yellow, with hideous pineapple motifs – from a distance they looked like small grenades.

'That'll be a zircon, gold-plated, from Ratner's. *Gold-plated if you're lucky, Veronica.* He was not a generous man, our father.'

Suddenly her shoulders straightened and a blast of colour returned to her cheeks. She was pulling vigorously at her finger. 'You don't know everything. Take a look – it's a real diamond, and 18-carat gold –'

She pushed it across and the flies flew away and buzzed and worried round the lampshade. I picked the ring up disdainfully and peered at it in the sunlight. Unbelieving, I saw a miniature '18' take shape before my reluctant eyes. *Shit.*

But I couldn't allow her to beat me.

'9-carat,' I announced. 'Hardly worth having. So I'll get rid of it for you,' and – do not judge me, I am impulsive, she had tried to strangle me, I was under stress – in one bound I was across the kitchen and had thrown the ring down the kitchen sink, which was the original 1930s number, I told you my father didn't like spending money, and had just a single bar across the plug-hole.

The ring tinkled down the hole and was gone.

'No!' she shouted. 'You can't do that, give me my ring, Albert will kill you!'

'Too late for that!' I merrily quipped, and she was wrestling with me at the sink, and both of us saw it, about three inches down, a glint of gold in the nexus of darkness, and before she could stop me, I turned on the tap and her nails on my wrist could not prevent me and the water poured down and the ring disappeared.

'Oops!' I said merrily. The Girl started weeping and sank down on the kitchen stool which my mother had used when she was drying up.

'Get off that stool, it was our mother's.' I pushed her rudely back to the table.

When she looked up again, her eyes were strange, red and fixed and furious. 'When I tell him, he's going to kill you. You're going to wish you had never been born.'

'Tell who?' I sneered. Her father was in prison, according to my colleague, with a ten-year sentence and no early release.

'I'll tell Albert! I'll tell Albert!'

Had she gone mad? A tiny wire of fear buzzed through my belly, cold, electric. Taking a gulp of air, I suppressed it.

I had seen my father dead, one eye like a squashed tomato, propped on a bed that was drenched in blood.

'Tell Albert?' I mimicked, 'tell Albert? Oooooh, I'm scared, she's going to tell Albert! Don't you know that Dad is dead?'

From a sack of flour, damp and flabby, she instantly quickened into a demon. Her eyes burned with triumphant knowledge. 'He isn't dead. You think he's dead? Oh no, Albert isn't dead.'

'He isn't dead? No, you're mad.'

Again the silver wire of fear, a sharp thread puckering my stomach.

'He's recovering. He's a lot better. He's strong, Albert. "Strong as an ox." That was what the hospital said.'

And then I knew. I was a bath of horror, my whole body flushed with blood, I wanted to pee, I wanted to vomit.

I saw again his half-askew eyelids, dark awful slits in the mess of his head that had seemed, for a second, to be staring back as I looked at him across a lake of blood.

He must have been conscious. He must have seen me. What if he thought – what if he assumed – like all my siblings, what if, what –

The thought was too terrible to formulate.

First, the Girl, get rid of her.

'You can take your clothes from upstairs and get out,'

I managed to draw in a breath to command her. 'And don't say anything to the police. If you do, believe me, I'll know and I'll find you, if it takes twenty years, I'll track you down.'

Keeping me in view over her shoulder, she left the room, and I followed her. I had learned from my father the procedures of terror and as she went upstairs I was hard behind her, every so often giving her a nudge. Most of her clothes were on the bedroom floor, where I had left them when I ransacked the cupboard. I kicked them towards her.

'I'll need a bag,' she said, ridiculous, her little, girlish chin pushed out, and I laughed in her face, I wanted to hit her (but note: I am not that violent).

'Do you think I'm going to run and get one for you?' I asked her, and scooped up her sickly ragtags of clothes, as light and flimsy as butterflies' wings, dropping one shoe, a scarf, a handbag, yes, it was pastel-smart but plastic, and opened the door on to the balcony, stepped into the sunlight and threw them out, and they fluttered helplessly down in the breeze and spread out over the lawn like flowers, big limp flowers. I added more, they looked quite sad but I couldn't help laughing.

'Out, out,' I was pushing her, quite amiably, now that she was evicted from the bedroom, but sometimes I hardly know my own strength and Veronica nearly fell downstairs which, I assure you, was not my intention, why should I want collateral damage?

Part of me was enjoying this bit, but part of me, the submerged two-thirds that I wouldn't have time to attend to until later, was frozen with fear, changed for ever.

Dad wasn't dead. If Dad wasn't dead…

''Bye,' I shouted, too close to her ear, as I propelled her towards the garden. 'Give him up, Ronnie!' (She had never been Ronnie, so far as I knew, but now she was, the name was a token of our new friendship, the sweet nothings of the morning.) 'He'll never love anyone except our mother and he's fucking everyone in Margate.'

'Shhhhhh,' she begged. Now we were out on the lawn, she was evidently easily embarrassed. Then she was trying to pick up her possessions.

'There are worm-casts on my white blouse,' she said, which shows you what a whinger she was! I'm surprised our father hadn't smacked her (but perhaps he had, probably he had, he always liked pathetic women).

'Diddums!'

Veronica looked so funny as she scampered about trying to retrieve her knickers, which were white and plain, not what I expected. I kept laughing, which may have seemed unhinged, but there are health benefits to laughter, it lowers blood pressure and fights off cancer – not in the victim, unluckily for Ronnie, but excellent for me, for the active laugher.

Veronica was not a good sport.

Once she'd managed to get the whole pile in her arms, which left her looking like a wobble-doll with a tiny head and a great round belly, dipping now to this side, now to the other, as she reached out desperately for something she'd dropped – (I thought, with joy, I could push her over, but no, don't worry, the thought sufficed, better not make an enemy!) – she stood, unsteadily, glaring at me.

'You'd better watch out. Albert will avenge me. He's getting better every day.'

'I doubt he'll even remember your name, if he's had a head injury. There've been lots like you. You're not special.'

I could not bear it if she was special. Fairy had always been the special one. In some repellent way, the girl was like Fairy, not beautiful like Fairy, but mopey and fragile.

Now Wobble Doll was bouncing back again, her arms braced around that vast coloured tummy from which bits of clothing were slipping like petals. The sun was the fierce thin glare of November and her little pink face looked unnaturally bright, shining with injustice and hatred. 'You think you know everything. You don't. You can't! None of you children understand him. And you – you've never had a real man.'

I had to hold back the boiling moil of unpleasant feeling this unleashed within me. There was a little chink – a crack – of truth. I'd frequently clicked on Toyboy Warehouse, and something melted when I first saw Rupert. But striplings were not for long-term pleasure. Maybe a Ginger had more to offer? I knew I must change, but I wasn't ready…

'I've had my father. That was enough.' (She would never be able to call him her father.) 'You were a slag at school, I know all about you, your brothers became religious maniacs because your father's a criminal.'

She backed away towards the gate, quite a neat manoeuvre down the crazy-paving path, of course she had been a hockey player – until she missed the last bend and tripped over the 1920s boot-scraper that was placed by the gate for those who had trudged the muddy woods. Well played, garden, it had hacked her ankles.

Veronica sprawled backwards and lay there winded, her girlish clothes all around her. Utterly helpless. I could have killed her. 'I'm bleeding,' she said. 'What have you done?'

But I belong to the nation of Sir Walter Raleigh, who laid down his cloak for his queen in a puddle so she could protect her small powerful feet, so I pulled her up with a boisterous tug that sent her flying vigorously forward, helped her scrabble the clothes together in as much of a muddle as I could manage (some got trampled underfoot as we did a kind of dance to collect them, she shouldn't have snatched, she should have let me help her), and I smiled at her as I waved her off.

So on the whole I think that went well, though later I found blood by the boot-scraper. I felt – ashamed. Sorry, Veronica.

34

After she left, I sat in the garden. I didn't want to go inside. Dad was alive. My whole body was uneasy. How was it possible? The deed was done, I saw him aslant, toppled, bloodied –

It felt important to stay somewhere where I could keep an eye in every direction, the line of blue sea beyond the leylandii (taller and blacker since yesterday?), the private road where the detached, shuttered houses crouched in their gardens like waiting animals, the wilderness at the end of the garden, and Bay House, unreally bright in the sunlight, close to me, too big, too close.

Surely at least he'd have brain damage. He had always claimed to have a thick skin, he thought it was desirable. Did he have thick bones as well? For a man in his sixties he was superfit, true. He went to the gym three times a week, and on off days, worked on the machines in his study; we heard them creaking and his breath roaring as we tiptoed past. He rarely got ill. But this was different: a head injury. It would surely be months before he was better. By then the police would have caught the perpetrator. Ginger, I trusted him, DI Parkes-Woods –

'I'm treating you as a witness, not a suspect.' How many times had I replayed that sentence. But now I wondered: had he really said it? Played too often, it had lost authenticity, and all I heard was a mewling mini-me. He wasn't on my side. I had imagined it.

Suddenly I felt quite alone.

Friends. I've sometimes thought they're overrated. Most of them retreat when I show my sense of humour. With men, most of the time, there's little talking, they get alarmed when I confide, and are never certain when I am joking. Women are more ready to cackle. New teachers sometimes suggest a coffee but 'you fuckoffee' pops into my head, I don't know why, and I fear I've said it – and laughed alone. Besides, it's not easy to make friends in the staffroom; senior management's not supposed to go there. In the end I am the Deputy Head, and it's my job to keep them in order, though I make a point of allowing free speech, and especially encouraging it about Neil.

In some families, people are friends with their siblings, but we were frightened into separate tents, trying to keep the front zipped at night against the minotaur pawing outside, you couldn't see him, you could only hear him…

So I sat on the step outside the French windows, my eyes taking in the untidy garden in restless swoops, here a sock, there a shoe, the overgrown grass, the red scabs of roses that clung, frosting, outliving their leaves, the blue-black of the leylandii like toothless battlements rearing up around me, the ribbon of road where no-one drove, the houses where I saw no-one moving, the blue-white glitter of the sea, but no, no, it was fine, I was happy, everything was known and clear to me and, reader, you can see I have no secrets, I am Monica Ludd, and unafraid.

I wouldn't let myself be frightened.

I had routed the Girl, outwitted Ginger.

I could certainly manage without friends if need be.

Then I noticed my hopefulness petering out, the faint flurry of a distant absence, as if a tiny wind sprang up. The winter sunshine on my back withdrew and the sharp colours of the morning faded. When I looked up, white cloud had spread and hauled dull muslin across the sun.

Who would be there if Dad comes for me?

35 Adoncia

Yes, I know he crazy when we fuck and he like to talk about wife, children. 'I love my fucking wife,' he hissing as he push his *porra* into me. 'A family is beautiful. Adoncia, do you have a family?'

At least I not tell him I have a daughter. I manage to keep her out of it, I keep his dirty hand off her. She out of everything, in fact, in institution, she never marry, my poor Juanita, she don't see no-one…

Sometime my heart break for her.

No more sex after he do the implant. After he do that to me, it over. Why, why I let him do it? All out, all in, the same day, everything, and then I suffer like never before, when the drug wear off, I crazy with pain, and my face swell up ugly like a great balloon, my pillow, sheet, everything, drench with blood.

Blood on the floor, pyjamas, towel.

And then, you think he talk to me? You think he answer when I ring his mobile, his special mobile he keep for me?

One day I meet Esmeralda in the market. We talk before, *a veces*, at surgery. I say, 'You look *muy guapa*, very pretty.' She look like shit, but I smart, I fool her.

'You looking ill,' she say to me.

I say, 'Esmeralda, you like a drink, you like to come down the pub with me?'

'I never drink no more,' she say.

'Never?' I say. 'You no live a little?'

'Only maybe birthday, Christmas. When I younger maybe I drink too much.'

Then I ask her, what her favourite? And she tell me *champán*, and I buy us a bottle, then another bottle. Esmeralda start to sing. First, she say how Albert wonderful. Then she tell me how he cheat and lie. He cheat her, and wife, and taxpayer, though I tell her everyone cheat taxpayer, that not a crime, that being brainy.

Then I say, 'I think you know what Albert do to me, when he feel like it, when I in his chair.'

Then at last I see she listening to me.

'You too?' she say. Her face look more ugly. If possible.

So then I know he fuck many more women.

'I see,' I say. 'So that always happen. Señor Albert take double pay.'

She angry and she say, 'No, three time.' Then she tell me the tricks he do, on the National Health Service, the NHS, very stupid system, they trust dentist. He claim double, maybe three time. 'He do that on his own,' she saying. 'Maybe he try to blame me though.' She say, 'Maybe we go to the police together. Once I love him, but I hate him now.'

Ojo! Watch out! Police mean trouble. Oh ho oh ho, no police,

I say. (I not explain, Spanish police know me too well.) 'Maybe you get in trouble for the National Health Service claim,' I say. 'Esmeralda, you the one in office. *Ojo*.'

She finish second bottle, she grow a little nasty, she say some nasty thing to me, she falling over but she try to hit me, I can flatten her but it too easy.

Esmeralda and me, we not friends no more. She stare at me as if she like to kill me. Why should she call me prostitute?

I an independent woman. I make my own plan.

Because my boy leave me. My boy, my boy. When I always in pain, Luis not happy. New teeth like nails into bone of head. Sometimes I lie awake and cry.

My Luis leave me. I like my boy, though he unfaithful and take my money, I like to keep him, I like to sleep with him, sweet sweet breath and young shiny body, I stroke his black hair like feathers of *mirlo*, but no, he go, he no sing no more, he say he hate me, he say that no-one, no one, never, *nadie, y nunca mas*, no man love an ugly old lady.

So then I lonely, and I get crazy. I start to think of how he laugh at me, the demon dentist laugh at me, I hear him laughing as the pain bite me, the pain bite me every day.

Albert Fucking Ludd, *ojo, ojo*.

I a decent woman or I go to his house right after he do it, before Luis leave me. I know where he live, I find some friend, some very old friend and kick his door down. I leave it too late, I not want trouble. But the pain never end, and Luis gone.

I come back to Margate for *Maroween*, 'Alloween Day', English call it. In North Spain where I born can be three days. Third one is *Día de los Difuntos*, Day of the Dead, when dead souls come back. He made me into mask, like a dead woman, my teeth like tombstone and I smile like skull, and after I pay him £20,000!

Yes, but now I come back to him.

I think, if I punish him, my soul return. Yes, if he die, I live again.

Part 6

What Are We To Do?

36   *Monica*

Self-care. I teach a lesson in it, it's part of PSHA for Years 7–9. Our Head prides himself on being 'caring': I was one of the applicants for his job, but of course they preferred a plausible outsider, an older man, Neil, the greasy little weasel.

'Perhaps your style was too abrasive', was part of the feedback I received, after the mockery of an interview. 'Phrasing things more positively' was also recommended. When asked about the 'challenges' of the job, I'd said, 'We have to stop the kids stabbing each other!' but I cracked a nice smile because it was an interview, and some people find my smile frightening, it's all to do with my big front teeth, and the Chair of Governors, a lying accountant, looked thin and disapproving and said, with a sneer, 'We have hardly come to *that*, Mrs Ludd.'

My 'Don't you think so? They have got knives,' was seen as 'being negative'. That was the feedback from the formal notes.

We *have* come to that, haven't we? Everyone's at it, Muslims, Christians, soldiers, civilians, children, parents, they all have a stab, but PLEASE remember, *I, Monica, am not a killer.* I care about the children I teach, also my siblings, and little Ma, though sometimes, yes, I've had dark thoughts.

They asked, at the end, if I had questions. I thought, 'There's nothing you lot can tell me. I've been more or less running this school for years, I love this school, I'd die for Windmills.' Mrs Al-Khamissi looked startled, oh, no, it had happened again,

I had said it aloud at the wrong moment; they all shuffled papers and stared at each other. 'Ahem,' said the Chair. 'Well, if there's nothing...'

Something of interest popped into my mind. 'Actually, I do have a question. What are we to do if ISIS can't be stopped? If they come over here? To Kent, I mean? What option have we got but absolute violence?'

'It's not quite the sort of question we meant.'

'Well, it's the sort of question you've got.'

Uneasy silence, so I continued. 'When the Romans came over, they attacked the Britons, then the Britons attacked them and chopped them up, then the Romans went away and came back again, and then the Romans chopped up the Britons.'

'I don't quite see the relevance —'

'The relevance is, we are living in Kent. That's where invaders have always landed — that's why people voted for Brexit. That's why illegals land here at night.'

'Illegals is a dehumanising term.'

'Yes, sorry, course, but what if they're ISIS?'

'We really can't discuss political issues.'

'What's the alternative to violence? The Romans and the Britons just slogged it out. They did try bribery, it didn't work. What am I supposed to teach the children?'

'It's time for the next candidate. Thank you!'

When Neil got the job, I was disappointed. Disappointed, but not surprised.

(Since then, the 'incidents' at Sandwich and Canterbury. That day, I was offering the Ludd Crystal Ball! But no-one could think of an answer to my question.)

After Neil had been in post for a few months, he suggested

we have a 'nice long talk', over a sandwich lunch in his office. He had installed a very fine cream carpet, and I'm not always the tidiest eater! I couldn't have predicted the Marie Rose sauce, and Neil should not have let himself become distracted. He said he liked to 'listen', as well as 'care'. 'We should be a listening, caring school.' Listen? Had he heard Year 8 in the canteen, the appalling din like a thousand elephants in *must*, stamping and trumpeting? They were too busy shouting to eat their food, and some of them only got crisps at home.

That was why I'd started a silence rule at lunch with a fixed penalty of detention, but Neil did not think that 'caring'. 'They have a right to self-expression.' He tried to assure me he was 'there for me', that 'pastoral care' was for the staff as well, 'and you in particular, my trusted lieutenant'.

Lieutenant? Mon is a brigadier!

(Where are you, Neil, good shepherd, when I need you? Cowering on the phone in your office.)

In any case, I teach 'Self-care' to two year-groups of teenagers. Basically, it means 'How to wash yourself', though the theme at the heart of it is 'self-respect', which rings a bell with some of them, although they have no respect for others. They have been taught 'First love yourself', which sounds like terrible advice, to me, probably thought up by some selfish adult. 'Take care of yourself' – that sounds all right, but what if it just means, 'Piss off, I won't do it'?

Why don't adults look after their children?

Why does that give me a faint grey ache?

Washing's an important skill for later life, and some parents don't teach it, they're too busy tweeting, LOL, OMG, and Lynx is no substitute for soap. I also teach exercise – 'going for a walk' can mean more than 'out on to the step for smoke' – and nutrition: 'add an apple to your Coke and chips' and 'baked beans isn't a vegetable'. I try to teach dressing for self-respect – their little skirts hardly cover their bottoms, they try to make up for it by wearing black tights but all their fundamentals are in the shop window; it's probably the way the Girl trapped my father, but I don't want the whole sixth form to get pregnant.

I talk to them about 'dressing for interviews' (though I leave 'interview technique' to others!), I tell them about 'clothes for the office', I try to teach them that appearances have a different meaning in different contexts, but I see them staring at me, lips curling, or curling as far as the little wimps dare, which is about half a millimetre –

Because they are afraid of me! Fear is often part of love! I always get my chocolates at the end of the year, seven or eight boxes, two dozen cards – 'Thanks Miss Ludd! Luv Kriss xxx' – that was a milestone, three years ago.

Kriss smelled of periods, at first, and was bullied, although she's clever, a very bright kid. I hope my 'Self-care' lessons changed her life. I didn't get taught it, I learned it myself. Washing my hands after using the toilet, having a repertoire of clean pants, it's taken me time to get it off pat, no thanks to Ma with her clinking bottles.

But the cool ones stare at me and form opinions. I've found the best garment for school is a tent, a black tent over black stretch trousers, and in cooler weather a bright-coloured jacket, though there's not enough choice in size 18, and a 'hip-length' jacket ends around my waist, baring my hips to their callow glances, so I often wear full-length coats as jackets and the sleeves stop somewhere just below my elbows.

I feel the acid of their adolescent judgement. I was young like them, once, I was young and scornful and boiling with murderous resentment, against my parents, against my teachers – I understand them, I love the rebels, that's not an overstatement, it's true, my heart nearly bursts with fellow feeling, *I was like you, I'm still like you* – but never tell them: you have to quell them.

As a furious pre-teen I began reading books. In books I discovered other people, other families who weren't like mine. I refuse to use the fashionable emp-word, but I felt a painful, pleasurable link to the characters, made-up ones nicer than people I knew. I liked them, and I pitied them. Parents in fiction cared for their children, or, if they didn't, other people noticed. People did well from terrible beginnings, like Becky Sharp, though she happened to be pretty, and lucky, too, because her father died. I read poetry. I started to write. That was how I came to meet Mr Stredder, the Head of English at my grammar school. He saw beyond the trouble I was in for scribbling a long obscene poem in the toilets. (It wasn't bad. There were some brilliant rhymes! As he remarked, when we met in detention.)

Knowing Mr Stredder changed my life. Somebody, a man, was not a maniac. I told him about what happened at home. He seemed to believe me, he didn't shut me up, he said the words, 'I'm sorry, Monica.' He said, 'Your father's wrong about you. You're far from stupid. Your English is terrific, though obviously you shouldn't write in the toilets.' There was a definite hint of a smile. 'You could be a teacher yourself, you know.' He was impressed by the books I had read. Mr Stredder is why I became a teacher. Thank you, Fate, for making someone listen. Maybe you'll call again one day.

Listening is still what the little thugs need. But today's teens aren't writing poems: some can't write and can barely read, they are ignorant, not innocent. Just a small step from that to violent.

(And if you read books, maybe two steps.)

37

The Veronica episode left me unsettled. Fear of Dad. Horror, terror. I felt empty and stunned inside, though half of that may have been hunger, I'm a big girl, I need my food. By the next morning, the cornflakes were gone and so had most of the tins in the cupboard.

I thought, 'Get food. And go and see Ma. No matter what, Dad was once her husband. If that old gossip in Reception tells her, Ma will get a shock, she'll be upset. Best if she hears what happened from me.'

It all depended what state he was in. How fast was he recovering, or preferably, dying? What if he'd been in touch with her?

Maybe she'd gone to visit him. Maybe she already knew too much. Might he have said something about me?

(Possibly I just wanted to see the look on her face at the sound of Dad's name. To check her out? Ma had always been a mystery. You couldn't reach her. She was only half there. Where was the other half, with us or against us?)

Outside the window, sunlight came and went. I couldn't settle in the house. My stomach rumbled; I had to get going. Using Gunilla's car was a risk, the daughter might have reported it stolen, she was agoraphobic and couldn't drive but she played table-tennis with her carer in the garage…

Shanks's pony! as Ma would have said. I swathed myself in

careful layers, topping the lot with a waterproof cape (plus optional hood) that made a good disguise, swaddled my chin in my old grammar-school scarf and tucked my hair away underneath it, then picked up a rucksack to bring back food.

Down on the beach is the realm of dog-walkers, the very old and a few truanting teenagers. Which was a risk, of course, for me, in case my picture had been in the papers. Some of them would be loyal to me, others would gladly dob Miss in.

Less of a risk, though, than the main road, which Ginger might be whizzing bossily along. The tide was out, I checked on my phone, Southeast Tide Tables, ultra-useful. (God, I was dependent on my phone. Better to keep it switched off than junk it.)

The Home, my mother's new home, Cliffetoppe's, was in Ramsgate, near the Terrible Two's green mausoleum. I could gallop along the beach in an hour.

Weather forecast: sunshine and showers. In my pocket I'd stuffed a woollen hat that the Boys must have left in Bay House two decades ago. Now I pulled it down over my eyebrows, checked visibility in the mirror, and carefully layered the hood on top.

I was a huge dark shape like a Christmas Tree, but we're used to the oversized in Thanet, it was one of the things Fairy always remarked on when she did a brief fly-past to brush us with stardust, 'I can't believe how huge people are! No offence, Monica.'

'None taken. I am very fit, as you know, Fairy. For example, I could break your arm like a matchstick.'

She knew I meant it from my smile.

'Sorry, Mon,' she giggled, nervous.

Actually, I would never hurt her. Too many people have hurt

Fairy, including me, but that's long over. Sister, sister, such a little sister, what happened to you, what did Dad do? Why are you so very frail and narrow? It pisses me off but it makes me pity you. What did he do to all of us?

Dad, Dad, Dad in my head. He had wormed back in now he wasn't dead.

I hove off down our path to the beach. Paper was blowing along the promenade, all of it covered with small blue writing, the archive of someone's life exploding. I planted my great foot on a scrap that twisted in a cross-wind, and scanned it quickly – I believe in chance, I believe in Fate, was it a message from some god of the multiverse? Did someone out there have time for me? – but though from a distance it looked neat, obsessive, close up it was partly illegible, 'I love you if…' Italic scribble. I hoped the scribble did not involve a sex act. Had my offer of sex made Ginger love me? I screwed up the paper and threw it in the bin.

'I love you if…' Had my parents loved me?

I decided to eat in the Bone Bay café, a ramshackle outfit on the sand. Till recently they'd closed in winter, but winter is getting shorter, warmer.

They hadn't a single customer. A blonde juvenile, just possibly a teenager, not one I recognised, thank God, was waving a damp rag in absent-minded circles. I ordered a Jumbo All-Day Breakfast, wolfed it down, almost choking myself, then went to the counter to order another.

Mistake, mistake, I have appetites, but when you're on the run you can't slake them.

The child had disappeared to play with her toys and the radio was shouting from the kitchen. I called 'Hello' several times, the last time as near to a bellow as I could get with layers of egg-smeared wool over my mouth. Finally she appeared, reluctant, saying, 'Sorry, we were listening to the radio, there's been a terrorist outrage at Gatwick.' She emphasised 'Terrorist Outrage' as if it were exciting news.

'All-Day Breakfast,' I grunted through my scarf, and as an afterthought, 'Sorry about the terrorist outrage.' It was second nature to me as a teacher to make an attempt to console the young.

'Oh, were there two of you, sorry,' said a woman who emerged from the kitchen behind her, carrying a pink radio.

The child asked, 'Did you say Extra Sausage?'

'No,' I muttered. 'Terrorist outrage.'

'So should that have been two breakfasts? She's new,' the woman said, pointing accusingly at the child, now pretending to clean a nearby table. 'Josie!' she shouted, and to me, aside, 'We got distracted. There's lots of people killed, have you heard? Including a little baby in a pram. Two hours ago. At Gatwick. Not far from here…Josie, there was two of them breakfasts!'

Josie had a yellow shaved head like a tennis-ball. She turned and stared blankly around the café. I said, 'There's just one of me. But I'm hungry, I had a lot of exercise earlier.'

Then both of them stood and gawped at me. Though a Jumbo Breakfast isn't that much food: three eggs, three sausages, two hash browns, two rounds of toast, three rashers of bacon, two slices of black pudding and a healthy tomato.

I told myself they would soon forget, transported by the horrors of Gatwick.

Yes, the terror and the horror. I mustn't forget it's everywhere, not just at home with the Ludd family. We get upset when there are 'little babies', though surely it's even worse for the adults. The radio sat and blared on the counter.

Eating my second Jumbo Breakfast – I took my time, I wanted to enjoy it, though the new lot of sausages were undercooked – I listened to the reports coming in. The number of dead was going up. The baby had been blown out of its pram. A woman came on to deplore violence. The interviewer was bored by her. What everyone wanted was more stories, preferably horror or selfless courage. In the background the sirens whined as ambulances tried to get to the wounded. 'This is the eighth or ninth incident this year in Britain...' – even the news was losing count. (Obviously, no-one turned a hair, or listened, when it happened in Afghanistan or Iraq, thirty dead here, forty dead there. Yes, we were losing interest in elsewhere.) One of the bombers was still at large, wearing an unexploded suicide vest. He or she might be in bulky disguise.

Then I realised the infant was peering at me, and whispering to the other woman. When I glared back, they both looked away. Leaving a twenty-pound note on the table, a generous tip for a dim young person who should have been at school today, I heaved myself out of the café at speed with an over-the-shoulder mumble of 'Thank you'.

'What did you say?' one of them shouted, and then, 'Your change? Your change, sir!'

It was warm for November. The cape was hot and heavy, the hat felt clammy and ridiculous. I drove myself along at a lick. I was practising the words I would use with my mother. 'Dad has been gravely injured, Mother...' It's a terrible model, 1930s' film. What did she really feel about him? Did she feel? Did she ever feel?

On, on, across Viking Bay, on to Louisa Bay, one of my favourites, beige and pale blue and glistening grey, and the sand is combed through with brighter mica that shines like gold dust in winter sunlight. I used to come here and read and feel happy, but that's in the past now I'm on the run.

All down this coast the cliffs are crumbling, great chunks and slabs of calcium that lie on the sand like Roman ruins with a snowfall of smaller pieces fringing them. The houses on the cliff that you see from the sands, mock-timbered Victorian, look anxious. Will the sea flood under and creep up their skirts? *Ave atque vale*, middle-class villas.

Actually, they're still twenty metres from the edge. But everything falls; given time, it falls. And when things fall, the sea is waiting, and all the time the sea has been helping, sucking and licking beneath the foundations, and Dad had to fall, he had to fall, but would we fall too, was it the end of us?

Bay House was closer to the cliff-edge than this, twenty metres away, maybe thirty. But Dad would have been careful when making a purchase, in some ways he took care of us, he had his points, he was the man of the house...

(And yet, those thumps and bangs in the night. What were the cracks between wall and ceiling, what were the gaps along the skirting boards, why was there a line between the door-frame and the plaster?)

The Ludds, the Ludds. We would stick together, we would not be afraid, the house would hold. Or else I was whistling in the dark. Yes, that was something my father did when he got up in the night and didn't put the light on. That terrifying whistle, *tantivy, tantivy...*

I tried to remember: someone else whistled.

But no, keep going, thank God for daylight, stride out, Monica, brooding is bad.

I'm a fast walker, I was almost at Dumpton, where Coleridge had a 'glorious tumble' in the waves. I've read the letters. I could read all night if I wasn't preparing for school, or escaping. Yes, we have culture, and poetry, in Thanet! Coleridge loved to 'Ramsgatise'! I've tried my best to impress this on Neil. I've suggested lessons on our local artists, but Neil's from London, and ignorant, and says, 'Yes, most interesting, Monica. Thank you. Your suggestions are always very welcome. Though modern figures may be more relevant. If there were a local, so-called, "dub poet"...' Flushing with pride at his own daring.

Two dogs were dancing against the sea, cut-out black against the glitter, and their manic energy leaped into me. Without thinking I ran across the stones to join them, sinking, at the end, into the sand, and I saw, as the drag of the wet beach slowed me, that they weren't dancing, they were yapping and fighting, the smaller one yipping on a high thin note as it carried on harassing the bigger dog for the dripping red ball he gripped tightly in its jaws, scattering curtains of bright water. I wanted to join in: I tossed them a stone. But though the big one whined and dropped his ball – maybe my stone accidentally glanced off him – they didn't want to play with me.

Brace up, Mon. You are quite alone.

Just after Dumpton, fifteen minutes from Cliffetoppe's, a black knot of worry began to grow. Dad was alive, in some vile new form. Ma, like me, would be afraid.

Or else my mother knew everything already, and I was the only one out of the loop?

No, no, not possible.

The clouds had darkened to navy ink, melodramatic against the sunlight. Soon I had reached the beginning of the promenade that led into Ramsgate. Above, out of sight, Ma's Home crouched, set back from the sea on the crown of East Cliff. The brochure with its twee 'artist's impression' made it look baronial, its handsome frontage fringed with pines, but it was a Victorian Gothic hotel cheaply converted into tight little boxes with washable floors and disabled toilets. The pines were chopped down ('Our ladies like light!') and had been replaced by pine disinfectant. Old women would be sitting in festering rows along the wall in the TV lounge, waiting for lukewarm, overbrewed tea. Thank God my mother had her own kettle and a 'Superior', second-floor bedroom which Fairy claimed our father paid for.

I had a sudden quiver of terror. What if she had reconciled with Dad? What if she were talking to him on the phone at the moment I walked into the room? What if Ma gave me away? At least out here I could spot the dangers. Here on the beach, no killer could hide. No shadows, no corners, no long corridors, no Dad hiding behind Ma's door.

Did I really need to talk to her? What did I owe her, after all?

No, I wasn't taking the steps up from the beach that would have taken me back to my family. My feet kept walking, I accepted their choice. They were big strong feet, I trusted them, whereas I didn't trust my mother, or myself, or this strange new life, with Dad not dead.

Sand was mute, sand was my friend. I went on walking towards the town.

38

Soon I had almost reached Ramsgate Harbour. Yes, provisions, feed Monica. I should have veered right towards King Street and

Iceland, but I couldn't face throngs of the unemployed, probably pupils some school had failed, women sporting fat boyfriends and babies like great rosettes of normalcy, getting in the beers and hotdogs for later.

But gaaah, Waitrose: the wealthy couples who had bought the big houses in Nelson Crescent and whizzed down 'from St Panks' every Thursday after their four-day week was over, doing their virtuous middle-class shopping, fluting to each other, 'Adam, can you see organic chicken? Darling, Free Range is *not* the same. Have they got quinoa?' Pronounced *Kin-wa*. I am *au fait*, but it just makes you fart.

Still, the food is better in Waitrose.

So I marched on towards it, around the harbour where cafés and shops have bloomed like bunting since the fast train from London began. The sun was piercing the clouds again, which made me feel more visible, and the wind was whipping at my cape. Right turn up the long flights of steps which Coleridge must have scaled before me. (*Porta Arietina*, he called Ramsgate. I won't bother passing that on to Neil. Or maybe I will, it would annoy him.)

Through the car-park into Waitrose. So close to people, I felt uneasy. Nobody could see my face, and most people who knew me were in Broadstairs, but all the same, I attracted attention. Nobody else was in a balaclava, or fully covered, like a Taliban woman. I hurried through the aisles, head down. The security guard watched me with interest: I realised I looked like a shop-lifter, and smiled at him would-be reassuringly, but somehow it turned into a vacuous leer, and he moved away at speed to bother someone else. Those supersized breakfasts had quelled my appetite, but knowing it would rebound later, I threw random items into my trolley: baked beans, eggs, bread, cakes, biscuits – oh, and gin was a good idea.

Then, another thought: I was short of knives. Bay House, for some reason, had only ever had pearl-inlaid dessert knives some hopeless godmother had given Dad, who swore about them but was too mean to change them, plus a bread-knife doubling as carving-knife that couldn't manage either job. I needed a knife to protect myself.

Fortunately, we were coming up to Christmas and the over-priced blocks of Sabatier knives were on sale as 'Gifts for the Man in Your Life!', next to port and stilton, red candles and tinsel, 'Gifts for Mum', 'Gifts for Dad'.

I'd give the knife to the Dad in my Life, if I had the chance, and if I had to I would wave it right in his face and stab him. A knife disappeared into the trolley. I was contented to have found it. I thought, 'I am behaving like a woman in a book, I have someone after me, I've bought a weapon.' Yet I also thought, 'I'm going to make a mess, if there's going to be blood, I will have to clean it.' I picked up bleach, salt, a small bucket.

Monica may be an unusual woman, but she was raised a woman, nevertheless. I went to a grammar school with other girls. It takes a long time to shuck it off, the dead chrysalis of feminine habits – smiling, flattering, cleaning things up – so the live imago underneath can flourish. *I will be beautiful, a butterfly*: that was what I thought until I was six.

By the time I was thirteen, I knew different.

I am real though. I am alive.

Blood. I'm afraid that more is coming. Hurry, hurry, Monica.

I paid my bill, a virtuous shopper.

39

Soon I was back on the beach again, hoicking my shopping back towards Broadstairs. The sea was lively; it was chilly but bright. Far out, the waves were dark greeny-grey with streaks of sunlight on their sides and every so often, a crest of white. The clouds were running faster than me. I shivered inside my hulk of clothes. Good job I had dressed up after all. Would I ever escape? Could I be forgiven? Briefly, I wanted to drown myself.

But what a waste of Monica! Back, back, I must try to get back, back to normality, home, work.

There were figures on the promenade above me. Every distant male had a look of Dad, black and hulking in the low grey light.

Then I noticed a man on his own in a raincoat. Square, sturdy, indeterminate hair, he was on his phone. Oh God, was it Ginger? Had he seen me, was he calling reinforcements? I slid the hood further over my head and walked faster, my heart beating hard, away from Ramsgate, my eyes on the sand.

Then a bright flash of movement caught my eye. To my right, up on the edge of the promenade, a drab little cluster of people stood, but beside them were others in white, scarlet. Red robes, black hats. Darker red banners. Good God, something was about to happen. The figure in the mac was keeping pace with me, though he couldn't have recognised me in this outfit, it wouldn't be Ginger…

It could be Ginger.

The megaphone barked, a poncey voice, pruney. Priest, must be. A laundry-load of priests, white robes flapping in the wind from the sea. For a second the sun dazzled on the whiteness.

Then a gust brought singing to my ears:

> 'Da da da-da-da da da saves/
> for those in peril on the waves.'

Oh, OK, they were singing for the migrants. A boat-load of Albanians *en route* for Thanet had been picked up off Deal last week. Lots of them had drowned on the way. Our school has a policy of welcoming 'newcomers', the language of the policy was carefully chosen; of course I support it, blah blah blah, I prefer new people to the ones I know – but who the fuck wanted to save Albanians? I'd slept with one once. He lacked finesse.

Still, I was curious. I edged up the beach, crab-wise, avoiding eye contact with the huddle of Christians in dingy raincoats, their mouths opening in time to the singing. No-one would stare at an enormous black crab. My eyes peered out between hood and scarf, two crab-eyes peeking out on stalks. I couldn't see the man in the mac any more.

That must be the mayor. And another mayor. And no, a third one. What was going on? Red robes, black hats, gold chains of office. One had a nineteenth-century Nelson-style hat like an upside-down boat, another, fatter one, a wide-brimmed black number with black ostrich feathers that billowed wildly as if its wearer was about to take off.

There were further oddities. Three very young women – no probably girls, God, I hoped they weren't some of mine? – were wearing floor-length ice-blue satin frocks under capelets fringed with rabbit fur. Their hair was dragged back into identical topknots – leave those in and they'd be bald at twenty. One of them wore a plastic tiara. Then I got it: they were beauty queens, or a queen and two princesses, in Thanet sashes.

I edged nearer, staying on the sand, half-hidden by the rim of the promenade, and, to be extra safe, after one last crick of the neck to check for Ginger – nothing, unless he was disguised as a mayor – turned my back squarely to the land. Then I called up sideways, cautiously, to a very short woman at the front of the crowd, 'This is very nice, excuse me, what is it?'

'Who's there?' she cried.

'Just a passer-by.' I disguised my voice by trying not to shout, I had started to think I recognised her. Unfortunately, I burped in the middle, the sausages were giving me trouble.

'It's a service to bless the sea,' a man hissed. 'Could you pipe down a bit, we've got three mayors, the mayors of Broadstairs, Ramsgate and Margate, all the churches are here, we're trying to pray.'

'Everyone except the servers please turn towards the sea,' the fruity-voiced priest was telling them. Now everyone would be staring at me. I was already facing seawards, but I bent at the knees, a sort of half-crouch I hoped looked reverent, rather than a prelude to 'Emergency Beach Toilet'. Now we were praying. I didn't know the words but I joined in boldly with the 'Amen', just to reassure them I had only good intentions.

A little bunch of them was coming down the steps towards me, the three priests in their blowing white nightgowns, one of them swinging a thurible, another clutching the megaphone, minions carrying the dusty red standards. Maybe they were coming to exorcise me? No, they walked straight past me. Bringing up the rear was someone unexpected, a white woman holding a child by the hand, a beautiful black girl-child, maybe eight or nine, with a bunch of roses; what was I reminded of? – yes, a painting by Burne-Jones when I did A-level art a lifetime ago and thought my future would be hopeful, not rage and loneliness and bloody murder.

I did want a child, I'd take that one.

The bright flowers against her black silk skin. I managed not to lunge at her and swoop her away in my big ape arms.

The odd procession went down to the sea, vivid verticals getting smaller and smaller against the sea's vast blue horizontals. The child, the child, with her red and white roses. I hauled out my phone, switched it on, took a photo.

The wind was cold now, fiercely cold, it must have been, my eyes were streaming. Something I wanted, longed for, lost. Dad had prevented me from loving men, because I was afraid of them. I risked another look along the promenade and didn't see the figure in the raincoat, but as my head swung back towards the sea, rustling and straining in its stupid cloak, I spotted a beige mac among the congregation and broke out in a sweat, despite the chill wind.

The priest was on the megaphone again, explaining. 'I shall sprinkle holy water on the sea and bless it, then a bouquet of flowers will be thrown on the waves. But first, let us…'

The wind was against him, but there were more prayers, Catholic ones, in staccato gusts, '…ineffable Virgin…Give thanks…blessed mercy…'

Something peculiar was going on. A youth in red leathers on a big red quad bike was driving between the little group and the sea. There was plenty of beach without him driving on our bit. I nearly ran after him and pushed him off his bike but the days for such innocent fun were over. I didn't dare draw attention to myself, and he revved obnoxiously away.

The thurible was shaken over the sea. The drips that came out can't have made much impression on the long hard muscles of the waves. Then the woman led the little girl forward. With surprising strength, she drew back her arm and in an impressive overarm bowl, chucked the red and white blossoms outwards. She had given it her all, but their group was so tiny, the sea so big, the waves so wild. She watched for a second, then turned away just before a large wave brought the bouquet back again and deposited it neatly on the sand. The humans were already struggling back up the beach.

The young girl's face was proud and happy. She hadn't seen the sea reject her offering. She must be a migrant. Yes, I loved her. I would do anything to help. It was an act of grace, gracious. My temper vanished, and just for a beat, I felt no fear, I felt only love, the crowd behind me weren't hiding Dad, these were good people, and on my side, I was part of them, the curse was lifted

Now the megaphone was booming again as priest number one came up the steps beside me. 'Psalm 130,' he was just intoning when I saw the man on the red quad bike coming zooming back along the edge of the water. I thought in a split second, 'He's going for the flowers. He'll either nick them or run them over,' and then I was charging down the beach, my rucksack banging against my spine. Monica Ludd is acts, not words, I didn't care about my own safety, I got to the bouquet just after the lout, I watched him stoop from his arrogant saddle to scoop the girl's sacrifice from the sand, the roses still beautiful, glossed with dark water, I shouted, 'Oi, leave it alone!' and he swayed back up with a 'Fuck off, I'm just looking!' On the promenade, the happy singing faltered.

Then the biker was gone in a skirl of foam that left my shoes and trousers drenched. It was freezing cold. The sea retreated further. As the water fled, the flowers looked abandoned.

On a swell of good feeling came a bad idea: I thought, 'I'll chuck the flowers further out.' The singing had stopped. People were drifting away, but a small group was bearing down on the sea. The ice-blue maidens were wearing heels, which slowed their progress across the sand. Before I could stop myself, I put down my rucksack, bent over and picked up the flowers, meaning to throw them back out on to the water to perfect, or correct, the girl's gesture.

But voices began to scratch at my ears as I stood there waiting for the next wave. 'It's a homeless woman,' 'She's stealing them,' 'Put those down!' 'She should be ashamed,' and another one said, 'I think I know her.'

There was nothing for it but to hoof it! I shouldered my rucksack and turned and ran, a loping charge under the weight of my shopping; there was a feeble hue and cry behind me, I upped my speed, something scratched my palm, oh God, I was still clutching the flowers –

I outpaced them all long before Dumpton. By then the wet flowers were in a bad way from being swung like a relay baton.

The bouquet was evidence, I 'd have to lose it.

I climbed some concrete steps to the prom. The toilets were closed, but I was not alone. A man with a dog and a silly red beard was watching me with a little frown, a big panting woman with a dripping bouquet.

'My beard is not silly,' he said, sulkily.

Fuck, I was thinking aloud again.

Avoiding his eye, saying sorry to God, whoever he is, the god of flowers, the god of pretty, mysterious children, and praying no-one else could see me, though all the same, this was not OK – I sidled up to the nearest dog-bin and stood with my back to it, meditatively, as if I was going to sit on it, or perhaps do another Emergency Beach Toilet (Red Beard looked hastily away), then stretched one hand behind my back to raise the lid; impossible, my rucksack prevented me, I swore loudly as I shucked it off, then with would-be nonchalance repeated the manoeuvre, this time it worked –

With the other hand I stuffed in the roses, forced them down, crushed them down, sorry, sorry, you have to go down.

> *Down, down, carry on down.*
> *Go too far and it's carry on down.*

40

By the time I had hauled myself back to Bay House I was dripping with sweat beneath my disguise. Right, 'Self-care' and 'Personal Hygiene', although it felt lonely and exposed in the bathroom, taking off my clothes in the empty house. The boiler kept thumping and groaning below as I lay in the bath and thought about Ginger and watched, through the dirty latticed window, the sky's indigo turn black. Unease melted into dozing as the friendly heat spread through my bloodstream.

Evening: dozed. Failed to write diary.

No sign of police. No sign of Ginger. But it's not Ginger I'm worried about.

I went to bed hoping I would sleep like a baby; it was only 10 p.m., I had applied 'Self-care', I had taken healthy exercise, particularly with the Girl, in the garden –

I had followed procedures, yet I was afraid.

Dad had survived. He was alive.

10 p.m.; 10.30 p.m.

And suddenly my phone was ringing. Yes, shit, I had taken the photo then somehow forgotten to switch it off.

Phones in the Ludd family were always loaded with anxiety, because our father was hostile to anything that breached his kingdom from outside, callers, schoolfriends, telephone calls. When mobiles arrived, they were out of the question: that would only have meant more ringing.

Whenever my phone rang, I was afraid. Now the same thing fifty times over.

Brrrrr! Brrrr! It went on ringing loud as doom in the whispering house.

(If Dad had allowed people to ring me, I might have had schoolfriends. Though not having friends made me read a lot of books, Peacock, Mary Shelley, the whole of Dickens, Becky Sharp, that delightful sociopath…Did Dad ever read? Just the *Daily Mail* and an obscure small-format publication called *The Weekly Weasel: Everything about the Mustelidae.*)

Brring! Brrring! It could be my family, *it could be Ginger,* I thought, as I lurched in search of it –

Brrrring, brrring, my father would kill me.

Brrring, brrring, and then suddenly silence.

Just as I found it, it went dead.

I had gone ten paces when it rang again. I put it to my ear, but didn't speak.

'Mon, I know it's you.' It was Angus's voice! My cheeks flushed hot with relief and pleasure.

'How do you know, you clot?' I asked, happy to be back

186

with my family. Insults are a good way to show affection.

'Because it's the number Boris told me to ring.' That tells you everything about Angus, the missing dimension, the literalness. It also made him lovable, yes I, Monica, love my brother, but Dad could never see it, he despised his son. How could he have called Angus 'Anus'?

'Somebody might have stolen my phone.'

There was a silence. Angus was thinking. Then, 'Has someone stolen your phone, Mon?'

'Oh for Christ's sake, Angus. Can I speak to Boris?' Boris nearly always did their phonecalls, being at the nearer end of the spectrum.

'He's in the bath. He says he's worried about you, and we should pick you up and bring you in.' I could hear Boris roaring from the bath in the distance. Angus must have been too truthful: lasso me to a horse and bring me in to justice.

'Hmm. I'm not ready to go, Angus. But it would be nice to see you buggers. In fact, I'm not that far from you –' The boys' enormous green arts-and-crafts-house stared across the sea on East Cliff, Ramsgate.

'Mon's coming to the house,' Angus was relaying, followed by trumpeting sounds from the bath.

'No,' said Angus. 'No, no, no, Boris thinks the police are watching us.'

'Come to mine tomorrow. I'll be in Bay House.' Shit, I shouldn't have let him know. But surely my siblings would have guessed. Stick together. We would stick together.

More discussions, this time muffled. I was very tired, it was getting late.

'Boris says coming to Bay House might be, you know,

what did you say, Boris? – intimidating.'

A roar from the bathroom which I heard quite clearly – 'Incriminating, Angus, you oaf!'

We agreed to meet in the Harbour Brasserie, eleven o'clock tomorrow morning. I pulled up the bedclothes, which felt damp and chill.

I would never sleep.

I did not sleep.

On the balcony, someone might be hiding. Was it just mice, the noise on the landing?

41

So, next morning, I was tired and nervous.

If he was alive, he could come back.

Don't be stupid, he's in intensive care. They will keep him in for weeks or months.

No, Mon. They will need his bed.

Yes, I would take to the beach again. Yes hat, yes glasses, yes yes yes yes waterproof cape, at least I had got my disguise off pat.

I left at 9 a.m., so I got to the Harbour nearly an hour before my brothers. An hour to kill in this stupid disguise. Maybe I would take a turn on West Cliff. I walked past the sail-maker's and harbour office and on to the long stretch of nothingness that borders the abandoned ferry-port. So many people used to work here, it wasn't their fault they were unemployed. I sent a mental apology to all the dossers buying beer in Iceland.

If I were to be sacked I'd have nowhere to go. I enjoyed my job, I didn't want to lose it, I'd found somewhere that suited me, with Neil usefully afraid of me...

Two things happened: a wasp or a bee began buzzing un-pleasantly close to my ear and I started jogging but it followed me and I shrugged my bag off to flap at my head, and the bee, which must have been drunk with cold, fell off and whizzed in a dim half-circle on the concrete like a broken toy, and pity or horror made me stamp on it. I don't like suffering, I'm not a bad person, I didn't know Dad was only half-dead and I stamped, stamped like a maniac dancing, it was stuck to my shoe, *get the bloody thing off me*, I charged on through the port and away.

My subconscious was giving me Gloria Gaynor, 'I Will Sur-vive', on the road by the sea. Once it had been jammed with drivers making for Belgium and greater Europe, but now it was empty, the link had broken. The little beach beside it had come back into use now the ferries were no longer spreading oil and rubbish. Once or twice I'd come here just to be with the bodies, not to lust after them or pick them up, though I wouldn't have looked a gift-horse in the mouth, *Monica, be ready for action*. But it was November: too late for that.

The tide was out, the rocks black with mussels. I thought, if you had to, you could live off those. I was learning to think like an outsider, an outlaw. But no, that would obviously be disgust-ing. I doubled back up the zigzag path that would take me along the top of West Cliff and thence down to the Harbour Brasserie where I had a date in half an hour.

Half a dozen seats are spread along the cliff-top because there are views towards Deal and Sandwich. I didn't usually come this way. Most of the seats, I noted now, had curious crests of red and orange and yellow.

This brilliant plumage turned out to be flowers: plastic flow-ers in plastic containers ingeniously fastened to the seat-back.

I stopped to look at one more closely. There was a note in a transparent folder stapled to the plastic flowers. It shook in the November wind. 'For "Gav",' it said. 'Corporal Gavin Shepherd. Died "doing his duty" in Afghanistan. Proudly remembered, not forgotten.'

Something rushed up and choked my throat before I could think, 'That's tautologous.'

That's what we should have done for Fred. There was still time, he would not be forgotten, we would club together to get it done, we would sit on his seat, pressed close together, thinking of Fred as we gazed across to France –

Water was streaming down my cheeks again, that winter wind affecting my eyeballs, I walked on towards the next seat, which remembered 'Miriam, who loved Ramsgate, welcomed here after Second World War, nursed QE Hospital, Loved by her Patients.' Lonely spinster? 'Loved by her Patients'? Miriam received a plume of pink silk orchids.

(Monica, too, was loved by her students. Even the pretty ones got used to me.)

I marched past the next two seats without looking, *do not be fazed by sentiment.* I did not want to be late for the Boys, but then the compulsive side of my brain made me go and peer at the very last seat.

This time the plastic flowers were bright scarlet, symmetrical, a bunch at each end. At first, I could only see the blank side of the paper inside its simple plastic folder but when I flipped it over, it struck me in the chest.

> For beloved Dad, the Best in the World,
> Mr S. Shepherd, 1919–2008.

Dad, we think of You every Day.
Wife, Kids and grandchildren
XXXXX

Dad, we think of you every day. What would it be like to do that and feel happy?

Dad, I think of you every day – I did that too, every day, and often, but for me that had meant three decades of terror.

And then I started to smell a rat. Yes, the seat was pious garbage. He'd died at eighty-nine, his wife had survived him, they were so fucking old the whole family must have hated them. They'd put up the seat to impress the neighbours and never thought about their father again. They couldn't write clearly – big childish letters   they couldn't spell or punctuate   Yes, these Shepherds were chavs and liars.

Only then I noticed that the red roses at either end of Mr Shepherd's bench were not plastic. They were living and fresh, there were buds to come, they must have been put there recently.

They did think of him every day.

So fucking what?! Who were they looking at?

Lessened by love, I limped away, back to my hopeless family.

42

The Harbour Brasserie is a building which clapped-out journalists would call 'iconic'. It sits on the far prong of Ramsgate Harbour, a fair walk, with ten minutes to get there. I strode along the quay, past the Main Sands and the Wetherspoons pavilion with lounging Grecian gods on the roof, past two old men with fishing lines and a trio of surly young Eastern Europeans leaning and complaining on the harbour wall, black leather jackets, cigarettes, too engrossed to set up the fishing gear which was half unloaded from a rusting trailer. They look at us as if we hate them now that we've voted to chuck them all out, but keep your glares to yourselves, morons. I don't have much against Poles or Latvians and even Lithuanians can be OK, although Albanians – a bit of a stretch.

On the right, the yachts in their silted-up moorings; keep going along the narrow mole; I would be late, it was five to ten, but a gust of wind caught my cape, unsteadied me and spun me round, and I saw two blond boys below on the sea, dropping anchor from a pale-blue yacht, still fifty metres from the pier and the little beach that lay beyond it.

They were slight boys, lissom; it took both of them to heave the anchor, with an effort, over the side. I glimpsed the yacht's name, 'The Racing Greyhound', and for a second I longed to be with them, blond and innocent and just eighteen, but I turned away, no point in yearning, and spotted my brothers' new Aston Martin, long and silver like a single cigar-case, parked in the shelter of the Brasserie wall. Good brothers, they were there already. Below me, the blond boys had climbed from the yacht and were rowing a little boat gracefully in towards the curve of sand beneath the Brasserie.

I could keep them as pets, in a golden cage, but no, I must go and meet my brothers.

The Harbour Brasserie looks like a ship, with an open upper deck that has views to Calais on a good day, and the sea runs past it through the harbour mouth, with Ramsgate behind at an elegant distance, the beautiful line of its two long cliffs and the town between them, rose and white, its military crescents curved to the light. In spring or summer I sometimes sat here, it was fun, fun, I would sit there alone but sometimes I would meet a man. All in the past, Mon, now, all gone.

Boris and Angus were sitting inside, cheek by jowl in the long sea window, backs to the cold light tossed off the waves so their long, identical faces were in shadow, two magnificent jaws like Desperate Dan from the *Dandy* comic we loved as children. Even in the morning they were dark with stubble.

'Mon, thank God!'

'Thank God, Mon!'

Yes, my brothers were unanimous.

'Boys!' I said. 'Bozzer! Angs!' And to my surprise they surged up and hugged me, proper big hugs that made an ache in my ribcage, and hung on for a second before we all sank down.

'Did you do it, Mon?' Angus said at once, and Boris nudged him in the side so hard that Angus stopped and stared at him, hurt, then enlightenment dawned and he covered his mouth and then said, 'Oh, sorry, Boris said I mustn't say that you did it, not even to the police.'

'*Especially* to the police,' Boris added.

'You lummox!' I said. 'And keep it down. The bar staff are listening.' A thin-faced youth was staring our way, probably at my bulky burka. I have no truck with anti-Muslim prejudice, Christians with tambourines are worse.

'Him?' said Boris. 'No, he looks retarded.'

'We have to stick together,' I said and smiled at them, my peculiar brothers. (I had missed my family, missed calling them names, which was our main way of showing affection. But Dad – his nicknames were cruel, foul. I will write it one day, will record it all, oh *ars, artis*, help me redeem it.)

'Got that,' said Angus, and, 'He's got it,' said Boris.

'Yes, yes, I'm not thick,' boasted Angus.

'He isn't, Mon,' echoed Boris.

Angus and Boris smiled at each other, the pleased, deep, tender smiles they used when, rarely, they looked directly at each other, rather than confronting the world side by side, and I smiled too: what delightful brothers.

Encouraged by this, Angus continued, 'But still, I'd like to know – *did* you do it?'

Boris and I groaned together.

But, 'I have a point.' Angus was obstinate, and after a pause, while Boris stroked his great chin, 'He has a point,' Boris confirmed, his opaque brown eyes briefly sharpening.

'He's got as much point as a broken pencil. I'm hungry,' I said, like a child asking, 'I want something to eat. I haven't had breakfast.'

'You always want something to eat, Mono,' they roared in unison, and shook with laughter.

'Breakfast,' said Boris. 'Go order, Angus.'

Three Ludd specials, which meant doubles of everything. The barman brought it over politely enough but again he stared hard in my direction; despite my cape, he must have admired me. 'I need ketchup,' Angus told him, but instead he went back and talked on his phone, eyes still riveted on me.

The three of us ate companionably, distributing food according to known preferences, so I got Boris's extra mushrooms and he got my fifth rasher of bacon, and Angus ate both our second tomatoes, and none of us had butter on our toast because when we were growing up it was forbidden, or rather, only our father was allowed it, a knob of gold butter on his own blue dish.

Angs and Bozzer: they would not desert me, we had suffered everything together...

But they thought they knew what was best for me. After all, they were fifteen years older. They wanted me back within the pale, not hiding from the police and worrying the family.

Angus said, 'I need the toilet. Don't tell him anything until I come back.'

'What are you, Angus, nine years old?'

I chomped down two more mouthfuls of breakfast and then began explaining to Boris. 'I'm not guilty, I'm not a criminal. But the truth is I was there, I saw him, it was hideous, he looked like a gargoyle, all bloodied on the bed, and I had an axe, I can't deny I had an axe.'

'Whoa there, Monica, this sounds bad. You can't admit to the axe,' said Boris.

'But I did have an axe. It got splashed with blood. That is the problem with explaining. I mean, I don't think I would have attacked him –'

'If he hadn't what?' yelled Angus, excited, freshly returned from his toilet trip. 'What drove you to it, Monica?'

They both leaned forward like twin inquisitors. Was this the news they were hoping for? Maybe we all wished one of us had done it. Did they just long to feel proud of me?

'Boys, get this into your great thick skulls, I am a witness, not the guilty party.'

The long faces opposite curdled with doubt. We were all talking louder than we meant to, but when we came in the Brasserie had been quite empty, it was a weekday morning in November and Ramsgate must have been having a lie-in, and now both of them were practically yelling, their identical brown eyeballs

195

fixed on my face: 'But the axe, Mon!' 'Fuck it, a fucking axe!' –
and I sensed that the café wasn't empty any more, it was filling
up, there was a scraping of furniture and murmur of voices
behind my back, so I pointed my finger at my lips: *ssshh*.

'So I took my axe and drove to the house, after the night of the
Party. I was furious –'

'That's very interesting, Ms Ludd. Perhaps you should explain
the rest to me?'

A familiar voice, with a Midlands twang, the associations
not unpleasant, and I turned round and saw, first, a uniformed
policeman, oh God, the fucking police were here, then beside
him Ginger, standing right behind me in the beige belted mac of
a TV detective. His collar was turned up; there was a bulge in his
pocket, and I let my eyes linger on that.

His expression was pleased, imperturbable, his pale-grey eyes
had a glint of triumph, but I thought I saw a slight change in them
as I managed, hardly missing a beat, 'Are you just pleased to see
me, officer?' Which would have been lost on everyone else.

'I'm afraid this is a firearm, Miss.' Then Ginger laughed, two
short, contained barks, and removed, from his pocket, notebook, pen, voice recorder. 'Only joking. Good morning, Miss
Ludd, and Mr Ludd, and Mr Ludd. Perhaps I should call you
Messrs Ludd?'

I knew that Ginger was a man who loved language. But Boris
and Angus stared, unsettled – was the man disrespecting them?
Boris stood up, to show his size. 'You'd better call him Angus,' he
grunted. 'And I am Boris. Would you like to sit down? I'm hoping
you aren't going to shame us. This is the county where our sister
teaches.'

Boris, you were magnificent! Boris showed poise, and *savoir vivre!* Suddenly I saw why Buoyant had thrived, despite Angus's psychotic streak.

Ginger sat down but his henchman stood, looking nervous and officious. Ginger kept giving me sideways looks. I tried to read them; did he bear me a grudge? No, it seemed more like intimacy, the complicity of two people playing a game, and he had just scored a victory.

'We need to talk to your sister,' said Ginger. 'We were talking to her but were – interrupted.'

I wanted to laugh, remembering that day, but turned it into a choking cough. Everybody stared at me.

'There are calls on her time,' Boris said, firmly. 'As a Deputy Headteacher, she has to preside.'

'And yet she's not at work today?'

For a moment Boris looked baffled.

'Officers, would you like some tea?' I asked. 'I could go and order some.'

'I'll go, Mon,' Angus offered, but Boris stared at him repressively and said, 'You might as well let Monica go, wasn't she just saying she needed the toilet.'

Boris! No longer handing me in, Boris was trying to help me escape!

Ginger, though, was wise to that. 'I'll accompany you,' he offered. 'To help you carry it back, Ms Ludd,' he added in a tone of grim amusement.

For some time, I had been far too hot as the meat sweat from the sausage and bacon spread through me. I turned to my man in the detective mac, my bane, my swain, my nemesis…

When in doubt, showcase the breasts. I slipped off my enormous cape and stretched, elaborately, shoulders back. This was just between me and Ginger: I let him have the breasts, both barrels. 'Wouldn't you feel cooler if you slipped your mac off?'

'I'm still a bit chilly from outside,' he said, but his eyes had done what I wanted them to do, they had slid over my front, and back again.

'You won't get the benefit.'

'I might.'

We set off together across the café. My mind was racing. I had half a plan.

By now the room was crowded with late brunchers, big blonde women hailing each other and miming orders across the room, anxious new couples in tight new clothes scraping their chairs as they squared up to the future. Pungent smells of chemical attractants. Gel like sticky honey smeared in adolescent hair.

Had a lover ever wooed me?

For some reason Ginger was leading the way – did he not know it was ladies first, did he not know I was a lady? – but as that question transformed to pain, he turned and briefly smiled at me. 'We'll have a little chat on the other side,' he said, and one big, square finger tapped the side of his short, straight nose, which I instantly decided was his best feature. Now he was having a word with the barman.

Monica, you have a chance.

Ginger seemed to have – forgiven me. Perhaps he – liked me? He might not, of course, after what I did next, and for some reason that gave me qualms, pale wormy squirmings under my ribcage – not like me, I just did what I wanted.

Mon, you need a friend in high places.

We paused beside the dessert cabinet with its tempting

puffballs of cream and chocolate beside the corridor to the toilet (we don't truckle to Feng Shui in Thanet).

'I need to talk to you, Monica.' He was talking quickly, urgently, and there was a line of sweat on his upper lip. 'I want to be sure that you're all right. You know your father isn't dead?'

'Yes.' He was concerned about me! I felt – womanly. The cream was thick. Maybe he wanted to buy me a gateau. Yet I was about to run away.

'We've got another suspect. You say you didn't do it. I do need to hear your account of things, and by that I mean your honest account. We are poised to arrest a Spanish lady. Though 'lady' is a misnomer. There are other crimes we are looking into. But my colleagues have issues regarding your car…Are you going to order tea?'

'A Spanish lady?' I saw black curling hair, red satin, a lace mantilla. Did Dad have one of those as well? Then I remembered the rancid blonde. Of course, that hideous accent was Spanish. Foul smells of musk that reminded me of ferrets, my mind was racing, but I couldn't show it –

'Ginger, I told you I wasn't there.'

'Yes, yes,' he hissed, 'but can we cut the crap? You'll have to trust us, Monica. Order the tea, I'll help you carry it.'

Us. In 'Us' I can never trust. The first 'us' I ever met was my parents. 'Drinks later, toilet first.'

'I'll wait outside, Monica – I can't trust you not to abscond.'

I reached down – no-one was looking, we were in a corner, pressed close to the glass of the sweet cabinet, which was smeared with that cream *I'd flirted, but not come across* – and I lightly patted the front of his coat, roughly at the level of his penis. 'See you later, Ginger,' I said, and I swear he half-guessed what I was going to do, there was a look of sharp interest, swiftly tempered with resignation.

Then I was in the dark corridor that led to both the exit and the toilets, and I went into the shrieking pink Ladies, a dank single room which was papered with a fashionable design of cerise loo rolls, and at once I saw an end to my plan, for there was no window, *there was no window*, and I had no choice but to come out again, saying, 'Ginger, I'm afraid that loo was disgusting, I will use the Gents, I'm not bothered.'

This visibly excited him. 'Monica, I see you have no boundaries.'

'That's as maybe. See you in a mo'!'

Yes, thank God, though it smelled of male urine – testosterone, and not a type I liked – there was a sash window by the single basin, the glass thick with salt from the spray of the waves, and of course the bloody sash was painted shut, or maybe just glued with brine and dirt, and I used all my strength (from weight-training days) to heave, heave on the lower pane while trying to hold it steady so the glass wouldn't rattle, and as I pushed, putting in so much effort that my eyeballs throbbed and a headache started, a voice in my head was chattering with worry, trying to remember the height of the tides; it was low enough for me to have walked along from Bone Bay, but was it going out or coming in? If the beach this side of the mole had gone, there was nothing for it, I would have to swim.

Someone was whistling outside the door. Oh, it was Ginger. Yes, he'd whistled before. What was the tune? 'The Something White Sergeant'. Fuck, I'd broken a fingernail. 'The Dashing White Sergeant'. How appropriate!

The window wouldn't move. I felt despair. Soon I'd have been in here for three or four minutes and Ginger would be hammering at the door.

Then I heard his phone ring. Great! That would distract him. I was surprised by how close it sounded, as if Ginger had his ear to the wooden panel.

Right, the upper sash, I was desperate now, although that meant I could only get out by standing on the basin, which looked fragile. I heard Ginger talking, 'Yes? Really?' then the window shifted, *yes, thank God*. I wrenched the sash down and cold air flooded in and then I was heaving myself up on to the basin, via the toilet, which rocked alarmingly, and, trying to save myself, I caught the chain, which instantly flushed, the feeblest gurgle, and I called, 'I'll have to wait for that to fill up', but outside, Ginger was almost shouting, '...fucking awful! You're breaking up!', so obviously he was still distracted by his phonecall, and I tried again, gently, nervously, levering myself on to the basin while leaning half my weight on the window frame; there was just about room for me to wriggle through but first I needed to look down; there was a wide ledge along the side of the building, and then, oh, a drop of eight feet, ten feet, a dozen, extending below. Could a body fall twelve feet and not be broken?

There it was, waiting, a thin strip of sand.

I hesitated, I wanted to live, I felt like an idiot, perched on the basin. What was he shouting – 'Fucking *dead*!'

Dad was dead? Dad had died? A flood of relief poured through my body. Yes, he was dead, I would be saved –

'Speak up!' he was shouting. 'Are you sure she's dead?'

Sure she's dead. Had I really heard it?

A seagull screamed, the air was cold, I scraped my hand, I hung between worlds – crushing my knee, banging my forehead,

I pushed myself through into the world beyond. I could still get back, but no, outside was freedom, I was Monica Ludd, I would not be beaten and for a split second I fell like a comet and knew it was the end, *you will be dead*, but I was hit by something huge and flat, ouch, the beach, and there I sprawled, huge, alive, totally winded.

Slowly, painfully, I raised my head. I felt like an enormous tortoise.

The blonds were on the beach. With their backs to me. Drinking something from a flask. I do like toy boys, but this wasn't the moment, my need to escape was far more pressing. Their yacht gleamed palely, not too far out. Raising my head had made me tired.

I lay there and panted, panted for air, but Ginger was somewhere, impatient, behind me, no time to relax, Monica – I hauled myself up on to my elbows; now I was a Komodo dragon.

One of the boys turned round and looked at me, but unsurprised, as if I'd always been there. I managed to smile, this was going well! (Nothing, remarkably, seemed to be broken, and so much of my body was bruised already from my cross-country escape from Dad's house in Margate that I could hardly tell if anything had worsened. Yes, it had: one foot, one knee, but there was no time to attend to them.)

'Good afternoon,' I yelled at them.

They looked improbably young, too ash-blond to be English. Maybe no more than nineteen, twenty? Yes, they must be language students.

'Sailors?' I said.

'Students,' they said. 'We hire a boat. We are Swedish.'

'Where did you come from?'

He looked puzzled. 'Yes, Sweden. It is in Europe.'

'Where did you come from *today*?' I pressed, thinking, 'I'm fucking European, too, mateys,' and their faces fell, had I said it aloud? There was sand in my mouth, I spat it out, and smiled warmly, so as not to put them off. They both stared back at me, young, puzzled.

'That way,' one of them said, and pointed. Great, he was pointing down past Broadstairs.

In two minutes, we had arranged it, they would give me passage back to Bone Bay. At first, they refused my offer of money but when I insisted, they accepted. The taller one looked at me doubtfully as I heaved myself into the rowing-boat: I seemed to fill up most of it. They tried to push the boat the few feet to the water but nothing happened, I was stuck fast. They muttered in Swedish, then politely in English. 'Now get out, please,' and one of them offered his hand to help me but the other one just turned away, his shoulders shaking, oh, he was laughing. I don't object to people being cheerful.

We tried again on the edge of the water. The boat wobbled wildly as I climbed aboard, but then they joined me, this could be fun, they almost had to sit on my lap, but they rowed to the yacht with surprising strength, they hauled me on board, we were on our way. Once they upped anchor the winds took us, and the power of the water made me a swan!

Although I have never been a confident sailor, although we might be pursued by Ginger, I thought, 'I am happy, now, in this moment; a woman is dead' (please could it be Dad?) 'but I have been saved by two blond gods.'

Soon the journey lost its glamour as the waves steepened and the winds got up and the short, choppy, nervous motion turned into a kind of grim running on the spot. It took half an hour to round Dumpton Point, another three-quarters to get past Broadstairs, and how odd and quaint the land seemed from the sea, dots of people and eggshell-light houses that looked as if they could be blown away...

And what could be happening in the Harbour Brasserie? Would my Dashing White Sergeant ever forgive me?

By the time they cut in to the sands of Bone Bay to drop me off, my legs were like rubber from bending and jouncing to the power of the sea.

Each one bowed formally as we shook hands and, trying to be tactful, I passed them their money. 'Here is the dosh.'

'What is dosh, please?'

'Brothers?' I asked. I was thinking of my own. These were so alike they could be twins. 'Friends,' one said, and the other laughed and said, 'Very good friends', and their eyes met in a smile of approval.

What would it be like to love one's appearance? I dragged myself away, up the cliff, along the road, off to the little local shop. I had to see the local paper. How had the barman recognised me?

I went into the oddly named newsagent: 'Dirk Whites' of Kent'. Oh, unruly apostrophe! The shop window had a flock of union jacks around the National Lottery symbol, and below it, a framed *Daily Mail* front page, very yellow, from the day after the Referendum – 'TAKE A BOW, BRITAIN: WE'RE OUT!'

A rat-faced man lounged on the counter, looking vaguely pleased with himself. He only stocked the *Express* and the *Mail*. I am not a snob, and to err is human, *humani a me nihil alienum puto*, but, sorry, the *Express* is for sub-humans. The *Mail*'s headline was 'NEW BREXIT HOPES', which I knew I'd seen many times before. I grew quickly bored and glanced at page two. Which led me, logically, towards the middle: ah yes, something on poisonous mothers. The best bit of the *Mail* was always the features. I started reading. They must know my mother!

'Are you going to buy that paper?' the man suddenly asked, with elaborate sarcasm. His closely set eyes rolled across my body in a way that said there was too much of it.

I could have swatted him like a fly. 'Hmm, on balance I don't think I'll bother.' I went on reading for a minute or two. His wall-eyed sneer had got through to me, though, so I took a long look around his shop, being in no hurry to vacate it. There was a crude statuette of Winston Churchill on the counter, and behind him, on the wall, a black-and-white photo of Churchill in a pinstripe suit, cradling in his arms a large machine-gun.

'Do the local right-wing nutters meet here?'

'That's highly offensive language, that is.'

'Still, I expect it's accurate.'

'You look like a lesbian. You look like a Remainer.'

'You look like a cross-eyed idiot boy.'

'Old Slag Cunt!'

I quite liked his spirit. 'And by the way, the sign outside is misspelled.'

Suddenly he looked uncertain. A frown trisected his yellow brow. 'My sign? I think I know my own fucking name.'

'Yeah, but you don't know English grammar. Whereas Winston Churchill was a very good writer.'

His eyes fell, unsynchronised, and I moved in for the *coup de grâce*.

'Winston Churchill would be ashamed.'

His mouth opened, but no words came.

Two to me! I felt elated.

Outside the shop, I breathed in deep. Mon on form, Mon on top!

Happy adrenalin went coursing through me, but Bay House beckoned in the thin blue sunlight.

43

All that fresh air had left me tired: the perfect time to read the paper, except that, damn, I had left it behind, and so, instead, I went to the bookcase where we Ludd children kept a few holiday books.

Why did I have to slide out *The Shining*? No, I dared not re-read that novel. Jack Nicholson's manic-eyed, wide-nostrilled face, baring his canines with glee and hatred, grinned at me from the paperback cover. The film had obsessed my elder brothers but I had never wanted to see it. The actor stared at me knowingly. *Monica, what did you do to your father? What will your father do to you?*

But I wouldn't be afraid of a fat old actor. I read for a bit. They were all cooped up together. Johnny, the father, was possessed by anger. Now they had managed to lock Johnny in the larder. The boiler was going to explode. An hour slipped by. I couldn't stop reading. But now he was out, he was coming for his family...I jumped to my feet in a sudden convulsion and dropped the book face-down on the table.

I made some sandwiches for lunch and stared at the bright, normal garden, but the colours looked lurid and artificial and the branches waved with too much vigour. I forced myself to go back into the lounge, picked the book up between thumb and finger, stuffed it away at the bottom of a pile.

Yet after that I couldn't quite settle. I moved restlessly from room to room. I had always been large, I was proud of it, but I rattled around in all that space. I missed having lessons to prepare. Yes, I should have got on with my diary, but my laptop languished upstairs in the bedroom. I wasn't eager to go up and find it. What if someone was hiding there? The golden-red light of late afternoon shone brief and bright on the wallpaper, a palimpsest of rusty stains.

Monica, you are a great sad booby! I shook myself hard and jumped up off the chair. The house stretched round me, it was four, half-four, the shadows were growing on their own, and I made myself move as the sun went down, a red dim flash through the sitting-room window.

Dark comes early in November.

Was it so mad of me to go round checking, pushing the door of each bedroom open with a little, darkening lurch of the heart, putting the light on, *thank God, no-one?* Opening, peering, shutting again.

No-one in the old-fashioned bathroom with the claw-footed bath that someone had wrecked (the Girl, the Girl, it must have been the Girl who had painted the feet with matt blue paint).

No-one on the long windy balcony where a plastic chair banged and nagged at the railings.

No-one – this door was especially hard to open, it was Dad's lair, we weren't allowed inside – in the separate lav with the high cistern and the old-fashioned chain. Swinging, swinging, as if Dad just used it…

If only the house were completely quiet. No-one drove down

the private road, you didn't hear normal dogs and children. But it wasn't quiet. Age fretted away at it, constantly creaking and settling, twigs were knocking and scratching at the windows, clasps and latches rusting and flaking, radiators knocking, banging, pumping, pipes were straining, had the boiler been serviced? – curtains were sighing in gasps of air that slipped through gaps, and any of this could have been the sly creepings of a living being, watching and waiting.

But no. I emerged from the very last room. There was no-one in the house, no-one and nothing.

I would make a cup of tea and go on with my diary.

In fact, I sat down at my laptop and slept, lulled by the walk, my escape, the fresh air. I woke with a start; my phone was ringing. I couldn't get the hang of this security business. I was almost sure it would be Ginger.

He'd have fooled Angus into giving him my number.

But no, it was the husky whisper of my sister. 'Mon? Monica? Are you on your own?'

I was on my own, and the shadows were moving. I shivered slightly. 'Yes, I am.'

'Can I come and see you?'

I paused, surprised. 'Well, it's a bit awkward, I'm not at home.'

Fairy so rarely came to see me. Oh fuck, she would demand real coffee, or poncey flavours of herbal tea, and she was always in the middle of some crisis, though maybe that had all changed, with Rupert.

'Mon –'

Then I realised Fairy had been crying.

'Yes, all right, but no-one knows where I am, well hardly anyone, you'll have to promise –'

'– to keep the secret, right? Angus told me. I'm actually parked at the turn of the road.'

Although I knew she was almost here, I still jumped when the doorbell rang. It had an eccentric, unpleasant tone, an electronic chime from the eighties or nineties that went 'tantivy-tantivy-tantivy', a vague simulacrum of a huntsman's bugle, the tune Dad liked to whistle at night or sometimes in the garden in summer as he went around spraying insecticide. The tape had stretched into a minor key so the end fell horribly away. Mum had found it in a shop in Margate and given it Dad as a birthday present. 'A bloody doorbell? We've already got one!' 'But Albert, it plays your favourite tune. I thought we could put it in Bay House.' I remember he was pleased, for once, and kissed her. Hearing it now made my skin prickle.

But I went to the door and there she stood, long and skinny in the light from the porch but bulked out by the bush of her hair and the glossy mass of her creamy coat, a shimmering landslide of cream-yellow pelts, each of which kept its separate shape, the outline of each tiny body slightly darker, the tail-tips tapering to a point, as skinny and perfect as the tip of her nose which was white-blue-transparent with cold.

She started to do the little scream of excitement I supposed she'd learned from her modelling contacts, but I cut her off in mid-whinny.

'Yeah. No, OK come in, come in.'

And then she was hugging me, which was strange, and the coat had a faint ammoniac smell which was overlaid with her tobacco-flower perfume.

When I pulled away I saw the rest of her face. She had a jagged red line across one cheek as if she'd been hit by a hard object, one eye was half-closed, her mouth was swollen. 'God, Fairy, what happened?'

'It was Rupert,' she breathed, pushing on past me so I couldn't look. 'I refused to tell him or the police where you were and all at once he lost his rag completely and the next thing was, I was on the floor.'

My sister had stood up for me! 'Thanks, Fairy!' I said, surprised. 'Has he ever done that before? – Bastard.'

'He's, you know, a black belt at Judo, and he represented Marlborough at fencing, that's, you know, really a *very good* school,' (that stupid lisp – '*a very good thchool*'), and he trains with the Reserves. But no, he doesn't actually hit me, or only when he's completely drunk.'

She was still half-boasting about the brute! Yet at the same time, she was silently crying, a glittering track running down one cheek, and she moved her hands to cover her face.

'I'll tell our brothers,' I said, fist clenching. I hated the thought of a Ludd getting bullied. 'Boris will lay him out for you.'

'No, no, that's not why I came – Mon, it's Veronica, I came to tell you –'

'Oh yes, she came here, can you believe it, the silly bitch attacked me, so I whacked her!' The memory of Veronica's pathetic summer pastels blowing all over the lawn was a good one. 'Result!'

'Mon – Mon –' She was staring at me through a cage of fingers and I saw her terrified eyes, enormous. Her lips parted: she struggled to speak.

'What's the matter?'

'Mon, do you know Veronica's dead?' She took a step backwards: two; three. 'Mon, do you mean – did you – did you?'

I was trying to absorb this new information. The call Ginger took outside the toilet, I was halfway through the window, I thought I'd misheard. Someone had died. But Veronica? The Girl, the Girl, so hatefully young, who would take Dad's money and outlive us all. So now she wouldn't. Good, she was dead.

'Fuck's sake! I'm not a murderer.'

She looked doubtful, but stopped backing away.

'Don't you know your own sister?' I demanded.

'That's the trouble,' she wailed. 'You don't know your own strength. That day when you suffocated me in the cupboard –'

'That was just high spirits,' I patiently explained. 'No, I just showed the Girl what's what. She was perfectly healthy when I last saw her. Just a bit rumpled. Is she really dead? Sit down, Fairy. Take that disgusting coat off.'

She took the tea as good as gold, not making her usual mad requests, and drank with only a faint grimace of distaste on her poor, beautiful, battered face. After a few sips, she started talking.

'The police told Rupert when I was out jogging, Rupert told me, then he hit me. Because I wouldn't say where you were. The Girl was found dead at Dad's house, this morning. It's totally awful. Rupert said Ma found her –'

'Ma found her? She never leaves the Home.'

'She came to the Party, didn't she? Anthea saw weight-training stuff in her room.'

I had seen it too. My mind was racing. Nothing made sense. 'You don't suppose Ma…?' I said, slowly.

'Ma found her. She called the police.'

'Maybe our mother wee-ed her to death?'

Fairy, who always shrank from familial crudeness, buried her tiny face in her teacup.

'Tell me what you know, Fairy.'

'Everything's second-hand from Rupert. It was just, like, the Girl bled to death. She was lying on Dad's study floor. Ma went in to feed the ferrets. Veronica was there before her. One of the ferrets was glued to her neck.'

'Disgusting things! They were probably half-starving.'

'The policeman said there was a lot of blood.' *The pleethman thed there woth a lot of blood.* Her lisp made the whole thing ridiculous.

But then I imagined it: a sea of blood, spreading outwards from that terrifying doorway, the forbidden room, Bluebeard's study.

'Bled' and 'death', they were becoming common, they were part of my new, lurid lifestyle that had begun the day after the Party. I hadn't had time to unpack my knife.

'I just want things to go back to normal,' I heard myself saying, and Fairy nodded, though had her lifestyle ever been normal? 'I miss Windmills. I can't go in. Neil told me to take all the time I needed. I think he means, "Don't come back."'

I missed the girls shrieking when I entered the classroom and they stopped whatever bad thing they were doing, I missed my raids on the staff biscuit-tin, I even missed my tussles with Neil as I explained what he should have been doing. I felt I had been away for a lifetime. Yes, the girls. I was fond of them, harridans, swots, geeks, doxies! I felt it sharply now I couldn't see them.

Suddenly I pitied Veronica. Not long ago she was a schoolgirl like them. Once she had run up and down playing hockey…I remembered the blood on the steps of the Hall, after we ejected her from the Party. Yes, and blood on the boot-scraper after our little spat in the garden. Why was she always bleeding on us? Honestly, what a fucking nuisance! I imagined a hockey-stick battering her skull but no, no, the Girl was a victim, Dad was forty years older, it was disgusting.

She wouldn't have a life. She would never be a woman.

Then just for a second: what about me? Had I grown up to be a normal woman?

Something pushed me to my next question. 'Why is this house full of pictures of you?'

Fairy shrugged, uneasy. 'He collected them.'

'Isn't that creepy?'

'Well, I am a model.' Not what she wanted to talk about.

'There's only one group photo with me,' I pressed. 'And one or two of Anthea. There were three of you, just in the bedroom.' (Not true any more: I had turfed them out; I had thrown them, cracking the glass, into the dustbin.)

'The Girl bled to death. She was only twenty,' she said, sadly, stroking her cheek, where the red mark was like a flaming arrow. 'She was a teenager when it started with Dad. Much too young. It's like, abuse.'

The forbidden word, so over-used, so meaningless, so full of meaning, so hard to voice, so mealy-mouthed, the red pennant that poked out from corners and always had to be shut away.

Our eyes met. We stared at each other. 'Our father was a terrible man,' I said. I left it lying there. Once she would have defended him.

We both jumped when Fairy's phone rang. 'I'm at Bay House with Mon,' she said. Then, to me, 'It's Anthea. Here she is.'

'I need to see you. I've got things to tell you –'

'She's here, tell her yourself,' said Anthea.

When it rang a moment later, it was Boris:

'Well done, Mon, I have to hand it to you! He got in a temper, the ginger-haired bastard, after you gave him the slip in the lav.'

'I quite like Ginger, as it happens. To be fair, I was quite annoying. How are you two, in any case? Both all right? I didn't get a chance to ask.'

'Since you ask, I'm not at my brightest. Did you hear what happened about Marija? She's already looking for a job in Riga. Angus and I thought we might come and see you.'

So then the whole family was coming round – yes, of course, when I didn't need them and had lots of other things to do!

I didn't need them. I was doing fine.

But the dreams, the dreams, and the repetitive questions. Itching and crawling like fleas or beetles. No rest for anyone till there were answers.

Had the Girl really bled to death?

My family are murderous.

Part 7
Tantivy

44

Wildlife. There were mice at Bay House. I feared nothing except my father, so all I felt was a little distaste when I first smelled that smell. Strangely enough, it's not animal, it was like cold metal souring the air in the kitchen by the green enamel bread-bin. Then I found droppings in the bathroom upstairs. Tiny black seeds like grains of rice. So some of the rustles, some of the runnings, some of the clicks and shivers and tremors that made the house so hard to sleep in were small animals fleeing me. Maybe some of the traffic was the other way. Maybe sandflies and crabs and lugworms and piddocks that can turn a rock into a lump of Swiss cheese were crawling busily up through the cliffs that held the foundations of the house, advancing further as the tides crept up, maybe they enjoyed each minuscule inroad of wind and water, and followed it. Maybe Bay House was the next to go. Yes, the Fall of the House of Ludd, it was way past time, goodbye, good riddance.

Now suddenly the house surged with people, all of the Ludds, full-on, full-strength, and the thunder of our feet must have unsettled the rodents. Anthea pounded off to the kitchen to open the bottles of Rioja she had brought (red, red, Ludds only drink red) while the rest of us shouted in the sitting-room, exchanging amicable jokes and insults. I had offered tea, but been outvoted.

'Who wants to help me?' Anthea called through. Without

Kelly she evidently found opening screw-top bottles a challenge.

'Fuck sake Anth, you can open bottles.'

Fairy, the sucker, trotted through to give assistance. Kitchens, remember, were my sister's element long before she discovered catwalks. Shortly afterwards, a long thin scream. A brief silence; we looked at each other. Then, 'Quick, Angus, come and kill the mouse!' Anthea called, and we all rushed in, and Fairy was backed into the corner by the door, Anthea was doubled up with laughter, and Angus, big face concentrated, blond hair shining over lengthening roots, was kicking and stamping at something on the floor, and Boris was pulling at his arm, 'Come on Angus, no need to do that,' but one look at Angus as he put the boot in, pale eyes fixed, intent, ferocious, told us all that he did have to do it, he had to finish what he had started 'Now you'll have to get that mess off your boot.'

I had seen enough. I thought of Dad. If only the attacker had finished what they started.

As the bottles of Rioja slipped down our throats a false glow of animation began, intimacy, love for each other, the beginning of perfect understanding, we had always been Ludds, we had always been together, surely now at last we could love one another.

For the first half-hour, no-one talked about Dad. Then Anthea took her empty glass and clinked upon it with her knife. A bell for silence. Something was starting. Whatever we'd come for, pell-mell, unthinking, magnetised filings, it had begun.

'I might be a bit drunk?' she said, to cheers. 'I want to talk about the parents? It's the first time ever we've been together, all of us, without Ma or Dad being there.'

Chorus of surprise and approval. I alone remained silent.

'Dad's getting better but he doesn't want to see us. I've talked to the hospital. The only visitors he wanted were the Girl and our mother, and Fairy, of course –'

'Did you see him, Fairy?' I asked, furious. Why was Dad asking for her? Why hadn't Fairy told me before? Why should Dad be asking for Ma?

'Because Fairy's his favourite,' Boris answered, equably, as if his answer wouldn't make us all jealous. Dad was hateful but belonged to all of us.

'It's not my fault,' sighed Fairy. 'Is it?'

Anthea just ploughed on with her toast, if this rambling speech was to be a toast. No, it was a Crime Digest. 'The police officer told me they've located the suspect? And Monica, I don't think it's you. Then this awful thing with Veronica dying, I suppose everybody knows about that?' (Several people didn't. She explained, badly.) 'Monica says the Girl turned up here –'

Yet again they were mixing me up in a death! I shouted robustly, 'Ages before.'

'Must have been less than a day?' said Anthea.

I frowned a warning. Vengeance is mine. Alas, my mouth was full of biscuits.

'Did you do it, Mon?' Angus said, on cue, though with less conviction than before, as if he half-remembered he had been seen off, and Boris pushed him, but amiably.

'It was Ma who found her. In Dad's study. Monica was a long way away?' Anthea said, and I nodded, sulkily. I wanted to talk about something else, Veronica was of limited interest. 'Our father won't fully recover, will he? You're the only one of us who's seen him, Fairy.'

'He looked horrible,' Fairy shivered. 'He was all – bandaged.

Like something from, you know, a horror film. He was walking a bit. But his voice was, like, mental. Look, I meant to tell you, it's partly why I came here, Mon –'

Oh, the wispy little whisperer was talking to me. I was a little drunk. I raised my glass. Everyone was looking at me: nice. At family gatherings, I was often ignored. Or was I getting too much attention?

'He kept on talking about Monica. Just sort of roaring out your name. I said, "Dad, do you want to see her?" but he said – I couldn't make sense of it, he was barely out of intensive care – he said, I can't actually remember the words, but it was something like, "No, I'll bloody find her." And then he kept repeating it. And – his voice was all wrong, his throat was hurting, but it was almost like he was happy again. He was sort of smiling with his eyes. And – laughing,'

'So that's good,' Angus said into the long, thoughtful silence that followed that. 'That's good, Mon. All friends again.'

Anthea was looking puffy and worried, but she had a glass half-raised in the air. 'Let's drink a toast to –' she petered out. None of us could help her. Then she had an inspiration: 'Surviving our parents!'

'Our parents!' roared Boris. We drank to that.

After this I went and switched the light on, I needed clarity before things went wrong, yet the evening was already blurred at the edges.

Family anecdotes began. Everyone had their 'Dad' story. They were horror stories – we vied with each other to show how outrageous Dad was, how capricious, they were stories of childish humiliations, and yet we all laughed and interrupted, capping each other's dreadful tales. 'No, he didn't!' 'He did, the bastard!'

The Boys were laughing particularly heartily, shaking their shoulders in unison, plonked on the sofa side by side, though the stories they had to tell were the worst. Fairy giggled hysterically, at random.

Suddenly I saw it all differently.

Ever since Fairy's revelation a part of me had been cold, watchful. Something very bad was hidden somewhere, here in this room where we were shouting and laughing. I looked at the Boys and their eyes were dead.

Who were these people? Why was I with them?

My siblings sat there, these people I knew, people that I had known for ever, yet knew not at all, arranged round the room like ventriloquist's dummies being operated from another planet. Their arms and jaws were in constant motion but someone else must be pulling the strings. I loathed the dummies! They were all insane!

It was Dad speaking through us, mastering us. This wasn't our life, these weren't our voices.

'There's no-one like him, the old fellow!' The dreadful chorus of the Boys.

There was a loud bang outside the house. For a brief moment, the laughter stopped. Dad, I thought, then instantly dismissed it. Since Sandwich and Canterbury, we were all nervous. The Gatwick gunmen had not been caught, which added to a long line of unsolved crime; ditto the Oxford Street terrorist.

'It's Firework Night,' Anthea announced. Everyone gasped and smiled: of course.

Fairy's voice whispered. 'Oh, I'd forgotten. I'm meant to be going to a party with Rupert. He said he would come and pick me up.'

'You're not going near that prick any more,' I said, as calmly as I could manage.

'I have to go. They're expecting me. It's a fund-raiser at the Turner Centre.'

'With your face like that?'

'Oh, you know, make-up.'

Obviously the beatings had happened before, probably more times than she could remember.

'I'll knock him down,' Angus announced. I was proud of him, but Fairy started crying.

Just at that moment, the doorbell rang. Tantivy-tantivy-tantivy, it squawked, in horrible run-down arpeggios.

'I'll go,' I said. 'I think it's Rupert.'

I swear I had no fixed plan in my head, but opening the door and seeing him there, immaculate in his cashmere overcoat, the over-door light on his yellow hair –

I don't know what happened, but a moment later he was lying flat on his back on the floor. 'Cheers, Rupert!' I shouted, politely. His nose was bleeding. My right hand tingled. I was breathing hard, I felt terrific. I gulped in air. I must have remembered my boxing lessons. Excellent. It was just a reflex. Hahahahahahaha.

Hahahahahahaha.

HAHAHAHAHAHAHA!

'Who is it?' Boris yelled from the lounge.

I held my bruised hand behind my back. 'Er – it's Rupert. He's fallen over. Actually, I think he may be unconscious.'

Yes, it was time to stick together. Anthea came out with a jug of cold water and poured it over his head to revive him. It was cold outside, but her intentions were good. I watched it all through the porch window. She was wiping his face with a tea-towel, not a clean one, I checked that later. It soon turned pink, but his face looked passable. 'I'm calling the police,' was Rupert's first reaction, but my brothers convinced him otherwise as the two of them walked him back to his car.

'It didn't take very long to persuade him,' said Angus when they came back inside. Boris was grinning, and fist-bumped me. He must have learned that from Marija.

'Don't hit her, Boris, she did right,' said Angus.

Everyone groaned, then we saw he was grinning. Angus had managed a joke. Well done!

We drank some more. Fairy grew miserable. 'I think Rupert loved me.'

'He didn't, moron.'

The evening seemed to be in decline.

I had an idea. 'There's something on at Broadstairs. Firework Festival. It's meant to be a sort of reprise of summer, lots of things happen in a giant tent. Why don't we go?'

The Ludds don't like surprises. They sat and stared at me, tentative, nervous. Outings at home had been rare, and pre-scheduled.

'What's a reprise?' Angus asked.

'You know, a re-match,' Boris said. 'Play it again, this time we win.'

I guessed that everyone was going to say 'No', and suddenly I knew it was the right thing to do. 'It's ages since we did something together.'

'Did we ever? Do something together? After we left home, I mean.' The truth-telling voice of Anthea.

Uncertain faces, avoiding glances. Then I had an inspiration. 'This evening we've talked about Dad –' I began, and Angus actually yelled, 'The Man!' I ignored him. 'I think our father would want us to go. Remember, he always said, "Stick together."'

Ten minutes later we were on our way, dressed in a puzzling range of costumes, Fairy (skin painted porcelain again) nestled in her shimmering, glimmering coat and tiny silver ballet slippers, Anthea in vile red cashmere tracksuit, black leather cap and sparkly trainers, the Boys in their new, immaculate, matching Hong-Kong-tailored houndstooth frock-coats, me concealed beneath raincape and dark glasses, with a pair of Dad's wool gloves against the cold which I had found lying in the summer-house. My hands looked enormous, strangler's hands!

(I had molecules of Dad all over my fingers! This time I felt a grim pleasure. So I could be as strong as him.)

Oddjobs, weirdos, we were still the Ludds, five out of six of us, side by side, we packed into Anthea's jeep together, four big bodies and an elegant skeleton, someone remembered how Dad used to try to pack all us kids into his Jaguar, the jeep barrelled through the night, we were flung together, we felt the body warmth, we laughed at each other. Anthea had been drinking, yes, but she wasn't drunk, and suddenly she shrieked, 'Afterwards, let's go and see our mother!', and because we were all in a dizzy mood, nobody said 'No' to her.

And a cold little light shone in my head: Ma's shrivelled, grim white face on a pillow. Who did we blame for the state of her?

Dad, the bastard. It was his fault.

But then there was the Girl. Who found her dead?

Ma. *It was Ma*, with all that blood.

Ma, on her feet, in the house in Margate.

45   *Adoncia*

Señor Dentist, I come for a visit!

'Alloween, like I tell you 'Maroween' for Spanish people, nice new fiesta for witches, is my day! I take off Ryanair from Malaga Airport and fly like witch to find my Albert, two bottles of best *Rioja* in my bag, has the tan in, like you say in England, has the tan in, red-black like his blood. I book myself in the Sands Hotel, why economise, I plenty of money.

Next day I take hire car, I go to Tesco to buy *cigarillos* and one roast chicken, ready *cocido*, make dinner easy. I see Esmeralda by fridge of cold *vino*, she stare inside, light make her face green, she stand like statue, I think she not see me. I walk by quickly, but after a bit I go back again because I need my *cigarillos*. This time she nearly see me because she gone to the *bricolaje*, she have to do her own do-it-herself because no man never do it for her! She very ugly, frowning at a hammer. It look too big for her, little old woman, if I take one breath I blow her away. She go through the till. *Adios para siempre.* I hate these stupid victim women.

I call at house I still own in Margate, have stupid tenant but I keep one room with key and, in it, many useful *cosillas*. Including bag with Luis's little secrets, things he use when he visit people's houses and story go wrong before he leave, people no sense, they come back too soon, and sometimes he has to stop them shouting, because, fair do, no-one want trouble. Little bang on head. Sometimes a big one.

Then I turn up like holy saint on Albert doorstep, good as gold, in a short fur coat and black stocking like I know he like. 'Surprise, surprise, Señor Albert!! See how Adoncia beautiful!

See how she bring you cigar, chocolate!'

And I smile at him, show him big painful teeth, they still hurt like death, five years later, until I mad from loss of sleep, and they not pretty, too big, too white, like white tombstone, and I lick my lip. Like white tombstone on the dirt pig's grave. I lick my lip, I show him long red tongue, he think he do what he want with me. After five years, perhaps he miss me, the nice little things I let him do, like I miss Luis, my beautiful boy, when we first together he touch me, lick me, I melt like chocolate, like warm sweet chocolate, *oh chupa, chupa*, like silk he suck me but no more sugar, never no more, Albert drive him away from me.

'I have a date,' Albert say, on his doorstep. He look old, the dentist. He look startle. I come like a whore, I give him no warning, it winter already but my coat open and I wear a top that show my booby, I let my hand slip down to my bum, I smile at him, I say to him, 'I come to give you a present, Albert. You know the one you always wanted?'

'I've got a date with the family.'

He always want it, though. Is his favourite. Albert like to hurt people. I know if I offer he can't say no, although he miss visit from Queen of England. So his face go red, and I see he excited, and he ask me in, he open my wine, though he say, 'I'll have to go out later. Family business. Family comes first.'

But Albert never go out later. Albert come first, his needs, every time. I make sure Albert busy in the bedroom.

That night I give him things but not the final one. Some things Albert Ludd must wait for. The best thing, the worst thing. I make him wait. I smile like *bruja* in the darkness.

'Yes, Albert, tomorrow morning. Before you get up. Something special.'

46

Lights, camera, actors, music! The Ludd family was on the road!

Neil calls me 'excitable'.

Broadstairs flamed with remembered glory, a last bright flare against the coming dark, its annual Firework Festival. In huge marquees overlooking the bay they had gathered the best of their summer attractions. A dozen different sets of musicians were reprising their gigs at the Folk Festival: Irish fiddlers, white-haired rockers, hard-eyed sisters with long grey dreads singing Joni Mitchell in wiry soprano, duelling with nearby Cajun Blues. Outside in the night, beyond the lit tents, other musicians huddled near the canvas, Iraqi folk-singers wailing something, their story scribbled on pieces of cardboard, by a plastic carton with a few 10ps, and two hungry-looking teenagers singing Bob Dylan, the boy wearing a dirty top hat, the girl with red lipstick, down-at-heel slippers and an old Labrador without a collar. (I gave them nothing; it would just encourage them, but Anthea is suggestible – obviously she hasn't worked hard for her money and doesn't mind giving it away. 'I had a chat to them,' she said, rejoining us. 'Nice couple? They voted Remain?' 'So fucking what, Anthea?')

'Fireworks at eight,' Angus announced, happy to have some shape to the evening. It was half-past seven, we were out to have fun, walking arm-in-arm in a line that made oncoming people break ranks and scatter. I heard a regular clacking or crashing somewhere over to the side of the tents. In the same direction, there was wild, free music, manic music that spoke to my instincts and made me want to dance towards it –

Dancing. Could it be in my blood? – though my games

teacher claimed I had 'no sense of rhythm' and no-one ever wanted to dance with me. 'Choose your partners' – that horrible mantra.

Nobody. Not once. Not ever.

Which is their loss! I'm a red-hot dancer! I'm just waiting for the perfect partner.

'Why are you lunging about?' asked Anthea, who had her arm entrapped in mine.

'What do you mean, lunging?' I asked. True, I had started to rock to the music.

'You're sort of lumbering about. You're pulling me into other people! Did you finish off the wine before we left?'

I danced her off to the side, and back, pulling her arm away from Angus, and we nearly fell over, and she shrieked and laughed, or maybe it was a cry of pain, and we were almost kids again.

Without our father to terrify us, without our mother genteelly ignoring us, did we have a way of being together? Could we big children survive our parents?

The wild music was getting louder, driving and thumping into my brain, making my heartbeat jump to meet it. I'm a wild woman! I am Monica! You have never seen the half of me! *Thump-ah, Thump-ah, Thump-ah, Boom* –

I spotted a leaflet lying on the ground and swooped to read it. 'Morris of the Night. Featuring: the Hooden Horse…'

There they were, suddenly, Morris Dancers, in the guttering, swooping light of a strobe that only deepened the darkness around it, cloaks of uncertainty swashbuckling their movements, can you believe it, did I really see it?

There. We did really see that. A long white face on a tall dark pole, not a face, a skull, the skull of a horse, and another, a third, three tall dark riders cloaked in black. Just for a second I thought *jihad*, under the cloaks, machetes, machine-guns, but no, this terror was much older, this kind of terror had always been here, hiding at night, in our heads, in our houses. Morris of the night: I had seen them before. As soon as I met them, I had known them for ever. The Black Morris. Lords of misrule. Household gods of the Ludd family.

'Who's that?' roared Angus.

'Fucking mime,' said Anthea. 'Mime is shit.'

But I knew my sister, she tried to sound sophisticated when she was nervous, and one horse turned its head towards her, trotted over and nudged at her hair with its long white glimmering bony nose, and she screamed, and the man-horse laughed a high whinny, and Anthea fled behind Boris and Angus.

The Morris dancers were a piggyback of manic high spirits on funeral-stately. They crossed and whirled, totally free –

Had I ever been free? Would I ever be free?

People have called me 'unrepressed', but that hasn't given me my freedom.

Nice, how their thighs leaped and spread, the flash of their teeth that said sex and power, and anarchy, and revolution, and yet there was also, underneath, an ominous low beat, a funeral measure, and for the next dance, they huddled down together, then straightened up all holding sticks, long serious sticks that could stave a head in, and now we were in a minor key and the pulse of the drum grew more insistent, and as the dancers ran towards each other they clashed their sticks, once, twice, they crossed their sticks like a demon kiss, loud, hard, and they weren't smiling, this was a war-dance done in earnest, they were winding up, now, to something bad, the end of order,

of parliaments, kings, the end of Europe, it was England dancing, old, old, furious England, ploughboys dancing against the
farmer, Breke-ek-ek-ex, BREK-EK-EK-KEX – then the light on
the dancers suddenly died.

It reappeared, a brilliant shaft round a very old man who had
wandered in. He was stooped and fat, with a yellow-white beard.
No, wait, he wore a pink smock, pale baby pink, and blonde hair
in bunches, and frilled pantaloons, it was a very young girl – but
dangling from its hand was a tankard –

It was both. Someone shouted, 'That's the Molly.' Someone
else said, 'No, the Fool.' Its movements were slow, uncoordinated. Did it rule the dancers, or was it their victim? I felt queer,
confused. It was fat and pink. No, it could not protect itself.

'I thought Morris dancers were, you know, nice,' said Angus,
puzzled, to his brother. 'We saw them last summer. They had
hats with flowers –'

'It's "Morris of the Night",' I told Angus. 'Shut up.'

'I don't like it. It's, you know, weird. Can we get ice-creams?'
Fairy was squeaking. She flinched from meals but she liked ice-
cream, and tiny-teeny cakes and sweeties.

'It's a story, concentrate,' I told her. 'Maybe they're going to kill
the Molly. Maybe the Molly will kill them.'

The dancers moved like knives or scissors, the Molly or Fool
moved like an old man, they were all together, he was alone, and
my heart lurched, but I was powerless to change it, the story
crept slowly onward in front of us, the Molly wove pink and
uncoordinated between the hard leaps of the black dancers, and
very soon it would be too late –

In a snap decision, with the advantage of surprise, I yanked our little group round ninety degrees so all of us were staring at the foodstalls.

'What are you doing, Mon?' Angus roared. 'I was just getting into it.'

'Angus was just getting into it. What are you doing?' Boris echoed.

That was the trouble, I was into it too, I could see we were heading for another murder, and there had been one and a half already, seeing as Dad was only half-dead.

'Moving on,' I said to my siblings. 'Fairy's hungry, Fairy gets food!' Feeding her was a family obsession. But three black horses were following us, tall and deaf, three cones of malice, pursuing us in a dance of death, and, in the end, I faced them down, Monica alone: 'Get away from us!' Only then I realised they were just collecting; one cape flourished a yellow bucket. I found a crumpled twenty-pound note. 'OK, sorry, but now fuck off.'

We were quiet, for a bit. The Morris had subdued us. We queued sedately for soft ice-cream cones like the one Ma bought us on the beach one summer. She gave us ice-cream, she must have cared. We had to share, though. Was she short of money?

We sat in a row and schlooped with gusto, on plastic seats, under cruel lights that made us prematurely old, but it didn't matter – was I happy? A whole cold creamy ice of my own.

The fear had moved slightly further away.

'Great,' said Angus.

'Well done, Fairy.'

'Yuck, Mon, it's all down your front.'

'Give us a lick, mine is finished – '

'Sod off…oh all right, just a small one, no, *stop*!!! GIVE IT BACK!'

Yes, we were sisters and brothers again, I was on one end, but still included. I thought, 'Quite soon I might be arrested but, Monica Ludd, enjoy the moment!'

As I said, I am only human.

'It's eight o'clock, we're nearly late.' One of the Boys remembered the fireworks.

To the cliff-edge, still hand in hand!

By the railings there were hordes of people, standing about between us and the view. If it had just been the Boys and me, we would have forced our way straight through, no trouble, but we had to think of Fairy, who was wet and fragile, and Anthea, who got embarrassed.

But, 'Up the Ludds,' said Boris, softly, and, 'Ladies, come between Angus and me,' and then we were off, in a solid phalanx, a line of genomes like a battering ram; we slid through the crowd like a key through a key-hole, I was in a gang, it was happiness! Then the fireworks started, and words were useless.

No-one has ever called me romantic. Are they fucking blind? Of course, I'm romantic. Sparks from the rockets fell in flower-like sprays of purple and silver over their reflections, wrenching oohs and gasps from the crowd, melting even the drunk and disgruntled, the DFLs, Down From London, in their 'cool' vintage tweed overcoats, the loud teen couples getting pissed before a shag, the shrunken pensioners eking out nothing, the dog-tired teachers and longing artists. My humungous brothers, my titanic self, all for once lifted out of ourselves as the fireworks built to a multiple climax where all the balls were shot into the air – (score, Thanet! Thanet scored!) and the sky was a blazing palette of planets, and all of us were laughing, cheering, sighing. Yes, I, Monica, with all the rest, I sighed with my fellows, not an awkward guest, not a giant spare part in the universe.

And as the fireworks faded away, I saw the thin web of actual stars. Far and remote, but I still saw them. I saw them because we all looked at the fireworks. For one split second, I could feel small. When you're big as I am, that's a miracle.

'That was the dog's bollocks,' Boris said, and Angus laughed and said, 'Fuck yes, Boris.'

After it's over, though, you feel empty. Fireworks can only last twenty minutes. 'It's the most people can bear,' our school caretaker says, who, in another life, worked for Northwest Bangs and Flashes, the Midlands' biggest fireworks company. 'You're full of shit, Dan,' I said at the time, but now I think I see what he means.

Life's ninety per cent hell, and ten per cent beauty, and too much beauty might burn us out. But a little more. That's all I'm asking. A tiny bit more for Monica.

Maybe a boyfriend. One who dances.

As the crowd ebbed, I thought I heard children, multiple harp-strings of high thin voices; then the forced blare of a children's entertainer, 'Are you ready, girls and boys and undecideds? Let's have some hush for the very last performance!' We were ready to part, we were on our way home, but the sound of children always alerts me. 'Hang on a second,' I said to the others.

And then I saw it, at the very front of the second tent of the Festival: the red-and-white stripes of a puppet show. 'Punch and Judy!' I shouted to my sibs.

'It's, like, so old-fashioned,' Fairy complained, but soon we were standing, a wall of tall adults, watching the show, behind a cross-legged bunch of children, while parents leaned against walls looking anxious.

There was Punch, the father; Judy the mother; Baby, the baby;

and PC Percy, or whatever his name was, the useless policeman, with his big truncheon and outsize helmet. (Had Ginger ever worn uniform? Probably not, he was too bright.) Then there was the dog, and the string of sausages.

When we joined the audience, the Baby was getting it. Yes, everyone was hitting the Baby. One of the mothers in the audience had a pale gormless-looking boy on her lap and constantly commented on the action in a whisper: 'Isn't that naughty! *Isn't* that naughty! Isn't that silly? We don't do that.'

'It's not, what-d'you-call-it, PC, is it?' Boris said to me with a chuckle.

Naturally, all the Ludds adored it. Even Fairy was screaming and rocking about and some of the children turned and watched us; why were those grownups laughing so much? Thanet's essentially a quiet place. Things happen, though, behind closed doors, they happened to us, they will happen to others –

Children, learn to speak up for yourselves. If you stay silent, you have no chance.

We were all laughing uproariously as if nothing could be funnier than battering babies (of course, funny because Not Allowed). The worried mother in the audience was in full flood, 'Oh POOR little baby! Oh NAUGHTY Punch!' Every time they hit him, the Baby bounced back again. But then Judy stopped and chipmunk-twittered indignantly at Punch, who took no notice, and suddenly Judy had snatched the baton, and Judy hit Punch, and Punch hit Judy. We Ludds couldn't get enough of it, we were the riotous gang of giants at the back of the crowd of pale, puzzled children, looning and shrieking and falling about and clutching each other: it was SO funny, the funniest thing I had seen in my life, I was doubled up, wheezing in utter abandon, yes that was the way we'd survived it all, our demented childhood, laughing like monkeys –

Bish! Down again. Boing! Up again, there was Judy, there was the Baby, Judy long-faced with a frilled mob-cap, the Baby in an improbable striped onesie, Punch with a furious red face and a nose and chin that touched in the middle...

Bash! Now he had bounced back from the jail to which PC Plod had dragged him and yes, after a brief kiss with Judy the Baby started loud bleats of complaint and out came Punch's long enormous baton and bash, crash, thrash at the Baby till suddenly Judy had had enough, she snatched the stick and beat Punch in earnest, bash-bash-bash, BASH BASH BASH, and Punch was down for the very last time. Boris and Angus were barking and hooting, rocking, weeping with baritone laughter, my big stiff brothers, dissolved in joy –

Judy settled to nurse the Baby. But after a few seconds of contentment, there was worry. 'Where is he where is he where is he where is he?' squeaked her little electronic mouse of a voice.

And horribly, we saw Punch creep back, his movements furtive, damaged, baffled, sneaking up slowly on the mother and baby. 'Where is he where is he where is he where is he?' till Anthea could no longer contain herself and shrieked, 'He's behind you!' and we all joined in; none of us could bear it, 'Behind you, behind you, look out, he's BEHIND YOU!'

Now even the quiet parents of Thanet were trying to warn little worried Judy as she gibbered and jittered with Baby in her arms, 'WHERE IS HE WHERE IS HE WHERE IS HE?' she crescendo-ed, and then two things happened one after the other: Punch did a sudden leap on to her shoulders, and grabbed the baton, to screams from the crowd, then began to tug and wrench at the Baby, and after a minute Judy gave in and handed the Baby over like a present with a single weak little electronic mew – Fairy clutched my arm in horrified protest – but the Baby, transformed into Baby Hercules, reached up deftly and grabbed the baton back, BASH-BASH-BASH-BASH-BASH-BASH-BASH-BASH, Punch's head bounced about like a punchball, and yes, this time Punch was finished, the Baby had done it!

The crowd stayed silent – would he rise again?

But it was game, set and match to the Baby.

I could hardly believe it. Our side had won!

47   Adoncia

Next morning I tell him I go out for some milk. 'You want it from behind?' I say to him, 'You stay in bed and close eyes, Albert. Just ten minutes, you enjoy waiting, you think about it until I come back.'

I go next door to find bag in suitcase, the special bag that hold Luis's toys. Believe me, I ready to give it him. Yes, do it so quickly he never see me.

Métetelo por el culo, dentist. Up yours, Albert. From me to you.

But something funny come over me. I think of my daughter, and I not so happy. I need a little *pausa para fumar*. I take my *cigarillos* outside in the square, into miserable garden where dog is barking, miserable garden with too many trees.

I think, is Sunday. Juanita is praying. They take even the stupid ones to the *capilla*. Maybe I go away, leave Albert be.

But sun is bright, as if God is staring.

Vengeance. Is mine, like Bible say.

48

BISH BASH BISH BASH BISH BASH BOSH.

And then, starting slow as rainfall but rising to a storm of approval, relieved applause, whistles, cheers, with Anthea and I loudly 'Woo-woo'-ing.

Hot-cheeked, aerated by laughing and clapping, I turned to the others – my posse! my tribe! I was out on the town with my sisters and brothers – Boris, Angus, Anthea, but, oopsy, where the hell was Fairy?

Then I spotted her, head on one side, at the exit.

A blinking green EXIT sign coloured her curls and gave her snowy coat a grass-green glow: she looked like an extra-terrestrial, with her skinny legs and oblong body and hair like green and white candyfloss.

'I didn't like it, I didn't like it,' she was saying over and over again, thin fingers covering her eyes, waiting for somebody – Rupert? – to rescue her. 'It was so violent. I couldn't stand it.'

'Well that was the point of it,' I said, but I had a bad feeling under my ribcage – please note, Monica Ludd felt pity. Of course, I was impatient, why couldn't she enjoy it, any normal person enjoys a bit of bashing, but she looked as if she were about to fall over, as if Punch and Judy had drained all the current that made Fairy, the model, electric. The make-up had worn off her face and the livid red marks were like alien writing.

'We'd better get back,' Anthea called, though we had nowhere to go together (but we'd been somewhere: we had been out: the Ludd children had all gone out). 'Shall I give you all a lift, folks?'

No, the Boys had other ideas. 'Angus and me are off for a drink.' The boys exchanged one coal-black glance and started shifting from foot to foot, pawing the ground in unison. Anthea and I looked at each other: we knew that meant they were off on one of their once-in-a-while, tremendous pub crawls. (And no, we don't know how often that is. Was it once a year or once a week that the two jut-jawed Herculeses marched off blindly, into the night, into the bottle, to be carried home in a taxi at breakfast from one or other Thanet drinking club, legal, illegal, it didn't matter, totally, paralytically drunk?)

But who was to judge? Not me, not Mon. I liked a drink, I liked my gin. My Big Brothers had their giant battles, they were mountainous, rock-like, they could take it all and still get up sometime tomorrow morning and go to the gym, sore, roaring, but back on the treadmill, working their bulk into more blank muscle.

Oddly, this time Fairy went with them. My little sister with the two great boys. Angus called for a minicab. I managed to take her cold paws in mine and felt a sharp dig from Rupert's ring. 'Be careful, Fairy. Don't go back to him.' She didn't say anything for a long time. The mark on her face like a cattle brand. Her hands felt like the hands of a corpse, but at the last moment they twitched in mine.

'You be careful too,' she breathed, whispered. 'Thanks for, you know...Thanks, Mon.' And her long fingers slipped through mine, ten long bones, a skeleton, yet under the skin, her blood was mine.

Boris had something to say to me. 'Are you all right on your own?' he asked.

'What do you mean, all right on my own? I live on my own. I'm always fucking alone.' It sounded sad, but I gave him a grin.

'There's weird stuff happening,' he added. 'First Dad, then Veronica.'

'No-one would dare attack me,' I boasted.

Boris agreed. 'We all know you're fearless. When you went for Dad that time…'

'It was because he broke Fred's glasses.'

'He couldn't stand Fred having glasses –'

'Because he wanted him to go into the army –' All of us were talking at the same time as we walked along towards Anthea's jeep. The minicab was picking them up in ten minutes. The smell of cordite was still in the air and rocket-shells lay dead at our feet.

'It was because he didn't understand that Fred just had an astigma-thingy,' Fairy whispered.

'*Astigmatism*,' I shouted, strictly. 'Honestly, Fairy, get it right! Which wouldn't have affected him in combat. And the row was because Fred was watching TV and Dad had told him to rest his eyes, and I was next to Fred on the sofa –'

(I wanted to tell my moment of glory but Boris took over, talking louder.)

'And you went over and picked up Fred's glasses, and yelled at the old bastard, "You shouldn't have done that," and he was so surprised he stopped hitting Ferd and started on you, and you just took it!'

Bish Bash Bosh BISH BASH BOSH

Angus's turn. 'Yes, you're fearless.'

'Yes,' said Anthea, 'you are. Got to say it? Respect, Monica.'

So that was a full house. Monica was fearless. They thought I was, they needed to believe it.

We smiled at them as we put on our seat-belts, Fairy flanked by Boris and Angus, Fairy's head on a level with our brothers' because of the dizzy heels on her shoes, but her head still drooped towards one side and their big inflexible arms were round her: yes, the Boys were holding her up, and as we drove off, both Boris and Angus raised the hand of their outside arm at a perfectly identical angle, a synchronised salute to us.

Anthea and I drove away in silence.

'What time is it?' Anthea asked.

I looked. 'Only half-past nine'.

'Shall we pop and see Ma before bedtime? Tell her, you know, we've all been on an outing?'

I didn't like her coming on like a dutiful daughter. 'You just want to ask her what happened to Veronica.'

'Yes, don't you?'

'And about Dad. Yep, let's go.' Anything was better than back to Bay House for another long, long night alone.

'It's a bit late, though?' Anthea said doubtfully. 'What if she's asleep?'

'Wakey – WAYYY-Key!' Just a family joke, some radio catch-phrase from before we were born, the thing Dad yelled through the bedroom door when we were little and he shouted us awake to do our chores, and if we didn't answer…

Not a joke, a threat. Why didn't Ma wake us? Why didn't Ma do some of the chores?

'Anth, let's go.'

We were on our way.

49

Cliffetoppe's was already in semi-darkness. We peered into the foyer. No-one. Bells are for ringing. I rang, hard.

No-one appeared. I rang harder.

On my third assault, the lazy receptionist shambled out and pressed her face against the glass. Ma's friend. Name on the tip of my tongue.

'Don't be frightened,' I shouted, in case she was deaf. 'It's only me, Monica! Me and Anth! We've come to see Ma!'

'She will be asleep, sorry.'

'We want to see her! She is OUR MOTHER!'

'April is a resident. And my friend. Come back tomorrow.'

Yeah, fuck that.

I started rapping hard on the glass, I knew she wouldn't want a fuss, and sure enough, after a few seconds she opened the front door, and peered at us through a six-inch gap. The name wouldn't come. Was it Lizzie? She wore an unsuitable pink tracksuit.

'April's very tired. She's been under stress.'

This is when Anthea showed her mettle. 'Let us see our mother or we'll call the police?'

No reaction on Lizzie's fat face. I must have been about to punch her, because Anthea was staring at my clenched fist. Suddenly her tanned arm shot through the door and paused inches from the idiot's nose. 'Stop annoying my younger sister! She'll come back tomorrow if you tell us what's happening!'

'With reference to?'

'I'll have your wig off!' Anthea was a Ludd at last. She had actually got hold of a lock of hair.

I put my arm around her shoulders. Had I ever done that before? So long ago that I had forgotten. 'We want to know what happened to Veronica. Our father's girlfriend. It's OK, we know our mother found the body.' I was trying to sound calm and mature, easier to do when others are losing it, then I can come on like Mary Poppins. 'Anthea, let go of this woman's hair.' But I slammed my foot into the gap in the door.

There was a silence, then the ratbag yielded, talking to us in a silly stage whisper. 'It was very upsetting for your mother. She went round to your father's to feed the ferrets –'

'Why?' Anthea interrupted, and I gave her a hard, restraining shove. 'Let Lizzie get on with it, Anthea.'

'Lizzie's not my name, by the way. Your father is very ill, as you know.'

'How bad is he?'

'Recovering. He asked April to feed his ferrets. I offered but she said he only trusted her, then it turned out he'd asked Veronica too. Poor April found Veronica lying on the floor. Both the ferrets had bitten her. Wrist and neck. There was blood. Lots.'

'Ferrets are tiny. I don't believe it,' I said, thrilled, but my skin was crawling; we had always been frightened of going into Dad's study, and then I felt dizzy, because if we had done, his fucking pets might have actually killed us. I pulled back my foot to keep my balance.

'She had some problem, haemo-something,' the ghoul added with a burst of excitement. 'When ferrets get a grip on you, they can't let go. April had nothing to do with it.'

'Haemophilia,' Anthea said. 'It can't be true. I know it's not?

I've done personal training, the medical side? Haemophilia's just in men.'

'The policeman just rang. He said the same thing,' the woman blurted, forgetting to whisper. 'I don't believe it,' and the door slid shut.

We stared through opposite sides of the glass. She didn't look happy; her mouth was open. I stuck my tongue out at her as a joke, but then decided it was immature and tried to pretend I was licking my lips and pushed right through by accident. I couldn't tell if she'd got all that, she was walking firmly away from me.

My sister drove me back to Bay House. We hardly talked on the short journey. Dread was in the car between us.

I had left a standard light on in the kitchen, but as I opened the door to get out, the laurels blew between me and the beam so the lamp itself seemed to move and flicker. Briefly, it disappeared altogether.

Then it was back. Thank God it was back.

If haemophilia was just for boys…who had killed Veronica?

'Will you be OK, Mon? You'll be OK?' My big sister called through her car window. OK, she's thick, and fake Australian, her lips are fake, her tan is fake – but still, thank God, I have a sister.

Yet I was walking away from her. A younger Monica wanted her to stay, wanted her to come in with me and check each room, corner by corner.

But I would never ask her, and she would never offer. Loud and proud, I ploughed over the gravel. 'No, I'm fine, of course I am!' And as an afterthought, 'Safe home!'

'Same?' she twanged, and her engine gunned.

But she drove away, and I was alone.

50

A quiet night, surprisingly. I went to bed, I went to sleep. I had a dream that my phone was ringing, someone was trying to help and warn me, someone somewhere was looking out for me…

But I was missing it. Who was it? Yes, I had known, in the dream I knew, but as consciousness leaked back, the certainty faded.

Still it left a brief glow of happiness. A bird, confused by the light in the lobby which I'd left on to keep me safe, started a loud territorial song, although it was only 4 a.m. I tossed and turned. I thought about Fred, I thought about the family.

(Would the Boys and Fairy be rolling home, furry-throated, half-unconscious?)

I have a watchman, I thought to myself, the last thought before I slept again. This time the dream was clear. It was Ginger.

10 a.m. I had woken late. I had to hear the news. I hesitated then switched on my phone. Surely Ginger wouldn't track me down during a ten-minute bulletin?

Oh dear, the news was terrible. Another attack in Manchester. An 'Ecumenical Peace Council' had 'reached out' to other faiths. Three men had slit the speakers' throats and a fourth had shot at the audience, most of them university students. Mugshots of the dead had the open, well-meaning, shiny look of young Christians. Two others looked like the kids at school. My kids, yes. Monica's kids. What were the fucking adults doing? Nobody was saying who the killers were, though obviously they weren't Quakers. Suddenly I had to get outside. Everyone was mad, Britain was mad, something was wrong, in the house, in the garden.

I sat out on the verandah reading, wearing all my clothes, pyjamas underneath, jumpers, cape. By midday the sun was so unseasonably warm I was peeling off layers as the sentences came and eventually my blood pressure dipped and drowsiness dropped like a cloak of bees. Mon should sleep, she needed it… dull birds cooed in low comfort, the lawn was long, Dad was far away and Mum in a Home, home, hum, don't think about her, mum, mmmm, something too awful to think about, no, nonsense, enjoy the sunlight, someone was blowing leaves nearby, two or three houses along, or closer, or was it the sound of an engine idling, someone stopping in the road outside? But the sun was hot, I couldn't stay awake and then my lids were half-open again and something woke me up with a startle, a tiny ringing, a tingling, the twitching of some nerve-ending –

Now I was completely awake. I had sat too long, it was afternoon. The colours in the garden were always off, Ma had always moaned about it, red roses next to some Japanese tree that was yellow in spring and orange in autumn. Dad, of course, was colour blind. Not totally, or he couldn't have been a dentist. You have to be able to see the blood, you have to be aware of the damage. Now all the bushes seemed to loom towards me. The leylandii were like great blue truncheons, the sun shot spiteful spears through the gaps. Dad had planted them thoughtfully so the shade fell mostly on other people's gardens, but a line of dank shadow crawled over the lawn. Surely it wasn't getting dark again?

Somewhere near by, a phone was ringing.

My mobile sat safe in its black shroud on the table.

OK, it was the land-line.

Slow prickle of each hair on my body.

Only the family knew this number. It was ex-directory.

Was it our mother? Did she guess I was here?

Even worse, was it our father?

Then I was hurrying into the house, I tripped over the step and had to clutch at the wall as the dark of the hallway left me blinded, I charged on into the sitting-room where the black headset squats like a frog. It stopped in that second. I stared at it, willing it to ring again, but there was just an echo. The round old-fashioned dial was a sightless eyeball.

Probably just someone selling insurance.

Still I was rattled. I walked through the pines, down to the sea, doing big strides, looking straight ahead at November sun on wintry blue water, everything was clear, everything was open.

I eased myself down on to the steps by the beach huts and pulled my big knees up to my chest. The winter sun began to lull me again, as did the occasional passing of benign humans, no-one knifing or shooting anyone, young parents not hitting their children, dogs not shitting on the sand, old people not moaning or falling. Sometimes one of these paragons nodded, sometimes I nodded back to them. I am not a misanthropist, you see, though once I thought, 'Why is he with her?' about a dark athlete with a clapped-out woman wearing a fluffy angora hat, and the woman doubled back and said, 'Because he's my husband!', but as soon as I heaved myself up from the step for a chat, they hurried off in the opposite direction.

No, my afternoon was tranquil.

There is absolute horror, but I remain hopeful. I was still young, we could all recover.

I mustn't think about Ma, not yet. I mustn't think about them as a couple.

All the parents would grow old and die, all the old tyrants, if we only waited. Everything could only get better. Children would be taught to speak up (though not to shout out in the middle of my lessons). Justice would stop the terrorists: it had to happen, somehow, somewhere, history would let us look back on our actions and see what we were doing wrong (no, I should never have bought the axe, without the weapon I'd be in less trouble). Women would learn to stand up for themselves, and only suck the cocks they wanted – Ginger was a case in point. Adults who rape children would be executed. Monica would be in charge of the school. Monica would be in charge of most things. Dad would die in hospital and it would all be over. Maybe the Ludds could be a family again. Maybe I could have a family of my own?

Ginger, in fact, would sort things out. Ginger, fearless, with hair, taller…I started to snore, I was dozing again, but the stone of the steps was a little chilly –

I liked deck-chairs, I wanted a deck-chair. I wrenched a deck-chair from the neatly chained stack. It took a long while, and did a bit of damage.

I put the thing up, hacking my shins and trapping my fingers between the sides. Eventually I had it at the right angle – the rest of the pile was strewn about at random like a pile of cards, but it wasn't my fault. Errors were made, I would see that in time, but I *just had to sit in that fucking deck-chair.*

Yet it didn't feel right. I was trapped in it. Once I was down, I could not get up. Deck-chairs aren't very comfortable.

If anyone came after me, I couldn't escape. The other deck-chairs were a cubist mess. It hadn't improved my afternoon. I looked for another source of pleasure.

Parking my cape and sunglasses, I walked the twenty metres

to Bone Bay Café to buy the ice-cream Dad had refused us. The woman who had served me double breakfasts didn't recognise me at first.

'Isn't it a bit cold for ice-cream?' she said.

'Thanks for the advice. Strawberry Ripple.'

'Small or large?'

'Family Tub.'

'How many spoons?'

'One will do.'

She looked at me again and her mouth dropped open. 'Oh yes, I thought it was you!'

I lowered myself cautiously in my deck-chair and hung there like a great baby in a cradle. But I'd put the ice-cream down too far away. I prised myself up again, peeled off the lid, moved it closer, with a happy sigh, settled back down into my seat, reached out my hand for the ice-cream – FUCK!

'YOU FUCKING BASTARD!'

A giant seagull, hook-beaked, quick, eyes a-glitter, was trying to fly away with my ice-cream, the tub clasped in its strong yellow beak, but it couldn't rise more than a foot above the ground, and I shot out of the chair so fast I nearly charged off the edge of the prom.

OK, I kicked it. The flurrying bird. My foot connected. Bones, feathers. It dropped the ice-cream – more waste, more mess. The promenade looked like a battleground. I watched the seagull. It wasn't flying straight.

Yes, yes, I know that seagulls are endangered. But bear in mind, I had been assaulted, it wasn't serious, it might still recover…

How much is justified in self-defence?

51 Adoncia

I sit there in the square and my heart drum fast, so I smoke some more, it always helping me. I think, no matter what I do, he deserve it, he spoil my *cara* and I lose my *cariño*, my face get ugly and I lose my darling. I mad with hatred for the dirty bastard, and yet, part of me still not decided.

Then I go upstairs and I hear him shouting. Maybe he complain that I not there? Soon he get something to complain about!

I leave Luis's toolkit outside bedroom door, and as I bend down to get *cacheporra*, I hear him calling. 'Adoncia! Donkey! What are we fucking waiting for?' Yet he not too angry, is a laugh in his voice.

I open door quiet, very quiet, and see him from back and side in the sunlight, poor Albert, he helpless in bed like baby, he can't see me, he can't hear me. For a moment, *me duele el corazon*, I don't know why but my heart hurt me, almost I go to stroke his hair. But then I realise I have cosh in hand, so now I happy he can't see me.

I hit him, hard, again and again. He never see me, he quiet straight away. I hear myself shout, *'Dios mio!'* He groan two times so I hit him again. Soon he like a squash strawberry.

52 Monica

That night again the checking, the re-checking. Nobody was in the house (it was just me, the mice, the spiders, and Monica Ludd does not fear THEM). Which made me think about our mother: how often did she scream for me to save her from spiders? She would be on the sofa with her feet pulled up, 'Oh Mon, Mon, it'll run on me, get it!' Once the poor hairy thing had been reduced to a black, tangled squidge of limbs, Ma would be tearful with gratitude – 'Mon, Mon, you're never afraid' – though that never lasted for more than two seconds.

(Why should I do her dirty work? Why should I always be the one?)

When I can't sleep, I sometimes make up crosswords, little 3 x 3s, a cube of three-letter words. MA wouldn't do it, but MAD could. MAD across the top, MUD down the left side, I didn't want it but DAD across the bottom and then the right side had D blank D and all I could see was DAD all over it, DAD was everywhere, I fell asleep.

I dreamed the Girl was a part of me. She was in my belly, trying to get out of me. She had to get out before her periods started or all of us would be drowned in blood. I wanted to protect her, but also escape her, because something horrible was trying to engulf her, a huge red shape just out of sight…In the dream I half-knew it was already too late. Too late for me, too late for her, he had us all, we were all done for, they held me down by the hair, on the floor…

I woke up on a tide of terror and was relieved to find it was 8 a.m., the room was square, normal, full of sunlight, there were angles of sky in the three-part mirror, it didn't matter that my parents once slept here, that Dad had had sex with the Girl, and my mother, and who knew how many women before her?

Mon, Mon, stand up to him.

Stand up to him, stand up to her.

Yes, I had to go and see Ma.

I took a taxi: thank God I had money.

I pressed the buzzer – 'It's Monica' – and strode into Cliffe-toppe's bold as brass. Yes, I was a normal next-of-kin, I wasn't wanted by the police. There was the old woman in the pink tracksuit, her skin looked scaly in the sharp daylight, I should know her name by now, shouldn't I? Yes, it was Liz. She stared at me.

'What are you staring at, Liz?' I asked her. (Actually, I fear I slipped, and said 'Lizard'.) It didn't matter, I was past her already.

'Nothing.' She started writing on a pad. When I was far enough away, she said, 'My name is Nikki. I reminded you quite recently. Usually guests sign in in Reception.'

'Really? Sorry. Don't be over-sensitive. Liz and Nikki, it's an easy mistake.'

'No, it's not, they're nothing like.'

She was quarrelsome! We had to sort things out. I made an effort, I doubled back, stood very close and looked her in the eye. 'Right, *Nikki*. You seem edgy with me.'

There was a pause while she trembled, then she spoke up bravely. 'Have you forgotten you and your sister punched me?'

Oh God yes, at the end of Fred's Party, she must have been the person who tried to interfere in that small disagreement Anth and I had in the toilets. 'Must have been Anthea. She was grieving. You should let bygones be bygones, Lizzie.' It made me laugh to remember that night; we were both so drunk, and she so sober, surely she would see the funny side? But she just stared resentfully.

Upstairs, Ma was dressed and sitting at the table.

'Well done, Ma, you're out of bed.'

'So people like to tell me', she said, almost slyly, with a lift of her head. I pecked her on the cheek. She avoided me.

'Do you want a sherry, Ma?' As soon as I'd said it, I remembered. 'Sorry.'

'No,' she said. 'I'm not an alcoholic. Some people try to make me drink.'

'We never had to make you, Ma.'

'Other people, friends of mine, say those people don't have my best interests at heart.'

I happened to know she had no friends. She must be talking about Lizzie. No, *Nikki*. (I can learn, there's hope.)

'You haven't been around much, have you,' she continued. 'Somebody told me you're in trouble,' she added, and covered her little mouth, and giggled. 'Somebody said you'd gone on the run.'

I didn't like people laughing at me. I wanted to believe my mother loved me. The boys remembered her breastfeeding me. ('You were a greedy great thing, Mono! She couldn't get you off the tit!') And she had read to me. Hadn't she? She sat there, tiny and shrivelled, my mother, and I thought, she's a complete enigma.

'What do you know about Dad?' I asked her. 'Anything? I need to know.'

She drew herself up like an indignant meerkat. 'What do *you* know?' she snapped back, and suddenly her eyes looked very sharp. 'I'm visiting him. In the hospital.'

'Have you really seen him, Ma? How is he?'

'Dad asked for me. Naturally he would. Nikki drove me.'

She called him 'Dad'. It was an age since she had called him that. 'Naturally he would.' There was nothing natural.

'I thought you were afraid of him?'

She looked obstinate. 'You exaggerate. Children always exaggerate.'

'You haven't seen him for years. Have you?'

'How do you know? We have interests in common. Just because he made a few mistakes.'

Who was this new, hostile mother? I swallowed hard. There was a lot to take in.

Then she continued, more conciliating, 'I thought he'd want to talk about dying. You don't refuse to see a dying man. And wills. We have to think about them.'

'He's definitely dying?' Blessed relief. She'd always had a good head for money.

'No, he's recovering. His jaw is bad.'

'How bad is he?' A wave of fear. The blood was banging in my head. *Thud, thud, Monica Ludd.*

Her teensy face screwed up like a lemon. 'Looks like a monster,' my mother said with a definite smack of satisfaction. 'Tubes. Monitors. Charts. Bandages.'

Phew. I relaxed a bit. But then she sat straighter and peered at me. 'He's getting better every day. Why does your father keep mentioning you?'

'What's Dad saying about me?' It came out between a shriek and a wail, the fear was boring through my entrails, I wanted to shake the truth from her, I was on my feet, I needed to move, but the room was so small I only stepped two paces, I was standing right in front of her –

No, I must never frighten my mother, never upset or worry her.

'Don't shout at me.' The familiar whine, a reversion to the voice of my childhood.

'What happened to Veronica?' I asked her. 'I hear it was you who discovered her. What were you doing in Dad's house?'

'Dad's house now, is it? Half that house belongs to me.'

'You said harsh words about Veronica the last time that I came to see you.'

'I never did,' she insisted. 'Don't go telling these wicked lies!'

'Ma, did you murder her?' I couldn't believe I had managed to ask her. The words, painful, enormous, hideous, clogged the room like horse-apples. In the background, the radiator ticked. I stared at the spongeable brown carpet that covered the washable vinyl floor, they could get anything out, any stains, any mess, but what I had said would sit there for ever.

Ma was pulling herself to her feet, blue-veined, bony, tiny hands gripping the shiny arms of her plastic chair. 'Did you try to kill your father?' she shrieked (which was shocking – little Ma never shouted.) Her wild hair shone like thin white silk in the fluorescent light and her eyes flashed red. I had a sudden vision of Albertina, the first ferret Dad had kept, a lone white animal and therefore vicious, ferrets need exercise, companions – it tried to bite Dad and he brought it out and explained all this as he broke its neck, then left the body in the kitchen sink. 'Dispose of it!' Dad had shouted. 'Why are you looking at me like that? These kids must learn!' Yes, we had learned.

'Did you attack him?' her thin voice wheedled. 'He says you did. He's sure of it. The first thing he remembers, you were there.'

The words ran through my innards, my organs, wiping my brain, curdling my blood. I found I was leaning against the door, clutching myself, wounded, winded.

Maybe she saw the effect she had had. Slowly, she sank back into her armchair, patting her hair, trying to look demure, her mouth shrinking on its prim drawstring. 'I told him he might be wrong,' she whispered. 'I said, she's always been a good girl.

You've always been a good girl, Monica. Always been a good girl to your mother.'

I had a sudden desire to vomit. Monica Ludd has a strong stomach, but had they always been in it together, my meek little mother, my raging father?

'Toilet,' I muttered, and made for her en suite, but she raised her mouse-paw in agitated protest. 'Use the one in the corridor.'

'What?'

'They haven't been in to clean it yet!'

I had a vision of senile hell, the sterile white walls covered in shit, the two of them up to their eyes in it –

I plunged out of the door and down the corridor, trying to control the surge inside me. I was starting to close the peach-pink door of the air-freshened 'WC' on the landing (silhouette of a crinolined lady) when I heard the sound of whistling. God, it was him, my Dashing White Sergeant, no, not possible, couldn't be, but then I glimpsed him through the crack, marching down the corridor, pink, healthy, grimly confident, DI Ginger, my bold pursuer, and in an instant I slammed the door shut.

Thud-a, thud-a, thud-a, Monica. The urge to vomit instantly died, stifled by my urge to survive. I heard him knocking on Ma's door. Then a long pause. I was poised to run. Mum would be wondering what was happening. The instant I heard her door open for Ginger – 'Ah, good morning, Mrs Ludd!' – I was off my marks and down the stairs, then pounding powerfully out through the lobby.

Yes, there was a brief unfortunate spat with a wicked old biddy on a walking frame, I may have knocked her slightly off course but pensioners really shouldn't say 'cunt', hahahaha, HAHA-HAHA, in other circumstances we'd have been pals – and then I was out through Cliffetoppe's front door, the briefest snapshot of two covered women gawping at me as they alighted from a taxi, I pushed them aside and threw myself in, one of them shouted in Arabic, or no, I realised, extremely poor English, and pushed her complicated face into mine, head-scarf, spots, lipstick, glasses, they paid their money with agonising slowness, making ill-phrased remarks about me, I gave orders to the driver, we were away.

Quite enough excitement for one day.

53

One more night, one more night of scribbling, then I'll be ready to hand myself in, hands in the air, 'I'm Monica, sorry to give you the runaround, Ginger!'

One more night and I'll be done.

My family, the Ludd family – yes, I will have told our story. We are not like other families.

Why did my father have to die? I corrected myself – he wasn't quite dead. The biter bit; the beater, beaten.

Tempting, now, to finish the job. If I could smuggle myself into the hospital where he lay plotting to murder me.

> *Monica Ludd, Girl-with-an-axe,*
> *gave her father forty whacks –*
> *When she saw what she had done*
> *she gave the cunt another one.*

But no no no. It's not the way forward. Only violence comes from violence. Nothing can come from nothing, Mon.

Violence, though – it's not nothing. Do something and you exist. You exist, your victim doesn't.

They must feel joy, the runaway killers, the lonely American classroom shooters, the ISIS slicers, the Islamic State Haters, the loonies who attack the mosques, boys who unleash their dogs of war – now in an instant, total freedom, hearts pounding, drugged to the eyeballs, a chest full of ecstatic air exploding into that single second.

ISIS. Odd that they had that name. I knew about Egyptian gods from teaching. Isis was the Egyptian goddess of wisdom, wife of Osiris in the *Book of the Dead*. Isis helps the dead on their journey.

Way back when I first started teaching I got some Year 7s to copy sections from the Living Egypt website on to cardboard. 'Copying teaches them to concentrate,' I assured a mother who complained – well, one of the mothers who complained. I was very young, I was still learning. 'It also teaches accuracy. Your Jodee does not lead the field at either.' (It also let Monica catch up with her marking.)

'Isis, she who gives birth to heaven and earth, who knows the orphan, knows the widow, seeks justice for the poor and shelter for the weak.'

Did ISIS once believe in justice? Were they driven mad by what happened to them, the bombs raining down, with no recourse? Bursting in from outside, in their land, their space?

Dad did not see us, he did not hear us, he would not stop, there was no appeal, he was in our face, in the bedroom, the bathroom, he burst in on us, we had done nothing, nothing could shelter us from his blows.

Till we grew up. Till we grew stronger.

I could have done it. I would have done.

54 *Adoncia*

Then doorbell ring like God bringing vengeance. I drop my *porra* and go to the window.

My stomach hurt like I having baby. Albert bleed everywhere. He moaning again. I look down from window and see her, big woman, big stupid lump of woman on the pavement. I have to get rid of her to finish the business, it only half done, no stopping now. She shouting up like she wake the dead, and I run downstairs before neighbour get nosy, and she say, 'I come to see my father,' and then I realise she look like him, she have his blood, she have his bone. This must be poor ugly daughter Mono, the one he tell me like chimpanzee. I try to talk to her very nice but she stubborn so I close door in her face.

Then I hit the head of Albert again, he never respected MY head, did he? He never respected no-one's head, no-one was safe from Señor Albert, he steal from mouth, he steal from jaw, he steal from patients while they asleep, he steal Adoncia's youth and beauty away from my Luis who one time adore me, but now I fix him so he steal no more.

Funny thing – after I hit him for a while, it no longer feel like anyone there.

I start to feel tire, I almost bore. It seem like hours, but the head not break. Few time in Malaga when some little thing happen, some small problem I have to settle, I always have my people do it, quick, get job done and tell me nothing.

I never realise how long it take.

I never know how hard to get clean.

I never know, how sad, how untidy. When I smell hand, it still bloody.

Then I sit him up like big doll on pillow, I pull up jacket like frame for his head, I take my *porra* and run to my car.

Asi, I learn about bad dream.

Is so much blood. Oh Jesus and Maria.

Part 8

The Final Door

55 Monica

I've tried everything to help me sleep.

I dosed myself with tepid milk, DISGUSTING, made my bed-time round of the house, which never got easier, that heart-trip moment when adrenalin pushes a door open. Everything in order, I was ready to drop, lay down on the bed for a read before bedtime, chose *The Castle of Otranto* and fell asleep on the very first page.

Of course, I was awake thirty minutes later, semi-darkness, alas not morning. The light still on on the bedside table, my eyes heavy but my limbs twitching, doze, dozing, with fluttering lids.

Then I jerked fully awake again. Dim, in the distance, among the low hum of traffic passing on the Margate road, a car engine was getting louder, a car engine was coming nearer, someone had turned off towards Bone Bay, someone was driving down our private road, headlights veered across the window through the curtains, someone was coming to this end of the road, *no, no, don't come here*, then the long rolling crackle of tyres on gravel. There was gravel where the made road ended, the part that served the last two houses.

No, of course, it would just be the neighbours. Good, my neighbour, I could do with one.

But there was gravel right here as well. The drive ran up to the back door.

Yes, the fear. I do feel fear, it was here, huge, under my ribs, squeezing ever tighter down the back of my head, my throat, my thighs…

But then, nothing. Not a sound.

I listened, intent, my whole body an ear. I imagined, awaited, the car door slamming. No, nothing. No slam, no footsteps. Slowly the terror leaked away, my angry heartbeat returned to normal. Silence, surely, meant no-one was there.

Yes, it must have been next door. Who was the man? Some kind of lawyer? Lawyer, yes, his holiday house. I seemed to think his name was Horace, I had met him once by chance in the road and asked him not to tell my father; yes, it was he who insulted me! 'I've come to tidy up as a surprise for Dad,' I explained, lying through my teeth. 'Were you thinking I was a burglar?' 'Hardly, you're the image of your father.' 'Dick-brain!' I said. I don't think he minded.

It was a good thing he was here.

All the downstairs windows were closed. I remembered closing them, one by one, though I wasn't absolutely sure about the kitchen window, but no, I'd closed it, I must have done. Could there be someone there, in the car, sitting outside, breathing, waiting?

Dad must be in the hospital, rails on his bed, drugs in his bloodstream, lying impotent, dreaming, brooding.

Mustn't think about our father brooding. 'They won't get away with *that*,' was his mantra. 'I won't let them get away with *that*.'

Oh, I won't get away with it. The wind was creaking in the tree outside the window, groaning and rustling as the night grew colder. I didn't like it when things rubbed against the glass, but it was just the magnolia.

Dad got away with everything, always. Till someone stopped him. The yellow-haired woman? Someone hit the nail on the head. He would never be the same. And I was glad.

But oh, the thought of him hideously damaged. How would I look at him again?

No, I couldn't stay in bed. Any action was better than none.

I got up, went over to the dressing-table, connected the friendly green light on my lap-top, sat myself down in that strange vain posture, writing towards myself in the mirror, slightly askew because I was too tired to cram both thighs into the well between the drawers. I could see, in the glass, the door and the landing stretching away behind my powerful head, my poor big head with its fizzing brain, crammed with the last great upchuck of thought –

Go on, Monica! Get it out!

Everything will be done by morning.

So I began. There were things to say. Simple things that needed saying.

Things about the importance of order: no justice without order.

That's why our wars were such a disaster: Britain and America destroyed order. We didn't have anything to put in its place. Ditto, later, the Brexit posse. Ditto Erdoğan, Putin, Trump. Tear up the law and then – whoopsie!

I, Monica, avoid that error. I scare my classrooms into silence. Once they are quiet, they can hear their own voices, one by one, in orderly sequence. Without order, there is just the dark. I fight my way out of it every morning. I struggle not to be a maniac, I have a job, I hold it down, I try to preserve order for others, I try to keep order in my head.

That isn't all.

I breathed, I yawned.

I leaned my elbows on the dressing-table, folded my arms, rested my head. It was a quarter to one: I was not unhappy. I knew, somehow, though I didn't know when, DI Ginger would come and find me. And when he took me in, I'd be safe, because society has rules and procedures and Ginger was a part of them – wasn't he? Well, he did let me suck his dick – a bit unorthodox while on duty – but my bad for suggesting it, and basically, he was the law. Human beings seem to need it. Whereas life under Dad was random chaos, shouting, beatings, humiliations.

And then the chaos came for him. Dad on the bed, great sprays of blood, spattered on the floor, the wall, the window, pyjama jacket round his bludgeoned head, his eyes like button-holes, black, winking, under the dreadful bloodstained hood.

Something was moving behind the lid.

I had slipped into a loop of terror, I was in his house, the bloodied chamber, I must have been dozing, it was just a dream, but then something was moving outside the window or inside the window, a flicker, a tic.

I jerked upright and looked in the mirror. Nothing. Three panels of a static triptych, artificial light, sharp shards of shadow, the normal doorway, the normal landing which rounded a corner, true, into darkness, but I had already checked the rooms, the normal curtains with their chintzy patterns, a very slight swell where the small upper window was slightly open, normal, so normal, its bar impaled on the second hole.

263

I settled back in my seat again.

One more look for reassurance.

The curtain was moving. *The curtain was moving.*

Yes, that's fine, the window's open, the little top window, it must be the breeze…I was perfectly safe, they were leaded windows, the casement window was firmly closed.

But the orange curtain was moving oddly. It was poking out like a veiled erection, as if something stiff was pushing beneath it, forcing it inwards, into the room.

My chest was thumping like a drum. Two beats then a missing one, a missing one, a missing one. *Don't be thick, Mon, it's just a freak, the way the light falls, the Thanet breeze.* But my heart was pounding, my chest was heavy, I fell headlong into another story, not the one I was just concluding with happy thoughts about law and order.

In the new story, I was quite alone.

The lump behind the curtain had gone. But I had seen it.

I did see it.

No! There would be nothing behind the curtain, out on the balcony, trying to get in…

But I couldn't quite make myself get up to confirm it. I sat there staring at the window. Nothing.

Then another slight shift in the orange patterns, my legs were trembling, then stillness again.

Oh, did I hear something heavy and hopeless, slowly dragging itself along, the very faintest shifting and sliding, somewhere outside, just outside the window, heavier than leaves, heavier than branches?

As I looked, the curtain poked out again –

I realised, God, God, it's the bar that holds the little top window open, someone has unfastened it, someone is forcing it, that's what's pushing the curtains out, *soon a hand will be reaching through and trying to undo the main window –*

If I stayed frozen, it would happen, it would always happen, it would happen again

I knew it was Dad

Dad would get in

he had not been stopped, he had come for me

and cold ice strangled my voice, my legs, I was closing down, I was locking up –

but I burst to my feet with a great effort that left me with my chest exploding, would I die of fear, of a heart attack, '*Mon, our sister, she was always fearless*' – did they not realise I was always hurting? I was on my feet, my strong legs and feet, if I had to die, I would die standing, I would fight the bastard, I would try to survive him –

I ran to the window shouting, 'Who the fuck's there?' My voice was huge and raw and strained, the voice of a woman who was a man, I'd be a man and stand up to him –

I wrenched apart the curtains: my own reflection, cut into diamonds by the leaded panes. Beyond it, the night, the clouds, the moon, moving trees; nothing, no-one.

In a few long moments, my heartbeat slowed. I tried to look sideways along the balcony: the moon shivered on the leaves of the tree and shone white on the painted table. The last metre of the balcony was out of view, but no, there was no-one.

No.

I was wrong.

I stood and breathed. And breathed again. Yes, I was cold, but I was sweating. I told myself, You're all right, Mon. It's just your fucking imagination.

I could have gone further, I could have actually unlocked the glazed door on to the balcony and checked the garden, *I should have done*, but no, I still couldn't bear to do it, I could not unlock the final door for absolute terror of what I might find there.

I'd built a life. I grew up. I am Monica.

I bought a house. I am a Deputy Headteacher. I do my duty. But the fear's always there.

56 *Adoncia*

I do it all but my pain still here. His head so hard, same like his heart.

His teeth all smash, and his eye, I think. I tired after as if I dig garden. I wish I dug grave and put him in it, but no, I must run once Monica come there.

I drive to Gatwick and catch plane back to Malaga.

Not even for one day I happy.

On plane I remember how I dream, at first, I going to have a new life in England. No crime, nothing, nothing bad.

We went little drive in my car one day. Everything new and sun was shining. Luis still behave as if he love me. We drive near Broadstair, big nice houses, garden with roses, everything. I see the name: 'Western Esplanade'.

I think one day our café make money and Luis and I are living in heaven.

57   Monica

Everything would be OK in the morning. Just five or six hours left till daylight. I only had to get through one night, then the sun would come and make everything normal. I'd drink a mug of strong tea in the kitchen (I needed some now, but could I go downstairs? No, I dare not go downstairs) – I would hear the sea and those fat birds cooing, Dad would be safe in the hospital, sedated, wheezing, tied down with tubes – I'd finish my diary, I'm nearly there, another page or two will do it. I'll telephone Ginger, he'll drive straight round.

1.30 a.m. I had closed the curtains. Maybe I should call Ginger now? I had my mobile in my trouser pocket, the scrap of torn paper with his number – did I?

Have you still got it, idiot? My fingers were suddenly clumsy and eager, but yes, a tiny scrap of paper no bigger or stiffer than a chewing-gum wrapper, something very small can save your life, something very small and quiet. Yes, I had it.

No, tomorrow. Let him sleep. I'll cope alone.

This is the thing I want to tell you. Dangerous fathers, complaisant mothers, porn addicts, phone addicts, alcoholics and online gamblers and ordinary parents with no fucking clue, all of them deaf to the small and helpless, never listening when the children speak – soon those kids will have their turn. The future's overrun with them: brutal soldiers, violent preachers, butchers, beheaders, battering husbands, screaming harridans, social misfits, all of them screaming, Look! Listen!

Me, Monica. Walking damage. Trying to contain myself.

Somewhere here I'll find my ending. Wait till tomorrow. It will all be clearer.

Birds hooting. A fox screams. Or else it was a human scream. Long, wild, utterly despairing. Flesh crawls on my great tired arms. Suffering is everywhere.

No, it must be the sound of vixens.

But in a quick blind rush I charge down the corridor, passing closed doors on every side, tugging the light-cord on in the bathroom. Flat dull light of 2 a.m. Do a great piss like a sleepy horse. Back up the corridor. Why undress? Sleep in my trousers.

Head on the pillow. Blood thumping. Door locked, house checked, no-one there.

And yet, and yet…no hope of sleep. You know that, Monica. Yes, yes.

Now, wakefulness, be my watchman.

Monica Ludd will play a game, dear little crosswords, 3 x 3s. What to do when sleep eludes you. Easy game for a genius. Little boxes of nine letters.

First 3 x 3: across the top, GIN, left going down, you can't have GER, it's not a word, so yes, let's try GET.

(Yes, GET GINGER, Monica, listen. No, don't listen to a voice in your head.)

Right side now, going down: NOT. Not get Ginger, not till morning, not too late.

Across the middle we have E blank O, the E in GET, the O in NOT.

EGO. Let the child speak. I cried to Anthea, she pitied me, one day she stood up for me. Yes, my sister tried to save me.

Bottom three, I was just a TOT. But down the middle we have garbage, IGO, I go to sleep *long for sleep... will never sleep*

But I must have done, because not long later I jerked awake in absolute terror, something was shining on my face, Dad was coming through the open door from the landing, pulling one damaged foot behind him, black against the oblong of yellow light, and I tried to scream but nothing happened, tried to swing my legs off the bed before he was on top of me, couldn't move –

Then I really woke. No, there was no-one. My heart was going so fast I might die, desperate, racing hooves in my temples –

The chink of light on to an empty landing. I timed my pulse by the chill moon of my watch-face. Nearly 200 beats per minute. Terrible numbers. 2.20 a.m. Five hours left. I would not survive. I had slept for ten minutes. It was inhuman. *I could not get through this night alone.*

Before I could make a conscious decision, I had grabbed my phone from the bedside table, switched on, naked, ready for Ginger, and pressed Anthea's phone number.

Her sleepy voice. 'Monica? It's the middle of the night? You've woken me up?'

'Antler, please. Sorry, Anthea…Anthea…' I couldn't say it.

'Monica? You're sounding weird? Are you all right?'

'Anthea, it's just – Anth, I'm scared.' The childish word was easier to say. 'I don't suppose – Could you come to Bay House?'

'Mon, are you joking, you're never afraid!'

I said nothing. Then, 'Yes. I am.'

'I'll come in the morning. I'll come first thing. Have you had a bad dream?'

'Something like that.'

'Want to talk about it?'

Talking wouldn't help. 'No, fine, see you in the morning.' And I rang off.

Damn, damn, I wished I hadn't rung her. Now I was more awake than ever.

No, I could not lie there in the dark. My eyes ached, I longed for oblivion, but every part of me twitched and resisted.

I slid out of bed and a sudden clatter pronged at my ribcage – it was just my mobile, fuck, I had knocked it on the floor. Yes, I was insanely jumpy.

Put the light on, Monica.

OK, get up and write some more before you finally fall asleep. Yes, the dressing-table, yes, the mirror. No, I didn't want to see my own face, huge, haggard Monica.

Yet she is always waiting there.

Monica, sullen, yellow-skinned, haunted, hair hanging down like hanks of dark wax (when had I actually last washed it?). Monica Ludd, slovenly, shapeless, a mountain topped by a great flat face, her one striking feature black frowning brows, that V of anger and fear between them. Now I remember with a leap of rage something Dad said when I was twelve or thirteen. 'I'm ashamed of you. Have you looked at yourself?' It was when I first started putting on weight.

Who cared about him? I refused to care. I wanted to be fat, I needed to be large, then nobody could make you – nobody would make you –

The mirror flickered. The darkness moved. Infinitely quietly, some-one was whistling. It was in my head. I was going mad. *Tantivy, tantivy* – it was in my brain, an echo of that mocking doorbell. I listened again: absolute silence. In the mirror, only stillness.

A split-second pause, then I heard my name. 'Monica?' And then, louder, in a mocking singsong, 'Mon i-ca? Mon-i-ca?'

Then he emerged in triplicate, horribly multiplied, coming for me, a hideous mummy-wrapped head in the mirror but he was actually twelve feet behind me, closing, closing, it was really happening, freezing horror, he was running, limping, stumbling fast down the corridor towards me –

I spun round to meet him, his leg was dragging, he bounced off the wall, no, he recovered, he was in through the doorway, an inchoate roar, the knife I had bought was on the bedside table but oh, I didn't know how to use it, and God, what if my father seized it – I saw it happening, blood on the bed, blood on the carpet, the wall, the bedding –

Yes, my phone, quick get the phone. I managed to press 'redial'. Anthea answered but before I could speak the phone was snatched like a toy from my hand –

The bull was on me, tripping me, tupping me, bearing me down with the force of his rush –

I fell backwards on the bed, yelling, 'Get *off* me,' his hot raw meaty breath on my face, 'You wanted to kill me, Monica?' His strong steel hands were gripping my shoulders, lifting and dropping me on the bed as I struggled to get my strong legs underneath him to knee him, anywhere, push him off. 'Did you want to kill your dear old father? Did you think you'd get away with it?' He shook me every few words for emphasis, his fingers digging in like metal bands, his bulk blocked out the bedside light; he pushed me down into the bed-covers which smelled of dust and stale feathers; I was going down into the dark of the past but I turned my head and bit him hard, I bit his hand like a joint of chicken, I had strong teeth, I would not let go till they closed upon my father's bone and, 'Fuck, fuck,' he roared, he raged, 'You fucking bitch, I'll finish you,' but with the biggest effort of my long harsh life I pushed up my knees and half-heaved him off me. I knew he was hurt, but he wouldn't let go, his one good hand was gripping the mattress, but my thrust had made him lurch to one side and for the first time I saw him clearly, the bedside light fell across his face and I saw the dressings, one leaking yellow, the bruises everywhere, blue, maroon, his whole face sore as a rotted fruit, his broken nose, the line of red stitches, rusted, crusted, two front teeth gone – I could have punched him but I *could not* punch him –

Oh God, I was grappling with a mess, not a man, a great heavy doll, horribly broken

he thought that I was the one who broke him

It's what he shouted at us kids, *'I'll break you'* –

a great uprush of fear and pity. I had one hand across his bandaged throat, pushing hard at his Adam's apple, I was nearly up, I
could roll him off me, what if I tore away those dressings? – no,
not yet that final horror, it would all flood out, stinking, festering

no, please no, I had something to say, I was his daughter, *I was not
guilty* –

'I didn't do it,' I found myself panting, 'I DIDN'T ATTACK YOU!
It wasn't me!'

He had never listened, he wouldn't now I had to say it, but
his gaze didn't flicker, the savage red of his one good eye, so I
squeezed his throat with desperate power, he released his grip
with a gasp of anger and quickly I slid sideways off the bed and
both of us somehow stumbled to our feet, standing on opposite
sides of the bed, panting, sweating, regrouping, swaying, and
Dad was coughing with pain and fury.
    'Maybe you have a point,' he panted. He was leaning forward.
I thought, 'I can see you, now I could punch you,' but the bandages, the small yellow leak now blooming into a big sour flower,
growing wetter and pinker as it spread outwards, his wounds
were bursting, his stitches torn, all the vileness, all the foulness,
nothing for it but to bring him down, but

*no, Monica, breathe and listen. You are an adult, a Deputy Head, you
believe in dialogue and justice.*

'Maybe there are things we could talk about,' he said, straightening up with an effort. His face was straining, hideous. Oh, I realised, he was trying to smile. 'You've got blood on your mouth. Are your teeth all right?'

Yes, of course, Dad was a dentist, but it got to me, it actually moved me, my father showed concern for me, diddums, Monica, don't let him do it, Dad has always been an actor, but I put my hand to the wet on my face, and looked at my fingers, and they were red.

I said, 'It's your blood.' The blood we shared. I looked with shame on his damaged face. Why did we all have to hurt one another? Just for a second, I closed my eyes. Hide us all. End the horror.

In that second's blindness, Dad was upon me, he lunged across and brought me down, now this thing would go on for ever and there was no other kind of ending *him or me, the cheat, the liar*

But I rammed my elbow on his punctured hand and as he moaned with pain, I crawled away

I was back on my feet, I was through the door, he was after me as I ran downstairs, his gait sounded odd, of course, he was wounded, I was doing well, I could get away

I would run next door and wake the lawyer and he would call the police, call Ginger –

Out in the road, the sound of a car, or was it two, more neighbours arriving? That is what saves you, police, neighbours, hope, but no, there had never been a neighbour, cars were passing on their way to Margate, the only one that had stopped was Dad's, he'd been parked there for hours, waiting for me, *he'd been out on the balcony, sweaty, near-silent, trying the window, trying the door,* and now he was tearing down the stairs behind me into the kitchen, my bare feet skidding, round the table, skate to the door –

but the door was stiff, it would not open, open, *open*, I begged it, then

his great male arm was round my vulnerable throat and his other hand was wrenching, dragging my hair. The pain brought a flood of water to my eyes, God, he had forced me to my knees, pain of my knees on the flags of the kitchen, now I was kneeling on my bones, the pain poured through me, I knelt for my father, the beast was laughing, out of breath, triumphant, panting, 'Did you think you'd get away from me, Mono? – We'll see about that – We'll see about that ' Every time he spoke, he tightened his grip – 'Now I'm going to fucking finish you off.'

And I was in the red pass of horror. The hard gibbet had trapped my throat, hot blood stretched my cheeks, exploding, no more air, my nose, my eyeballs

no, there was just a sea of scarlet – floating out, going down, going under

I'd always known my father would kill me

58

Then I was lying on the floor, face down, my throat hurt badly but I was conscious. Legs and voices were around me, above me, there were sounds of people pushing and struggling but then a great shout, not Dad, Angus: 'Did you think we'd let you murder our sister?'

Anthea was crouched down beside me. 'Mon, Mon.' She was calling my name. 'Mon, we're here.' She was actually crying. 'Mon, it's all right. The Boys are here.'

I half sat up: she supported my head. Yes, the kitchen. We were in the kitchen. We were in the kitchen of Bay House.

One by one, I took them in. Anthea. Boris. Where was Angus? I could hear him but I couldn't see him. Anthea was trying to explain something. Then the door opened on the dark and Fairy came in, followed by Ma in a strange patterned coat, pale and tiny. Both of them looked around, astonished.

Yes, I must be dead, or dreaming.

'Sorry, Mon, so sorry, Mon? I told Kelly about your phone-call and she said, "You should go," so I got my clothes on. I was almost ready when the second call came and there was just silence, you said nothing, but in the background I heard a weird roaring which had to be Dad, so I knew he was here, and I was so worried I called the boys, but Fairy was still staying with them, and Fairy went to pick up our mother –'

'I wanted to come,' Fairy breathed. 'I got Ma because, well, you know, sometimes Dad takes notice of her. I told that woman, that Nikki woman, it was life or death. I didn't explain. She got really mad about her dressing-gown. Ma has come in Nikki's dressing-gown.'

There was Ma, white and tiny, perched on a cushion, high above me, biting her nails, in an unfamiliar flowered dressing-gown.

Where was my father?

I stared around. Then I saw his great hams of legs under the table, terror and horror. I twisted slightly and there he was, down at the end of the table, sitting on a chair restrained by Angus who held both Dad's arms behind his back and had his head pressed down on the table-top. Every now and then Dad bellowed with anger and Angus shoved him down harder.

'I think she's all right,' Anthea said to the others. 'Do you think you can get up, now, Mon?'

'Have you called the police?' I asked them, and was shocked by my reedy, damaged voice.

'Well, that was a difficult one,' said Boris. 'Ma doesn't want us to get the police. You've been avoiding them yourself, Mon.'

'I don't want trouble,' Ma's little voice wheedled.

'Help me up,' I said. 'I've got a number.' I was quite clear what we must do. There are laws, procedures that will save us. Police, lawyers. Civilisation.

Several hands were helping me. I must have had my eyes on the floor because all I remember next was noise and somehow Dad had surged up off the chair and landed a great blow on Angus's nose, Angus's nose was spouting blood, Boris was shouting, 'Get down, you bastard,' and they were brawling in the open door and Angus was holding the side of his head and Dad was trying to head-butt Boris and everyone was joining in, cold night air blowing in through the door, cold wet air, was fog on the way? – and father and son half-fell out of the door, then Boris was hauling him back in again, and Angus joined in, and Dad was panting and straining at the table.

For the first time I dared to look at him.

He sat there and glowered, a mess of dark cherries, bandages unravelling, the lines blurring, pullulating, but not dead yet, ready to come back, ready to hurt, ready to pull us down like a great bramble, you could not get it out, the roots went on for ever –

Only one way of stopping it.

My phone lay forgotten on the table.

I dared to look, but not meet his eyes. He was so hurt. No, horrible. Both his eyes battered. No more contact. Then, for a second, a bolt of hatred.

'What do we do?' I don't know who said it.

Then we were all staring at our mother. She was the mother. She should know.

If there is no authority…

She sat there, small, immensely powerful. Her mouth opened and closed again. There was just the noise of the men's heavy breathing, Boris and Angus using all their strength to hold Dad down, the rest of us silent. No, there were no words for this. Everything burst. Everything broken. Nothing could be put right again.

I made a great effort. We must have justice. 'I've got a number. I will call the police,' I said, but my voice sounded unconvincing, we were too far out, no-one would come, or they would take too long to save us, and my hand didn't move, I did nothing, I believed in justice but I did nothing.

'Ma. Ma?' It was Fairy's tiddly-widdly voice, a wavering plea. 'What do we do?'

Ma rose, holding the arm of the chair, clinging to it, her thin back bent, crawled up like ivy, indomitable. Her hands distorted. She still wore his ring. She looked at him, and then away, but her arm still stretched in his direction, her arthritic fingers poking towards him.

Then she made a gesture.

Palm down, arm straight, a slow claw fanning from left to right.

It said he was done for.

Then she did it again, to make certain. Her ring in the light.

And then she pointed the boys to the door. Her small bright eyes; her half-closed lids. 'Not in here.' That was all she said. 'We don't need to see it.'

The horror: the horror. My heart blundering against my ribs. Did she? – could we? – No, not possible.

'Not in here. Do it outside.'

And it was already happening. The boys were manhandling Dad towards the door, a shoving, mauling, knot of maleness, the same stock, the same flesh, a thin spatter of the same blood from someone's mouth or someone's eye.

A voice spoke. Yes, it was mine. 'Ma – Ma.' Something warm as grief grew from my chest, some swelling plant. 'Ma – Ma.'

'What's the matter?' she hissed. 'He hated you. He would have strangled you at birth.'

'Oh!' That pain. She didn't care. 'Oh, but Ma. He did love you.' I can't believe I said it, but it was true.

'Fuck off, Monica,' her little voice said. 'You were always soft. He's asked for it.'

And yes, that's when the end began. The hopeful plant in my chest withered, there was just the red petal on the stone of the steps in Margate where it all began, when I stood there, raging, ringing the bell.

Time for death, then. Time for murder. The men were through the door, and then gone. Alas, Monica followed them, driving Dad back to where he had come from, down to the horrors and the darkness, the bare knuckles, the grunts, the panting.

But if the children kill the parents?

Carry on down, lads, keep on trucking.
Fuck Dad up, fuck him over,
Fuck our father,
Fuck our mother.

I was following on down the summer-house path, it was 3 a.m., only hours till dawn, and then I heard the sound of the fog-horn.

59

Out in the dark, everything was different. Out in the dark, no law, no policemen, no neighbouring lawyers, only the chaos. We had to beat him; we had to subdue him. We had to vanquish this great damaged thing.

Or else he would come back again
always come back   mad, roaring

We were stumbling down the path to the beach, driving him onwards like a bull at Pamplona. The fog-horn bellowing, sea-smells, salt-smells. Blood smells very like salty water, blood runs away into the sand, the sky over the sea had faint pink blood-stains, we had to hurry, the dawn would come, the weather was changing, a light wind rising.

And now the Ludds stuck together. All of us did it, all the chil-dren, we struck together, we clubbed together, we had no option, we had to do it, he kept on fighting, he would never lie down. Panting, thudding, the grunts of a body, nobody could see what we were hitting, was it that he was no longer human? But he would not stop. Perhaps if he'd yielded –

I was still clinging on to my phone, I was still clutching my piece of paper – at some point Boris said, urgently, 'Monica, no, it's too late for policemen.' He meant, we had all done too much damage. Yes, but we didn't see what we were doing. Only the fear, the fog,

Bish-bash-bosh, bish-bash-bosh, *bash-bash-bash-bash-BASH-BASH-BASH* –

Anthea and I went back to the house. But not Fairy. Fairy stayed. She says it was a long time before he stopped struggling.

Anthea and I sat slumped in the kitchen, drained, exhausted, everything hurting, *what had we done? Out there, what was happening?* Ma had gone upstairs 'to see the house', as if she was inspecting her inheritance.

I started telling my sister how Dad had attacked me. She put her arm round me. It didn't feel awkward. Both of us were shivering.

Rat-tat-tat on the kitchen door.

'Open, it's us.' It was Boris, urgent. 'We've got to get him into his car. You can't imagine how heavy he was. It's all over. We'll need two vehicles.'

Vehicles. Boris! – his stately language.

Fairy had had a good idea. Maybe her only good idea – she had always been the least clever of us. ('Well it was obvious,' she said to me, after we had done it, after it was over, as the pinky grey light crept over the horizon and spread like spilt red wine through the fog, with the air around us grey-white, mysterious – 'our father was a terrible driver. Anyone who knew him knew how bad he was.')

We looked after Dad. Heavy, so heavy, as once again we all tried to lift him. A great heavy sausage of stones and blood. The door of his car, waiting on the gravel, had been left open for a quick getaway. Yes, that was why I didn't hear it shut, he'd eased out of it in silence and come for me –

Now he was over. Over for ever. First one shoulder, then the other, then the legs were rolled in like a giant grub.

Angus was in the driving seat. In the back, Boris, Fairy, me, shoulder to shoulder, the warmth of their bodies, we were the Ludds, somehow we'd done it. Anthea was following in her jeep. The fog made keeping to the road difficult, but that meant we had the road to ourselves, and fog, the fog, was what we needed. At one point we veered, and Boris said, 'Don't kill us, boy,' to Angus.

'I'm a better driver than our father.'

Eventually we reached Dumpton Gap. It's an awkward place, unfortunately named. It had once been the dump for all Ramsgate's rubbish, but if you go down and walk west a bit, the beach at low tide is glorious, the light perfect, it's all washed clean, everything's white and pastel bright, white cuttlefish, white cliffs, white chalk, and one day that was how life would be – if we could only get rid of the horror.

But now there was fog: only the fog. And the tide must be up. It had still been rising when we were struggling down to the beach. Fairy jumped out of the car like a dancer and went to the edge of the cliff to reconnoitre. She disappeared after a few paces, then came back pointing at a tangent. 'That's the way. It'll have to be fast. There's just a small fence, then he'll go straight over.'

There was a house with a tower fifty yards from the edge, but we saw no lights, there was no car outside. Behind stretched a mild suburban estate with a wide private road that led straight down the hill from Ocean View to Seven Stones Drive. We drove quietly up the quiet mild drive behind which civilised people were sleeping. Then we got out. It was Angus's turn to get into the car's front passenger seat. We hauled Dad's body out and stuffed him behind the driving-wheel.

So, yes, that's how our father went, how he always wanted to, driving, driving, in his great big fuck-off dentist's car, Dad had to be in the driver's seat but it was the kids, at last in control, it was Angus who clasped Dad's hands round the steering wheel, his stiffening hands, *Dad, you take over,* it was Angus who put the car into drive and his foot on the accelerator. Angus went bucketing down the road and straight for the cliff, straight for the cliff-edge, the rest of us ran horrified, thrilled, behind –

Yes, thank God, then our brother dived out, slamming the door, falling, rolling, and the car was off, gone, careering downwards, and in another second, the fog swirled between us, and all we heard above the roar of the engine was the twanging impact with the chain-link fence, the fence-posts yielding in a split second, we heard the engine roaring through space, I counted but only made it to *one,* and then we heard a great smack, smack, splash, and the engine died as the car went under.

And then we were hugging each other, shaking. Fairy said like a child, 'Well done us.'

Bish-bash-bish-bash-bish-bash- SPLOSH.

Never, never think it was easy.

I still don't know what it has cost me.

60

Linked by the horror, we couldn't part.

Everyone came back to Bay House. In the mad kitchen where too much had happened, I put the kettle on, offered drinks. The kettle roared, or the wind was getting up. I didn't know what I was saying. 'Tea? Coffee? Beer? Juice?' I tore open a packet of biscuits which spilt, helpless, all over the table. Yes, there were tiny specks of blood.

Blood? You'll find it's thicker than water.

In the cupboard I had bleach, a bucket.

Everyone sat there, very quiet.

Somebody's voice broke the silence. 'He wouldn't have been happy in a Home.' That pious tone. It had to be Ma.

'Are you fucking having a laugh, Ma?' That was Angus. But 'Language, Angus!' – that was Boris.

'He wasn't very happy in our home,' I said.

A short pause, then, 'I made your father happy,' Ma put in from some other planet. 'Well, at first. And later, you kids did.' She was eating her biscuit like a rabbit, little paws in the air, blank face twitching, the crumbs falling, her pupils blank.

Explosions of scorn. I reminded her. 'You said he hated us. I haven't forgotten.'

'It was YOU he hated, Monica.' Ma's top lip lifted in a little smile. Underneath, her false teeth glinted. 'He loved Fairy. He loved Fred.'

That was a blow beneath my giant ribcage. 'He loved Fred? He fucking murdered Fred.'

Yes, there seemed to be a lot of murder. Teaspoons were clinking against cups. I heard Angus breathing, hard, heavy, as all of us stared at our small white mother. How did we all come out of her? Maybe she was just one vast vagina covered in clothes, white head on top.

Now the pale creature spoke again. 'He wanted Fred to be like him. Ai don't know whay. It was his last chance.'

'He spoiled Fairy,' said Anthea.

'Yesss…that,' Fairy said. Under the fluorescent, she was changing. Candle-wax. Melting, hissing. I couldn't bear to look at her. All her features were disordered, her maddening prettiness twisting, warping, insects writhing beneath her skin, grief, anger, shame erupting. Something was oozing into the open.

'Ma, stop messing with that biscuit!' I shouted, furious, at her.

'He was a SICK FUCK!' said Angus. 'Face it!'

'Shut up,' said Boris. 'All of you. Shut up! Not in front of our mother.'

Long pause. Ma went on mouthing her biscuit. What was happening underneath?

'Maybe it was her all along?' said Anthea. 'Maybe the two of them were in it together?'

'MAYBE WE KILLED THE WRONG ONE!' bellowed Angus.

Ma's terrified face. 'Only joking, Mother,' said Boris, leaning heavily forward, heavily, heavily over her, the pale, squirming, misshapen queen, her hive broken open, the daylight in, and all of us hung there, suspended, crushed.

We didn't dare uncover it.

How far do you go? How far dare you go? We had gone so far. Off the edge of our world. None of us could have survived going further.

We had to preserve some kind of order.

Outside the room, the wind was howling. We cleaned the house, closed it for ever.

Part 9

Try to Forget

61

Claw your way back. Back up the slope. Try to forget. It could not have been different. I apologise. Mistakes were made. I know we made the right decision.

My nails, bloody. The slope, endless.

62

What does it feel like to kill someone? I often wondered before it happened. Vengeance is mine – that I imagined. Maybe it would be exciting. Then guilt, yeah. Of course, you'd feel guilty.

In the weeks that followed, I started to learn.

What did I fail to imagine? Pity.

Odd that Monica could feel pity; so few people had pitied me. Maybe I learned it from pitying Fairy? (I should have a Doctorate in Psychology, an honorary one, I award it to me.)

But pity – if you can, avoid it.

Pity's the thing that will gnaw you away. Dumb beasts stumbled down through my dreams along the endless path to the sea, beaten, brutalised, on and on, it must have been ages before he weakened. Pity twisted a blade in my entrails, yes, we did it, yes, he died. Dad was a pig, a lion, a bear, a great roaring animal, but he bled. His thick skin split. Bruised and split. I wasn't there for the final stretch, it was dark, foggy, we could hardly see him. Now

I would see it every night. Hour after hour, minute by minute.

Yes, I failed. I failed to stop it. So I would always, always have failed. Because we drove Dad down into darkness, I abandoned order, we failed, I failed. And so the terror came upon me. Night after night, day after day, I sat and shook with fear and pity. Shivered, sweated. Moaned aloud.

For the first time in my adult life, I was incapable of working. My doctor was a skinny middle-class twat who had hinted once that I was overweight and misunderstood when I laughed in her face. I went to see her shortly after Dad's death and asked for something to help me sleep. Halfway through asking, I changed my mind and blurted, 'Actually I've got depression.'

'You, Monica?'

'Who else would it be?'

'It's just that you're so…well, you seem so…'

'What?'

'You know, cheerful. Er, strong.'

(I remembered then she had a child at Windmills.)

'Well, I don't know, I'm not a fucking doctor, but I feel frightened all the time.' I remembered too late the 'Polite Notice' in Reception that said, 'Verbal abuse of our staff will not be tolerated.' 'Sorry,' I said. 'No offence meant. I only swore because I was depressed.'

'Any other symptoms?' She was looking down, her puddingy face tight and sulky.

'I can't be bothered to get dressed.' I started to pull up my top to prove it – I hadn't put on a bra that morning – but a mere glimpse of nipple had her writing on her pad. 'I can't face going into work,' I added.

I left with a prescription and a sick note.

Soon I couldn't get any of my clothes on. I lay in bed naked, on wrinkled sheets. The blood beat and beat in my head, too loud for sleep, *thud-a, thud-a.* I did feel bad about letting school down, but naked Monica was 'not right for Windmills', as Neil always said of Latin.

Vengeance had come. Dad's vengeance on me. I almost longed to be arrested. But nothing happened, no-one rang on my door. Week followed week. Christmas came and went. Anthea, Fairy, Boris, Angus, barely got in touch with me. We avoided each other, my siblings and I.

Yes, quite gloomy, but there's better stuff coming.

Because, one day, Ginger came round. For some reason I answered the door, a duvet carelessly wrapped around me, baleful glare at the ready.

But it was him. Pink, healthy, grey-blue eyes alert and gleaming. I was so shocked, I dropped the duvet.

'A Spanish lady has been arrested.'

Various things then went on. Stick around, I'll tell you later.

63   Adoncia

The police come knocking at my door.

Soon I in *feo* cell in Spanish prison, and *feo* detective come from England. He big and bald with little bit red hair. Spanish police tell me they find a body. Albert's body. Why it take them so long?

And then they tell me *extradición – como se dice*, extradition.

Then I am flying back to England.

He ask about my life in Malaga, link between Malaga and Thanet, as if I some big criminal! But no, I only know couple bad people.

'I just a woman, dentist break my heart,' I say. I cry a little. Baldy ignore me, he really want to know my friends, he talk blah blah about mafia, and I give him names, most of them invented. But I tell him the name of that bitch Esmeralda, I say she thick as thieve with Albert, I say, 'She worst of lot of them,' and he say, 'I know her, she's been most helpful. Esmeralda not germane to this.'

I start to realise, she talk about me. 'I not a German either,' I say.

But he take no notice, just laugh as if crazy. English don't like foreigners.

He tell me Albert was attacked with hammer, but I tell him *cacheporra* not same thing. He smile a lot and say, 'I see, you hit him with *cacheporra*, thank you for that information.' 'I not say anything,' I tell him. 'I tell you fact about Spanish language.' He ask me when I last in Margate? I tell him that I not remember. He say, 'I remind you. You were seen in Tesco Westwood Cross at the beginning of November.' I say, 'I a lady, I not shop in Tesco.'

Then he say Albert run from hospital and disappear. 'Do you know his whereabout?' he asking. I shocked to know Albert alive, but I hide it. He say, 'You not look so happy now.'

I say, I know nothing, I very happy.

He say, 'Maybe Albert Ludd coming for you.'

Why Esmeralda have to see me in Tesco?

Part 10

A Victorious Sound

64   Monica

Drumroll. We're getting to the main event. What most people would see as the main event, though from my point of view, that's already happened, cannot be undone, will not be undone, he'll come no more, never, never. Please, God, help me. Never, never.

Drumroll! Play louder, drown it out. Drums, make a victorious sound.

I want to tell you about what happened on the morning I started back at Windmills. It may be the only thing you know about me. My moment of fame, Fairy-style. Only, let's face it, a thousand times better. Sorry, Fairy, you lose, I win!

When in the spotlight, you're supposed to be modest. It was a small thing, my action that morning, I merely followed the logic of events. But when I say that to anyone, they contradict me, and say I'm a hero. And so, I wonder – was I a hero?

Did I have love? A hero needs love. I loved my students unreasonably, given their spots and ignorance. They were my class: OK, my children. Adults must protect their children.

Luck, fate had never been with me. No, I have been a klutz, a clown; ice-creams, deck-chairs, axes on buses, seagulls, hotwater bottles, mothers, fathers, the whole universe ganged up on me. Until the moment when glory was mine.

Never despair. Every dog has his day. And I, Monica, was ready.

News of the Spanish girlfriend in custody spread via a badly written piece in the *Thanet Gazette*. I was no longer the main suspect. I was no longer a suspect at all. And Ginger's visit, though uncourtly, shifted something in my gloomy brain. Daylight leaked back, bleak but brighter. For the first time, I felt restless. Was there a world outside my window?

I had a shower and put my clothes on. Then I was bored. I wanted work.

Neil rang up from school the first Monday after the story appeared in the paper and invited me to come in 'for a talk'. 'I hope you're on the mend, Monica? We have all wondered how you are.' I bounded off into a full explanation but realised too late he was still speaking. 'No no no, you don't have to explain, we under*stand*, Monica. Very distressing, a parent's death, foolish gossip, that sort of thing. The *Thanet Gazette* put a few things straight. Do pop in and see us soon.'

Neil had become more royal in my absence. 'How about today?' I asked at once. He sounded slightly alarmed, but agreed.

Soon I was back on his white fluffy carpet. I couldn't stop smiling. I wanted to kiss him. That urge didn't last, he was pink and sweaty, but just for a moment I felt so happy, fully dressed and out of the house! Back in Windmills, like a normal Monica. He looked small and cuddly, sat at his desk. Maybe I'd pick him up and whirl him round.

'Do sit down, Monica. When you stand up, you look so tall! How are you?'

'I'm good, I'm good, I'm very good.'

'Splendid! It's time to talk about whether you return "pro tem"?'

'Great, Neil, I'll start tomorrow.'

'We shouldn't rush this, Monica. Let's start with a sample lesson or two with some of your favourite young people. And then, if all goes well – if all goes well *from both sides*, maybe?'

It was partly because he had staffing problems, partly because the kids had asked for me. Yes, they asked for me! They loved me! When a rumour spread that I was banned from the premises they'd actually sent a deputation to Neil with an ill-written note demanding my return.

Neil showed me this and I laughed, loudly, then a small tear ran down my cheek. 'Miss Ludd talked to us about morrality, etc. It was intrresting. Yours sincerrly, the Whole 6th form.' I recognised Kriss's terrible spelling, she always favoured 'r's and 's's because they featured in her own name. I knew the 'Whole 6th form' did NOT like me, but I cleverly didn't explain that to Neil. I wanted to sob and bray like a donkey and cling to his knees, but I refrained. Instead I poured energy into thinking.

A newspaper was lying on his desk with a picture of Trump waving tiny hands. The headline was 'Trump Standing Ovation at NRA'. National Rifle Association, yes. Right-wing lunatics from Texas. Instantly I had an inspiration.

'I could give a talk about gun control. And weapons generally. It's topical.'

'Yes, non-violence, excellent,' he said. 'That will be viewed favourably by OFSTED. Feature it in your lesson plan.'

It was a yes. I was on my way back.

65

Two weeks later I went into school. I was feeling hopeful and high-spirited; it was a beautiful clear spring day. *Dum spiro spero!* Cicero. Neil had suggested I skip morning assembly because I might get 'unwanted attention'. 'That foolish gossip, Monica. Best to let everything calm down.'

Little did Neil know what was coming.

I marched in as I used to, though later in the day, and found the big doors at the front of the school left open. No-one was doing security checks. Behind the window of the office, the old cow of a School Secretary waved at me. She was on the phone, but her gesture was bossy, beckoning, frowning, signalling me with such stupid vigour that I ignored her, she must want to make me fill in some form. A backward glance: she went on waving. No, I was still Acting Deputy Head, I had no need to truckle to her. I waved back at her dismissively.

For some reason she looked shorter than usual, as if she was crouching behind the partition.

We must get security sorted out. Every other week the system went down.

Windmills seemed surprisingly quiet and calm. You didn't normally see empty classrooms; maybe there was a school excursion, or they had moved breaktime to ten o'clock, a ridiculous idea I would quash immediately, I hated Neil taking any initiative. Yes, I peered through the empty classrooms and saw crowds of figures streaming into the playgrounds. No matter as long as my class was waiting. They would be there if they knew I was coming, I trusted them, I knew they'd missed me.

The sun shone yellow through all that glass, the corridor

gleamed as smooth as butter, someone had spilled red paint from the art class – that messy young German performance artist who Neil had insisted on employing, she had better clear it up before the kids came back in or the school would be spattered with scarlet footprints…

Red, red. It made me uneasy. But no, I was safe, I was back in school! What did a little spillage matter? No, today I was perfectly happy. I was going back among my people, prodigal Monica, returned. I had a place in the world. I was useful.

A sudden misgiving. Might Neil have forgotten? Why wasn't he waiting to welcome me? Or warn me, as the case might be, he liked to drop little reminders in my ear about various 'stake-holders'' sensibilities. But no, he'd been keen on the non-violence idea, I'd write him the sodding lesson plan later, it was perfect for OFSTED, he would have remembered, he's desperate for a 'Good' instead of an 'Average'.

Up the staircase. More red splashes. Somebody had dropped paper tissues, which only made it look more of a mess. Someone had abandoned an old shoe! Standards had fallen while I was away. School still seemed pleasantly, unnaturally quiet, espe-cially compared to the world outside where I heard a complex chorus of sirens.

A little burst of adrenalin. This class, though lovable, was always a challenge.

Yes, they were there! I saw from the distance as I marched down the corridor their dear heads, neatly aligned. My God, they had actually sat down ready. They were not fighting, or dancing, or rioting!

Then I saw something more puzzling. A large dark figure stood in the front corner, beside the blackboard, and I heard him talking. Talking non-stop in a bossy male voice. What was he up to? Fuck off, Shouty!

Kriss, Mohammed, Dale, sat still, staring at him with utter fascination. He hadn't a clue how to teach, however, ranting and leaving no time for questions.

I paused for a moment outside the door, trying to recognise the teacher. No. He had a black jutting beard, a small pot-belly, arms like tree-trunks, and shone with sweat. Newbie nerves? A supply teacher. Neil, you worm, you fish, you vermin, you've ratted on our new agreement!

My first thought was to zoom down to Neil's office and find out what the fuck he was doing.

The sirens outside were becoming distracting.

No, it was my classroom, my class, my kids. I would pitch straight in and evict the man myself. Protocol would only slow things up.

He was surprisingly burly for a teacher. He had walked across the room to gaze out of the window, which had a good view of the road with the sirens – they seemed to be coming to some kind of climax. Time for me to take direct action.

No sooner had I thought it than I'd flung the door open, and Jutty Beard swung round as if stung.

In a second, I took in what was happening. On the teacher's table was a replica machine-gun. He was doing my session on Gun Control! Fucking cheek! He had stolen Non-Violence!

Several children shrieked with pleasure as I entered, no, for some reason they looked frightened –

'Hello,' I said. 'I'm Monica. I am their teacher. I'll take over now.' (Kriss claimed later I said, 'Hello Sunshine' – I might have done, it was a sunny morning.)

'No worries,' I smiled at the worried-looking class, some must have believed the rumours about me – but the supply teacher was not yielding, he looked enraged, he was actually yelling, 'Get back, something something' (it sounded like *binty labwa*) – everything was happening in slow motion, he was running across from the window straight at me –

'Sort it out with Neil,' I said to him. 'This is my class. I'm teaching it. Take this thing with you, I won't need it,' and I picked up the replica gun from the table and suddenly all the kids were screaming and it was horribly, shockingly heavy and my heart jolted and I knew what was happening

and maybe I had known all along, which was the way the story got told

FUCK, FUCK, it's a terrorist

and then I noticed Abdul was crouched on the ground, clutching his hand, over a pool of blood

I thought, 'Right, point the gun at Beardy,' but he had dived sideways and grabbed hold of Kriss (who was sitting alone in the front row of desks, I realised later, to be close to me) – he was holding Kriss in front of him, her face was mottled red and white all over, her mouth was open, her small grey teeth, his great thick arm across her poor thin throat, she looked at me with an abject plea, I could see her short fingers and pink bitten nails, she was gazing at me with despair and terror and something else – I saw she thought I could save her – and when I saw that, life stopped, life stalled, she trusted me, I had to protect her she was five feet tall, stunted in the womb by her mother's drinking, and don't all rush to slag off Kriss's mother, it was only because Kriss was so small that I got a clear view of Jutty Beard's face, glaring insanely above Kriss's tiny topknot, his eyes bulging, brown and bloodshot

but no, I hadn't seen the great knife in his hand with which he had severed Abdul's little finger

so I dropped the gun and in a moment of grace my boxing lessons swept into motion, my fist aimed a hard jab at his nose, bruising my knuckles as it cracked into gristle, a clean punch, a big punch, kerr-unch on the bridge, and his eyes glazed over and I spotted the blade and Christ, Christ, better punch him again and I hit him so hard that it bounced me backwards but Beardy was swaying, he had let Kriss go, the bright blood poured out in thick scarlet gouts as he fell, slamming his head on the side of a desk, and lay there bleeding on the ground, a rent in his black hair showing red and yellow bone, blood all over Kriss and all over the mat, and she wriggled away like a red, shiny tadpole as I thought: what next? as his great thighs twitched and everyone was screaming like a horde of seagulls – then I went with my instinct and sat on him, smelling him, sweat and metal and something chemical I didn't recognise, using my weight, using my size, I sat like a boulder on his terrifying chest with my great big body, Monica Ludd, my beautiful big strong powerful body, I kicked the long knife away with my foot, and he lay there limp but I felt him twitching and my heart lurched again and I yelled in terror to the paralysed class, 'Get the fucking knife!'

After that it's hard to remember.

Abdul ran forward, his eyes huge with fear, his mouth set with determination, and took the knife with his one good hand, then stared at it astonished, three of the girls took charge of the machine-gun, Deniece joined me on top of the terrorist and shouted to Zain to do the same, and everyone was sobbing and talking and explaining when the door burst open and the police came in.

Ginger was hanging around behind them.

Later I learned this was the terrorist who had been on the run since the events at Oxford Circus. The man was incompetent, but not, alas, a hoaxer. That morning he had slashed three members of staff before making hostages of my class. I had become the 'Brave teacher', 'Thanet's Hero', and all the rest.

It was my day. This dog had her day. Kriss's family posted on Facebook, 'We ♥ Miss Ludd. She saved Everybody. She is a Hero and desserves meddles.'

66

Of course, that fateful day changed me. (Are we ever different? Yes, I hope so. Neil sometimes looks at me wonderingly when I agree with something he says. I'm tired, you see. All that blood. If we ever get married, I'm changing my name. No, it's not feminist, but change is good. I never chose to be a Ludd.)

And I've written a whole new scheme of work for the sixth-form course on 'Civilisation'. Since it isn't examined, thought is allowed. My lesson plans will dazzle the inspectors.

I focus the course on violence, now. Of course, it's tangled in their heads already. The family, that's where it starts. And yet Deniece is doing better, and Abdul has been made a prefect and is aiming for catering college, while Kriss has applied to university. First choice Edinburgh – far from home. I can't believe it! Little Kriss! But she's statemented for dyslexia, and with help and support, I think she'll make it.

I tell them violence never stops. That we're all violent, underneath the skin, we can all be pushed to violence. But once you give in, you're lost for ever, because the tit-for-tat begins, the red tide rises, everyone drowns. I quote Seneca, and the Torah.

'But Miss, Miss! You punched the terrorist out!'

'Yes, well, I had a duty to defend Kriss.'

'Miss never killed anyone,' Deniece points out.

Deniece, Deniece, I wish that were true.

On, up, I have to get out – let the dead stay down, I have to get out –

I tell them stories, and ask the sixth-formers to try to think of alternative endings.

I get them to read about the Trojan Wars, which they do reluctantly: it's so far away. I do better when I talk about 9/11, and the bizarre tit for tat that followed, with Britain and America hitting Iraq, although it had nothing to do with it, then ISIS growing up like a hydra and hitting anyone in sight. Good job Neil wasn't listening! Bish-bash-bish-bash-bish-bash-BOSH!!

And then about a Turkish blood feud. A clever young Shia

female student fell in love with a Sunni boy. Her family forbade it, she ran away with him, her brothers came and killed them both, his fathers and uncles came and killed the brothers.

'It's about blood, and sperm,' I said. I didn't mean to say it; it just came out. They fell about laughing, joyfully embarrassed. At least, however, they were wide awake.

'Say *what?*' Joey Alvarez called out. 'Miss, I can't believe you said that!'

'It's about who is allowed to have children. Who owns the future. That's what blood feuds are about.'

Almost certainly someone would tell their parents and I would have to talk to Neil again, but Neil is a shadow of his former self, he lost whatever authority he had when someone revealed (not me, for once) that he had taken cover under a table when he saw the terrorist come in with his gun, or, as he insisted, 'went to a safe place so he could contact the emergency services'. Yes, he and I have got on infinitely better ever since Monica became a hero. A month later I got the permanent appointment, no longer 'Acting', but 'Deputy Head' – I gather the governors insisted. The 'Deputy' bit is a fig leaf, in any case: when anyone important phones – journalists, politicians – they ask for me, Monica. Windmills, for now, is Monica's fiefdom.

'How could this story have ended differently?'

'It would have been better if they weren't all dead!' Laughter. That was the bright, dark-haired boy who arrived this year from Syria: Zain, of course. But the laughter died away too quickly. Everyone remembers our own brush with terror, everyone remembers the Windmills victims, the old, brave PE teacher, six months from retirement, stabbed in the neck, the chest, the back, the passing cleaner whose tendon was severed, the sobbing cook who bled out on the floor. Everyone remembered the randomness. That's partly why we long for stories: things have a place; things have a purpose. Human beings prefer justice.

'How could a different ending have happened? How can people avoid violence?'

Silence. The class looks at me dumbly. Ever since the day when I took down the terrorist they think that I have superpowers, but inside I'm begging them *don't look at me, how the fuck would I know, I'm a fucking Ludd. My whole family is drenched in blood.*

'What do you think about the law?' I ask them. Yes, I know, I'm leading the witness, but they are young, they do need help.

(The law? What do they know of the law? The local police station has just closed down, there is only an answerphone on the door of the abandoned building asking them to leave a message.)

Oh, it seems the class does know something. Alison Gales, a very smart girl, though she'd do better if she worked harder and spent less time cheeking the teachers, puts up her hand and smiles at me. 'Ms Ludd, is it true you married a policeman?'

'We're engaged to be married,' I said. 'But yes.'

'Why are you with a policeman?' she asks. That's pushing it a bit, but I'm more relaxed with these growing teenagers, soon to be adults, soon to march out on to the world's pavements. I sense the class is listening hard.

I tell the truth. 'I had no choice.' Then there's a pause, because I can't explain all the complexities behind that statement. There are other things I can tell them, though.

'He saved my life,' I say. Some girls look happy – it's the way they think, the kind of thing they say to each other. Yes, they hear a romantic fiction. How can they know what I mean by it?

Ginger owns me. I have no choice.

But Kriss isn't having it – I've taught her different. 'Miss, Miss, he didn't. You saved us.'

'Everyone needs backup.' I cut her off. 'Let's get back to the blood feud,' I said. Sometimes hero worship is exhausting. 'Who do you think needed help?'

'The girl,' someone shouts. And another one, 'The girl and the boy.'

'Yes,' I say, but I'm still gathering answers, waving my hands encouragingly.

'Everyone,' a voice at the back calls out. Then Zain suggests, 'Maybe the brothers?'

'Yes,' I say, delighted. 'The girl's family. They needed help not to do it. But what helps us not to do things?'

'Parents.' Said gloomily by Priya Patel, whose father is a Hindu priest. 'Parents stop us doing everything.'

'Nah, the parents in that story were the worst,' says someone.

'Police,' says someone else. 'Supposed to be the police.'

'Yes. In theory. Yes, and laws.'

'But Miss, Miss, they closed our police station!'

'I know,' I said. 'It's a pity. My partner has to work somewhere else.'

He's not far, though. Never far away.

'Education?' suggests the Syrian boy.

'Love?' Kriss whispers, very quietly.

67   Adoncia

Life is *injusto, no cierto*? I do all that, but I don't feel better. Life is shit, if you are woman.

I miss my daughter, which I not expect. She dwarf, and simple, but she liked to see me.

68   Monica

We had sex on the day Ginger came round to tell me Adoncia had been arrested. You'll remember the duvet had let me down and left me standing before him, majestic. I naturally felt nervous around a policeman and so it seemed best to cut to the chase, oral, vaginal, and well, the rest, a Christmas feast of orifices. Ginger lavishly, loudly enjoyed it. To my amazement, I did too – I think I was bored with being depressed.

Afterwards we talked in the red front room where I had once left him *in flagrante*. Or more exactly, *in medias res*. He seemed not to bear a grudge about that; now we were both relaxed and sated, and chatted almost as if we were friends, though I remained wary. Ginger can be tricky.

How had he caught Adoncia?

Turned out she was on his radar already. 'I'd been tracking the old harlot,' he said. An excellent word, when not applied to me! He'd been investigating Dad for a year or two before Adoncia attacked him. 'You wouldn't believe what there was in Albert's background. Generations of crims. Subhumans, Monica!' He laughed, loudly, in cheery amazement, then reddened in an instant, and covered his mouth. 'Er, sorry. I forgot it's your family.'

I didn't let him get away with it. 'There must have been plenty of brains, as well. Boris and Angus got them from somewhere. And there must have been some sensational lookers – my sister Fairy! I rest my case.' Of course what I actually wanted to say was: 'Your lot were ugly, bald and ginger.'

He looked at me earnestly, his grey eyes softened. 'You are a looker yourself, Monica. Not too skinny, like your sister. And I'm not handsome enough for you.'

He 'wasn't handsome enough for me'! Great, that gave me a clear advantage. My spurt of temper fizzled out. 'I must have mis-spoken in the heat of the moment. I've always found you attractive, Ginger.'

He sat and glowed, I glowed back, companionable glow-worms in growing darkness.

It was time for a trip down memory lane. Ginger said, 'I first met you half a lifetime ago, when we were both just teenagers.'

'Really?'

'Don't you remember, Monica? I'm pretty sure you do remember. We don't have to pretend any more.'

Someone had knocked out his teeth in a fight; he went to my father in a terrible state. Dad had used his best selling techniques to persuade Ginger's mother to get him gold crowns. 'You'll want to give the boy a chance,' Dad roared at her, a single mother who had saved up a few hundred pounds over a lifetime of being a cleaner. 'You want the best for him?' ''Course I do.' She had handed him her life savings.

'He made me look like a gangster. Idiot police cadets dubbed me "Grillz". It made my way up through the ranks a lot harder. OK, I bore your father a grudge. But you – you were sitting there in reception, curvy and gorgeous, writing down appointments.

Every time you looked at me you started laughing and once the other woman sent you out. But I knew laughter meant sexual attraction. That was it, Monica, wasn't it?'

I didn't tell him I barely remember that strange month of work experience. Just the weird sense that something was wrong, Esmeralda kind but nervous, the drunken revelations that followed and cast a shadow over it all. I must have laughed at scores of people, it was the happiness of having a job. I let Ginger cling to his illusion. He knew enough of the truth already.

After an hour or two he put his shirt back on, buttoned it neatly, straightened the collar. He cleared his throat and made an announcement. 'Monica, you're a remarkable woman, and I am very grateful, but till the case is settled, I'd better not visit. Now we have another secret,' he concluded.

Every few weeks, though, my suitor had phoned and asked me if I was feeling better, and when I might go back to school. I think he likes me being a teacher.

And then the Day of Reckoning arrived: the day when Monica took out the terrorist, and so achieved beatification.

Not long after that, he rang at my door.

It was a Sunday and he looked very neat, almost 'smart casual'. I saw he had dressed up for me! Or else he dressed carefully when poised to arrest. But surely he'd be reluctant to arrest a hero? I felt both flustered and pleased to see him.

'Monica, put the kettle on.' I knew by now he liked Earl Grey – Ginger was aspirational. 'Your father's body has been found,' he said.

I started as if he had kicked me on the shin. Until they had a body, Dad was just a missing person who had discharged himself in the middle of the night, refused to listen to worried nurses, taken his car from the car-park, and vanished. Thus far, we'd had the luck of the devil. The day after the car went into the sea, Anthea got the fence repaired, claiming she'd hit it on her bike in the fog, and she said there was no sign of the car on the beach. A storm had blown up out of nowhere. The sea was wild, with tiny boats like corks, bobbing about on a chaos of white froth. We thought we'd get a week. It had been many months.

'You needn't pretend to be upset,' he added. 'I think we all knew he was probably dead.'

I made an indistinguishable moan, something between 'No,' and, 'Yes maybe.' Curiously, I *was* upset.

'Better sit down,' he said, quite gently. 'He was washed up on the Goodwin Sands.'

'Fuck,' I said. 'I mean, sorry, sorry. How – I mean who – I mean, what happened?'

'He was in his car. A freak wave, perhaps? The storms have been very bad this winter. You'll remember the recent incident when four people were washed into Ramsgate Harbour.'

I nodded, dumbly. I did remember.

'Your father's car is a write-off, Monica. Though in theory the family could claim it?'

'Er no, don't think so.' I had poured him some tea. My hand was shaking. Tea flooded his saucer.

'We're trying to confirm the dates,' he said. 'The date of your father's presumed accident.'

'The dates? I've never been good with dates. But he was a terrible driver,' I said. 'Anyone who knew him would tell you that.'

His eyes seemed to be laughing at me.

'Maybe it was foggy,' I offered.

'Poor visibility,' he agreed, and again, he smiled knowingly. 'You may be interested to know that, after such long exposure to seawater, the body won't tell us about the cause of death.'

'Which must have been drowning,' I tried to say. My mouth was dry, my tongue was too big, a sound like a mouse in a nest of dust. I took a suck of my cup of tea. Then I tried again, and it came out halfway between a hiccup and a yell – 'which must have BEEN DROWNING!'

He nodded. 'No need to shout, Monica.'

'No, my tea went down the wrong way.'

'You had no contact with him that evening,' he said, and it was more a statement than a question, as if he had decided what he wanted me to say, what he needed me to say if life were to go on.

'Er, no,' I agreed. 'Which evening?' A patch of sun lay between us. That familiar feeling that we were fencing.

'And nor, it seems, did your sisters and brothers.'

'Really, have you asked them?' I said, surprised. He said nothing. I understood. 'Though probably it's not worth the trouble.'

'Were you children actually estranged from your father?'

That sounded like something I should deny. 'No! My sister visited him in hospital.'

'Fairy, yes. The rest of you didn't. But the hospital wouldn't have wanted a crowd.'

'No.' Then I had an inspiration. 'Maybe my father was missing us. Maybe he was coming to see us!'

'In the middle of the night. Surprise visit,' Ginger said,

I sat uneasy, my eyes on the floor, but I suddenly thought, 'You're enjoying it! You know everything. Everything.'

'Are you saying I'm a know-all?' God, it was still happening, the blurting out, but it was OK, Ginger was smiling.

'I was wrong about one thing, Monica. Haemophilia. Your father's girlfriend. There's a female variant, after all. Haemophilia C, or Factor Something. Milder than the other kind. Veronica had it. Two little bites and she bled to death. Your mother may not be a murderer!' He laughed heartily, and I smiled back, trying to get in the spirit of things, though sweat was pouring down my neck. 'Though there's something a bit odd about it, Monica. So far as we can see, from the CCTV footage which shows the times when both women came to the door, it was ages between your mother's arrival at the house, and her telephone call to the police station. Do you think she was too upset to call an ambulance?'

I said nothing. I imagined it, how Ma sat watching the Girl bleed to death.

'But for you, that's a side issue,' he said. 'You'll be more concerned about your father.'

That day I waited for the punch, the crunch, the moment when he revealed what he knew and the force came in with tracker dogs and DNA tests and all was lost.

In fact, after half an hour of talking about arrangements for the body, he got up, straightened his jacket, smiled.

'So that seems to be that,' he said. 'It will be some time before the case is closed, but no need for a Home Office post mortem.'

'No need for a post mortem?' I gabbled, astounded.

'So much time has gone by, there's not a lot of him left, if you don't mind me putting it like that.' He smiled, and his gold teeth flashed. Something sharkish, flesh-eating? Great, as long as he disposed of the body.

'Not at all, Ginger,' I confirmed.

'And besides,' he said. 'People need heroes. We don't want them thinking you have feet of clay.'

There was a silence. We looked at each other. Despite that one afternoon of energetic sex the relationship between us had stayed curiously formal. Of course, I was afraid of him, and perhaps (who knows?) he too was afraid – *my family is murderous.*

'So maybe we could – go out?' he asked. 'Now that's behind us, so to speak.'

'I think I might like that,' I blushed and tittered, idiotic with relief. 'Where would we go?'

'Oh, around Thanet. That's my stamping ground, of course.'

Stamping ground – I saw it, suddenly, the five of us hitting, kicking, shoving.

'My stamping ground, as well.'

He picked up *The Shining*, which lay on the table, where I had been re-reading it. 'We both like books,' he said. 'Sometimes we could stay in, as well. In fact, we have a lot in common. Do you like dancing, Monica?'

I was hot with pride, fear, guilt. I was a criminal wooing a policeman, as well as a hero whom Thanet idolised. Did we have enough in common? He stood up, slowly, against the light. Just for a second, I saw my father. Could there be a slight resemblance?

'I love dancing. I thought you'd never ask.'

'Maybe we could make a go of it,' he added. 'Come on, Monica. You'd better say "Yes".' Just for a moment there was something in his voice – something less playful, more definite.

Why did you marry a policeman? That canny question from my class.

You see, I had no choice.

'Yes,' I said. 'I think I have to say "yes".'

'But I'll kill you if you're unfaithful,' he said, and he crossed the room, laughing, and took my hands, and pulled me playfully to my feet, my smart suitor, my swain, my pain. 'Would you care to dance, Monica?' We gambolled heavily around the room.

69

And so, we got away with it. The storm coincided with a record high tide. That car had given Dad a wild last ride, and he ended, flayed, on those pale sands.

There was a flurry of coverage in the local papers – 'Hero Teacher's Father's Body Found' – and speculation from a gobby doctor: the brain injury must have affected his judgement. It was far too soon for him to drive.

After a few months, the story died.

So that was the beginning of what I have now, the day when I knew we would not be accused, the day I had longed for, when we would be free.

Instead, something else had started.

Jazz dancing, Laban, hip-hop, street – that was what I had always fancied. But Ginger found a line-dancing class. He's the only man, so he has no rivals. With his perfect memory and big neat feet, he quickly became good at it. I'm more of a challenge for the teacher.

Ginger chats to her at the end of each session. 'What does she say about me?' I asked once. 'Oh, nothing,' he said, startled. 'Nothing much. She recognised you, of course, from the first. Very proud to have you in the class, and so forth. She's still quite happy for you to keep coming. At first she worried you might fall over. But now she's become quite a fan of free dancing.'

Part 11

Speak, Hecate

70

I've been with Ginger for a few years now. He's been good for me, some would say. I am the Incredible Shrinking Woman – I weighed seventeen stone, I went down to eleven. I no longer raid the staff biscuit tin. Ginger says he always found me beautiful, but I suspect he prefers me thinner, smaller, less of a hero, less of a handful, laughing less loudly, *less*.

A lesson! Few men like women who are louder, larger, more irrepressible, stronger than them. Not many people want to live with a hero, though lots of people smile at me and give me a thumbs up, I am used to hearing, 'Good for you, Monica,' I'm used to people wanting to shake my hand, or give me a hug, or do a selfie with me. Then conversation dies away.

Yes, it cheers me, yes, it soothes me, yes, I had always wanted people to love me, and Ginger, at first, was very impressed, and it helped to equalise the power balance. He wasn't just a policeman shagging a suspect.

Adoncia Martinez – Dad's blonde floozy – was extradited to the care of HM Prison Service, East Sutton Park, Middlesex. Ginger spent days listening to her. 'She really had it in for your father.' Her statement ran into thousands of words. 'Actually I think you'd quite like her, Monica. She had the gift of the gab, like you.'

Once she had been charged with attempted murder, the road ahead cleared for the Ludds.

I became calmer, I think; less tense. Easier to work with than before. I have my thoughts, but I don't always show them. Sometimes I've said too much to him.

Say too much, and you yield your power. I was incautious because I loved him. Ginger fancied me at first because I wasn't prudish, then fell in love with me because I was a hero, but underneath, I was still a suspect.

Now I am taking stock again.

My weight is creeping back up, slowly. Better to be visible, audible. If you're visible, you can't disappear. Safer to be a larger woman.

Yet it is true, Ginger saved my life, and not just with police back-up, that day in the classroom. He saved the Ludds, my whole family. Oddballs, drunkards, murderers. He saved our bacon, pulled our fat out of the fire, whatever metaphor you want. With a man like Ginger, you get what you asked for. He likes our home life. He likes to stay in. He likes stability, and order

Out, out   I have to get out

He's a clever man. He's read a lot. Sometimes I think he reads everything. Sometimes I think he's read my diary, even though it is password protected and the password is written in a hidden notebook. He's a policeman though. I think he'd look. It's part of loving me; he's everywhere. Yes, there's no getting away from Ginger.

'Knowledge is power,' he said to me once, tapping the side of his neat pink nose, smiling at me with his sharp blue eyes. 'No need for you to have secrets from me.'

Where is the truth? In the news programmes, in the tabloid papers that sanctified me, in the smiles of the parents who will always be grateful? Or is the truth about me in my diary, notes and scraps, password protected? Is it in the head of a man who was staggering, maddened, bruised, beaten, towards the beach?

Only our father knows everything he did. How many people were in his chair? How many adults, how many children? So many women: them too, us too, when we lift the curtain, it all crawls out. And stretching away, the maimed generations, dragging themselves along the edge of the sea, following him, waiting for him. Surely it all had to stop somewhere?

Did we stop it or did we join them?

No, forget it, we had to survive.

Monica has long been ready for love, and now a man has offered his heart, so yes, that must be my happy ending. The others have theirs: Fairy left Rupert, and dates another handsome man with eyes as bright and clear as cocaine; Boris still dances alone with Angus; Marija never came back from Riga; Abdul's taller, more confident, with a job as a chef in a Margate restaurant where every few months we like to eat (Ginger and I never pay for dessert); Kriss and Zain are in their last year at university, and Deniece, having trained as a Norland nanny, will very soon be richer than me.

Ma – interesting. She's still sober. Sober as a judge, but her mind is clouding. For years she faked it, now we think it's for real. She's still living at Cliffetoppe's, but recently she moved in with Nikki. Nikki – yes, I've learned her name. Apparently she was attached to it. And another thing. She may love Ma, or why would she look after her?

There is love. People give and receive it. Ginger gives something of the sort to me.

Aarash Zubair, the deranged, dyspraxic former hospital porter who attacked Windmills, was sent to Belmarsh after a trial that forced me to take time off school. He was an Afghan, furious for justice. Why was the great Satan in Afghanistan? Brexit Britain revolted him, the immorality of the *kufar*, et cetera. He had a point but he made the trial so fucking boring as he ranted on, though he turned out to be cheating on two different British women and had stolen drugs from the hospital.

He won't get out till he's a very old man, and he'll be seen by many in prison as a hero. Doubtless he's nurturing *jihad* in Belmarsh. Nothing will change until there is justice, but let's pretend, let's lock him away.

Anthea broke up with Kelly and moved to Byron Bay, where she teaches yoga and counsels people – she's a counsellor now; she earns good money. She's with a Kylie, so she hasn't gone far. 'There's a lot of pain, you know, Monica?' She says things like that when she calls at night, long distance. Sometimes she's drunk, sometimes she's high, sometimes she seems to be all right.

(Ginger has stopped me drinking gin. Yes, I've swopped one addiction for another. Bye-bye gin, hiya, Ginger.)

He'll always know, and I'll never leave him.

No-one, ever, gets away with murder.

Carry on down, keep on trucking…

We dropped Fred's ashes into the sea, down near St Ives, off a green, green cliff, a very long way from the sandbanks of Thanet, on a clean blue day, the five of us, the five of us Ludds, the Ludds for ever, and Esmeralda, our little aunt, who's been looking better since all this happened, and has a job in a hardware shop. We stopped for lunch in what Boris called 'a hostelry' by the side of the road. The boys were buying, and both my sisters were doing things to their faces in the loo. Esmeralda and I sat alone in the garden. 'Have you been all right?' she said to me. 'Are you all right now, Monica? Is it better, now that your father's –' She stopped. Her wrinkled finger flicked a leaf from the table. She looked right at me. Her big brown eyes. That tiny face had colour, for once.

'Yes. You?' I needed to know.

'Life's more boring. But I sleep at nights…Happy they put that bitch in prison.' She was still staring intently at me. 'We all have a right to get away, darling.' She'd never called me darling before. Her carmine lip-line softened, trembled. 'All the same, I do – miss him –' Then I reached out and held her hand.

'Ow, Monica, you're crushing me.'

'Thanks for talking to the police, Aunty.'

Ginger let me go on my own, alone with my siblings, that one time, but he said, 'You'd better behave, Monica. I know what you lot are capable of! Remember, Monica, you are a hero. You have a reputation to live up to!' Ginger and I are both great laughers. Sometimes, when we stop, there's a silence.

Through pastures green we led our brother. I read it aloud, the 23rd Psalm. Justice and mercy; quiet waters. Grace for Fred, for Fred at least. To die bravely, and be at rest. Yes, Fred did have love for his comrade. Where did he learn it? Was he born with it? Did somebody – did we? – love him enough to make up for our loveless parents? I long to see him, I long to ask.

When I swim in the sea, alone, alone – I never tell my fiancé I'm going, but it's fine, the sea's at the bottom of the road, there would only be problems if I went further – the currents bring Fred near to me, cold small molecules of my brother, through miles of blue sunlight, miles of sand. Stretching my hands out under water, I hold him in my arms, my brother.

71

And now, stop press, there is another surprise, another, surely more hopeful turning! Monica's been in the news again. 'Classroom's Ms Courage Becomes Mother. '

Bleats and rustles from the room next door reach the sunny room where I just stopped dancing, boogeying down to Radio One, which I only have on when Ginger's not in. Yes, our child is one and a half. Time to wake her from her afternoon sleep. She likes it at the same time every day.

Warm, tender, slightly damp, a copper-haired cherub with delicate features; she looks like Fred, she looks like Fairy, though Ginger insists that it's me she resembles, and after a beat, I return the compliment, but really, all she has from him is red hair. I hug her to me: happy gurgles.

Yes, she's mine. Something for me.

She's big for her age, and astonishingly bright. Sometimes I worry that things will go wrong, that all we can do is repeat, repeat, but little Hecate has something about her, not just her name, which is a cracker, Hecate Artemis Gaia – yes, we both smiled at the initials. Hags, *brujas*, give her your gifts. And oh, my heart: a great thump of love.

'Hello, Mum,' Hetty says, clearly. 'Hello, Mum-mum-mum. I see you.' The infant prodigy is talking early. Nearly sentences, not just words. Help us, Hecate, goddess of crossroads.

'You're the baby, baby, baby, Hetty.' I tell her the same thing so many times, and crush her closer, though we're both too hot. I can never get enough of her.

But Hecate has ideas of her own, Hecate, my small warrior.

'*No no no,*' she gurgles, burbles, '*no no no no no, Mmaa,*' and with a strong small hand and an adorable smile that shows two pearl teeth, she will push me away.

Yes, my girl. Speak, Hecate.

Acknowledgements

Thanks to readers of early drafts for their encouragement and criticisms: in chronological order, to Nick Rankin and Rosa Rankin-Gee, Barbara Goodwin, Peter Sheldon Green, Deb McCormick, Bernardine Evaristo, Omar Al-Khayatt, Rhodri Jones and Julia Harrison. Thanks to John Waite, sharp-eyed linguist of La Losa, for help with Adoncia's Spanglish. Special thanks to Lyndall Gordon and Elaine Showalter. Thanks also for the early editing eye, intelligence and enthusiasm of Anna Wilson. Grateful thanks to a police informant who I will not name lest he be blamed! Most of all, thanks to Katherine Bright-Holmes, who did so much to make it happen.